DETACHED

Saphera Nyx Book 1

ELICIA HYDER

Inkwell & Quill, LLC
Print ISBN: 978-1-945775-26-0

Edited by Nicole Ayers
Edited by Kit Duncan
Cover by Christian Bentulan

For More Information:
www.eliciahyder.com

DETACHED

Now is your chance. Grab some coffee or tea and find a quiet spot to settle in. This magical adventure will keep you reading all night, and it will stay with you long after the first book ends.

Don't worry. Book two and a support group will be waiting.

Are you ready?
Welcome to the world of Saphera Nyx.

For my loving husband, Chris.
Who's always wanted me to write about
zombies and orgies.

Sorry, babe. This still isn't it.

CHAPTER ONE

My breaths whooshed, shallow and quick, against the body armor cinched tightly across my breasts. I leapt over a fallen tree, clanging the bones in my ankle when my boot landed hard in a puddle. Thick, heavy mud slashed my pant leg as the flashlight beam danced wildly through the tall pines.

Neither of us could keep up this pace for long. My lungs burned as I sucked in the crisp fall air.

"Suspect considered armed," dispatch said in my ear.

I swore, panting, as I sidestepped a rotten tree trunk. "Teek . . . don't make me . . . shoot you!"

He gave a high-pitched squeal. "You'll never take me alive!"

I swore again.

In the moonlight up ahead, Corbin "Teek" Fleming was slowing. A good sign for me and my screaming thighs. I slipped the hood off my holster. "Let me see your hands!"

He tripped and pitched forward, losing his bag of potato chips in an explosive shower above his head. I caught up as he tried to scramble to his feet. Securing my gun, I tackled him into the pine needles and dirt. "Don't you fight me!"

Teek squirmed, his torso making a loud *crunching* sound. More chips, I assumed. Something was in his left hand. I straddled his back, holding his arms with my knees, and shined my flashlight on what he was holding. It was long and black, with a green tip. I looked over the rest of him. Bright red T-shirt, pants barely hanging onto his ass, and one safety-yellow sneaker. The other foot was bare.

I panned back to his hand. "Is that a sock over a cucumber?"

"No."

I reached for his "gun." He twisted, and I rocked forward on my knees until he yelped and stopped moving. I yanked the vegetable away and pulled off the sock. "Oh, you're right. It's a zucchini." I tossed it onto the ground and pulled his arm back behind him. "Anybody else might have shot you, you know that?"

"I'm a lone wolf, Nyx. Wanted, dead or alive."

"Yeah, yeah." I handcuffed his right wrist and called into dispatch. "Delta Three, suspect in custody."

I pulled Teek to his feet. "What were you thinking?"

"I was hungry." A potato chip was lodged in the strawberry-blond scruff that hid his chin dimple.

"So you held up the Mini Market with a squash, while an army of police officers hung out in the parking lot? Genius."

"They're gonna write books about me."

"Sure they are. How'd you get here?"

"I ran."

I rolled my eyes. "I am fully aware of how you got in the woods. How did you get to the gas station?"

"Oh, I walked." He lifted his face toward the moon and howled. It was a long walk around the lake from the Boro, and Teek didn't have a driver's license or a car.

Officer Brian Everly, the newest member of the eight-person Delta team, met up with us halfway through the woods, on our way back. He was young and lanky, in desperate need of some protein shakes and a treadmill.

"You got him?" He was panting, doubled over to grip his knees.

"Yeah, I got him. Are you gonna make it, Everly?" I slapped his chest as I escorted Teek past him.

"I was right behind you."

"Yeah, when we left the parking lot." I flashed a grin over my shoulder.

"You're so funny." Everly started after us. "Hey, where's his shoe?"

"Who knows? Apparently, lone wolves don't need shoes. Right, Teek?"

"That's right," he said proudly.

Everly fell into step beside me. "Did you get his weapon?"

I laughed. "Yep. I'll probably make a salad later."

"What?"

"He wasn't armed."

"I have arms," Teek said, rattling his handcuffs.

"Is he high?" Everly asked.

"The story is he's been high for a couple of years. His friends say he ate a handful of acid tabs and never came back."

Teek stumbled. "Drugs are bad. Just say no."

Looking at Everly, I gestured toward Teek as if to say, "See?"

"Wow," Everly said.

"Get used to seeing him. I've taken him to Sterling Heights at least three times this year."

"No Sterling *Frights*," Teek said, cringing. Sterling Heights was the mental health center.

"Oh, you're going to jail tonight, my friend. That's what happens when you rob people and run."

Only three squad cars remained in the parking lot of the Mini Market when we emerged from the woods. Eric Jones was standing by his door, eating a corndog. Jones was tall and thick muscled. A fellow combat vet with a shiny, bald black head.

Bright-yellow mustard was smeared from the corner of his mouth up his cheek.

He swallowed the bite in his mouth and grinned at me. "Beefing up your resume with an armed-robbery capture?"

"Yeah, I'm sure the board will be very impressed by a suspect armed with a zucchini."

"Huh?"

"It wasn't a gun. It was a zucchini inside his sock."

Jones bit down on the insides of his lips.

"You said it was a squash," Teek said.

I closed my eyes and took a deep breath.

"You got him?" a woman yelled from the door of the convenience store.

I waved. "We got him, Sally!"

"Thank you, Nyx!" Sally Penrod, the night-shift clerk, held up a thumb and walked back inside.

"Where's everybody else?" I asked Jones.

"Called to handle a 'delicate matter'"—Jones used air quotes—"at the Drexler. So, of course, *everyone* is headed that way."

"You going too?"

"Bet your ass."

I chuckled.

With lakeview chalets going for over $10,000 per night, the swanky resort, golf course, and casino drew an always-interesting clientele. The last time we were called to handle something "delicate," a hammered and *naked* Hollywood A-lister (not naming names) was tearing up the hotel golf course with a Bugatti.

Needless to say, no one was missing out this time.

Jones looked down. "Where's his shoe?"

I tugged on Teek's arm. "Did you stash it somewhere around here?"

Teek lifted both shoulders and his eyebrows.

"Guess you're going to jail without it. Come on." I walked

Teek to my unmarked black patrol car and opened the back door. He stepped into my back seat, and as I reached to hold his blond head . . .

Kaboom!

All our heads whipped in the direction of the lake. Smoke billowed up through the moonlight from somewhere around the Drexler Resort and Casino.

"That wasn't me," Teek said, breaking our stunned silence.

"Officer down!" Corporal Mason Baker yelled, breathless, over the frequency.

My heart stopped.

"Explosion at the Drexler, north side, near the chalets. We need medical!"

Jones tossed what was left of his corndog into his car.

"Who else is there?" I demanded as I hurried Teek into the back seat.

"Sarge and Rivera, I think," Jones replied, getting in his driver's seat.

Everly was still frozen to the concrete. "Get in your damn car!" I yelled at him as I got behind my wheel.

"I've never driven Code Three by myself." His eyes were as wide as the moon above us.

"Go!" I slammed my door and flipped on my lights and siren. Then I floored the gas pedal.

My radio beeped as I followed Jones onto the highway. "Delta One," a deep, winded voice said.

My heart eased a bit.

"Go ahead, Delta One," dispatch replied.

"All officers are OK and accounted for," Sergeant "Sarge" Essex said.

I exhaled fully for the first time since the explosion.

"Roll medical and fire. Possible casualties inside Chalet One-Ten on the golf course."

At ninety miles per hour down the winding mountain pass,

Jones, Everly, and I peeled through the entrance of the Drexler before Sergeant Tyler Essex even stopped reporting over the radio. In my back seat, Teek wailed along with the siren, the perfect soundtrack for the adrenaline surging through my veins.

"Holy shit!" I said when I rounded the steep curve toward the back of the golf course.

The chalet, once a bi-level, wood-and-stone marvel that faced the sixteenth hole on one side and Sapphire Lake on the other, was now split down the middle. Raging flames devoured the crevice, pumping black-and-gray smoke toward the few visible stars. Even at the bottom of the hill, the smoke stung my eyes, giving the flecks of rising embers a watery glow.

I parked beside Sergeant Essex's unmarked black SUV and opened my door. "Teek, sit tight."

He didn't answer; his face was plastered to the polycarbonate front wall of my caged back seat, the flames dancing in his pupils.

I pulled my undershirt up over my nose to block the acrid smoke. "Everly, watch Teek!" I yelled as I ran past him toward the scene. Jones was right behind me as the first fire truck pulled in.

The silhouettes of two men, one significantly larger than the other, were coming down the hill toward us. The smaller one was limping. When I was close enough, I made out a black police uniform and a black suit. The officer was my boss, and the giant dressed like a penguin was my older brother, Ransom, head of night security for the hotel.

Ransom had grown a short beard since last I'd seen him, and his dark-walnut hair had some kind of faux hawk thing happening in the center. Something I'd definitely give him shit about later.

For now, all I cared about was that he and Essex were safe. "You all right?" I asked both of them, carefully searching my brother for blood.

Ransom shook my hand off his arm. "I'm fine. You?" he asked Essex.

My boss's face was covered with ash and a few small cuts. "Yeah, I'm OK." His limp down the hill said otherwise.

Ransom peeled off his jacket and tossed it to the ground. His ruined shirt was only recognizable as white by its sleeves. "Damn, that was close though."

I looked back toward my car. "Everly! There's a case of water in my trunk. Bring some over."

He nodded.

Officer Jadon Rivera jogged down the hill behind them. Rivera was our shift's reigning asshole, but I was thankful to see him in one piece.

"You good?" Essex asked him.

Rivera gave a thumbs-up. Soot streaked his face.

"What the hell happened?" Jones asked.

Essex took a few deep breaths. "Some people walking on the beach heard screaming inside the unit. They called hotel security." He tipped his head toward my brother. "When Ransom couldn't get an answer, they called us."

"There was nothing but silence by the time I got here," Ransom said.

"Why didn't you go in?" I asked him.

"I knocked, even tried my master key, but the lock was disabled. It was like all the power was out in the chalet."

My brow lifted with surprise. "You didn't break down the door?"

In his wilder days, my brother had been an MMA fighter. And at six two and two hundred five pounds of solid muscle, a door couldn't have stood in his way if Ransom had been determined to get through it.

"It's company policy to call the police before forcing entry." He looked back at the building. "Maybe that was a mistake."

"Or maybe it would have gotten you killed too." I squeezed his arm, thankful he was alive.

Rivera looked from Ransom to me and back again. "You two know each other?"

"My brother." There was no time for formal introductions.

Everly came over, cradling an armful of water bottles. As he passed out water, Corporal Mason Baker joined us.

A former semi-pro linebacker, Baker towered over the rest of us, even Ransom. In addition to our normal patrol shift, Baker and I were both part of the SWAT team, a specialty unit called out to resolve high-risk tactical situations.

Baker swiped the back of his hand over his brow, leaving a sweat smear through the ash speckling his forehead. "Sarge, I've got units blocking the roads up here, but we probably should put someone on the beach."

"Everly, go down and block beach access—"

I stopped Essex. "Everly's busy."

"With?"

"Guarding my suspect in custody."

"Babysitting seems about Everly's speed," Rivera said with an eye roll.

Essex spoke into his radio. "Delta One, I need units blocking beach access. Nobody on or off the golf course."

"Delta Five, en route," Chris McCollum responded.

"Delta Six, en route," Cameron Legieza said.

"Ransom, does the hotel have barriers handy?" Essex asked.

"Already on the way," Ransom answered.

The firefighters were knocking down the flames, but it was clear the chalet was a total loss.

"What caused the explosion?" Jones asked.

Essex turned toward the dying inferno and shook his head. "No clue. I was looking in the front window when it blew. In seconds, the whole place went up in flames."

"Gas leak?" Rivera asked.

"The hotel doesn't use gas," Ransom answered between sips of water.

"Did you see anything inside?" I asked Essex.

"Just the glass blowing at me."

I walked closer to him and examined his face. Blood drizzled from a cut across his cheek. "You're bleeding." I reached into my pocket and pulled out the napkin left from the gas-station dinner I didn't get to finish. I dabbed it against the cut.

"I'm fine, Nyx." He took the napkin from me and held it against the cut himself. "No way the same is true for whoever was inside."

"Who was it?" I asked.

"We didn't get that far." Essex looked at Ransom. "Who was staying in this chalet?"

Ransom looked nervous, a rare emotion for my brother. "Ryder Stone."

"Who?" Essex asked, because if someone was famous for anything outside ESPN or crime action drama, he was lost.

I leaned toward him. "The son of country singer Shooter Stone. They had a reality show called *The Family Stones.*"

Essex lifted both shoulders.

Baker looked down at me and cocked an eyebrow. "I'm a little surprised you know that, Nyx."

"Our grandfather loves that show," Ransom said.

"I heard he was in town with his girlfriend, filming an episode of *Romancing the Stars,*" Jones said.

We all turned to look at him.

My mouth gaped. "Big fan, are you, Jonesy?"

"Hey, I have teenage girls," Jones said.

Rivera laughed and crossed his arms. "Whatever you say, man."

Essex shot us all a *look*, and the amusement died immediately.

"Stone checked in with Amber Stevens yesterday," Ransom confirmed.

"Anybody seen them today?" Essex asked.

Ransom tipped his chin toward the blaze. "Heading straight for there."

"Damn," Jones said, looking at the fire again.

Two firefighters in full gear dragged a hose past us. "Essex!" a voice boomed.

We all looked back as the captain of the fire department waved him over. Essex winced as he limped in that direction, taking my napkin with him.

"You didn't see anything?" Jones asked Rivera.

Rivera shook his head. "I was lakeside, checking the back of the unit when, *boom!* I hightailed it back around front and found Sarge lying against the rock wall."

I followed the direction Rivera was pointing. The wall that lined the driveway was nowhere close to the front window.

"That's more than five feet," Jones said with a grimace. "No wonder he's limping."

"At least his first few days on night shift were calm," I said, walking back to my car. Teek's scruffy face was smushed against the back window, and his eyes looked like they might bug out of his head.

"Anybody hurt?" Everly asked.

"None of us." An ambulance screamed into the lot. I leaned toward Teek's window. "Teek, you good?"

His wild smile indicated he was just fine.

When he finished speaking with the firefighters, Essex joined us and looked in the back seat of my car. "You caught Butch Cassidy, huh?"

"Yeah. About halfway up Reyna Peak."

"His dad wasn't with him, was he?" he asked with a chuckle.

"No, you're safe." Borg Fleming was still in lockup last I

heard, but that reminded me to ask, "Are you sure you're all right?"

"I told you I'm fine."

"You also said you were fine when Borg knocked a molar out of your jaw."

The corner of his mouth tipped up. "You know me well." With a grimace, he leaned to one side. "Might have a couple of broken ribs."

I cringed. "God, I hope not."

"I know, broken ribs are the worst. I'll be fine though. Thanks for worrying." His tone lightened. "You know whose fault this is?"

"Whose?"

"Rivera's."

My brow lifted in question.

"Back at the Mini Market, he said it was a quiet night."

Our laughter was cut off by the roar of a powerful engine. A silver car with an emblem that boasted "I cost more than your condo" sped through the tidy golf-course grass to bypass the driveway clogged with emergency vehicles.

"Harlan's here," my brother announced.

Real-estate tycoon Harlan Drexler had almost single-handedly built the mountain town of Sapphire Lake. As the heir to the biggest lumber-mill fortune in Nevada's history, Harlan and his late father had converted the family's 20,000-acre estate between Lake Tahoe and Carson City into a booming economy. It all began with a golf-course resort built around the manmade blue lake that once supplied the silver mines with water and timber.

These days, Sapphire Lake was the seventh-largest city in the state. It now included ski slopes, two outdoor shopping villages, three schools, and the biggest casino between Las Vegas and Reno.

I'd never met Harlan Drexler in person, despite Sapphire Lake having been my home on and off for big chunks of my life.

Ransom spoke highly of him, and he had the reputation of being as charitable as he was enterprising.

The sports car parked sideways on the imported sod, and Harlan tripped over his own slippers as he scrambled out of the driver's seat. He caught himself on the door, staring in horror at the flaming chalet. "My god. Was anyone hurt?"

Essex and I walked to meet him. "Mr. Drexler, I'm Sergeant Tyler Essex. We're waiting on the official word from the fire department, but I'm afraid this fire was deadly."

This was news to me.

Harlan ran both hands back through his wild silver hair. "Oh no."

Ransom began speaking to Harlan in a hushed, soothing tone.

I tugged on Essex's sleeve an jerked my head to the side. We stepped away from them, toward our guys. "They found a body?" I asked quietly.

He scanned the area to make sure we were out of everyone's earshot. "Two bodies so far. The fire captain thinks it might be arson to cover up a homicide."

"Shit, really?" Jones asked.

"Yeah. The first body was charred so badly it was unrecognizable."

"And the second?" Rivera asked.

"A female. Only partially burned, but—" Essex had to pause for a breath.

"But what?" I asked.

"Her torso was ripped in half."

I took a small step back.

"Never seen a fire do that," Jones said, his dark eyes dancing with the dying flames.

Unease stirred inside me. The whole situation felt eerily familiar.

Something caught Essex's eyes behind us. "Shit."

I turned to see a news van stopped by some of the hotel's security guys.

"How the hell do they get here so fast?" Essex asked.

"I'm on it," Jones said, starting in that direction. Rivera followed him.

Ransom walked over, passing Jones and Rivera. "The vultures are here."

"We'll handle it," I said.

My brother offered his hand to Essex. "Good to see you, Corporal Essex."

The two men shook hands.

"He's a sergeant now," I said.

"Congratulations. You two are on the same shift now?" Ransom looked down at me, the corners of his mouth fighting a smile. "Isn't that convenient?"

I withered inside.

"As of Monday," Essex answered. "But we won't be for long. Your sister has a big promotion coming up."

"So I hear," Ransom said.

"It's not for sure. I'm not even finished interviewing," I told them.

"But we all know Nyx has it in the bag," Essex said to Ransom. "There's even a betting pool. I hear the pot is over five hundred now."

"Seriously?" I asked.

Essex nodded. "That's what McCollum said."

"Sarge!" Rivera called from the news van.

Essex groaned. "Excuse me. Nice to see you, Ransom."

"Hope to see more of you, Sergeant."

I wanted to crawl under my patrol car. When my boss was out of earshot, I backhanded my brother's chest. "You're an asshole."

My brother smiled. "I know." He lowered his voice and looked toward the chalet. "What happened in there?"

"Not sure."

"Did I hear someone say one of the bodies was torn in half?"

I nodded. "But you're not supposed to know that."

"Damn." Ransom stared up the hill. "Mutilated bodies and a fire cover-up . . . You know what this looks like."

I shook my head. "Don't even say it."

He looked at me with his lips pressed in a hard line. We were both thinking the same thing. I hated we were both thinking the same thing.

"Ransom!" a man yelled. Another car had pulled up behind Harlan Drexler, and a red faced bald man waved to my brother.

"That's my boss. You gonna be here for a bit?" Ransom asked me.

I glanced toward my car. Teek was still smiling in the back seat. "Yeah. Gonna stay as long as I can."

Half an hour later, the fire was almost out and hotel security had pushed all the media back to the hotel's entrance. The guys and I were waiting around our patrol cars when a fireman walked toward us. He removed his helmet.

"What's up, hose dragger?" Jones asked.

"Your momma's risk factor for STDs," the fire captain replied as he stopped in front of Essex. "You definitely want to get your investigators in here."

"They're on the way. Why?" Essex asked.

"We found a third body missing its throat. The bit of wall left standing in the living room is covered in blood." He put his hands on his hips. "Whatever happened in there, it was brutal, man."

Nausea churned in my stomach. This had absolutely happened before.

Harlan Drexler rushed toward us. "Is there an update?" He grabbed the fire captain's arm.

"The coroner is on his way, Mr. Drexler. We've recovered three bodies."

Harlan's knees went out, and he would have fallen had I not been there to catch him. "Come with me, Mr. Drexler," I said gently. "Let's find you a seat."

Harlan leaned heavily on me as we walked toward a bench on the golf course. "What am I going to do? What am I going to tell their poor families?"

I patted his back. "I don't know. It's a terrible thing that's happened."

"Do they know how the fire started?"

"There will be an investigation."

"Do they have any suspects?"

"Not that I'm aware of."

"Who was in the back of the patrol car?"

I smiled. "No one relevant to what happened here tonight. He's harmless, mostly, but he did try to hold up the Mini Market down the street with a zucchini."

Harlan's bubble of laughter seemed to surprise him, and he walked the rest of the way to the bench on his own. When we reached it, I held his hand until he sat down. Sweat drizzled from his hairline, and his face was freckled with soot.

He glanced at my name tag. *Cpl. S. Nyx.* "Nyx. Are you related to Ransom?"

"My brother, sir."

"What does the S stand for?"

"Saphera, but my friends just call me Nyx."

He grabbed my hand and squeezed my hand. "Thank you, Nyx."

I really hadn't done anything, but I smiled and said, "You're welcome."

Ransom's boss joined us. I stepped out of his way and turned back toward the chalet. It was an eerie sight poised against the moonlit clouds over the lake, and another cold chill took my breath.

"It's happening again," someone whispered behind me.

I spun on my boot. "What was that?"

Ransom's boss looked up from his smartphone. "Pardon?"

Harlan's eyes were glazed over, looking past me at the chalet.

I blinked. "Sorry. Thought you said something."

Maybe I was hearing things. Or maybe my imagination was making this into more than it really was. After all, my father was still safely behind bars. That much had been reconfirmed by the state penitentiary only days before.

But when I turned back toward the chalet, the sinking feeling in the pit of my stomach returned like the recoil on a shotgun.

This wasn't a coincidence.

And I knew it.

"Nyx!" Essex called from near my car. I walked to him, and he jerked his head toward Teek. "He says his wrists are starting to hurt. Better go book him in."

"The guy's harmless. Can't we just call somebody to come get him?" Everly asked.

"Under some circumstances, sure, but he held up a store clerk. Made her fear for her life," Essex said.

I opened my driver's side door. "Don't worry, Everly. I'll make sure they call his brother or Gramma T."

"Gramma T?" With worried eyes, Teek's head whipped around like his grandmother might be in the parking lot.

Essex held onto my doorframe. "I'll see you back at the station. We should wrap up here soon."

"10-4."

He stepped back and shut the door.

I wound through the labyrinth of emergency vehicles along the path to the exit. Seven different news vans had gathered at the closed front gate. One of them, I recognized. Sapphire Lake's premier newswoman, Marianne Clarke, and her cameraman from News 4 ran toward my patrol car as I drove past. "Looks like you might make the news, Teek."

Silence.

"Teek?"

The interior lights flickered, all the doors locked around me, and my surveillance cameras shut off.

From the back seat came a chilling voice that didn't belong to Teek Fleming.

"Hello, Saphera."

CHAPTER TWO

*W*ith a loud gasp, I grabbed my heart to make sure it was still in my chest. Then I looked around to see if anyone had seen me freak out.

I drove away from the Drexler and stopped on the shoulder up the road. I turned all the way around in my seat and slid open the dividing window to the prisoner in the back. "You swore you wouldn't do this to me anymore."

In the back seat, Teek's doe-eyed bewilderment had faded. His expression was soft and pleading. Teek's mouth moved, but it was my father's voice that came out of it. "You haven't replied to any of my letters."

"Because I haven't opened them. What the hell are you doing here?"

It was no secret (at least to me) that Elias Nyx had the power to *detach*—to leave his body during REM sleep and travel. Like a ghost, his spirit could lurk undetected, taking eavesdropping and espionage to a whole new level. It was a small part of why he was in prison, even admitting that PIN numbers, safe combinations, and computer passwords were *never* safe with him around.

He could also commandeer the bodies of others to interact

with the waking world, but at my insistence, we hadn't seen each other like this in years. His control now over Teek Fleming was unnerving.

"I'm dying, Saphera."

"I'm aware. Ransom called, and my work told me."

"Your work?" He sounded surprised.

"Yes. They've kept tabs on you since I joined the department. A consequence of being the daughter of a cop killer."

"I'm sorry if I've made your life difficult."

"No, you're not. I thought they were treating you."

"They tried, but the disease won't respond. I'm afraid my body already looks like a corpse."

I'd heard he had some form of flesh-eating disease.

To anyone else, I might have said, "I'm sorry." To Elias, I asked, "What do you want?"

"I haven't been strong enough to detach on my own in quite some time. I'm using extreme measures to accomplish it now because it's imperative that I speak with you and your brother."

"Well, Ransom is about five minutes that way." I pointed behind my car. "Go talk to him."

"I plan to, but this directly affects you as well. Have you found the *hypnox* yet?"

I gritted my teeth. "I knew this whole thing reeked of you."

"You also know those three humans were killed by a night-walker tonight."

"Elias, what did you do?"

"Nothing. When I got to the fire, you were already there."

"You sure you didn't cause that explosion? Because hypnox, fire, and dead people all sound a hell of a lot like you."

"Saphera—"

"Did you start it?"

"I did not."

"Then who did?"

"It might have been Orion, but there hasn't been time for me to find him to ask."

"Who's Orion?"

"Someone I hope will help you when I'm gone. He left a letter in my cell stating he found a woman, Norina Grumley, detached inside the Boundary in Seneca Park. He confirmed she'd used hypnox. She didn't die, nor was her body breached, because he returned her spirit in time."

"What does that have to do with you?"

He looked away. "Hypnox grows in Earth's fertile soil when magical blood is spilled within the Boundary."

"So this *is* your fault."

Guilt flashed across Teek's face. "I fear it was my blood that created this danger."

I faced ahead. "I knew it." Gripping the steering wheel, my knuckles turned white.

"I tried to warn you, but you wouldn't answer my calls or my letters."

My eyes darted toward the mirror. "Warn me about what?"

"The necrosis began when I was attacked inside the Boundary. I was stabbed in the back with a shadow blade. It was a miracle I didn't die then, but it's clear now I won't survive it."

"So what is this? Some kind of deathbed confession?"

"No. I'm here to impress upon you the danger the whole world now faces."

"The whole world," I repeated with an eye roll so hard it hurt my head.

"Yes. The nightwalkers know there's vulnerability here. One was killed in the fire tonight. And I have plans to kill another."

"Nightwalkers," I muttered.

He leaned toward my seat. "You may not believe me, but soon, I promise you'll know the nightmares are real."

If he was to be believed, Elias was a primordial scion, the direct descendant of the Goddess of Night, Nyx. Hence our unusual—and, it should be noted, legally fabricated—last name.

He said our bloodline was meant to protect the Boundary, the space between dreams and reality where nightmares were tangible, bloodsucking monsters called *nightwalkers*.

Elias had probably told me other things too, but I was just a kid when his wild stories were part of my life. To my young ears, the horror of nightwalkers had overshadowed anything else.

Now, despite my grown-up disbelief, goose bumps still rippled my skin.

"I'm no longer strong enough to fight this war. When I'm gone, you will have to—"

"*I* will have nothing to do with it," I snapped.

Frustrated, he huffed. "Fine. Your *brother* will be thrown into this war soon. He'll need your help. You must promise me you'll take care of him."

"I *must* do nothing for you. Ransom is a grown man, fully capable of looking out for himself."

Elias snorted.

"Well, Ransom is a grown man, anyway. And he knows a hell of a lot more about your shit than I do."

"That was your choice."

"I'm sorry, did I give the impression I was upset about it? I can't wait until all this is no longer part of my life."

"You can't wait for me to die."

"I didn't say that."

Watching him in the rearview mirror, I saw him look out the window. "Soon, I won't be around to bother you ever again."

Somehow, I doubted that. Elias Nyx seemed to own permanent real estate in my mind. I wasn't even sure that his death would free me of him completely. As if to illustrate the certainty, my heart gave an unwelcome tug.

I shifted uneasily in my seat, gripping the steering wheel with both hands. "You think it will be fast?"

"I will be dead by morning."

My heartstrings danced, despite how desperately I wished not to care.

"Listen, please," he begged. "For Ransom and Amelia."

I swore under my breath. Elias knew there wasn't much I wouldn't do for my brother. Even less that I wouldn't do for my niece, Milly. "Fine. How am I supposed to help him?"

"First, don't forget the basics. Never detach at night."

"It's nighttime *right now*," I reminded him.

I expected him to launch into a "do as I say, not as I do" speech, but he didn't. "I am well aware. May I continue?"

I shut my mouth.

"The detached *must* assimilate, rejoin the body, before sundown. Those two things are absolutely essential."

"Right. So essential you would choose to ignore them yourself."

"Saphera, please!"

I flinched, but I shut my mouth.

"Any vacant body, including my own, is an open door to the dangers of the Boundary. I'm aware of that risk, which is why I would hope you might take me seriously." He took a deep breath and calmly continued. "Finally, remind Ransom to keep his mouth shut."

I smirked. "Are you afraid people will think he's crazy? That they won't believe him?"

"No. I'm afraid they *will*." For the first time I could ever remember, fear filled Elias's voice. "In the wrong hands, this gift—"

"You mean this *curse*."

His tone of concern shifted to annoyance. "It can be very dangerous."

"I know. Maximum security kind of dangerous."

In the rearview mirror, I saw him hang his head. "Saphera, I won't ask you to ever forgive me. God knows I'll never forgive myself. But for Ransom's sake—for *your* sake—please don't let your hatred for me dismiss the very real threat of this power. Every day is a battle, a constant choice between good and evil."

"Do you think that's something exclusive to your precious bloodline? Elias, we all have that choice. Every single day. I wouldn't have a paycheck without it."

"You're right, but what is exclusive to my bloodline is the power to operate in secret. Keep your brother accountable. Work together. Don't let him end up like me."

"Anything else?"

"Someone knows the power of my blood. With nightwalkers in the area, I fear it is the God of Nightmares. My attacker stabbed me with a weapon from Imera."

"From where?"

"The spirit land across the Boundary. Whoever it was could see my detached spirit, and they'll be able to see my heir once I'm gone."

That worried me for Ransom.

"You must be vigilant. And you must find the plant before anyone else dies."

"Well, if it grows where your blood was spilled, where were you when you were stabbed?" I merged onto the freeway, checking my blind spot before changing lanes.

Elias didn't answer.

"Well?"

"Well . . ." Teek Fleming shoved his face through the window.

The car swerved as I flinched at the sudden change in voice behind me. Teek was back in control of his mouth, and my father was gone.

An hour later, Elias still hadn't returned. I booked Teek into jail, specifically asking they call his brother or grandma to come get him.

Essex was waiting for me when I walked out of booking. It was still jarring to see him so often at work. He hadn't asked to be put on nights, but when our sergeant, Sharon Gregg, was moved to narcotics, Essex was next in line to make rank.

"All done?" he asked, looking up from the paperwork in his hand.

"All done."

"Good. Take the rest of the night off, so you're fresh for tomorrow."

"That's really unnecessary." I started toward our wall of mailboxes.

"Consider it an order."

"Thanks." With a grateful smile, I reached into my box.

He leaned against the wall and crossed his arms, and the short sleeves of his black uniform strained over his shredded biceps. "Did you take my advice?"

I forced my eyes away. "Yes, but it feels arrogant."

"It's not arrogance if it's true. You're a badass, and the committee needs to know that."

"I've been with this department for over two years. Shouldn't they already know that?" I sorted through memos and mail.

"Most of us do." He looked around the hallway and lowered his voice. "But the brass only see what comes through on paper. Your arrest record speaks for itself, but they probably haven't seen the history in your file since you were hired. It definitely wouldn't hurt to remind them you're one of the most highly trained officers on the force."

I stopped sorting and looked up at him. "Why are you so invested in this?"

"Because I know your value. And, as your boss, it's my job to help you succeed professionally."

I narrowed my eyes.

He chuckled. "And I may have put fifty dollars on you beating Morris."

I laughed and rolled my eyes. "I appreciate the confidence." I glanced over the department newsletter before tossing it in the trash.

He looked over at my mail. "Ooo. Department of Corrections. What's that?"

Shit.

He leaned closer. "Is it from your father?"

"Excuse me, but is that your business?"

"No." He grinned. "But is it?"

"He's been writing a lot lately."

"Because he's dying?"

"Beats me. They've all gone into the trash." I moved the letter behind another stapled intraoffice memo.

"You're not even curious as to what he has to say?"

"Obviously not as curious as you. I could give you his address. Maybe you two could be pen pals." I walked past him toward the exit.

"Touchy?" he teased as he caught up to me.

"Not even a little bit." The tension in my jaw and shoulders probably told him otherwise.

"Will you see him before he passes?"

"Not if I can help it."

"Sure you won't regret that?"

I stopped walking and turned toward him. "Not everyone's father is on the Wall of Heroes."

Essex came from a long line of cops. His father had been chief of police in Sapphire Lake when he was killed on duty. Even the man who would become his stepfather had been appointed acting chief when James Essex died.

In stark contrast, Elias went to prison later that very same year for fraud, grand larceny, possession and distribution of a schedule-one narcotic, and first-degree murder of a law-enforcement officer. Having a felon for a father was something my boss would never understand.

We started toward the door, and when we reached it, he held it open for me. Outside, his SUV was in its reserved space. My car was still parked at the booking entrance.

It was drizzling, chilly drops that in a few short months would turn to snow. I held out my hand to catch a few raindrops on my palm. "Be safe out there tonight."

"I'd better be, since you won't be watching my back."

I laughed.

"I'll probably see you in the morning," he said, unlocking his car.

"Why? You're off this weekend."

"Word has gotten out that a semi-celebrity died in Sapphire Lake, so we're all prepping for blowback. My life is about to be nothing but one meeting after another."

I smiled, walking backward away from him. "And you wonder why I don't want to make sergeant."

He laughed and opened his door. "If you want overtime, I'm sure they'll approve all we want once the national media rolls in."

"Cool. I'll probably do that."

Before I could turn around, he pointed at me. "Have at least five copies of your qualifications in hand when you go into that interview tomorrow."

I gave a snarky salute.

He laughed. "Goodnight, Nyx."

"Bye, Sarge." It was still weird calling him that.

I got in my car, locked the doors, and waited for him to leave the lot. When he was gone, I pulled out the letter stamped "Nevada State Penitentiary" in bright red ink.

With a shaky breath, I opened it—something I'd sworn I'd never do.

Dear Saphera,

I've written to your home address a few times without an answer. Perhaps this letter will find you at work. At your request, I've left you alone for as long as possible, but it is now essential that I speak with you. I don't have much time left, and there are things you should know.

Things you must know.

Please visit as soon as you are able. We should talk in person.

Elias

I sat back in my seat. What the hell was suddenly so important? I pulled out my phone and tapped my brother's name in my call history. It went straight to voicemail. "You've reached Ransom. You know what to do."

"Hey, it's me. Had a weird night after I left the fire. Call me when you get this." I ended the call and pulled out of the lot.

I pulled my radio to my mouth. "Delta Three, 10-7," I said, signing off for the night. I got on the highway back toward my place.

It was a quiet trip, unusual for a drive in my patrol car. I loved music, and it always echoed the ever-changing demands of my job. At the beginning of a shift, rock or metal amped me up. Put me on alert. Kept my head on a swivel.

Pop or classical would bring me down for the drive home. Pop when the shift was calm; classical when I had to battle demons. It was a trick I'd learned from my training officer the night I worked my first suicide.

Tonight, there was no radio, only my mind replaying the bizarre conversation with my father. How could this be happening again?

Now, of *all* times in my career.

The exit toward home was empty; not surprising since most of Sapphire Lake shut down after ten p.m. I turned onto the highway and caught an oncoming car in my radar beam.

Alarm bells sounded through the car. I looked at the flashing radar as the car whizzed by me.

Sixty-six in forty-five.

Damn it.

I flipped on my blue lights and cut the wheel hard to the left, spinning up gravel as I crossed onto the road's shoulder. I touched my radio. "Delta Three, 10-81."

I sped to catch the car. "Please don't be drunk. Please don't be drunk. Please don't be drunk," I chanted in a whisper.

Tickets I could write and leave. Drunk people I had to take to jail, the same jail I'd *just* come from. I really wanted to go home.

Brake lights blazed up ahead as the driver finally slowed.

"Go ahead, Delta Three," the dispatcher replied.

"Sapphire Park Highway approaching Snow Valley Road. Nevada tag, eight-six-nine-victor-charlie-adam."

The piece-of-shit car eased onto the side of the road across the emergency lane. Its crooked bumper was covered with band stickers.

I pulled behind it, leaving the front of my car angled onto the pavement to protect me from any other idiots who might be out that muggy night.

I threw my transmission into park and unbuckled my seat-belt, carefully checking all around me as I got out. Then I closed my door and cautiously started toward the car.

Music was blaring so loud it rattled the back window. *What's that song? Oh . . .* "Apple Bottom Jeans." *Shit.* Drunk people love that song.

Erratic movement in the driver's seat made me slip the hood off my weapon and partially unholster it. The music stopped. I cautiously approached, counting only one head inside as I touched the back taillight to leave my fingerprints behind. I shined the flashlight on my shoulder into the messy back seat as I passed.

Is that a boom box?

The driver—White female, shoulder-length brown hair—waved through the hazy glass. Duct tape was holding it inside the window frame.

The girl pointed to the door. "Can I open it? The window doesn't roll down!"

I nodded as my gaze swept the empty passenger's seat.

The door creaked open. "Hi!" Two soda cans and a long, slender piece of plastic tumbled onto the asphalt. "Whoops. My bad." She moved to pick them up.

"Ma'am, please stay in the car," I ordered.

She held up both hands. "Sorry. Didn't want a ticket for littering too."

I frowned. *She has to be high. Nobody's this chipper.*

The car appeared to be empty. I kicked the plastic device over with my boot. "What's this?"

"A remote control." She glanced into her back seat. "The car speakers are busted. I dropped the remote when I saw the blue lights."

So weird.

"My name is Corporal Nyx with the Sapphire Lake Police Department. I clocked you doing sixty-six in a forty-five-miles-per-hour-zone. Why were you driving so fast?" *Pupils normal size.*

She clasped her hands beneath her chin. "I'm really sorry, Officer. There's been some kind of emergency at my work, and my boss needs me to come in and close the bar, and I *really* can't afford to lose this job because my ex moved out, and I'm already behind on my rent, and I—"

I held up a hand to stop her. "Where do you work?"

She tilted up the name badge on her white blouse. "The Drexler. It's the golf resort near—"

"I know very well what it is."

"I'm a bartender in the lounge and kind of on a final-strike basis with my boss, if you know what I mean."

"Where are you coming from?"

"My apartment." She jerked a thumb over her shoulder. "I live in Seneca Park, the older complex behind the—"

"License, registration, and proof of insurance, please."

When she leaned across the car to open the glove compartment, I took a deep whiff inside. No pot. No booze. No cigarette smoke either. Just coffee and pizza. A half-eaten slice lay on the center console.

She gripped the car-owner's manual with her teeth as she riffled through her purse. Then she passed a Nevada driver's license through the window.

Bess Lincoln.

24.

Organ donor.

Seneca Park address.

The license had only been issued a few months ago. "You just move here?"

"From Charleston in the spring." As she flipped through the pages of the owner's manual, she rolled her hazel eyes up at me. "A *guy.* Guess how well that turned out? Whatever, though. It got me the hell out of South Carolina, and this place is—aha! I knew the registration was in here." She handed me a folded piece of paper with torn edges. "My proof of insurance is on my phone."

She pulled a phone out of her purse and swiped the cracked screen. Then she showed me a digital insurance card from a budget company.

The names and address matched, and the insurance was current, so I let her keep the phone. When I handed it back, she pointed at my arm. "Nice ink."

How is this girl not high?

I patted the roof of her car. "Close your door and sit tight. I'll be back in a few minutes." I backed toward the end of the vehicle.

Had she been going six miles per hour less, I wouldn't have given her a ticket, but fifteen over on this road was my limit. My code. And it was a rainy night.

No job was worth wrapping a car around a tree.

At least she wasn't impaired. Which, thankfully, meant no trip back to the station for me.

When I reached her bumper, I turned back to my patrol car.

Tires screamed.

Headlights swerved.

Crunch.

The last thing I saw was a flash of silver sailing straight for my face.

CHAPTER THREE

"Shit, Celise!" With a stifled yowl, through a clenched jaw, I pounded my fist against the side of the thin gurney mattress. "What are you cleaning it with? Battery acid?"

"Yes. It's been a while since we've had to patch you up." The syringe clanged against the metal tray as the nurse put it down. "We use battery acid on all our patients now."

I held up my middle finger.

"Classy." She bent so we were eye level, and her honey-blonde bob fell away from her face. "You sure you don't want the drugs? This isn't going to get any better."

"I'm sure," I said, gritting my teeth. "Are you about finished?"

"No." She picked up another syringe. "Does Paps know about this?"

"Not yet, and don't you call him. No sense in waking him up. I'll tell him tomorrow."

"What about Ransom?"

"I'm waiting on him to call me back."

"Sounds familiar." She laughed and hosed down the side of my head again.

I cringed, unsure of what hurt the most: the gash in the skin or the pounding inside my skull. Through watery eyes, I saw the lobby door open and my boss walk in.

Because he'd been on his way back to the Drexler when the 911 call came in, Essex had been the first officer on scene. He'd stayed behind with the driver of the car that had hit mine when I was taken by ambulance to the ER.

I muttered the F-word into the pillow, then steeled my nerves—and my face—as Celise bathed the wound in betadine.

Essex squatted beside me. "Nyx." A lot of emotion was packed into my name. Worry. Pity. Relief. All those feelings surged in his dark eyes. "Are you all right?"

"Do I look all right?"

He let out a sharp sigh. "You look better than you did. God, there was so much blood."

"Pretty common with head wounds," Celise said. "Lots of capillaries in the scalp."

The information didn't seem to help Essex relax. "When I pulled up, I thought you were dead."

"Right now, I feel like I'd rather be." I winced as Celise dabbed the deep gash with gauze.

"Didn't you numb her scalp?" Essex asked her.

"She refused," Celise answered. "I've learned better than to try to argue."

Essex scowled at me. "You know, Nyx, normal people aren't so well acquainted with the emergency-room staff."

"You know everyone who works days in here." Our job required regular trips to the hospital: suicide attempts, DUI blood draws, rape kits.

"Yes, but they can't identify my personality flaws."

I pointed at Celise. "Well, this one gave birth to my niece, so . . ."

Essex looked surprised.

"Don't let her fool you," Celise said to him. "All the other doctors and nurses know her flaws too. Are you new on night shift?"

"First week," he answered.

"Good luck," Celise said with a grin.

I made quick introductions. "Celise Kendrick, this is Sergeant Tyler Essex. Celise survived a short time being married to my brother."

They shook hands over my head.

"*The* Sergeant Essex?" Celise asked, casting me a teasing smile.

"What's that mean?" he asked.

"We've just heard a lot about you. Good things, which is rare coming from this one." She pointed the syringe at me.

My cheeks burned as he looked at me. "That's good to know," he said.

Ugh.

She touched my shoulder. "Be right back."

"Been talking about me, huh?" Essex asked when she was gone.

"Yeah. Complaining."

He smiled. "Did they do a head CT?"

"Let me sit up."

He grabbed my arm to help, but I wrenched it free and pushed myself up against the thin mattress. My whole body ached, and stars twinkled around my boss's face. I forced my squinted eyes to relax.

God, he's hot.

I was lightheaded. Must've been the concussion.

Touching my chin, he turned my head for a better look, then cringed. "Damn."

I pushed his hand away. "I'm fine."

"Your ear's dangling. You're *not* fine."

"CT was clear. No bleeding, but doc says I'll need staples to close my head and sutures to reattach the top of the ear."

I could feel the sticky blood dried on the side of my face and down my neck. Celise had tried to clean it off, but she'd mostly just diluted the mess, making it spread. As much as I could see of my undershirt was soaked in dark blood.

Essex was still visually cataloging the damage. "You're lucky that mirror didn't take off your head. You hurt anywhere else?"

"Mostly sore from the fall. My ass will have some spectacular bruising."

Red burned through his cheeks. He cleared his throat and changed the subject. "Do you remember any of it?"

"I remember everything until I blacked out. I didn't even hear the car coming until it was almost on top of me. It's like it wasn't even running."

"Electric motor."

"Was the guy hurt?"

"Not a scratch. Just shaken up."

"Was he drunk?"

"No. Said he thought he saw a person in the middle of the road."

"I was nowhere near the middle of the road."

"I'm sure he was distracted by blue lights and hit a slick spot. It's a good thing you parked where you did. He sends his condolences, by the way."

I'd woken up in the emergency lane with the chick I'd pulled over cradling my head in her lap. Blood had been everywhere. All over her. All over me. She'd called 911 before beginning roadside triage. "What happened to . . .?" I couldn't remember her name.

"The woman you pulled over?"

"Yeah."

"She's still here. Saw her in the waiting room when I came in."

"Really? She's been here the whole time?" I looked over his shoulder like she might be standing right behind him.

"I think so." He grinned. "Maybe she's hoping you'll let her off with a warning."

"Ah, damn it." Celise dropped her arms against her sides when she reentered the room. "Why did you sit up? Do you know how long it took me to fish all that black hair out of the way?"

"Got any scissors?" I asked.

Puzzled, Celise opened a drawer on the rolling cart by my bed. She handed me a pair of shears, and in two quick moves, I lifted up the right side of my long hair and sliced through it.

I handed her back the shears, along with the twelve-inch handful of blood-matted locks. "Here. Donate this to a wig program or something."

Celise's mouth was gaping. "This isn't Master Clips. We don't do that here."

Essex was staring at the clump of hair. "Is this part of the concussion?"

"Nope. This is just crazy." Celise dropped it in the red trash bag.

"The hair was in the way. Now it's not." I lay back on the pillow. "Gonna have to shave it off anyway."

"Why?" Essex asked.

Smiling, I draped my forearm over my eyes. "How else will I show off the scar?"

I heard both of them snicker.

Celise pushed my face toward the pillow. "Now, be still."

I cringed as she pulled strands of hair from the wound again.

Essex lifted my arm off my face to look at me. "Take the damn drugs, Saphera. You're going to be off for a few days anyway."

"I don't need—"

"Calm down. It's our weekend off anyway," he reminded me.

"Oh, right. But I am going to my interview tomorrow."

"I'm sure they can reschedule it."

"Hell no."

"Fine, but get ready for a nice little vacation. The department's going to need all the details on the concussion, and you'll have to be cleared by medical before returning to duty."

"I'm OK."

"Keep saying that. Celise, at least give her lidocaine for the staples." Essex backed toward the door. "I need to make some calls, but I'll be here when you're done . . . unless you want me to stay."

With a groan, I covered my eyes again. When I heard the hallway door open and shut, I peeked at Celise. "Give me the drugs."

Essex returned when the doctor finally came in to discharge me.

Dr. Richmond read over her notes. "The headache may last a few weeks. Take the weekend off, and follow up with your regular doctor in seven to ten days to have the stitches and staples removed." She looked at me over the tops of her glasses. "If the headache gets worse, if you have a seizure, new vision problems, arm or leg weakness, or new problems with balance and coordination, come back in. Do you live alone?"

"Yes."

"Can someone stay with you tonight?"

I grimaced. It hurt too much to think.

"If not, it might be a good idea to keep you here for the—"

"I'll figure something out." Nothing in me wanted to stay in the noisy hospital. I *hated* hospitals.

The doctor didn't seem sure she believed me. Hell, I wasn't sure I believed me. "Head injuries are serious, Nyx."

"I'll make sure she takes it easy," Essex said.

I would have glared at him if it didn't hurt to look up. "When can I go back to work?"

"Typically one to two weeks. Who's your primary physician?" she asked.

"Dr. Pratts." I pointed to the ceiling. "She has an office upstairs."

"Ah yes. I'm going to let Dr. Pratts make the final call on returning to work. She'll also take out the stitches and staples after at least a week."

"I'll make an appointment tomorrow. Thank you, Dr. Richmond," I said.

"My pleasure. Stay safe out there," the doctor replied to both of us before turning back toward the nurse's station.

Pain radiated through my left butt cheek and down my leg as I stood. Before moving, I took a second to let the pain settle and the dizziness fade. At the triage door, I looked around for Celise but didn't see her anywhere.

"Looking for something?" Essex asked.

"My sister-in-law. Wanted to say goodbye. She must be busy."

"Probably. The waiting room is slammed. Do you have everything?"

I picked up my phone and keys off the counter. "Where's my weapons belt?"

"In my car. Figured I'd be driving you home."

"I'll call an Uber."

He gave me the side eye.

"You're on duty. There's no sense in you driving—"

"Stop being so stubborn, and let me help you for once." He held the lobby door for me.

Ready to argue, I turned toward him so quickly that the room spun. Black threatened to close over my eyes again, and I grabbed a fistful of his shirt.

He put his hands on my waist. When I focused on him again, his expression was begging, *"See?"*

He took a step closer. "Look, I know you can take care of

yourself. If any of the guys were here tonight and needed help, I'd offer."

To his credit, he was right. Unlike some of the other brass, I had no doubt Essex would always show up for his officers.

"I know, but—"

"But what?"

But there was also that *other thing* between us. That treacherous gray area where attraction rumbled like a loosely corked geyser. It had been there since the night we met, when he'd challenged the lonely girl at the bar to a game of darts.

Tonight, that gray area—along with everything else in the world—felt too unstable for me to be trusted.

He lifted my chin to look at him, and for a second, I couldn't remember what we were arguing about. Head trauma is tricky that way.

"Officer Nyx!" a young woman behind him shouted.

Essex released my face as the girl from the traffic stop hurried across the waiting room. She dropped her phone and a half-eaten Snickers on the way.

She grabbed them and covered her mouth with her hands. "Thank god you're okay."

And then she hugged me.

I was frozen with my arms at my side. Over her shoulder, Essex was enjoying my discomfort. "Please don't touch me," I said.

She took a quick step back. "Sorry, I was just so worried about you. I've never seen that much blood in my life."

"It happens with head injuries." I squinted against the harsh halogens. "Thanks for sticking around to call for help."

"Of course." She laughed nervously. "They would have found out if I ran, right?"

I laughed and it hurt. "Yeah, they would have. What's your name again?" My brain felt foggy.

She stuck out her hand. "Bess Lincoln." She leaned forward and winked. "No relation."

Essex chuckled. "We really appreciate your help tonight, Bess Lincoln, no relation."

Bess nodded, looking a little rattled. She still wore her white work shirt, though it was now red with my blood. "All joking aside, I'm really glad you're okay. If there's anything else I can do to help—"

"Actually, there is. Can you give me a lift home?"

She blinked a few times. "Um, sure, I guess."

I gestured toward her bloody top. "Doesn't look like you're going to work. Do you mind?"

"Of course I don't mind." She dug around in her purse, spilling a gum wrapper on the floor as she retrieved her keys. She jingled them in the air and picked up the wrapper. "I'll just go bring my car around."

"Thanks."

When she was gone, Essex frowned. "Seriously? You'd rather get a ride home from a complete stranger with a shitty driving record than come with me?"

No. "Yes."

"Why?"

"She owes me for not writing her a ticket."

He laughed. "She dragged your ass out of oncoming traffic. I think you're square. Try again."

A wave of nausea washed over me, and I grabbed the wall to steady myself. "Seriously, I'm grateful for the offer, but I just want to go home and pass out. If I go with you, we'll go over my interview *again,* and my nerves will never let me sleep tonight."

My words took him back a step. "Oh. Nyx, I apologize if I've pushed too hard about the job."

"You didn't do anything. I appreciate you looking out for me."

"You really shouldn't be nervous—"

I wagged my finger. "See? Here we go."

He grabbed my hand. "I only say it because I believe in you." He held my gaze for a second longer than was probably appropriate.

"Thank you," I said quietly.

He dropped my hand. "Who's staying with you tonight?"

"Umm . . ."

"Can your brother come?"

"I still haven't heard back from Ransom."

"What about your mom?"

"Mal? Ha. I'd rather stay here."

"I could lock you up in a cell for the night."

"I'd rather that too."

He lowered his voice and looked around to be sure no one could hear. "I'll sleep on the couch—"

"No, no, no—"

"We don't have to talk. You won't even know I'm there."

I sighed so hard it hurt my head. "I don't need a babysitter, Sarge."

"I'm not trying to babysit you. I'm trying to be a friend."

I put my hands up. "How's this? Call me every hour. If I don't answer, you can send the whole damn department Code Three to my house."

"Counteroffer. I call you every hour, *and* I post McCollum outside your place with a key."

"Deal." My brain was tired of negotiating. All I wanted to do was curl up in a dark, silent room and shut the hell down. "Tell him I'll leave a key on top of the doorframe."

"I'll get your stuff from my car. At least let me help you outside. You don't look so steady on your feet."

"I'm not." No point in lying.

He put an arm around my waist as we walked through the sliding-glass doors.

Bess pulled up under the overhang in her rattling, rusty green coupe. The gears *thunked* into place as she put the car in park. It backfired. Essex shook his head as he opened the passenger-side door.

"Hang on!" Bess called across the car, diving toward the floorboard. She tossed soda cans, food wrappers, and enough paper to fill a library into the back seat.

Essex lifted an eyebrow and lowered his voice. "Did they give you a tetanus shot in there?"

I smiled.

When the seat was clear, he protected my head with his hand as I eased into the car. "Be right back," he said when I was inside. I left one boot on the ground as he ran across the parking lot to his SUV.

Bess let out a low whistle that echoed in my ears. "That's your boss?" She gripped the steering wheel with both hands. "If he were my boss, I'd never be late to work."

"Speaking of work, are you going to get fired?" I asked, looking across the dark car at her. She had stars tattooed behind her right ear.

"Probably, but it wouldn't be your fault. It's been coming since the day I started."

Essex returned with my woven black weapons belt. He handed it to me, then checked the empty chamber of my gun before handing it to me with the slide open.

I checked the weapon myself, then closed the slide and laid it on my lap. I put the clunky belt between my feet when I pulled my right leg inside.

Essex leaned in the doorway. "Text me when you get home?"

"Yeah."

He checked that the door was clear before closing it. He stepped back to the sidewalk, and I held up a few fingers as Bess pulled away.

It was after midnight, but the world was too bright for my head. I shielded my eyes against the oncoming headlights. Still feeling like I might puke at any moment, I closed my eyes and reclined against the headrest.

"So where am I going?" Bess asked.

"You know Delaney's in Winter Village?" I asked because everyone knew Delaney's, the shiny new hotspot in my neighborhood.

"Sure. The Irish bar?"

"Yep. Go there."

"I don't know much about head trauma, but I don't think it's a good idea to be drinking alcohol right now."

"I live in the condos behind it." I prayed she'd shut the hell up, but if getting hit in the head wasn't indicative enough, luck was not in my favor tonight.

"Wow. Those are nice."

The condos at Winter Village were nice, too nice for a cop's salary. Half the units had private owners, mostly corporate executives from the Bay Area who spent their summers on the lake and their winters on the ski slopes. My side of the complex was owned by the developer, and the units were rented out by the week to vacationers with deep pockets.

I was the only long-term resident, and only because the management gave me half off the rent for helping keep the place secure. I generally responded to a couple of calls per month from my temporary neighbors. Mostly noise complaints and illegally parked cars.

"So do you have a real name? Or should I just call you Officer Nyx?"

"Corporal Nyx."

"*Oooo-kay*. Wanna listen to some music, *Corporal* Nyx?"

"No."

"Oh, right. Head injury. Bet it hurts."

"Getting hit by a car usually does."

"You get hit by cars often?"

"No."

"Don't really feel like talking?"

I held my finger over my lips. "Shh, or I might puke all over your car."

She laughed quietly. "Wouldn't make much of a difference."

Couldn't argue with that.

We rode for a while in semi-silence. Bess hummed "Miss Independent," tapping out the beat with her fingers on the steering wheel, until I considered shooting her. I changed my mind when I realized I'd have to drive myself.

The bars were still in full swing when Bess pulled into my neighborhood, on the mountainside, behind Winter Village. From the air or on Google Maps, Ransom always joked that Sapphire Lake looked like a saggy ass. By his description, I lived in the tramp stamp, on the long north shore of the lake.

When I'd started with the department, Winter Village, the lake's shopping and dining mecca, was where my team had introduced me to "Sunday Funday." The one off-day a month when we'd all meet up for deep-fried food and endless buckets of beer. The guys were now jealous because I could walk (or stumble) home after indulging too much.

Down the hill and directly across the street from my building, the patio of Delaney's Irish Pub faced my kitchen window. The pub's bay doors were open, and a loud and drunken "Whiskey in the Jar" blared from the stage inside. The crowd merrily sang along.

I pushed open the car door, taking a second to collect my wits before getting out. It was challenging, and the accordion whining from the bar certainly didn't help.

Bess ran around the car to assist. When I stood and the blood rushed to my head, I was thankful she was there. After a moment, the lights stopped twinkling behind my eyes, and I tucked my gun into the back of my waistband.

Bess looped my weapons belt over her arm. "Geez, this thing is heavy. You have to wear it every day?"

"Every day I'm on duty."

"Which way?"

I pointed to the last unit on the right, where I had a garage space on the ground floor. The front door was up a flight of stairs.

Stairs that were likely going to kick my ass.

"Do you know your neighbors?" She was looking down the row of condos.

"No."

"You want me to leave?"

Yes. As much as I hated to admit it, I needed her help. "Can you just make sure I get inside without passing out?"

"Sure. Lead the way."

We started up the steps to 130 Snowshoe Boulevard, Unit 9-C, my new end condo with a partial view of the lake over the roofs of the shopping village.

As predicted, halfway up the stairs, I had to sit down. And almost had to throw up.

"You OK?" Bess asked, stopping behind me.

I gave a thumbs-up and took a deep breath. The smell of fried fish and firepit smoke filled my nose, sending another wave of nausea through me.

After another second, I reached for the handrail to pull myself up. Bess grasped it instead and helped me to my feet. She didn't release my waist until we reached the door.

I fumbled with my keys to find the right one, and when I finally got the door open, she followed me into the entrance hall. My snowboard and a pair of skis were mounted above the entrance table. To the left, a short hallway led to the bedrooms I'd converted to an office and a home gym. A bathroom was between them. To the right, through the kitchen, was the living room, dining room, and my master bedroom.

I put my phone on the kitchen bar and tried to work my

house key free from its ring. Looking down, my vision rippled, and I dropped the keys twice.

Bess put her hands under mine. "Can I help you, please?"

I released the keys. "I need the big brass one off the ring."

"OK. Go change. You smell like blood."

"So do you."

"And I can't wait to get out of these clothes. Go. I've got this."

I started toward my room. "There's water and beer in the fridge if you're thirsty."

She looked up with surprise. "Thanks. Water would be great."

It was the least I could do.

I walked into my bedroom and froze in front of the full-length mirror. Freaked myself out a bit, if I'm being honest. I looked like Carrie at the prom, covered in blood, with Bride-of-Frankenstein hair. Part of which was missing.

I removed my gun and walked to the bed. On the headboard was a fake panel. When I pressed it, it slowly lowered back toward me. I stuck the pistol into the mounted holster and closed it before sitting on the bed.

Balancing my boot on the nightstand, I pulled the knife from around my ankle and put it in the top drawer. Then I unlaced my boots and unbuttoned my shirt. There was no saving it. It was soaked in blood with a hole torn in the left elbow. My scathed skin stuck to the sleeve as I stripped it off. With a wince, I yanked the fabric free and threw the uniform in the trash.

There was no way in hell I was pulling my blood-soaked undershirt over my head, past the stitches and the staples. So I walked to the kitchen to get scissors.

Bess gasped and clutched her heart when she saw me. "God, you look like an extra from *The Walking Dead*."

I pointed at her own shirt. "You should check a mirror."

"Your key is on the counter."

"Thank you." I picked it up and took it outside, reaching up to hide it on top of the doorframe. Parked across from my driveway, a patrol car flashed its lights. I waved to McCollum.

When I returned, Bess was holding a water bottle and looking at the only photo on my fridge. Hell, maybe the only photo in my whole condo. "Are you in the Army too?" she asked.

"I was."

"They made you shave your head?"

"Yep."

"Who's the guy? He's cute."

I sighed. *Questions* were the reason there weren't photos around. "A friend." I took the scissors out of the junk drawer and cut the center of my shirt's thick collar. "Listen, I need to jump in the shower and wash off this blood."

"Mind if I hang out till you're finished? You were pretty wobbly on the stairs, and I wouldn't feel good about leaving you alone. Probably wouldn't sleep a wink tonight."

As much as I hated it, she was right. "OK. I'll be fast."

"I'd rather you be careful. Maybe a bath would be safer."

"Noted." I gestured around the room. "Make yourself comfortable. The TV remote is on the sofa." When I returned to my bedroom, I grabbed the shirt's collar with both hands and ripped it down the front.

I stripped out of the rest of my clothes and turned on the shower. When I straightened, and the blood rushed to my head again, I realized a bath might, in fact, be safer. I leaned into the garden tub and plugged the drain before switching the shower back to the faucet.

I had to lean against the wall to regain control of my vision.

When the wash of dizziness passed, I heard my phone in the bedroom. I caught a flash of my backside in the mirror as I passed. A bright red, splotchy bruise was already blossoming from the top of my hip bone, halfway down the side of my ass. It was tender to the touch.

In my room, I checked my phone. There was a missed call

from the station—they didn't leave a message—and a text from Essex. *Make it home OK?*

I texted him back. *Safe and whole. The key is outside for McCollum. Thanks for your help tonight.*

Essex: *Did the doc say anything about sleeping after the concussion?*

As I was typing, he texted again.

Because I could come over and keep you awake.

My head snapped back, and it hurt. What the hell did that mean?

Essex: *That came out wrong.*

Me: *You think?*

Essex: *I just meant I could take off and keep you company.*

Me: *You should stop while you're behind. She said it's fine for me to sleep.*

Essex: *OK.*

I checked my call log again. Still not a damn word from Ransom. I put the phone on the bathroom counter and stepped into the tub. The water was hot as I eased down into it.

Carefully, I splashed my face and neck, letting red drizzle down my chest and arms. My elbow burned as the fresh blood clots melted away. When the water ran clear, I shut off the faucet and relaxed back against the wall.

Every muscle between my chin and my toes ached. The soothing heat seeped into my bones, and the room was dark and quiet except for the muffled noise from the TV in the living room. I closed my eyes, and a moment later, I was asleep.

And a moment after that, I was inexplicably *not*.

CHAPTER FOUR

$\mathcal{W}$ith a gasp, I bolted upright in the bathtub. Strangely, the water didn't slosh or splash.

It didn't even ripple.

In fact, I could feel its pressure around my legs but not its volume. Its heat but not its texture. My knees moved sluggishly as I drew them toward my chest.

And another set of knees lay dormant beneath the water.

Oh no.

My heart pounded in my chest, drum-line loud to my super-sensitive ears. The large bathroom seemed to vibrate with the sound. I covered my head with my arms.

Oh no. Oh no. Oh no.

This was a dream. A nightmare. A byproduct of a head injury. Absolutely nothing more.

It couldn't be.

Yes. Of course. You have a head injury, Nyx. That's all this is. Take a deep breath. Don't panic . . .

The lifeless legs in the tub were definitely mine. The outside of the left one was covered in patches of silvery-pink scar tissue from my ankle to my hip. And my toes were painted a glittery blue-violet, fresh from the day before.

Nausea fluttered through my gut as a distant dream danced across my memory. Me, standing beside my body, lying in a hospital bed.

Josh stood opposite the bed. Unlike my body hooked up to all the machines, Josh was pristine. No bruises. No road rash. No twisted limbs. When our eyes met, someone else was looking at me.

"You're not Josh."

He seemed mildly surprised, and he shook his head.

"You're Death."

He nodded.

"Are you here for me?" I asked, my voice steady and calm.

"No."

"For Josh?"

His eyes didn't waver from mine, nor did they blink.

"Is he in pain?"

"No."

"Can you take me instead?"

"No."

"Can I see him?"

"There is no time. You must return. Now."

The last thing I remembered seeing was his hand coming toward my face. At the time, I'd thought it was just a crazy trauma-and-drug-induced dream. But this—whatever was happening now—felt exactly the same.

No, no, no . . .

This couldn't be real.

"I'll be dead by morning," Elias had said in my car just a few short hours before.

If he was dead, his "gift" was tied to his bloodline, and upon his death, it would pass to his firstborn—Ransom.

Ransom.

Not me.

I cradled my head in my trembling hands. It was Ransom's destiny to carry on the demented family legacy.

Not mine.

Ransom wanted it. *Needed* it. Hell, he even had the word "DETACHED" tattooed across his knuckles. I daresay the gift was the only thing he clung to all those years of our parents being locked up. To him, it was a superpower soon to be in his grasp.

Not to me.

Never to me.

This . . . whatever *this* was had destroyed any shred of normality us kids were supposed to have. We'd been orphaned. I was born on the floor of a women's prison, for Christ's sake, because of this *thing*. This vile, wicked thing.

The body beneath me flinched, sending tiny waves across the surface of the water.

This can't be possible.

I needed to wake myself, but how?

I pinched my arm and slapped my cheeks, but nothing happened. In the movies, people always woke up from dreams by either falling or dying.

Falling, I was brave enough to try.

Gripping the sides of the tub, I pushed myself up. There was no headrush, no dizziness, no pain.

Not a good sign at all.

When I stepped out of the tub, I should have been dripping. I wasn't. Looking down, I expected my body to be transparent, ghostly. To the contrary, it was clear and in focus, unlike the rest of the bathroom. It was also very naked. My tattoos were bright and colorful, and the scars down the length of my entire left side were still visible.

I touched the side of my head. No staples or swelling. Interesting, since they were so fresh and the scars were so old.

On the chance I wasn't dreaming, I closed my eyes to avoid the mirror. If what Elias had once said about them was true, they could be dangerous. I couldn't remember exactly why, but the warning had freaked me the hell out as a kid. Something about getting lost inside—or stuck.

With shaking hands, I extended my arms at my sides. I took a deep breath, closed my eyes, and—

Bzzz. Bzzz. Bzzz.

My phone was ringing. Keeping my eyes off the mirror, I crept to the counter and looked at my bright phone screen.

Ransom.

I reached for it. When my fingertips neared it, the phone gave a violent sizzle. Then the pixels splintered across the display, and the glass screen cracked.

Shit.

Frustrated, I pressed my eyes closed, extended my arms again, and fell backward—a surefire way to wake oneself from a dream. Mid freefall, I freaked and caught myself, landing hard with my bare ass on the cold tile floor.

It hurt.

I wasn't dreaming.

I wasn't hallucinating from a head injury.

I was *detached.*

My consciousness, my spirit, was free.

I crawled back to the bathtub, where my body was hyperventilating and my heart thumped so hard I could see my pulse pounding in the side of my neck. The tendons strained between my jaw and shoulders, and my hands were balled into fists.

"I can't do this right now!" I panted, pulling my hands back through my hair. I closed my eyes again. *How do I make it stop?*

"So how do you get back in your body?" I heard Ransom's tiny voice ask, somewhere far back in my memory.

It was the year Gran had cut Ransom's hair at home. His bangs were at a crazy angle as Elias palmed his forehead across the visitation-room table. I was drinking chocolate milk out of a secondhand *Lion King* sippy cup.

"I hold my head like this . . ." Elias squeezed and gently jostled my brother's head until he giggled. "And I say"—Elias dramatically deepened his voice—"Self, go back in!"

I put my hand on my very real forehead and focused . . .

This time when I shot upright, water sloshed onto the tile floor. It was cold. I scrambled out of the tub, gripping the wall for support as I grabbed a towel off the rack. Wrapping it around my body, I stepped out onto the floor and grasped the counter to hold myself upright.

When the dizziness and stars faded, I stared back at myself in the mirror. My chest was heaving, and I was visibly shaking all over. On the counter was my phone. I hesitated before picking it up.

With a hard swallow, I reached for it.

Dead. With a crack that covered the screen.

I swore and slammed it onto the counter so hard a piece of glass skittered across the granite.

There was a light knock at my bedroom door. "Nyx? You OK in there?"

Holding the counter for support, two rogue tears dripped from my eyes and splashed between my feet.

"Nyx?"

I quickly dried my eyes with the edge of the towel. With a sniff, I walked to the door and opened it.

The news about Ryder Stone was on the television behind Bess. Her eyes widened as they drifted all the way to my bare knees. "Umm . . . everything okay in here? I heard a crash."

"Every—" I cleared my scratchy throat. "Everything's fine. I just dropped my phone."

"Uh oh. Do you have insurance?"

"Yeah. And I have another phone I can—" I stopped. "Shit. I *don't* have my SWAT phone."

"Need to borrow mine?" She patted her pockets.

"If you don't mind."

"Not at all." She pulled out a phone and handed it to me. Her screen, too, was shattered.

My hands trembled as I tapped the screen, and a locked keypad appeared.

"The password is holla, like Missy Elliott's version." Bess cupped her hand around her mouth. "Holla!"

Cute.

I tapped in the digits and touched the phone icon. Bess stepped out of view as I dialed my brother's number. It rang and rang, then went to voicemail. Gritting my teeth, I redialed. That time he answered on the first ring. "Hello?"

"It's Nyx."

"Finally."

"Finally? I've been calling you all night."

"If you weren't aware, shit's kinda been crazy at work. Celise came by the hotel on her break. Said I needed to call you. Is everything all right?"

"Did she say anything else?" I asked.

"About what?"

God bless Celise, who understood the right amount of family meddling.

"Ransom, I think Elias is dead."

Silence.

"Ransom?"

"How do you know?"

"He visited me tonight and said the treatments they're doing aren't working. He said he'd be dead by morning."

"Damn. Guess I'll be going home and popping some Ambien when I get off work." He sounded way too excited.

I frowned. I needed to tell him what had happened in the bathtub, lest he overdose on sedatives trying to detach, but I was keenly aware Bess was hovering right outside the doorway.

"Please don't." I sat on the edge of my bed and massaged my aching forehead.

"Are you OK? Celise said you were in the ER."

"I'm fine, but I need to see you. Can you come over?"

"With all the shit that happened tonight, I don't know when I'll be done here. The media is already like maggots on a carcass. And isn't your interview tomorrow . . . err, today?"

"Yeah."

"Are you working this weekend?"

"I'll be working overtime if they let me go back to work."

Ransom laughed. "What happened? You throat punch someone again?"

"No, smartass. I was hit by a car after I left the hotel."

"Shit. Really?" His voice jumped up an octave.

"Really."

"Are you OK? I'll leave work right now."

Part of me wanted to let him, but Ransom had a hard enough time keeping a job without having to take care of me. And Ransom *needed* his job. Joint custody of his daughter, Amelia, depended on it. "No. I'm all right and at home now. I'll see you when you're off."

"What happened?"

"I was doing a traffic stop and a car hit my cruiser. A piece of metal nearly took my head off."

"We heard sirens at the hotel. I had no idea it was you. Why didn't you call me?"

"I did, dumbass."

He was quiet for a second. "Nyx, I really don't mind taking off. I can be there in half an hour."

"Thanks. I'll call you if I can't hack it alone."

"Does Paps know?"

"No, and I don't want to worry him tonight. I'll tell him tomorrow."

"OK."

"Ransom?"

"Yeah?"

"Stay off the sleeping pills. If it happens, it happens."

He groaned. "I know."

My brother and drugs didn't mix. The first time he landed in jail on possession charges, he was only sixteen. Now in his thirties, he'd been clean for a while, but he also had enough sobriety chips for a game of poker. It was part of the reason I stayed clear of anything stronger than Tylenol.

What will happen when he learns the truth? Ransom wouldn't inherit the gift. And even bigger still . . .

His whole life had been a lie.

If I was able to detach, it meant Ransom wasn't Elias's first-born. Elias wasn't Ransom's father *at all*.

Nausea churned in my stomach again. "I'll see you this weekend," I said, my voice cracking with emotion.

"Yes, but I'm serious. Call me if you need help."

"I will. I promise. My personal phone is destroyed. I'll text you my SWAT phone number when I get it back."

"OK."

"Kiss Milly for me."

"She wants you to come visit."

"Tell her I'll come soon."

"OK. Bye, sis."

"Bye." I ended the call and stared at the phone.

"Are you all right?" Bess asked from the door.

With a nod, I stood and crossed the room to return her phone. "Yeah. Thanks for letting me make a call."

She didn't reach for it. "Do you need to call anyone else?"

I needed to call my boss, but his phone number wasn't one of the few I had memorized. "No, thank you, but can you do me a favor on your way out?"

"Sure," she said as she accepted the phone.

"There's a patrol car sitting across from my driveway. Can

you tell Officer McCollum that my personal phone is broken, and my SWAT phone is still in my patrol car? Also, ask him to let Sergeant Essex know."

"Essex. Got it." She rocked back and forth on her heels. "Are you sure you don't want someone to stay with you? I really don't have anywhere to be."

I forced a smile. "I'll be fine."

"Okay." She jerked her thumb over her shoulder. "I wrote my number on the whiteboard calendar in the kitchen. Not that it will do you much good tonight."

"Thanks."

"If you need anything at all, just *holla*."

I smiled and followed her to the front door. "I will. I really appreciate all your help tonight, Bess."

She turned with a hopeful smile. "Does this mean you won't give me a speeding ticket?"

I laughed, sending a wave of pain through my head. "Not tonight, but slow it down out there."

"I promise. It was really nice to meet you, Officer Nyx."

"Just Nyx. It's what my friends call me."

She beamed. "Okay." She waved and walked out.

I closed and locked the door behind her, and fell the hell apart.

CHAPTER FIVE

The next morning? Evening?—I wasn't sure—my doorbell rang. Disoriented, I looked at the clock on the nightstand. 8:19 a.m. My arms flailed across the cool sheets. I was, mind and all, still in my bed.

I pulled on a pair of sweatpants and trudged barefoot to the door. Looking through the peephole, I saw Essex in the breezeway wearing civilian clothes. Jeans and a fitted black tee.

I gingerly ran my fingers through my hair and pulled open the door. He held up two paper cups of coffee from Sapphire Java. "I come in peace." He offered one to me.

When I took it, I stepped out of the doorway. "Morning."

"Morning," he said as he walked inside. "How's the head?"

"Kinda feels like I drank a bottle of tequila and played drums on my skull with a hammer."

He grinned. "That good, huh?"

With a moan, I closed the door and led him to the kitchen. I squinted against the bright sunshine coming in from the sliding-glass doors to the balcony. I crossed the living room and closed the blackout curtains, shrouding the room in precious darkness.

I left the corner open so I could see to walk. "What are you doing here?"

"Doubted you should be driving yet, so I thought I'd give you a lift to your interview." His eyes fell to my sweatpants. "That is, if you're still going."

"Yeah. I'm still going."

"And . . ." He angled to the side and pulled my SWAT phone and some rolled papers from his pocket. He handed me the phone first. "Figured you might need this. I got it out of your car this morning."

"Thanks." I checked its battery level before dialing my personal cell phone number. "Is my car totaled?" I asked while my voicemail picked up. I pressed the pound sign to check my messages.

"No, they can fix it. Said they'd call me later today with an estimate of how long it will take."

"God, I hope I don't have to drive a pool car." I punched in my voicemail code.

"You have one new message," the robot voice said. "New message received at seven-sixteen a.m." Beep. "Hello, Corporal Nyx, this is Warden McCain from the Nevada State Penitentiary. Please call me back at your earliest convenience. We have an update about your father. Thank you." He left a phone number.

I stared at the phone in my hand. Elias was dead. No doubt about it.

"Everything OK?" Essex asked.

I put the phone on the counter. "Fine." I pointed to the papers he was still holding. "What's that?"

He handed them to me. "I thought you might want a copy of your accident report."

"Why?"

"Read it. Specifically, check out the statement from the guy who hit your car."

I skimmed the typed notes. *Driver reported that he saw a man standing in the middle of the lane. He swerved to miss the man, striking Officer Nyx's patrol car. When he looked toward the road again, the man had vanished. 'Like a ghost.'* I shook my head. "So now we've got ghosts to worry about? Great."

Essex chuckled. "Did you see a ghost?"

"I saw headlights coming at my face. If there was a ghost, I was too busy trying not to die to notice." I opened the cabinet above the stove and grabbed a bottle of ibuprofen.

"Didn't the doctor give you a prescription?"

"Yeah."

"Are you going to get it filled?"

"No."

He shook his head and sipped his coffee.

"What's the maximum dosage on this stuff?" I poured a handful.

"Not that many," he said with worried eyes.

I funneled a few into my mouth before leaning over the sink to drink straight from the faucet. Bending over was a bad idea. Lights twinkled around my vision when I straightened. I pressed the ball of my hand against my forehead and groaned.

"Maybe you should go back to bed."

I leaned against the counter. "I'm fine."

He grinned over his cup. "Looks like it."

The last thing I wanted was to go back to bed. I'd fought to stay awake most of the night for fear of leaving my body again. Sometime in the early hours, I'd lost the battle, but my nerves had probably kept me from REM sleep.

"You OK?" Essex asked, snapping me back to reality.

"Yeah. Head's just a little foggy."

Understatement of eternity.

I wished I could talk to him—to *anyone*—about what had happened in the tub, but my head was way too messed up to cross that bridge rationally.

"You made the news," Essex said.

"What?"

"Yeah. Small blip about your accident."

"Great," I said with a groan.

"It was buried in all the Ryder Stone coverage, but some people might mention it."

"Awesome. I'd better call my grandfather."

"Probably should." Essex looked at his watch. "What time's your interview?"

"Ten. I'll call Paps and jump in the shower." Even though I'd cleaned it the night before, I could feel the blood, water, and antibiotic ointment caked onto the side of my head again.

"Take your time."

"All right. If you hear a thud, come running."

"You still dizzy?"

"Only when I stand up, turn around, or think too hard."

"No problems with the last one, at least."

Laughing, I carried my work phone to the bedroom and flipped on the light. It burned my retinas and seared through my skull. As my eyes adjusted, I sat on the edge of the bed and dialed my grandfather's phone number.

Paps didn't answer, but he responded immediately with a text message. *JUST WRAPPED UP A TENNIS MATCH, ABOUT TO SHOWER. CALL YOU LATER?*

Paps couldn't communicate if it wasn't in all caps. I messaged him back. *I need to talk to you before you watch the news.*

My phone rang immediately. "Hey," I answered.

"I already heard about Ryder Stone." Of course he'd heard. Paps loved the whole Stone family. "Is it true? Was it really him in that fire?"

"I think so. They're waiting on official word from the medical examiner, but that's not why I called."

"Oh, what's going on?"

"Two things, actually. I was in a small accident last night. You might hear about it on the news. I'm OK."

"What happened?"

"A car hit my cruiser when I was doing a traffic stop. I was hit by some flying car parts. Tore up the side of my head pretty good."

"Are you all right?"

"Yes. I didn't want you to see it on TV and worry. Celise patched me up at the hospital last night."

"OK." He didn't sound convinced. "Maybe I should come over."

"No, don't. I promise I'm fine. Besides, I'll probably be pretty busy the next few days because of all the Ryder Stone stuff. I need you to keep an eye on Ransom."

"Ransom? Why?"

I lowered my voice. "I think Elias is dead."

Silence.

"Paps?"

"How do you know?" he asked.

"He visited me last night and said it would be soon."

"I really think we should come over."

"I'm about to head out to my interview, so I won't even be home. But I'm supposed to see Ransom this weekend. You should come too."

"That's right. Your interview is today. Good luck, not that you need it."

"Thanks, Paps."

"Remember, I'm here for you, Saphera. You don't have to be so tough all the time. I promise I won't tell anyone if you need to fall apart."

I smiled. "I love you, Paps."

"I love you, sweet pea. Let me know how the interview goes."

"I will."

I ended the call before my emotions got the better of me. I sent a text to Ransom. *This is my work phone. Use this number until you hear otherwise.*

Ransom: *10-4. How's the head? Empty as usual?*

Me: 🖕 *Head is fine. Have you taken any pills?*

Ransom: *No. Stop worrying, MOM.*

With a smirk, I put the phone down. Between us, there was no greater insult. Not that Malena Nyx had ever been much of a mom.

From under the sink, I grabbed my brush, a ponytail holder, and the electric hair clippers. When the whoosh of lightheadedness passed, I carefully brushed my long black hair and pulled everything but the right side up into a high ponytail. I snapped the longest guard onto the clippers and pressed the power button.

Buzzzzz . . .

Gently and meticulously, I buzzed off the hair from my right temple back behind my ear. Black hair fell in clumps in the white sink. When I was finished, I examined the work in the mirror. It could have been shorter, but that would have to wait until the gash started to heal.

After a shower, I slathered the staples with ointment and slowly dried my hair. I dressed in black slacks with a white button-up and a black blazer. I tucked my off-duty gun into an inner-waistband holster and returned to the living room.

Essex had moved to the sofa and had dozed off watching the news. I cleared my throat, and he bolted upright. He looked at his watch as he turned around. "Ten minutes, my ass." His whole body flinched when he saw me. "Whoa. A business suit?"

"I bought it for the occasion."

"Of course you did."

I turned my head. "Think the haircut will do?"

"Certainly shows off the steel. I like it. You sure you feel like going?"

Feel like going? No. But I wasn't getting promoted to narcotics by staying home. And what else would I do? Stay home and try *not* to sleep? Under the best of circumstances, an idle mind could be a dangerous one in my gene pool, and I'd definitely prefer work over falling asleep or overthinking anything with this headache.

"I'm sure." I picked up the file folder lying on the bar.

He grabbed the remote control and stood. A reporter was talking in front of the Drexler.

I pointed to the screen. "They're still at it?"

"Yeah. The media has been reporting on it nonstop. They've dubbed it a possible homicide—"

"What's the holdup with ruling it an *actual* homicide?" I asked.

He turned off the television. "Other than the bodies, they've found zero evidence of foul play. No murder weapon, no accelerant."

I started toward the door. "What about the mutilated corpse?"

His shoulders rose. "Who knows? They found drugs in the chalet's safe."

"What kind of drugs?" I asked.

"Gold heroin—"

"Gold?"

"Yep. Weird, I know. The bags were stamped with the Seven Kings crown, but it wasn't their normal stuff at all."

The 7 Kings, or *Los Siete Reyes,* was an infamous Las Vegas-born street gang, known for two things: bloodshed and heroin. Like so many other transplants from other cities, they'd recently taken root in Sapphire Lake.

"What makes this stuff any different?"

"Not sure yet, but unless it's laced with bath salts, it still doesn't explain mutilation," he said as we walked outside.

I grabbed the key from the door ledge and locked the condo. "Did anything show up on the cameras?"

"Only Stone and his girlfriend entering the chalet with the John Doe. He was wearing a hood, so still no confirmation on his identity."

"So he arrived with them?"

"Looks like they picked him up at the main parking lot of the hotel. He was possibly driving a vehicle that's now in impound. Its VIN came back stolen two years ago in Vegas."

"Prints?"

"None that were any good."

"Damn."

He unlocked his SUV. "I hope to find out more in the command-staff meeting."

I hoped they wouldn't find out more until after I finished my interview.

"You're fidgeting."

My knee was bouncing like it was hooked up to an electric current. I crossed my ankles under the chair.

"Why are you so nervous?" Essex asked. "This'll be a cakewalk today."

"Mmm-hmm." Talking about it would only make my nerves worse, and I'd already chewed a hole on the inside of my lower lip. "Don't you have somewhere else to be?"

He looked at his watch. "My meeting is in ten. You might have to hang out for a bit when you're done."

"Are you going home when you're finished?"

"Might grab some lunch and then go home. Gotta sleep sometime before I'm back at it tonight."

"You're picking up overtime?"

"Yeah. Don't have anything better to do."

"And you'd be at work anyway," I teased.

"Probably." Essex nodded to a stack of documents on my lap. "Is that your list?"

"Yep." I handed one to him. "Five copies, just like you

suggested, printed on expensive paper and bound with a fancy report cover."

He flipped to the cover page. "Nicely done." He read for a few seconds and handed it back to me. "You've got this job in the bag, Nyx."

I smiled, but my heart only beat faster.

The conference-room door opened, and Officer Stephen Morris walked into the hall. Morris was five years younger than me, was a rank lower, and had a year less on the force.

He stumbled a half-step when he saw me, and panic flashed through his eyes when they locked with mine. "Morning, Nyx, Sergeant Essex."

"Morris," Essex said with a nod.

My competition was decked out in a business suit and power tie. Thank god I'd bought a jacket.

"I didn't think you'd make it today," Morris admitted.

Bet he would have liked that. "I wouldn't miss it."

"Are you OK? We all heard what happened."

"I'm fine. Might as well have been a scratch."

Essex choked on his coffee beside me.

Behind Morris, Sergeant Sharon Gregg looked out in the hall. "Corporal Nyx, you made it." She looked almost relieved. "Whenever you're ready."

I stood, and Morris awkwardly offered his hand. I stared at it a second before accepting. "May the best man win," he said with a lopsided smile.

"Yeah. Something like that."

He gave a half-hearted salute to Essex as he hurried past us.

Essex stood and smiled down at me. "The best man will win." He bent toward my ear. "Little does he know your balls are bigger than his."

Laughter eased the tension across my shoulders. I took a slow, deep, steadying breath. "I'll text you when it's over."

"Celebratory beers later," he said with a wink.

With a forced smile, I straightened my jacket and walked into the conference room.

Gregg had reclaimed her seat between Terrence Henley, lieutenant of the narcotics division, and—*holy shit*—Joseph Magnus, the chief.

I only knew the chief by reputation. He was a native of Sapphire Lake, but he'd moved south many years ago to take a job with the Las Vegas Metropolitan Police Department. He'd worked his way up the chain by putting away some of the most hardened criminals in the state. He was the favorite to win sheriff in Las Vegas when he moved back to his hometown to work with us.

That was six months ago, and aside from one very formal introduction, I'd only interacted with him in passing. He hadn't been part of the interview process for this promotion thus far.

"Corporal Nyx." Henley stood, offering me his hand. I shook it, and he nearly crushed my knuckles. He was a tall, stout man with a dimpled bald head. Intimidating as hell but fair—or so everyone who served under him said. "None of us thought you'd be here today."

"Well, sir, I hope that shows how much I want this job."

He smiled. "It certainly does." He gestured across the table. "Have a seat. We won't keep you too long."

I started for the chair Morris had obviously just vacated. It was pushed back and catawampus on the other side of the table. "I hope you'll all forgive me if I do a lot of squinting and taking my time with questions."

"They said you had a nasty concussion," Gregg said.

"And a lot of staples," Henley added.

I turned my head so they could see. They both winced.

Gregg put her hand over her heart. "I'm thankful it wasn't worse."

"Me too."

Gregg folded her hands on the tabletop. "As you know,

Corporal, we've narrowed down the candidates for the open narcotics position. We're very pleased to have Chief Magnus with us today, here by his own personal request."

I couldn't help but wonder if Essex had something to do with that. The two men had played golf together the weekend before, and Essex had personally prepared me for today. Essex was a good friend and an even better boss—but he was also a meddlesome son of a bitch when he wanted to be.

"I'm honored you're here, Chief," I said.

He nodded but didn't speak. He hadn't said a damn word since I walked into the room. Instead, he watched me carefully, sizing me up the way most men do in this field.

I handed each of them one of the portfolios I'd made. "I hope you don't mind, but in addition to my resume, I've listed all my qualifications and commendations for you to consider."

"Very good," Gregg said as I passed one to her.

Even Henley gave an approving nod.

When I handed one to the chief, he put it down without looking at it. "You were in the military, correct?"

"Yes, sir. I was with the Army for eight years."

"And a Ranger, I hear."

"Yes, sir."

This was definitely my boss's doing.

Gregg was looking at my file. "Chief, she was one of the first female graduates of Ranger school in history."

"I'm aware. Very impressive." From his demeanor, I was surprised he thought so.

Henley and Gregg were busy reading through the list in their reports. "You were assigned to counterintelligence?" Henley asked, a note of wonder in his tone.

This shouldn't be new information to him. It wasn't the first time I'd applied for this job, but maybe Essex was right. If I didn't put my achievements in a bullet-pointed list, no one would pay attention to them.

"Yes. Just before I got out, I became part of the newly formed RMIB—"

"RMIB?" Henley asked.

"Sorry, the Seventy-Fifth Ranger Regiment Military Intelligence Battalion in Fort Benning, Georgia." Getting all that out made my headache worse. "We specialized in surveillance, recon, and cyber warfare."

"You sure you wouldn't be interested in working cybercrimes here?" Henley asked.

I bit back a smile. "No offense, but here in Sapphire Lake, cybercrimes means figuring out which website Granny put her social security number into because an email said the IRS was going to arrest her."

He chuckled. "Fair enough."

"What about CID?" Chief asked. "Criminal investigations is the natural step for someone of your rank."

"Investigations involves a lot of office work and talking to people. I don't think that's where I'd be most effective."

"Let me ask you a question, Corporal." Henley steepled his fingertips. "It sounds like you were pretty happy in the military. Why'd you get out?"

Was he for real?

Even Gregg turned all the way toward him, her boggled eyes begging the same question.

Henley looked confused. "What did I say?"

"I'm sorry, sir. I guess I've mistakenly been under the assumption that my history was some sort of highlight on the gossip mill around here."

I had been all over the news when it happened, after all.

His confusion morphed into annoyance. "Luckily, I'm not part of the gossip mill, so please enlighten me."

Gregg opened her mouth to answer, but I held up a hand to stop her. "It's OK. I don't mind telling it." I shifted on my sore ass, shielding my eyes against the halogens. "To be honest, sir, leaving the Army was never my plan. I loved my job and had planned to stay as long as they'd let me. But just after I joined the Seventy-Fifth regiment, I was involved in a fatal motorcycle crash. I suffered a broken arm, a dislocated shoulder, and a cracked spine."

That was the glossed-over version anyway. The drop of Gregg's gaze told me she knew the rest of the story.

Henley tapped a pen against the tabletop. "There was a fatality?"

"Yes, sir." A vice gripped my throat. "My fiancé and I were sideswiped by a car trying to pass us in the outer emergency lane. We were both thrown across the road. I was thrown past the oncoming truck. My fiancé was not."

Silence.

"I'm sorry, Nyx, I didn't know," Henley finally said. "I hope they caught the bastard who hit you."

"No, sir. It was a hit-and-run."

Henley sighed and shook his head.

"After the accident, I was medically discharged, and I returned to Nevada to recover with my grandparents."

"Your grandmother passed recently, didn't she?" the chief asked.

"Yes, sir. In the spring from stomach cancer."

"I was sorry to hear it."

"Thank you."

"Was the accident what made you want to become a cop?" Henley asked.

I almost laughed. A lost bet to Essex over a drunken game of darts was the actual reason I'd become cop. But I didn't think that would help my interview.

"It was part of it," I answered instead.

Gregg closed my report. "No one could argue that you have the talent and experience, but why narcotics?"

It was a fair question. I sat on my hands to keep from fidgeting.

"Narcotics is regularly the most active department here. They're drugs, vice, gangs, and organized crime all rolled into one. I'm ready for more challenging assignments, and I feel I've gone as far as I can with patrol."

Gregg looked at the chief. "She made SWAT right out of FTO, faster than anyone in this department's history."

Magnus nodded.

"I know it isn't a full-time position, but have you not been satisfied with SWAT?" Henley asked.

"SWAT has been great. I hope to be able to continue with them if the schedule allows . . ."

Henley's brow rose. "But?"

"Sir, I've trained my whole adult life to take down the worst villains in the world. I'd like to be trusted with taking down the worst here in Nevada."

"I fully agree," Gregg said. "Is there anything you can think of that might prevent you from fulfilling the role according to the rigid standards of this department?"

"No, ma'am. I'm excited for the challenge."

Gregg was all smiles. It was obvious I had her vote. "That's all the questions I have," she announced, then looked at Henley and the chief. "Anyone else?"

"I've asked all I need to," Henley said, closing my report.

Chief Magnus was studying me, perhaps searching for any sign that I wasn't up to the task. He sat forward. "I'm squared away too. It was nice to see you again, Officer Nyx." He reached across the table.

"You too, Chief."

"I know I speak for all of us when I say take care of that head, and if you need anything, let us know."

All the stress in my heart fizzled as I shook his hand. We'd made it through the entire interview with none of them bringing up my parents. Perhaps now that Elias was gone, that stress would be permanently behind me.

There was a knock at the door.

"Come in!" Henley called.

Valerie Leon from the administrative office stuck her head inside. "Excuse me. I'm sorry to interrupt." She was a perky Black woman with a bright smile and horn-rimmed glasses.

Chief waved her in. "You're not interrupting. We're just wrapping up here. What do you need?"

"I actually have a message for Corporal Nyx, and I was afraid she might slip out before I got to tell her."

The commanding officers looked as perplexed as I felt. "Go ahead then," the chief said with a curious smile.

She hesitated.

"It's OK," I said. "What is it?"

"We received a phone call from the warden's office at the state penitentiary. Your father was found brutally murdered in his cell this morning."

CHAPTER SIX

"I was *this* close." I held up my fingers an inch apart and flipped the passenger's visor down with so much force it smacked against the windshield. I slumped in the seat and covered my eyes with my hand.

My head was killing me.

"I'm sure you're worried about nothing," Essex said. "Everyone knows you weren't associated with him. Don't over-think it."

I shook my head. "Leave it to Elias to exit this life waving his freak flag one last time for all my superiors to see."

"Did they say what happened to him?"

"I need to call the warden for details, but Valerie used the word *brutally*, so . . ." I shrugged, fighting to not care. "I guess he finally got what he deserved."

"You really feel that way?"

"Elias was a madman. Everyone thought so, especially everyone in that boardroom today."

"Not everyone thought that."

"Elias confessed, and he apologized to the family during the trial."

"Doesn't sound like a madman to me. My stepdad said Elias was really remorseful. He didn't want anyone to die."

"The Green River Killer cried in court. It doesn't mean he was innocent."

"True, but just remember, we don't all believe the worst. I'm sure that's true for the brass as well."

"Rumors are the only thing people believe now. Anyone around more than thirty years ago is either retired or dead." As soon as the words left my mouth, I regretted them. "Sorry."

"Don't be sorry. It's true."

Before he died, Essex's father had been chief over the same officers who'd arrested my parents—and the one who'd died because of them.

Ironically, our family association had been the conversation starter when Essex and I first met. That night at the bar, he'd approached and had offered me his palm. He'd asked, "See anything in our future if I buy you a beer?"

Unimpressed, I'd lifted my own bottleneck to my lips. "If you only knew how *not* funny that pickup line was."

"I know exactly how *not* funny I am." He'd leaned against the bar. "Tyler Essex, son of James Essex, chief of police in 1988, and I'd like to buy you a beer anyway."

Intrigued, I'd glanced at the empty barstool beside me. "Have a seat."

I'd expected to drive him away with the same icy attitude I offered everyone those days, but two minutes into the conversation, he'd managed to make me laugh. We'd closed down the bar together, cementing our friendship for life.

"How much do you know about that night?" I asked, braving the questions I'd contemplated asking him for years.

"Not much beyond the official story." Essex looked across the car at me. "To be honest, I've always wanted to ask your take on it but didn't want to overstep."

I appreciated that about him.

"I doubt I know much more than you do. They'd been conning people out of money for a couple of years when Mal started drugging customers with hypnox. She marketed it as an out-of-body experience for people to communicate with lost loved ones. Of course, they didn't meet their loved ones. They met my father, or as they called him, 'a spirit guide', who told them whatever they wanted to hear."

"How'd he pull that off?"

I lifted my shoulders. "That's the question *everyone* wanted to know." It was a lie by omission, sure, but the less Essex knew the better.

"The police started watching them, and they sent an undercover officer in to investigate. The officer took the drug and never regained consciousness. When he didn't check in with his team, they geared up to raid the place. But they were too late. Elias blew up the house with the cop still in it.

"Mal got out but was taken into custody when she fled. Elias was carried out by firefighters, but it was widely believed he meant to burn himself up with it."

"Did he ever say why he set the fire?" Essex asked.

I shook my head. "I never really gave him a chance." Something I was starting to regret, given my newfound trouble sleeping. "Everyone always assumed it was to keep the truth of whatever happened to that officer from coming out."

"The truth of why his body was torn apart?"

I nodded.

"Is your mom still in the business?" he asked.

"As a psychic? No. One of the conditions of her parole was that she never practice again."

He grinned over at me. "You believe in that stuff?"

"Psychics?"

"Yeah."

"No," I answered with a laugh.

It was true I didn't believe in most things in the "psychic" business. But that's not to say Mal didn't have extraordinary abilities. She could a thousand percent see spirits. It's what drew Elias to her to begin with.

A true medium, Mal could not only see spirits that haven't yet passed *on*, but she could also see spirits inside the Boundary. She and Elias met when he was detached.

And unless, by some miracle, my out-of-body episode in the bathtub was some byproduct of a head injury, I could detach now too.

Fuck.

Nausea churned in my stomach.

"Do you ever see her?"

"Mal?"

He nodded.

"She was at Gran's funeral with her new husband or whatever he is, but other than that, she only pops in and out when she wants something. Now that Elias is gone, I expect my brother or I will see her soon."

Mal knew the gift would pass to Elias's firstborn. She'd want to use his heir the way she had used him. And depending on who she showed up to see first would determine how much she knew about Ransom's legitimacy.

For that reason, and for the first time *ever*, I was mildly interested in seeing my mother.

"Are you going to the prison?" Essex asked.

"I don't know. I need to talk to Ransom." I pulled out my SWAT phone. "Mind if I call him now?"

"Of course not."

I tapped the number in my call history. No surprise, Ransom didn't answer.

"I don't know why I bother," I muttered, dropping the phone onto my lap.

"We could drive over there."

"Nah. He'll call me back when he gets around to it."

"Didn't you tell me once that Ransom is an MMA fighter?"

"*Former* MMA, yeah."

"What was his name?"

"The Sandman."

"That's right. How far did he go?"

"He was working his way up to a title fight when he got booted out."

"What'd he do?"

"Failed some drug tests."

It wasn't the whole truth, but Ransom was my brother, and I didn't let anyone talk shit about him—even myself. He'd actually built a *very* lucrative career in the fighting world when he started testing positive for cocaine and marijuana. During one suspension, he was busted for possession on the Las Vegas strip.

After bailing him out of jail, Celise gave him an ultimatum: either clean up his act and return with her to Sapphire Lake or find a new family. He'd promised he'd change, but he couldn't leave Vegas because of his contract. As soon as his suspension was up, he was back in the octagon. Celise kept her word and moved with Milly back upstate.

Ransom fell apart then. Parties, drugs, gambling . . . the works. After another stint in jail, he finally returned to Sapphire Lake, and by some miracle, Harlan Drexler had given him a job. Celise still divorced him—Who could blame her?—but she didn't completely cut him out of her life or Milly's, which we were all thankful for.

"Is Ransom still taking care of your grandfather?" Essex asked.

"Sometimes I wonder if it isn't more Paps taking care of Ransom, but yes. Paps moved in with him when Gran died. They live down the street from Celise, the nurse you met at the ER."

Milly had a room at both of their houses. When both parents were at work, she stayed at Ransom's with Paps. For now, it was the perfect arrangement. Ransom and Celise slept while Milly was at school, and in the afternoon and evenings, she was always with at least one of her parents.

My phone rang. Ransom's name was on the screen. I tapped answer and put it to my ear. "Why do you even have a phone?" I said instead of a greeting.

"I was sleeping." Ransom sounded groggy. "We both work nights, you know?"

"Sorry."

"It's OK." He yawned. "What's up?"

"Have you heard from the prison?"

"Yeah. The warden left a voicemail. I just listened to it before I called you. Is Elias dead?"

"Yes."

"Huh."

"What?"

"I don't feel any different."

I couldn't talk about that now. "They said Elias was murdered."

There was a pause. "Murdered by who?" he asked.

"I don't know. The warden wants one of us to go there."

"Why?"

"I guess to discuss and make arrangements for the body."

"What are you going to do?"

"Why is this my job?" I asked.

"I've got one day off this week, so I can either come see you on Sunday or go see the warden. Which do you want?"

My shoulders fell. "Fine. I'll figure it out."

"Thanks. Call you later?"

"Yeah. Bye." I sighed when I ended the call.

"What's going on?" Essex asked.

"The prison needs one of us to go meet with the warden, and I guess the responsibility is mine." I leaned my good elbow on the window and cradled my forehead. "I wonder if they'd let me come after hours."

"You've got a badge, so maybe. Why? What are you thinking?"

"I might go tonight."

"Do you feel like going tonight?"

"No, but I won't feel like going tomorrow either. I'd rather get it over with."

"I'll drive you if you really want to go."

I hated needing help, but I hated the thought of driving myself to Fallon even more. "I'd appreciate it, if it's not too much trouble."

He lifted a shoulder. "What else would I do?"

"Work."

He laughed. "Probably."

"I'll call them now."

The receptionist at the prison put me straight through to the warden's office, which surprised me. A man with a deep voice answered after a few rings. "Warden McCain."

"Hello, Warden. This is Saphera Nyx. I know you've been trying to reach me, and I'm sorry I missed you."

"Oh, hi, Corporal."

Corporal? This guy had done his homework.

"We've been anxious to speak with someone from the family. Can you come to Fallon?"

"Would it be possible to come tonight? Late. I work third shift, so I'm about to go to bed now. I was hoping to come when I wake up."

"Sure. That'll be fine. I'll run a message up to the gatehouse so they'll be expecting you. What time, you think?"

"I'd like to leave around six, which would put me there about—"

"Eight or eight-thirty, depending on traffic."

"Yes, sir. How do you know that?"

"Well, your father told me you live in Sapphire Lake. You're part of the police department there."

"Yes."

"He was very proud."

Huh. Doubtful.

I wasn't sure how to respond to that, so I didn't. "Are you sure that won't be too late?"

"Positive. We always make conveniences for our friends in blue."

"Thank you, sir."

"You just ask for me when you get here."

Weird. "All right."

"We'll see you tonight, Corporal."

I ended the call and Essex looked at me. "Sounded like that went well. You talked to the warden?"

"That's strange, right?"

"In a place that size? Definitely. What'd he say?"

"He's expecting me at eight."

"Himself?"

"Yeah."

"Interesting."

"Is that cool with you?" I asked.

"Sure. Pick you up at six?"

"Sounds good. Thank you."

"Of course."

I leaned back against the head rest. "What do you think they'll tell me?"

His shoulders rose. "I have no idea."

The car was quiet for a mile or so until Essex looked at me with a curious smile. "Think it's possible Elias left you something?"

"What would he have had to leave?"

Essex looked back at the road, still smiling.

"What?" I asked.

"They say your parents hid a lot of the money they stole."

"Oh, geez. Not you too."

He chuckled. "What do you mean?"

"You think you're the first cop to ask me about stolen money?"

"Probably not. Your background investigation was a shitshow."

"Tell me about it. I'm pretty sure they staked out my grandparents for the entire six weeks of the hiring process."

"Longer." He draped his arm over the steering wheel. "They watched their place the entire time you were in the academy."

"And I just thought Gran was being paranoid."

We both laughed.

"You hungry?" he asked. "I think I'll grab Mexican before I go home."

I smiled, squinting against the sunlight. Essex needed few things in life to survive: oxygen, sweet tea, and tacos.

"Normally, I'd say yes, but I don't feel so great. If we're going on a road trip later, I should probably listen to the doc's advice and get some rest now."

"What? You're gonna listen to someone? Shit, I should call her and get some pointers."

"You're such an ass."

My vision was blurry by the time we pulled into my complex, and I was fighting hard to stay awake.

Essex put the car in park and opened his door to get out.

"Where are you going?" I asked.

He paused. "Nyx?"

I lifted my brow in question, unable and unwilling to open my eyes.

"Shut up."

I smiled and pushed open my door. He met me when I got out, and he closed the door for me. A grimace was plastered on his face when I forced slits in my eyelids. "Are you OK?"

"I'm fine."

"You don't look fine."

"Thanks?" I said as more of a question than anything.

We started toward my stairs. "Should we go back to the hospital?"

"No. I just need to lie down. I didn't sleep last night."

He smirked. "I wonder why."

If he only knew.

When we reached my front door, he took my keys and unlocked it. Then he walked in ahead of me and carefully checked both directions of the hallway, a habit for those who protect and serve.

"Are you sure we shouldn't go back to the hospital?"

"I'm sure."

"You're in pain though?"

I pointed toward my temple. "Twenty-three staples, Sarge."

He smiled, but there was no glint in his eye. He was genuinely worried. Before I could assure him of my resilience, he took a step closer. A *lot* closer.

"I don't have anywhere to be." His voice, quiet and rough, sent a rush of heat through me that curled my toes inside my boots.

My pulse pounded in my ears, partly from the headache, but mostly from the sudden spike in my blood pressure. Blame it on the head injury, but I *really* wanted him to stay.

I put my hands on his chest and instantly regretted it when his eyes fell to them. "Probably not a good idea," I whispered.

"You sure about that?"

No.

Our relationship had never been strictly platonic, but now that he was the sergeant on my shift, multiplying our time together exponentially, it was becoming glaringly obvious something else was there.

Something tempting.

Something sexy.

Something dangerous.

Add *this* to the list of reasons I wanted the promotion to narcotics.

"I'm sure." I dragged my fingers away from his pecs. "I'll see you at six."

With a nod, he took a deep breath and a step back. "Call me sooner if you need anything."

"I will. Bye, Ty—" I cleared my throat. "Bye, Sarge."

His smile melted into a salty mix of desire and disappointment. "Bye, Nyx."

When he walked out, I leaned against the door to close it.

Holy shit, Nyx. You're in trouble.

The pain and exhaustion—physical and emotional—was all too much. After choking down a stale pack of crackers and a banana to settle my stomach, I crawled into bed and was asleep before my head hit the pillow.

I wasn't sure how much time had passed, but it seemed like my body had barely settled into the mattress when my mind came fully awake again.

Panic twisted my heart, the same surreal fear that had always accompanied my nightmares. If Elias was right—and, unfortunately, it was becoming clearer and clearer that he *was* right—this curse was here to stay. The sooner I learned to keep my shit together, the better off I'd be.

Summoning every bit of stress-management knowledge I'd learned over the years, I focused on breathing. From PTSD training in the military to mandatory trauma counseling with the police department, deep-breathing exercises were all the rage among a variety of therapists.

Breathe in for 1 . . . 2 . . . 3 . . . 4 . . .

And out, 1 . . . 2 . . . 3 . . . 4 . . .

In, 1 . . . 2 . . . 3 . . . 4 . . .

Out, 1 . . . 2 . . . 3 . . . 4 . . .

After a few cycles, my heart rate had slowed to just below

stroke level. Finally, I allowed myself to open my eyes—my *meta-physical* eyes.

I sat up. My whole body felt light. Weightless, I guess because it *was*. My head no longer hurt. The staples no longer pulled at my scalp. And I didn't feel dizzy when I stood beside my bed.

The room was dim, the thick curtains just as I'd left them with light peeking around the edges. Glowing green numbers on the clock read 4:51. I'd been asleep hours.

I slowly moved my legs off the bed and eased my feet onto the floor. Looking down, I realized my spirit was clad in the same clothes I'd stripped down to before bed: my black tank top and panties.

With another deep, calming breath, I slowly stood. On the floor beside my feet were my combat boots. I eased my toe against one, but it didn't budge. It might as well have been bolted to the floor.

Before I could think better of it, I pulled my leg all the way back and kicked the boot with the inside arch of my foot, like I was going for the goal in the World Cup. Pain zinged through my foot, but the boot skidded forward a couple of inches.

Interesting.

I walked to the closed bedroom door, instinctively reaching for the brushed-nickel handle. I grabbed it but couldn't turn it.

Hmm . . .

Since I was essentially a ghost, maybe I didn't need to open the door at all. Maybe, like the boot, sheer willpower could move me from room to room.

I took a brave step forward. A brave and stupid step, I realized when my whole body *thunked* against the door. The door rattled against its hinges, and dazed, I fell back a step, grabbing my sore nose.

Huh. Defeated by a bedroom door.

Some superpower.

I turned around, and my eyes landed on the mirror. I had no

reflection. Childhood terror ripped through me, and I looked away before something dreadful happened. God, I wish I'd paid more attention to my father's crazy stories.

It was nearing dark. I went to the window and batted the curtains with my hands until they inched open enough to brighten the room. I stood in the corner and stared out at the sliver of the lake I could see from this angle. Golden rays of sunlight were splashed across its surface.

I splayed my hand on the window to see if I could leave a print on the glass.

My hand passed through it like it wasn't even there. "Whoa."

I guess that's one way out of the condo.

Carefully and slowly, I inched my head through the glass. Looking down, it was a long way to the ground. I jerked my head back inside. If I was ever going to leave home, I'd have to find another way.

Surprisingly, part of me wanted to venture out. The world looked the same for the most part, but everything was more colorful, brighter, and just hazy enough to remind me I wasn't exactly *present.* The haze shimmered with the sunlight.

The whole scene was beautiful. And otherworldly. Otherworldly, I realized, because I was still on Earth but inside the Boundary.

Errng! Errng! Errng!

My alarm clock. I ran around the bed to smack the snooze button. When I did, my hand swished through it, shaking the table. The clock sparked and went black in a puff of smoke.

"Damn it!"

I was running out of ways to tell time.

Time. My eyes widened as they turned toward the golden light from the window again.

"Soon, I promise you'll know the nightmares are real," Elias had said.

Before too much longer, darkness would creep across the sky. "Nightwalkers," I whispered.

I bent over my body and grabbed my forehead. A moment later, I opened my physical eyes.

Elias had been murdered—*brutally*—in his cell.

I needed to visit the prison.

t six o'clock on the nose, the doorbell rang. Essex had showered and changed since I'd seen him that after-noon. He was dressed in nice jeans and a button-up with the sleeves rolled up his forearms.

"Where've you been?" I asked, stepping back to let him inside.

"At home?" His answer sounded more like a question.

My brow crumpled. "You look ready for the club."

He laughed. "Do they let in people our age?"

"*Our* age?" I asked with a pitch of offense.

"Oh, come on. I'm like five years older than you."

I pointed at him. "And don't forget it."

He laughed. "Are you ready?"

"Just let me grab a coat." I walked to my room and put on a dark-olive jacket with lots of pockets. Then I checked my off-duty weapon before tucking it into the waistband holster inside my jeans.

"How's your head?" he asked when I returned.

"At the moment, my brain doesn't feel like it might ooze out of my ears, so that's an improvement." We walked to the door. "I slept for a while, so the pain eased off." I locked the apartment and followed Essex to his black truck sitting in front of my garage. I slowed as we neared it.

"What's wrong?" he asked.

"Nothing. I've just never been in your personal vehicle before." My mind flashed back to our exchange in my condo earlier that day. Now we were about to embark on an evening roadtrip alone.

Maybe I didn't think this through.

"Well, you're in luck. I just had it detailed." He opened the passenger-side door for me, which didn't help my raging apprehension. "Hop in."

My body ached as I pulled myself into the cab, and it took a moment to find a comfortable seating position with my bruised hip.

"You good?" Essex asked.

I nodded, and he closed the door. My eyes followed him all the way around the hood. He was clean shaven, a rarity on his days off.

The truck filled with aftershave, cologne, and testosterone when he got in and started the engine. *Oh boy.* "Mind if I roll down the window?"

"You warm?"

Not even a little bit. "Yeah."

"I'll turn on the AC." He didn't even question that I was still wearing a jacket.

Great.

He dialed the air-conditioning to arctic and put on his seatbelt. "The state pen in Fallon, right?" he asked.

"Yep."

At the exit of my neighborhood, he tipped his chin toward Delaney's across the street. "That place any good?" As usual, the pub was packed.

"You haven't been yet?"

He shook his head and turned onto the street.

"It's crowded, but it's all right. The owner's cool. He usually lets me drink for free after work."

"Drink for free? I love places that support local law enforcement."

"You love places that give you free beer."

He turned his palm over on top of the steering wheel. "Duh."

I laughed.

"We should check it out sometime when you're feeling better."

We?

"Unfortunately, I don't think Delaney's offer extends to *all* cops," I said.

"Oh, just the hot ones."

Heat rose in my cheeks. "Just the ones who flirt."

He looked across the cab, lifting an eyebrow. "You flirt to get free stuff?"

"Duh."

He *tsked* his tongue as he turned onto the highway.

"Did you hear anything more about my car?" I asked.

"I did."

"Are they going to be able to get it fixed before I come back to work?" I asked.

"They said they'd try, so no."

"That sucks."

"I'd be prepared for it to be out of commission for a while."

I held up both thumbs. "Awesome."

Whenever the city bought new patrol vehicles, the oldest ones in service were either scrapped or added to the "pool" to be saved for situations such as this. Pool cars were the cheap hookers of the fleet: at least a decade past their prime, worn out and falling apart, and reeking of ass and cigarettes.

I sank lower in my seat to dodge the direct blast from the air vent as we passed the "Welcome to Seneca Park" sign.

At the base of the Sierras, where the city limits of Sapphire Lake and Carson City bled together, the suburb of Seneca Park was the more affordable side of town. It catered to locals rather than tourists and second-home owners.

Paps and Gran had lived there for twenty years before she died. Essex lived there now, and "Bess Lincoln, no relation" had an apartment behind the old Seneca Inn. I wondered what had become of my Good-Samaritan speeder. "I gave that girl a warning last night."

"I should hope so. It was pretty cool of her to stay."

"I don't think she had anywhere else to go," I said with a chuckle. "I heard a *lot* about her life in the short time we were together." I tucked my icy hands under my thighs and shivered.

He looked over at me. "Are you cold?"

"I've been hot and cold a lot lately," I lied, avoiding his eyes.

"I'm worried about you. Are you sure you're doing OK?"

"Yes, I promise."

"Did you get some sleep?"

"A few hours."

"You can sleep now while I drive if you need to."

"I'll be fine. I don't want to disrupt my body's schedule too much."

When I'd first moved to night shift, convincing my body that nighttime was supposed to be daytime had been miserable. I never wanted to repeat that experience, so I kept to a nighttime routine as much as possible. But it wasn't easy in a city that was by no means nocturnal.

Bars and clubs usually stayed open until two a.m., but the rest of Sapphire Lake was dead after midnight. Fortunately, my neighborhood had a few twenty-four-hour establishments I frequented: a gym, a grocery store, and a tiny cafe called Night Watch. Sometimes I picked up extra shifts or security gigs, anything to fill the time and keep myself awake.

Not to mention, if nightwalkers were real, then until I

learned to control detaching, sleeping at night was going to be a problem. Maybe the shift change had been a rare stroke of good fortune.

"Why the sudden willingness to have anything to do with your dad?" he asked. "I've never been able to get you to even talk about him before."

God, I wished I could tell him the truth. "You'll laugh at me."

He smirked. "Try me."

"I had a bad dream."

The corner of his mouth tipped up.

"See," I said, looking back at the road.

"What? I'm not laughing."

"Sure."

"Come on, Nyx, tell me about the dream."

"No. You don't deserve to hear about it." And I wouldn't tell him anyway.

He chuckled. "Please?"

I ignored him. As we approached the exit, the bright lights of Sin City Tacos caught the attention of my stomach. "You hungry?"

"Always." He turned into the parking lot. "Drive-through?"

"Sure."

With everything from traditional tacos to ones with a southern spin, Sin City was one of the many Las Vegas seedlings that had sprouted and thrived in Sapphire Lake. They had an impressive selection of craft beers on tap, a full menu until two a.m., and a drive-through. They also gave officers half off our meals when we were working.

It was (surprise, surprise) one of Essex's most favorite restaurants. I had a sneaking suspicion it was a driving factor in his settling down in Seneca Park.

I ordered two honey chipotle pulled-pork tacos in cornbread shells with a water to drink. Essex ordered three crunchy catfish tacos with tequila creamed corn, a large sweet tea, and a side of chips and okra salsa for us to share.

The night-shift manager, Carly, leaned all the way out the window when we rolled up. "Hey, Tyler," she said, pressing her breasts together. Her uniform top was unbuttoned, exposing a low-cut red cami and so much cleavage I wondered if she used the cavern to stash extra packets of hot sauce.

"Evening, Carly," he replied, shifting into park.

She straightened when she saw me across the cab. "Officer Nyx."

I waved.

"I saw you on the news last night. You OK?" she asked.

"Peachy. Thanks." I shifted on the seat as my stiff body screamed otherwise.

She handed his tea through the window. "Twelve seventy-five."

"But we're not on duty," Essex argued.

Puckering her lips, she pressed her finger against them. "Shh. Our little secret."

I pulled a twenty out of my phone case and handed it to him.

"I got it," he said.

"Better let me. I'm pretty sure it was my half the bill she didn't comp."

With a laugh, he put his drink in the cup holder and took the money. He handed me my water and bag of food.

Carly leaned out the window again when she passed him his bag. "I stuck some banana pudding churro bites in the bottom."

He lowered his voice as he took it. "Thank you, Carly."

She held onto the bag a second and caught her bottom lip between her teeth. "My pleasure."

As he pulled away from the curb, I popped a chip into my mouth. "Looks like I'm not the only one who gets free shit for being pretty."

He shook his head as he got back on the highway. "Thanks for dinner."

"Thanks for driving."

Two hours later, we pulled up to the prison gate. Essex slowed near the guard post.

"Ask for Warden McCain," I said.

A burly guard walked toward us, and Essex rolled down his window.

"Can I help you?" the man asked.

"Sergeant Tyler Essex and Corporal Saphera Nyx of Sapphire Lake Police Department to see Warden McCain. He's expecting us."

"One second, please." The man turned away from us and used the radio strapped to his shoulder.

"Have you been here before?" Essex asked, looking up at the tall fence capped with coiled barbed wire.

"Not since I was a kid."

The guard returned. "Go ahead and put your car in park. Please remove all weapons from your person and from your vehicle. You'll check them in here."

Essex groaned as he put the truck in park. He hated being disarmed even more than I did. I got out and followed him inside. A second guard was watching a set of security monitors.

"Use any locker with a key in it. Put your weapons inside and take the key with you," the first guard instructed.

I pulled my gun from my waistband holster and put it in a locker. Then I bent and slid the knife from the strap around my ankle. My head swirled when I straightened.

"You all right?" Essex asked.

"I'm fine."

I locked the steel door and pulled out the key.

"Anything else?" the guard asked.

Essex patted his waist. "Feeling pretty naked."

"They'll pat you down and check your vehicle at the next gate."

Essex thanked him as we walked back to the truck.

Down the road, at a second gate, another guard walked outside with a long undercarriage mirror. "Please park your truck and step out of the vehicle," he instructed.

Two other guards came out. One got in the truck. The other patted Essex down. "Kind of late for a visit, isn't it?" the man asked.

"We work nights too," Essex said.

"Ah," the man said with a nod of understanding. He patted me down next and stopped on my right side. "What happened to you?"

That question was going to get old *fast*.

"Ninja knife fight," I answered as he ran his hands down my leg.

His face snapped up.

I just smiled. Essex was biting back a laugh.

"All clear!" the guard sliding out of the truck called.

The man who frisked me stood, still perplexed by my answer. "I'll be in the white truck ahead." He pointed through the gate. "Follow me to the admin entrance."

"Thank you," Essex said as we got back in his truck. He grinned at me as we waited for the gate to open. "Ninja knife fight?"

"What's funny is he wasn't sure if he should believe it or not. I'm calling that a win." I put on my seatbelt.

We followed the white truck onto the massive prison campus. The concrete building looked eerie in the moonlight with its watchtowers and searchlights. The truck stopped at a bright entrance under a metal overhang.

The guard got out and gestured for us to follow on foot. He pressed a button on the wall and looked at the camera over the door. "Escorting guests of Warden McCain."

With a loud buzz, the metal door clicked as the lock tumbled open. He pulled it open and went inside. Essex held it as I walked through, then followed me in.

The guard led us through a labyrinth of hallways and locked doors. Deep inside, we arrived at a cluster of offices and conference rooms. When we were buzzed through the final door, a large man with a white beard and a round belly walked out of an office to greet us.

He looked from Essex to me, then extended his hand. "Officer Nyx?"

I shook it. "Warden McCain?"

He nodded.

"I appreciate you letting us come this late. I know it's well outside business hours," I said.

"Happy to help out a fellow keeper of the peace." He smiled and turned toward Essex.

"This is my boss, Sergeant Tyler Essex," I said.

The two men shook hands. "Nice to meet you, Sergeant," McCain said.

"Likewise. Tight ship you run here," Essex said as the warden led us down another hallway.

"Has to be. We house some of the most dangerous criminals in the world."

My father had been one of them.

"You're doing a fine job of it," Essex said as we walked into a big office.

A woman in a business suit stood from one of the chairs facing the desk. "Sergeant Essex, Corporal Nyx, this is one of our attorneys, Margaret Pittman."

A lawyer? At this time of night?

She shook our hands. "We're so sorry for your loss, Corporal," she said to me.

McCain gestured toward the chairs. "Please, have a seat."

Essex and I sat. Margaret Pittman stood beside the warden.

He lifted a folder out of the rack on the corner of his desk. He glanced over the top of it at me as he laid it in front of him. "You're Elias's daughter?"

"I was," I said, my voice devoid of any emotion.

He held my gaze for a second, making it clear he understood my position. "Well, you should know that as far as our lifers go in this place, Elias Nyx was one of our favorites."

I would have been less shocked to hear Elias had murdered everyone on the block.

Essex was clearly surprised too. "Really?"

McCain folded his hands on top of the file. "Yes. He's been here a long time. Never caused us any problems, was always kind and respectful. I'm sure everyone here would say the same. He was well liked."

"Interesting." Essex crossed his boot over his knee and leaned back in his seat.

"How did he die?" I asked.

The warden took a deep breath and cast an uneasy glance at the attorney. "We're not sure, to be honest."

"But we are conducting a thorough investigation," Pittman added.

"We were told he was killed in his cell," Essex said, confused.

"He was, but we don't know how. We're still investigating."

"What happened?" I asked.

McCain looked at me. "I assume you know your father was very ill."

I nodded.

"The medical staff here agreed he was within days of passing, and the plan was to return him to Hawthorne Medical after the morning shift change. The night before, he asked to be moved to cellblock two hundred. We jokingly call them the condos, as they're the only cells in this entire facility with natural daylight."

Daylight.

"As requested, we moved Elias to Cell 203, and all was well when he was last checked on around three a.m."

"Was he asleep?" I asked, already knowing the answer.

"Soundly, I was assured, which wasn't unusual. He slept a lot in his final days."

I'll bet he did.

"Shortly after rounds, we had a system malfunction. On the other side of the facility, a security door between two general-population blocks was opened. The pods contained rival gang members, so you can imagine the fights we had on our hands."

"How was the door opened?" I asked.

McCain lifted his shoulders. "A system glitch."

I thought of my cell phone and my alarm clock. "Do glitches occur often?"

Pittman spoke first. "Like with any system, problems happen occasionally, but this is a secure facility."

"I'm not saying it isn't." I forced a smile. "We saw the level of security coming in."

McCain and Pittman visibly relaxed. "It's not flawless, but it's pretty damn good," McCain said.

"Clearly," I agreed.

"Still, our guards were quite busy wrangling the situation in gen pop, and the next few rounds were missed."

Oh . . . I suddenly understood the presence of the lawyer. McCain was afraid of a lawsuit.

He cleared his throat. "Elias wasn't checked on again until he was found dead around seven a.m."

The sun rose in Nevada before seven this time of year.

"I was told it was brutal. Can you explain?" I asked.

McCain hesitated.

"Warden, speak freely. You may have fond memories of my father, but I don't. I'd like to know exactly what happened. Please don't sugarcoat anything."

He studied my face for a moment before nodding. "There

were definite signs of a struggle. The body was mutilated beyond recognition."

I thought of the bodies at the Drexler.

"Mutilated by who?" Essex asked.

"We don't know. The cell was locked and could only be digitally opened by Master Control. Our records show it stayed closed."

"Would the records show if there was another system malfunction?" Essex asked.

"Yes. There wasn't. We found blood spatter outside the cell but no footprints leading to or from it."

"What about cameras?" Essex asked.

I already knew the answer before McCain said it. "The camera inside Elias's cell was disabled. The hallway cameras picked up nothing except a flash and smoke."

"Smoke?" Essex sat upright.

"There was a significant burn spot on the floor, by the cell door, and ash we're working hard to identify."

Nightwalkers were incinerated by sunlight.

Essex ran a hand down his face.

McCain's eyes fell. "His neighboring cellmates heard screaming and a struggle, but no one saw anything. There were no cells facing his. Only outside windows."

My mind was churning, trying desperately to recall all the conversations with Elias I'd tried to forget over the years. Nightwalkers—or night demons, as he sometimes called them—fed on human fear. They hunted at night and plagued human dreams to indulge on the fear they induced.

They were the reason Elias had warned against detaching at night. The body of a detached human formed a bridge between worlds. Nightwalkers could cross that bridge, tearing through the body to materialize in the human realm.

Here, they didn't feed on fear. They feasted on human blood, indiscriminately and viciously draining everything in sight. The more they consumed, the more powerful they became.

I gestured to the folder. "Do you have photos?"

Again, McCain hesitated.

I reached for the file. "May I?"

He handed it to me, and I opened it on my lap.

Essex scooted his chair closer to mine and lowered his voice. "You sure you want to do this?"

I looked him square in the eye. "I *have* to do this."

With an unsteady hand, I opened the file. The first page was a report with detailed chicken-scratch notes etched in blue ink. I skimmed it and turned the page. The photos followed.

Blood smeared and splattered all over the wall.

A close-up of a bloody mass only identifiable as a head because of the teeth.

Charred remains on the floor.

My stomach turned. I closed my eyes and felt a soothing hand on the back of my neck. "Can I see it?" I asked, my voice cracking.

"The cell?" McCain asked gently.

I nodded.

"Sure. Follow me."

I was keenly aware of the fingertips on the small of my back as the four of us walked through the jail. Essex kept step with me as we walked behind McCain and Pittman. The lights were dim, and everything was quiet, as most of the prisoners were asleep.

We entered a concrete stairwell and walked up four flights of stairs. After another loud buzzer, the door at the top opened to a deserted hallway lined with cells. Stale smoke and new paint lingered in the air.

The left wall was a long window covered with bars. I stopped and looked outside, carefully memorizing the lay of the horizon.

"Over here," McCain said quietly. He'd stopped at the third cell. Essex and I walked over to join him, and someone stirred in the second one as we passed. "I'm afraid there's not much left to see. The cleanup crew repainted this morning, and we just got new furniture moved in tonight."

"Don't waste any time, do you?" I asked.

"Can't. We're short on beds as it is."

"But we did follow proper protocol while investigating and cataloging the scene," Pittman added.

"Where are the cameras?" Essex asked, looking around the ceiling.

"Both ends." McCain gestured to the ends of the hallway. Then he turned toward the cell and pointed to the top-right corner. "That's the one that was disabled."

"Could it be an inside job?" Essex asked.

McCain and Pittman whirled around. "What are you trying to suggest?" the warden asked.

Essex crossed his arms. "Seems really convenient that no one saw anything and that the doors could only be opened by Master Control."

"Is that so?" A muscle was working in McCain's jaw.

Pittman stepped in front of him. "Perhaps we should return to the office and—"

"No, it's fine." I put my hand on Essex's chest. "What are you trying to do?"

"Just asking questions."

"As I told you, Elias Nyx was well liked." McCain was fighting hard to keep his temper in check. "We all want to know what happened to him."

"Of course," I said calmly. "Thank you, Warden."

"Whatever got him wasn't no human," a gruff voice said from a nearby cell.

McCain rolled his eyes. "That'll be enough, Bill."

I walked to the cell. "What do you mean?"

Beady eyes stared back at me. The old man was sitting on his bed in a white T-shirt and sweatpants. He rubbed his knotty knees. "I heard it, hissin' and sputterin' as it ate him. *Ate him*, you hear me?"

"What did you do?" I asked.

"Kept my damn mouth shut. Didn't want whatever that thing was gettin' in here. Ain't ashamed to tell ya, I hid under my bed."

McCain stepped in front of me. "Ignore him, Corporal. He's crazy."

"I'd like to hear what he has to say." I stepped around him. "What happened, Bill?"

Bill shuffled across the cell. "It was a goddamn vampire, you ask me." He pointed behind us. "The sun came up, and whatever got ol' Elias gave a screech and squaller, then *poof!* Everything was silent. Dead silent."

Essex chuckled.

McCain covered his eyes.

Pittman looked horrified.

I ignored them all. A chill prickled my skin. Everything Elias had told me about nightwalkers—*gulp*—was true.

McCain leaned against the bars. "Now, Bill, tell her about the faceless man who wanders the hallways—"

"Oh, fuck off, McCain," the old man said with a dismissive swat. He returned to his bed.

McCain was saying something about schizophrenia, but I wasn't listening. Chilled to the bone, I turned toward Essex. He was still grinning, but his eyes sobered when they locked on mine. Instinctively, he curled an arm around my waist. "Nyx? You OK? You look like you might pass out again."

I touched my forehead. "I'm OK."

"You sure?" He looked past me to McCain. "She got a nasty head wound yesterday."

"Master Control, open Cell 203," McCain called into the radio. With a loud buzz, Elias's cell door slid open.

"You may not believe me, but soon, I promise you'll know the nightmares are real."

Essex ushered me inside toward the cot as voices swirled around in my head. My legs wobbled, and his arm held me steady.

Elias's warning.

Bill's description.

Nightwalkers screeching.

Elias's death hadn't been a murder. It hadn't been an accident either. He'd died to kill a nightwalker—and to prove to his kids the danger was real.

CHAPTER EIGHT

he drive back to the mountains was quiet. My head throbbed from so much rolling through my mind. I wanted to call my brother, but didn't bother. He was at work and probably wouldn't answer even if he wasn't.

Before Essex and I had left the prison, I'd signed for Elias's body to be cremated and left with the state. The warden said he'd contact me when it was done, but because of the investigation, I had a few days if I wanted to change my mind.

On my lap were the only possessions Elias had left behind. I'd hoped for journals, notes, *anything* . . . but all that remained of my father's long and magical life had been reduced to a few trinkets in a shoebox.

It was after midnight when Essex took his turn instead of mine off the highway. "Where are you going?" I asked.

"My place."

"Excuse me?"

He looked across the cab. "You're clearly not fine, so either you're staying with me or I'm taking you back to the hospital. Those are your only two options here."

"I'm fine. I promise I'm not—"

"Nyx, you almost blacked out again in my arms."

"Did not."

He scowled. "Argue all you want, but I shouldn't have left you alone last night, and I'm not leaving you alone now."

"Why can't we stay at my place?"

"Because I have a dog who will pee all over my kitchen if I'm not home soon."

"I thought Karma stayed in the backyard?"

"He did until he figured out how to climb out of it."

I turned all the way toward him in my seat. "Karma can climb the six-foot chain-link fence?"

"Remind me to show you the video."

Essex had adopted the German shepherd when the pup flunked out of K-9 training. Karma was afraid of the dark and preferred humping assailants over biting them. Essex had transformed his entire backyard into a giant playland for Karma—a playland he could, apparently, now escape from.

"So is that a yes? You'll come peacefully?" Essex asked.

I leaned against my door. "You're lucky I like your dog."

Essex grinned. "He's always had a thing for the ladies."

"I've seen Karma in action. He is definitely pansexual."

"Yeah."

"Where will I sleep?"

Like me, Essex had transformed his spare bedroom into a gym.

"My bed." When I frowned, he laughed. "I'll sleep on the couch, but good to know where you stand."

Where did I stand?

There were rules about fraternizing within the department and serious consequences for getting involved with someone in your direct line of command. And, personally and professionally, I'd have hell to pay. As one of the few women on the force, it was hard enough to be taken seriously.

Then there was the new threat of getting moved to day shift, something I couldn't afford now that I was . . . *whatever* I was.

"Nyx?"

"Hmm?"

"Just wondering if you passed out again. You went freakishly silent."

"Sorry."

He turned onto his street. "You ready to talk about what happened back there?"

"At the prison?"

"No. At mile marker twenty-nine. Of course at the prison." Shaking his head, he draped one arm across the steering wheel. "What do you think happened to your father?"

"I think he died."

"But you have theories about it."

"What do you mean?"

"You had that *look* you get at a crime scene when you're on to something."

"I don't know what you mean." Guilt pooled like ice water in my belly. I hated lying. I especially hated lying to Essex.

"Why were you so interested in what the old man in the other cell had to say?"

"Because he was there. He heard everything."

"You don't think he's crazy?"

I sighed. "I don't know what to think." It was the truest statement I'd made in two days.

"Do you think it's possible Elias was murdered?"

"He swindled a lot of people out of a lot of money *and* killed a cop. I'm sure he had lots of enemies."

"Even after thirty-something years?"

I shrugged. "I wasn't even born when he did it, and I still haven't forgiven him."

Essex bobbed his head as if to say, "Good point."

After a couple of blocks, he turned onto the cracked driveway of his one-story beige house with dark-red trim. I slid out and met him around the front of his truck. We started toward the door. "Are you ever going to spruce this place up?" I asked, stopping next to the rocks and weeds that covered what was supposed to be a flower bed.

"It's a bachelor pad. It doesn't need sprucing."

I heard the beeps as he punched in the code to his electronic door lock.

"I really need one of those," I said, joining him.

Essex flipped on the living-room light, and toenails clattered down the hallway. Karma charged full speed into the living room, missed the turn, and slid headfirst into the leather sofa. Essex dropped his head back and sighed.

I laughed and patted my thighs. "Karma!"

"Bad idea." Essex jumped in front of me as the dog charged us. His paws collided with a thud on Essex's chest, knocking him a step back. "Oh, geez. *Platz*, Karma!" he commanded in German.

Sluuuuurp! Karma's long tongue dragged across Essex's face before he dropped to the floor.

I put the box of belongings on the table beside the door, then snapped my fingers. "Karma, *hier*."

Karma sat in front of me, wagging his tail so hard, his butt slid side to side on the tile. I got on my knees and scratched behind his ears. He licked the side of my face and immediately tried to mount me.

"Karma, knock it off." Essex pushed the dog down with his knee.

I hugged Karma's neck. "I've missed you too, boy."

Essex tossed his keys beside my box and walked to the kitchen. "You hungry? Thirsty?" He whistled and opened the back door. "Karma, *voraus*." The dog turned and ran outside.

I stood. "I'm good. Thank you."

The inside of the house needed a makeover as badly as the outside. The tile floors were worn and cracked, and the kitchen cabinets were stained a bright honey oak with white knobs to match all the appliances.

He filled a glass of water at the fridge spout, drank half of it, then carried the glass back to the coffee table. "How are you feeling now?"

"My head hurts, and I'm exhausted."

"Honesty; I like it," he said with a smile. "Come on. I'll find you something to sleep in."

"I'll sleep on the couch. I don't want to take over your room."

"Nonsense. Besides, you're in luck. I actually changed the sheets this week."

"Yippee." I followed him down the hallway. Collage frames of family photos hung in the hallway, something his mother had done when he moved in. We passed the room with his weight bench and treadmill, and I was officially the farthest down the hall I'd ever been.

I stopped near the hallway bath as he turned on his bedroom light. "This feels weird."

"What feels weird?" He walked to the wooden dresser on the other side of the bed and pulled open the top drawer.

"It feels like I shouldn't be here."

"Psh . . . do you know how many cops have crashed here over the past year?"

"In your bedroom?"

"Well, no. But why do you think I got rid of the guest room? To encourage the jerks to go home."

I inched forward as he rummaged through the drawer. The bed was unmade, with a charcoal comforter and light-gray sheets. His clothes from the day before were laying on the trunk at the foot of the bed. And all the finish off the side of the dresser was missing.

I walked over for a closer look. It was teeth marks. "What happened here?"

He looked down. "Oh, that's Karma's growth chart. He tried to eat it every day for the first six months I had him."

I laughed.

"These should work." He handed me a pair of navy drawstring gym shorts and a black T-shirt from his favorite gun range. "I'll brush my teeth and get out of your way."

As he walked to the master bath, I sat on the edge of his bed. I bounced a few times, making the headboard squeak and my cheeks burn with embarrassment. Karma barked out back, and I jumped up and raced from the room.

"You're gonna sleep great, Nyx," I muttered, walking back to the kitchen. My throat suddenly dry, I got a glass from the cabinet and filled it with water.

I let Karma inside and locked the door behind him. His water and food bowls were down the hall toward the garage. Both were full.

"Nyx?" Essex called from the bedroom.

"Com—" I cleared my throat. "Coming. Just let Karma in." On my way back to the bedroom, I grabbed the box of Elias's things in case Karma got curious. The dog trotted behind me.

"I put a new toothbrush on the sink counter. Do you need anything for your head?" he asked as I put the box on the bed. Karma plopped down by his feet.

"No, thanks. I'm good." I unholstered my gun, checked its chamber, and put it on the nightstand. When I looked up, Essex was staring. "Are you sure you want to sleep on the couch?" I asked.

His mouth fell open, but he quickly snapped it shut and laughed. "Is that an offer?"

"For me to sleep there," I answered with a smile.

He walked toward me. "I'm sure. You need anything else?"

"I'm good."

Standing toe to toe, he looked down and drew in a shaky

breath. "Well, sleep tight. I'll probably be up for a while if you need anything."

"OK."

"OK."

With a nod, he took a step toward the door. I grabbed his arm. "Hey." When he turned, in an unprecedented move, I put my arms around him. We'd never really hugged before. "Thank you for everything."

He froze for a second before his arms closed around me. My face nuzzled his neck, and when I inhaled, my legs wobbled for a whole different reason. I dug my fingers into his soft shirt as his hands trailed slowly down my back.

Danger sirens blared through my head.

I peeled my arms free and took a step back, resisting the urge to fan my face. "Night, Sarge."

He had a lopsided smile, and he shook his head. "See you in the morning."

When he closed the door behind him, I clenched my fists. My whole body tensed, and I twisted my arms in frustration.

The door reopened. I snapped my arms to my sides and spun toward him so fast my ponytail *phwapped* me across the eyes.

"You OK?" Essex asked, amused.

"Yeah." The squeak in my answer betrayed my attempt at playing it cool.

He clicked the side of his tongue. "Karma, *hier*."

The dog dragged his body off the floor like it weighed a thousand pounds. Slowly, he plodded through the doorway.

"Goodnight, Karma."

Essex smiled. "Goodnight, Nyx."

When I was ready for bed, I turned off all the lights except the bedside lamp. Then I sat cross-legged on the mattress and opened the box from the prison.

There wasn't much inside: a pair of thick, scratched eyeglasses; the world's smallest AM/FM radio; and a homemade bookmark with the handwritten quote: "Knowledge is your greatest POWER."

I closed the lid, and my hand lingered on top of it. Emotion swirled inside me like a whirlpool I didn't dare get lost in. "Goodbye," I whispered and placed the box on the nightstand. When I turned off the light, I rolled onto my left side, away from the box. I curled my arms around the pillow.

Tyler's pillow.

It smelled like his aftershave, sandalwood and cedar with a touch of eucalyptus. I buried my face in it and closed my eyes. Behind me, the door opened.

I froze.

What do I do?

My pulse quickened and my breath caught in my chest. I could almost feel his warm arms slide around me when . . .

Karma jumped onto the bed.

Daylight was beaming through the cracks in the blackout curtains when my spirit snapped free and I opened my eyes. For a second, I forgot where I was.

Then my eyes landed on the Cop Caddy perched in the corner. The front was engraved with a Punisher skull and the name ESSEX. A gift from his mother, the caddy was a custom-built piece of furniture that had a lockbox for his duty weapon, a rack for his pressed uniform, an arm for his body armor, and a charging station for his radio.

My spirit sat up, and I looked at the snoring dog beside me. Sleeping me didn't seem to mind. I was out cold with one leg wrapped around the comforter and one arm curled across Karma. There was a giant wet spot beneath my open mouth on the pillowcase.

Attractive.

But I'd slept all night, which was the important thing. I'd regret it come my first shift back on duty, but my head wouldn't heal without rest.

I stood, letting the cold from the hardwood planks seep into my invisible feet. The strange sensation moved up my legs until a chill rippled my whole spirit. I rubbed my arms and looked around the room.

I tiptoed all the way to the caddy in the corner until I realized I wasn't affecting the floor enough to make noise anyway. As I explored the room, I found a copy of the week's upcoming work schedule on the small desk beside the dresser.

All the spaces next to my name were blank for the upcoming week. With a groan, I turned away. The bedroom door was still open where Karma had let himself in.

I turned sideways to get through it, so I wouldn't disturb the hinges. Then I walked down the hallway, stopping to really study the photos on the wall.

It was a photo montage of my boss's life. As a boy, fishing with his stepdad. At a high school dance with a girl in a sky-blue dress. At his graduation from the police academy.

Essex got his good looks from his father, whom I'd obviously never met. In the photos, James had a generous dusting of white through his wavy dark hair and deep crinkles around his eyes. Surprising, given that Essex was still in utero when James was killed. But even with the age difference, there was no denying the genetics.

His smile he got from his mom. I'd met Clara once with his stepdad, Buddy Harris, at Essex's promotion ceremony. She'd been snapping pictures like it was his first day of kindergarten, and she was in over half the pictures in the hall. It was cute he was such a momma's boy.

I heard a noise in the living room and went to investigate. When I reached the end of the hall, Essex was lying on his back with his arm resting across his forehead. He was shirtless—a wonder I hadn't seen in a while—and he was staring at the ceiling.

When he sat up, I ducked behind the wall and slowly peeked out. The smooth, taut lines etched into his chest and stomach pulled and curved as he stretched. He scratched his head, leaving his hair standing on end. Wearing only a pair of navy boxer briefs, he stood and pulled on a white undershirt as he walked toward the kitchen.

I held my breath when he stopped inches in front of me. He looked down the hallway, and a small smile crept across his lips. I glanced back and saw my bare calf still wrapped around the blanket. He drew in a slow, deep breath, closed his eyes, and leaned back his head.

I knew that look. That restraint. I'd seen it the other night at my doorstep.

You shouldn't be here, Nyx.

Realization hit me like an asteroid. My first intangible brush with another human, and I was already spying. Making myself privy to information Essex clearly didn't want me to know.

Everything I'd accused Elias of over the years came rushing back so fast I felt dizzy.

I slowly backed away.

Essex walked to the coffee pot, and I crept backward down the hallway with Elias's warning replaying in my mind.

"Every day is a battle, a constant choice between good and evil."

Crazed barking made me jump. I spun, and Karma was standing on the bed looking right at me in the hall. He stopped barking as suddenly as he'd started and looked from me to my body and back again.

Holy shit. He can see me.

"Karma, *heir*," Essex said, snapping his fingers at the end of the hall.

Karma leapt over my sleeping body and landed on the floor

with a heavy *whomp*. He stopped in front of me. "Go see Essex," I whispered softly.

"Karma!" Essex said again.

Finally, the dog took off in a trot toward the kitchen, and I ran back to the bed.

"I'm sorry again about this morning," Essex apologized for the nine millionth time as we drove to my house about an hour later.

When I'd returned to my body, Karma had immediately started humping me.

I smiled. "Don't be. That was the most action I've gotten in a *while*."

"I hear ya. It's sad my dog has a better sex life than me." He turned into my complex. "Whose car is that?"

In front of my garage door was an old green coupe with a slanted bumper covered in stickers. "That would be Bess Lincoln, no relation."

At the top landing on the stairs, Bess waved from my front door. Couldn't miss her. She was wearing a fluorescent tie-dyed hoodie.

"Your speeder?"

"Yep." I opened my door. "You coming in?"

"Better not. I need to check in at the station."

I slid out of the cab. "Do you ever take a real day off?"

He shrugged. "I love my job."

"It shows." I grabbed Elias's box off the seat. "Thanks again for last night."

"Anytime. You know that."

I smiled because I did. Before I could close the door, a chill took my breath.

Essex must have noticed because he laughed. "You OK?"

I looked up at the cloudless sky. The sun was beating down, and even though it wasn't hot, it certainly wasn't cold enough for the gooseflesh on the back of my neck. "Yeah. I'll talk to you later."

He waved as I closed the door.

"Perfect timing!" Bess called down from upstairs.

"Have you been here long?" I passed by her car, which was packed to the roof with boxes, clothes, and god only knows what else.

"Just got here." She eyed me head to toe as I walked up the stairs. "Did you just wake up?"

"Is it that obvious?" I pulled out my keys.

She leaned against the wall by the door. "I recognize a walk of shame when I see it. Was that your hot boss in the truck?"

"This isn't a walk of shame, and the truck isn't your business." I opened the door. "What brings you by?"

"I haven't heard from you, and I wanted to see how you were doing." She followed me inside. "How's the head?"

"Better. Thanks for asking." I put my keys on the hook and deposited Elias's box on the kitchen island.

The toilet flushed in the master bedroom.

Bess looked as surprised as me. "I rang the bell. Didn't think anyone was home."

"No one is." I pulled my gun from my waistband. "Stay here."

"By myself? Nuh-uh."

"Then stay behind me."

She walked on my heels to my bedroom. I pushed the door open and carefully panned corner to corner across the room. Nothing looked amiss. I eased through the doorway, toward the bathroom. All the lights were off. I slid my hand along the wall, inside the door, to flip them on.

Bess jumped at our reflection in the mirror.

I peeked around the corner into the separate toilet room. It was empty, but the bowl was still refilling with water. The shower was clear as well.

"Must be something with the plumbing."

Bess gave a melodic sigh. "Oh my god. I thought we were going to die."

"Most home invaders don't break in for the facilities." I put my gun back in its holster. "What's with all the stuff in your car?"

She followed me back to the kitchen. "Oh, I was evicted."

I turned. "Shit. Really?"

"Yeah. I was hoping to get enough tips over the weekend to hold off my landlord, but ya can't do that without a job, so . . ." She turned her palms up.

"You got fired?"

"Yep."

"Because you didn't show up for work the other night?"

She nodded.

"Did you tell them what happened?"

"My boss didn't believe me."

My head snapped back. "Didn't believe you?"

Her nose scrunched. "It might not be the first time I've called in with a wild excuse."

"That sucks. What are you going to do?"

Her shoulders lifted. "Start the trek back to South Carolina, I guess. I think I've got enough gas money to make it."

But would her car make it? That was the real question.

"You'll move back in with your family?"

She grimaced. "With my mom until I get back on my feet."

I recognized that face. It was the same look I got whenever someone mentioned *my* mother. "You don't get along?"

"Mom's a train wreck. Lives off the state but could make a career out of marrying shitty men. She's on husband number four *and* she has a live-in boyfriend."

"The husband doesn't mind?"

"They're separated. Have been for years, but they're both too cheap to get a divorce. I moved out here to get away from it all. Start fresh and try to break the cycle of dysfunction, you know?"

I did know.

She hooked her thumbs in the belt loops of her jeans. "But a girl's gotta do what a girl's gotta do. The only thing worse than returning to Charleston would be hooking to get by, so I'm going home. I just wanted to check to be sure you were all right before I hit the road."

"Do you want to leave Nevada?" I heard it. The telltale tone of my voice right before I said something I was going to regret.

"No, but I'm down to my last hundred options in my wallet, if you catch my drift."

I sighed and put my hands on my hips.

"What is it?" she asked.

"Give me ten minutes to shower and change."

"What are we doing?" she asked as I walked to my bedroom.

"We're going to the Drexler."

"Why?"

"To get your job back."

Shredded black jeans. Check.

Studded belt. Check.

Leather jacket. Check.

Bess's eyes widened when I stepped out of my bedroom.

"Whoa. You're like one set of brass knuckles away from being a modern-day Xena: Warrior Princess."

"Thanks."

She looked down at her Bob Marley wear. "I am severely underdressed for this ass-kicking mission."

"Nobody's kicking anyone's ass." I walked to the foyer, and the overhead light flickered.

I paused and looked up.

"Did the power just blink?" Bess asked.

"I don't think so." I also didn't like it. The feeling of being watched spread through me like kudzu of the brain. Good thing we were leaving. I reached for my keys.

"Are you driving?" she asked, concerned.

"Yes."

"Is that safe?"

Safer than her behind the wheel. "No one said I couldn't. You need to move your car."

Bess moved her car across the driveway, and I reversed my blacked-out Jeep Rubicon—the perfect accessory for any ass-kicking mission.

Hiding behind her trunk, Bess changed into a black Metallica tee from her mobile storage unit, then opened the Jeep's passenger-side door. "Whoa, this thing is awesome."

"I know. Put on your seatbelt."

She obeyed as I closed the garage behind us. As I rolled out of the driveway, she leaned forward to read the subtle, almost camoflagued, black decal fixed to the dash. It read: *In this Jeep, boys ride bitch.* "That's hilarious."

I smiled, pulling past the other condos.

"You do this often?"

"Do what?" At the exit, I turned onto the street.

"Go all vigilante ballbuster, righting the wrongs of the American public."

"That's not what this is."

"Then what is it?"

I thought for a second. "Never mind. That's exactly what this is."

She laughed. "Do you do this a lot?"

"My niece was getting bullied last year, so I showed up looking like I might crack some skulls at her elementary school." I smiled. "Nobody's messed with her since."

Bess smiled across the car at me. "I really appreciate you doing this."

"I haven't done anything yet, but they shouldn't have fired you."

"My manager's an asshole."

"What's his name?"

"Clint Mitchell."

"I don't know him."

"I guess you would know a lot of people around here, being a cop and all."

I lifted a shoulder. "Some. My brother also works at the Drexler."

"Who?"

"Ransom Nyx."

"Your brother's name is Ransom? Did your mother hate him?"

I grinned. "She kind of hates both of us, actually, but she didn't name him. Our father did. He works security."

"We haven't met, but it's a big place, and I haven't been there long. Have you always lived in Sapphire Lake?"

"On and off. I lived here when I was little, but I went to grade school in Reno. We moved back when I was twelve."

Kindergarten had been hard for Ransom with everyone knowing what our parents had done. So Gran and Paps moved us to Reno, until Ransom got tangled up with some bad friends in middle school. We returned to Sapphire Lake then, and in the years that had passed, we'd mostly been forgotten.

"I left again when I went into the Army but moved back a few years ago."

"Do you like it here?"

"It's the prettiest place in the world."

"It sure is. The altitude is killer though. I had a headache for the first month I was here, and it's so dry I should own stock in my moisturizer."

"Don't forget about chapstick."

"God, yes." She counted on her fingers. "I literally have a car chapstick, a nightstand chapstick, a work chapstick, a bathroom chapstick—"

"And you haven't even been through winter yet," I said with a smile.

"I haven't really been through winter *anywhere*. I'm from the South, remember?"

"Before I get your job back, you might want to reconsider moving. Winters are no joke out here."

She leaned toward me. "My mother is no joke. Bring on the damn snow."

I chuckled. "I know the feeling."

Three news vans were still parked out front when we pulled into the Drexler's main entrance. And every head near the door turned when I stopped at the valet stand.

The valet opened my door, and I handed him a twenty. "Keep it up front, please. We won't be here long."

Bess clapped her hands when I met her on the curb. "This is so exciting."

"Keep your cool, and let me do the talking."

For Bess, I wasn't sure this was possible.

When we started for the automatic sliding-glass doors, a flash of movement to my right almost had me reaching for my weapon. Instead, I mom-armed Bess across the chest to stop her as Marianne Clarke with her News 4-branded microphone charged toward us.

"Officer Nyx!"

Strike one. I was a *corporal.*

"You were among the first on scene Thursday night at the Drexler. What happened inside Ryder Stone's chalet?" she shouted, shoving the microphone in my face.

The other reporters swarmed like vultures to a carcass.

"No comment," I said, pushing Bess through the door.

Questions flew from every direction.

"You were on scene the night of Ryder Stone's death!"

"Do you know what killed Ryder Stone?"

"Aren't you the officer who was hit by the car on Thursday night?"

"No comment!" I shouted.

One of the reporters—male, Hispanic, shockingly tall—realized I was determined to get through. He shielded me as the others crowded in, an unusually selfless move for anyone in the media.

"Thank you," I said as I pulled Bess past him.

Bess kept looking back as I dragged her into the lobby. "Holy shit! That was crazy. You're a celebrity!"

"I am *not* a celebrity. Come on. Where's your boss?"

"He could be at any one of the bars."

I gestured for her to lead. "Find him."

We drew stares from the patrons and staff alike as we wound through the swanky lobby. It was a massive resort, part hotel, part country club. In the third lounge, we passed a giant half-moon bar overlooking the first tee box. Bess grabbed my arm. "That's him. Brown hair, nine o'clock."

I turned left and saw a blonde woman shaking a cocktail. "That's not a *him.*"

Bess counted backward from twelve, drawing an arch with her finger. "Sorry. Ten o'clock."

To the blonde's right was a tall man with slicked-back brown hair, polishing a tumbler.

"Red suspenders?" I asked.

"Yep."

"Come on."

Bess hesitated.

"Come on," I said again.

Her nose scrunched. "I'm not so good with confrontation."

"Good. Then you won't have a problem keeping your mouth shut." I grabbed the front of her shirt and hauled her forward. She finally fell in step behind me as we walked to the bar.

When we reached the counter, I balanced a boot on the foot bar and leaned forward. Bess's former boss smiled and put down the glass he was polishing. "Hello, gorgeous. What can I getcha?"

I jerked my head toward the balding man to my right. "Do you call him gorgeous?"

Clint blinked. "Excuse me?"

"You heard me. Do you talk to all your customers that way or just the women?"

"Uhh . . ."

"Are you Clint Mitchell?"

"Who's asking?" His tone had shifted from flirty to defensive. Smart. Before I could answer, his eyes drifted behind me and widened. "You. Didn't I fire you, Ms. Lincoln?"

"You did. That's exactly what I'd like to talk to you about," I said before she could answer. The bar patrons around us inched closer. "Do you know who I am?"

He smirked. "Should I?"

After a pause, a woman two barstools down lifted a jeweled hand. "I think I know."

We all looked at her. "I saw your picture on the news. You're a police officer."

"That's right," the bald man said. "Weren't you hit by a car or something?"

I turned back to Clint in time to see realization dawn on his face. Still staring at him, I smiled. "I was." I pulled out my badge and slapped it on the countertop, then pointed at the side of my head. "Late Thursday night, I was struck on the roadside while on duty. Do you know why I survived?"

Guilt washed over Clint like a rain cloud had settled over him.

I jerked my thumb over my shoulder. "Because this woman held me in her lap on the side of the highway." I pointed at him. "And you fired her for it."

The people at the bar gasped and whispered.

"Gimme a break. It was a crazy story! It's not like it was the first time she—"

I cut him off with a wave before he said anything socially incriminating against Bess. "You called her a liar and fired her on the spot." I really hoped that was true. "Now, because of me and because of you, she's homeless."

"No!" Jewelry Lady, who'd guessed my identity, put down her martini in disgust.

"Yes." I leaned my elbows on the counter, immediately retracting them when the left one burned.

A dark-haired waitress, holding a drink tray against her chest, scurried past us. She leaned over the bar and whispered something to Clint.

His head shot up, and he stretched on his toes to look over his head. "Shit," he mouthed.

Jewelry Lady whispered something to the man sitting next to her.

When I turned, Harlan Drexler was stepping out of an elevator on the far side of the room. He scanned the lobby until his eyes locked on mine.

Harlan smiled.

I waved.

He waved back.

Clint swore.

Bess gave a tiny squeal and grabbed my arm.

I sat on a bar stool. "What kind of beers do you have on tap, Clint?" I patted the stool beside me. "Bess, have a seat."

She slid onto the cushion, hiding a giggle behind her hand.

Clint gripped the bar top. "Please, Officer . . . whoever you are. It was a mistake. Please don't bring Mr. Drexler into this."

"Clint, I'm afraid *you* brought Mr. Drexler into this."

"I'll do anything. Bess can have her job back. I'll give her an apron right now."

Bess perked up in her seat.

I shook my head. "Not good enough."

He shoved a hand into his pocket. "I'll even pay her out of my own tips. Just please don't get me fired."

I folded my arms in front of me. "You're terribly nervous. I'm guessing this won't be the first complaint Mr. Drexler has heard about you."

All the blood drained from Clint's face.

"I tell you what, Clint. You give Bess her job back, pay her every cent of her lost wages and tips out of that wad of cash, and give her first pick of the shifts she wants. Do all that, and I'll keep my mouth shut."

Bess leaned toward me. "And I'd like a better parking space."

"And a better parking space," I repeated.

"Fine. Fine." Clint started flipping through the roll of cash. "You would've made what? Fifty bucks closing the other night?"

"Try three hundred, on Thursday night and on Friday."

"Thursday you were only closing. And you weren't even scheduled to work yesterday," he argued.

"I think that's a little far past the point, Mr. Mitchell," she said.

"This is extortion."

"Bet your ass it is, sweet cheeks," Jewelry Lady said, sucking the olive off her toothpick.

Clint's worried eyes flashed over my shoulder again. "All

right, all right. I don't have that much on me, but I'll bring the rest when she comes in to work tomorrow night."

"I was supposed to work *tonight*," she said.

"Fine. Tonight."

Bess snatched the cash from his hand. "Deal."

Everyone at the bar clapped and cheered.

"Officer Nyx!" a voice boomed behind me.

With a smile, I stood and turned around. Harlan's arms opened, and I stepped into the bear hug, breaking out of my personal-space bubble on a matter of principle. "Mr. Drexler, good to see you again."

"Please, call me Harlan." Harlan smelled of cigars and scotch. "My pit boss recognized you from the news and let me know you were here. I've raved to everyone about how you and your partners handled everything with our tragedy the other night."

"I was only doing my job, sir."

He gripped both my shoulders and looked at my head. "I heard about your ordeal. Did you get my note?"

"Did you send it to the office?"

"Yes. I'll bet you haven't been in."

"No. I'm off work for a while."

"Well, there's a silver lining to every cloud, isn't there?" He snapped his finger over my shoulder. "Clint, please get Ms. Nyx a drink on the house."

It was hard not to smile.

"What brings you by today? Are you here with official news?" He looked so hopeful, I almost hated to disappoint him.

"Actually, no." I looked back at Bess. "I'm here with one of your employees. Harlan, this is Bess Lincoln."

Bess's face turned every color of pink and red in the rainbow as she extended her hand. "Hello, Mr. Drexler."

"Hello, dear. What part of the company do you work in?"

"Here, sir. I'm a bartender."

"Excellent." He put a hand on my shoulder. "Well, any friend of our brave officer's is a friend of mine. You should pop into my office and say hello the next time you're on the schedule. I'd love to hear about your aspirations in this company."

"That would be great. Thank you, sir." She was beaming.

Harlan turned his smile toward me. "Since you're off anyway, I could set you up in one of our best rooms tonight if you'd like to stay."

"Definitely won't be necessary, but thanks anyway."

He seemed disappointed, but it quickly faded. He looked past me again. "Seriously, Mitchell, anything these two girls want for as long as they want to stay."

Clint gave a begrudging nod.

"I'll see you again soon?" Harlan asked, squeezing my shoulder.

"I hope so."

When he was gone, Bess dug her nails into my arm and squealed. "Oh my god! You didn't tell me you *know* Harlan Drexler!"

"Gotta learn to keep your cards close, kid." I pried her fingers off me. "You want to drink, or do you want to get out of here?"

"Let's get out of here. Clint, I'll see you this evening," Bess said as she slid off her seat.

Grumbling something I couldn't hear, he ignored her.

"I'm starving," Bess said.

"Me too." I glanced at the bills she was stuffing into her pocket. "You're buying."

She laughed as we started toward the door. "Happily. I just wish you'd let Harlan get us a room. At least then I'd have somewhere to sleep tonight."

"You can stay with me," I said, not even believing the words as they came out of my mouth.

She stopped walking. "Are you serious?"

"Yes." I turned to face her. "But only until you get your shit straightened out. This isn't going to be a permanent arrangement."

"Cross my heart and hope to die." She drew an *X* over her chest with her finger.

"No need for dying."

"Thank you, Nyx!"

"You're welcome. But I sleep during the day, and I keep my house tidy. That shitstorm you've made of your car isn't going to fly at my place. Understood?"

"I promise."

I started walking again. "You've got a month to save up for a place of your own. And you should take Harlan up on his offer. Sounds like he'll help you move up at the resort."

"I will. I swear I won't blow it."

"Don't make me regret this."

Too late. I was regretting it already.

Back at my condo, Bess spent the next hour and a half unloading her car. When the last of the million boxes was inside, I carried a spare key to her new temporary bedroom. She met me in the hallway with her purse slung over her shoulder.

I looked at my watch. "Work time already?"

"Yeah. Thanks to you, I have a job to go to."

"Well, you'd better not be late." With a smile, I handed her the key.

She held it up. "Where was this the other night when you were wrestling with your key ring?"

"Oh." I hadn't even thought about it. I pointed to my head. "Blame the concussion."

We both laughed.

"Don't worry if I'm not here when you get back. I try to stay busy at night to keep myself awake. I sleep in the mornings, usually from eight until two in the afternoon. Please don't wake me up."

She put a finger over her lips. "You won't even know I'm here."

I doubted that.

Above our heads, the hallway light flickered again. She pointed up. "I can call your super about that on Monday while you're asleep, if you want."

My brow rose with surprise. One of the hardest things about working nights was not being around to get shit done during normal business hours. Having a roommate might have some perks after all. "That would be helpful."

"Sure thing. Just leave me the number. I'll set it up."

"Thanks."

"It's the least I can do. I really do appreciate your help, Nyx."

"I know."

When she was gone, I walked to the kitchen for a glass of water. Through the window, I saw Bess smiling as she got in her car. I smiled too. "Nyx, you can officially check off all your good deeds for the year," I said aloud.

A burst of cold stung my skin as something unseen cinched my throat. The whole world swirled to black.

When my spirit woke up inside the Boundary, the brightest blue eyes I'd ever seen stared down at me, inches above my face. The man's hand was still clasped around my throat, and I was pinned to my kitchen floor, with him straddling my hips.

My right hand reached across to grab his wrist as my left hand clamped onto his tricep. I pulled in my knees, trapping his leg between my feet. With a swift thrust of my hips, I toppled him over and rolled up onto my knees, then I drove my fist straight down into his groin.

He yowled and curled into the fetal position against the

refrigerator. I reached for my gun at my waist, but of course, it was on the floor, still attached to my real body.

My attacker pushed up onto his knees, and with a pained roar, he punched the refrigerator door. *Crunch!*

Before he could recover, I dove across the floor, grabbed my forehead, and disappeared back into my body. I bolted upright, alone—so it seemed—in my kitchen.

The front of my refrigerator was dented in.

"Holy shit." I panted. "What the fuck was that?"

CHAPTER TEN

I was tough, but I wasn't stupid.

After the attack, I abandoned my condo. I walked the lake trail until sundown, had a late dinner with lots of caffeine at Night Watch, and nursed a beer on the patio at Delaney's. I finally returned home when I knew Bess would be back.

Not that I thought she could protect me, but after hours of replaying the events leading up to my assault, I realized her presence was key in it not happening sooner. The chills I'd felt, the flushing toilet, the flickering lights—those were all signs someone was already there, just across the Boundary, waiting for me to be alone.

Bess was asleep when I crept inside, and I finally lost my battle against sleep at sunrise. It was a shallow and dreamless slumber, thankfully not quite deep enough for my spirit to detach. Sometime later, I awoke to singing.

With a groan, I rolled over and pulled the pillow over my head. Big mistake. The edge of the pillowcase snagged on a staple and pulled. Tears sprang to my eyes, and I sat up, gingerly touching my scalp.

Nothing was bleeding except my ears.

Somewhere in the condo, an off-key rendition of "Since You've Been Gone" by Kelly Clarkson was peeling the paint off the walls. I covered my eyes with my forearm. "Kill me now."

Something crashed outside my bedroom.

I threw the covers back and got up, opening my door with so much force it bounced off the hinges. I tore down the hallway to the office-slash-guest-room. The door was open, and the rolling office chair was lying on its back.

Bess plucked an earbud from her ear. "Hey! You're up!"

"Yes, and I don't want to be."

"I knocked over the chair." She grimaced. "Did it wake you?"

"Oh, it wasn't the chair. The caterwauling drowned it out."

Her head pulled back with surprise. "Was I singing?"

"Yeah."

She clamped a hand over her mouth. "My bad. Sometimes I get carried away."

Yeah, me too. Like with this offer of giving you a place to stay.

The twin bed I'd kept for Milly's visits was now covered with an oversized lime-green comforter and matching floral-print sheets and pillows.

Fine. Whatever.

But the closet behind her . . . oh my god. It was stuffed floor-to-ceiling with boxes, and my desk was piled with clothes and computer parts.

Perhaps she saw the smoke rising from my ears because her hands shot up in defense. "I promise I'll clean everything up. I'm just trying to sort through what I need and what I can leave in boxes."

Good. Don't get too comfortable.

Miraculously, I kept my mouth shut.

"Do you mind if I set up my computer on the desk?"

I gestured toward the computer parts. "It actually works?"

"When it's assembled."

"Sure." I picked up my laptop, remembering I needed to file an insurance claim to get my personal phone replaced.

"If you go back to sleep, I'll be as quiet as a church mouse."

I doubted that.

I looked at the clock on the small nightstand. It was almost noon, which meant Ransom should arrive any minute. "If you don't mind making yourself scarce, my brother is coming by today. He and I need to handle some family business."

Family business that I really hadn't thought through before inviting her to live with me.

"Of course. I was thinking of popping over to Delaney's for a bite to eat. Can I bring you anything back?"

"No, thanks. I'll probably go out with my brother while he's here." If he didn't storm out of my condo first.

"Great. You won't even know I'm here."

I doubted that too.

Shaking my head, I carried my laptop back to my room and closed the door. After brushing my teeth and changing into a pair of yoga pants and a long-sleeve tee, I grabbed my work phone and flopped diagonally across the mattress. There was a missed call and a text message from Essex. He didn't leave a voicemail, but his message said, *In the neighborhood. You up?*

I tapped his phone number in my call history. No answer.

A second later, the doorbell rang.

"I'll get it!" Bess called as I walked out of my bedroom. She was already at the door.

When she pulled it open, I expected to see my brother. It was Essex, in jeans and a blue T-shirt that said, "It's Taco'clock somewhere."

Bess leaned against the door. "Well, hello."

His head fell to the side with confusion. "Hi. Bess, right?"

"Yes, sir. Essex?"

"You can call me Tyler."

"OK, Tyler."

He looked from her to me then back to her. "What are you doing here?"

"I live here now."

"Really?" Surprised, he looked at me again.

"Only until she can get her own place." I walked to the door. "I just tried calling you."

"I was walking up the steps. Hope you don't mind my dropping by."

"Of course not. Come on in."

With a smile and a wave, Bess walked back to the guest room.

Essex followed me to the kitchen. "You have a roommate now?"

"It's a long story. Want some coffee?" I dumped the grounds from the day before in the trash.

"No. I'm going to try to sleep for a few hours before tonight."

"You didn't sleep this morning?"

"Nah. I worked till midnight with Bravo shift—"

"Crawling back into the womb already?" I asked with a grin. Bravo was the team he'd just left.

"Ha, ha," he said, unamused. "Chief is offering as much overtime as anyone wants, so I picked up some hours last night. Made the mistake of crashing when I got home."

I put a new filter in the basket. "Where have you been this morning? Wait, let me guess; a meeting?" I scooped fresh coffee grounds from the can.

He chuckled. "Yes. A meeting you would have found *very* interesting."

I looked back. "Was it about my job?"

"No."

With a sigh, I went back to scooping coffee grounds.

"Because of all the media hype, narcotics put a rush on the lab tests for the Seven Kings' gold heroin we found with Ryder Stone. Nyx, it was laced with melatryptophine."

I spun around, spilling coffee grounds all over the floor. "Hypnox?"

"Looks like it." He handed me the report.

My chest tightened as I read it.

"The department will want to question you about this."

"I don't know anything about it."

"I know, but your parents were responsible the last time hypnox was found in Nevada, so I'm sure they'll want to talk to your whole family. I know they're talking to your mother soon."

I slumped over the counter, bracing my right elbow against it as I cradled my head. I swore under my breath.

"But don't worry too much. Gregg is personally questioning Mal, and she's got your back. That should contain the gossip a bit."

That eased my nerves some. "Any other bombshells I should know about?"

"That's it. I assume you'll be on light duty for a while and riding with me."

I straightened. "I will?"

"You wanna ride with someone else?"

"No." Which was true, but damn. Was this a good idea?

He leaned toward me. "I know what you're thinking . . ."

You do?

"You're afraid you'll be accused of preferential treatment."

Sooo not what I was thinking. My brain was fixed on the recent skyrocket of the sexual tension between us. We could barely survive an afternoon alone together. How would being confined to a patrol car shift after shift go?

His mouth was still moving, but his words were going in one ear and out the other. I realized I was staring through him when he waved a hand in front of my face. "Earth to Nyx."

"Sorry, just dreading all the shit that comes with Mal," I lied.

"You really hate her, don't you?"

"Her name literally translates to *bad* in English."

He smiled as he got up from the bar. "Well, you might want to give your grandfather and brother a heads-up that they'll probably be questioned too."

"I will. They should both be here any minute." I finished filling the coffee filter with grounds. I was seriously going to need all the caffeine I could get. When I finished, I pressed start on the coffee maker and turned back around to face him. "I really appreciate you not making me find out about all this at work."

"You're welcome."

"Sure you don't want coffee?"

"Positive. Thanks." He came around the counter to stand in front of me. "Try not to let this all get to you too much."

"Too late. It's going to sink my chances at a promotion."

He closed the space between us. "No, it's not. And it especially won't if you're the one to bring this shit to a stop."

"What are you saying?"

"I'm saying, if you're cleared to return to work this week, you and I will be hunting some Kings. You up to it?"

"You know it."

With a smile, he looked at his watch. "I'd better get going."

We walked to the door together, and he opened it. He paused in the doorway. "Don't worry, Nyx."

"I won't," I lied again.

"Talk to you later."

"Bye." I watched him jog down the steps before finally closing the door.

"He's hot," Bess said behind me, causing my heart to leap into my throat.

"Geez, don't do that."

"Are you dating him?"

"What? No."

"Why the hell not? He's gorgeous, and he literally has"—she lowered her voice—"*sex* in his name."

I laughed and returned to the kitchen. "He's my sergeant. I couldn't date him if I wanted to."

"Is it against the rules?"

"Yes. And I already have to work twice as hard to be taken seriously because I'm a woman. That would be shot all to hell if I started sleeping with my boss." I pulled the bottle of ibuprofen out of the cabinet.

"I guess that makes sense. It sucks though." She slid onto a barstool. "What made you want to be a cop?"

At the filtered spout on the fridge, I filled a glass with water. "To help people," I answered without looking up.

She snorted. "OK."

I turned toward her. "Excuse me?"

"I mean, I believe you, but you answered like a parakeet. Are all cops programmed to say that?"

It was a common question. One I'd been asked since the day I turned in my first application. And my robot answer was the easiest response that returned the least amount of subsequent questions.

"Maybe," I said with a grin as I dropped a few pills into my mouth.

"Then what's the honest reason?"

I turned and leaned against the counter, giving the inquiry serious thought. "It is an honest reason, at least now. Nobody would stick with this job through all the shit we have to see and deal with if not for the glimmers of the good it does." The corner of my mouth rose. "But it's not exactly the reason I joined."

She leaned forward, ready for juicy secrets.

"I lost a bet."

"You what?"

"I left the Army and moved back here to recuperate from some injuries I got in an accident. My plan had always been to reenlist once I was healed, but my heart wasn't in it anymore. A friend was supposed to meet me at this bar one night to help me decide what to do, and he stood me up."

It felt too personal to tell this near-stranger that the friend was actually my brother.

"Anyway, this dude saw me drinking alone and came over cracking jokes. We started talking and playing darts, and he said he was a cop." I pointed toward the front door.

"Tyler?"

I nodded. "After a few beers, I spilled my dilemma. He asked if I'd ever considered police work. Then he challenged me to another round of darts and said if I lost, I had to apply to the police department."

"And you lost?"

"I was pretty drunk."

"You changed your whole life based on a drunken bet? That sounds like something I would do."

The coffee pot hissed and gurgled behind me. "It still made sense when I sobered up the next day, so I looked further into it. Compared to the military, the pay was decent, and the job required zero experience. They also offered me preference because I was a vet."

A smile crept across my face.

"And?" she asked.

"And here in the good ol' US of A, cops get to shoot a *lot* of guns."

Bess laughed. "I've never fired a gun in my life."

"Seriously?"

"They scare the bejeezus out of me."

"Then stay away from my safe." *And my headboard. And my mattress.*

She laughed again.

A knock at the front door ended the conversation. "That's probably Ransom."

There was another knock before I could open it. This time, it was lighter, faster, and accompanied by a giggle. I jerked the door open and shouted, "Who's banging on my door!"

My niece squealed and ducked behind Paps's legs, nearly toppling him over. Laughing, I grabbed his wrist to steady him.

"You trying to give an old man a heart attack?" he asked, panting.

Milly peeked around his waist and squealed again. Ransom palmed her face and pulled her against his legs. "Amelia, hush."

I bent and opened my arms. "Come here, you."

She ran and jumped, throwing her tiny arms around my neck. I picked her up and instantly regretted it as the blood rushed back to my head. I squinted and groaned. Even without a head injury, she was almost too big to be held. "I wasn't expecting to see you today. I figured you'd be with your mom."

"Someone overheard we were coming to see Aunt Nyx and then mysteriously became too sick to go shopping with Mom and Nana," Ransom said, following Paps inside.

I lifted an eyebrow. "You don't seem sick now."

Amelia shrugged her small shoulders. "It's a miracle."

I laughed and blew a raspberry against her cheek.

It was clear she'd spent the night with Ransom. Her long dark hair was in a lopsided ponytail. She wore blue pants and a stained orange sweatshirt, with rainbow-print rain boots despite the sunshine. Celise would have had a fit.

"Whoa!" Milly leaned so far to the side to look at my head, I stumbled sideways a step. "What happened to you?"

Paps grabbed my chin and turned my head to survey the damage. "Holy hell, Saphera. Looks like your head was caught in a bear trap."

"Paps, language," Ransom said, closing the door behind them.

"Kind of felt like a bear trap." I kissed my grandfather's cheek.

Paps was in his midseventies now, a retired Navy man and Vietnam veteran. Except for minor issues with his memory and a small irregularity with his heart, my grandfather was, as he'd recently told me in a text message, *HEALTHY AS A STUD HORSE.* He swam laps every day and played pickle ball at the community center.

Still, between arthritis and spine problems, Paps seemed to be getting shorter every time I saw him. Not so long ago, he'd towered over all of us. Now, standing beside him, my brother was slightly taller.

"Celise cleaned you up?" Paps asked, still grimacing at the side of my head.

"Yeah, she took good care of me." I gave my brother a one-armed hug. "You really never deserved her."

"Don't we all know it?" Paps chuckled.

"Momma says the same thing," Milly added with a wide smile. We all laughed.

"Look at me," I said to Milly. "Did you lose a tooth?"

She smiled, displaying the gap in her teeth. "Yesterday on the way to the park." She stuck her finger in the hole. "The tooth fairy brought me ten dollars."

"Wow. Even the tooth fairy has suffered from inflation." I carried Milly to the kitchen and set her on the counter. "Who wants a popsicle?"

Her hand shot into the air.

Bess was standing on the other side of the bar, waiting to be acknowledged.

Paps stopped walking first. "Hello. Who are you?"

With her hands clasped in front of her, Bess took a few bouncy steps forward. "I'm Bess. Nyx's new roommate."

Paps laughed *really* hard. "Try again. Who are you really?"

"It's true," I said, pulling a cherry popsicle from my freezer. "She's crashing here until she finds her own place."

With a crumpled brow, Paps turned toward me. "How hard did you hit your head?"

I unwrapped the bar for Milly. "Bess saved my ass the other night. She needed a place to stay, so I'm helping her out."

"Saved your ass?" he asked.

"She called the ambulance after the accident."

"Oh." My grandfather gave a slight bow. "Well, Bess, we are all in your debt."

"Bess, this is my grandfather, Paps, my niece, Amelia, and my brother, Ransom." When I looked back, Ransom was checking his reflection in the microwave glass. I cleared my throat as he raked his fingers through his dark hair.

When he realized we were all staring, he awkwardly stepped forward and extended his hand. "Hi, Bess. Nice to meet you."

"Nice to meet you too." She was downright giddy.

My brother had never had a problem attracting the ladies. Keeping them, however, was a different matter altogether. His longest relationship had been with Celise, but she'd always been a bit of a unicorn.

"Bess was just heading out for lunch, right, Bess?" I looked at her with raised eyebrows.

"Oh, right!" She scurried past Paps and Ransom, stopping next to me and Milly at the counter. "It was really nice to meet you all. Especially you, Ms. Amelia."

My niece pulled the popsicle from her already-stained mouth with a slurp. "It was nice to meet you too, Bess!"

"Hopefully, we'll see you again," Paps said.

She flashed a bright smile at my brother. "I hope so too!" With a wave, she disappeared down the hallway.

When she was out the front door, I pointed at Ransom. "Don't you dare get any ideas."

"What?" He feigned offense.

"You know what. She's too young for you."

"Is she over eighteen?" Paps asked with a chuckle as he walked to the couch.

"Don't encourage him," I said.

Paps sat on the sofa, and my brother lifted Milly off the

counter. "How about you go watch cartoons in Nyx's room?" He cast me a knowing look.

With a heavy sigh, she dropped her head back. "But Dad—"

He lifted both thick eyebrows in a warning glare.

She groaned. "Fine."

"Good girl." He put her down, and she trudged to my bedroom, squeaking her rubber boots across the dark hardwood floor. Ransom followed her, pausing in the doorway before closing it. "You know how to work the TV?"

I couldn't hear her response, if she even gave one. It was probably the "Duh, Dad" look I'd seen a thousand times. He closed the door. "You working tonight?" he asked me.

"No. It's my weekend off. I hope to go back tomorrow night."

"Is that wise?" Paps asked.

"It's better than sitting around here." In the kitchen, I opened the cabinet with the coffee mugs. "Anybody hungry? Thirsty?"

"Got any scotch?" Paps asked.

"Not a drop."

"Then no."

"Coffee?" I offered, grabbing my favorite mug from the cabinet. A gift from Paps, it said, *I like coffee. And maybe 2 people.* It was the most accurate mug I owned.

"No coffee. We need to talk," Ransom said, plopping down in an armchair in my living room.

I poured my cup full, then glanced out the window over the sink. Bess was crossing the street toward Delaney's. "So talk."

"What did you find out at the prison?" Ransom asked.

I told him what I'd seen and heard from the warden.

"You really think it was a nightwalker?"

"No human could've done what I saw in those photos."

"Why would he be so stupid?" Ransom asked.

"Good question." I sipped the steaming black coffee before remembering Bess had bought creamer. I opened the fridge.

"Elias lied to us."

I froze. "I'm surprised this is a newsflash for you. What did he lie about, specifically?" I pulled out the carton and got a spoon from the utensil drawer.

"The gift. It didn't transfer. Or it doesn't work. Or hell, maybe it never existed at all. I don't really know anymore."

With my back to them, I closed my eyes. "Why do you say that?"

"Because I've done exactly what he told me to do every time I've slept since he died, and *nothing.*"

My ears perked. "What did he tell you to do?" I poured a splash of Italian sweet cream into my coffee and stirred and stirred and stirred.

"He said if it didn't happen automatically, to lie in bed until I start to drift off, then to imagine a rope hanging above me. He said I could use the rope to pull myself out. Well, I tried that over and over and over again, and nothing happened."

I finally put the carton away and put the spoon into the sink. Slowly, with my heart jackhammering in my chest, I picked up the mug and turned toward my family.

Ransom's feet were on my coffee table, and his head was laid back in frustration. "I quit my job."

Paps's face whipped toward him, and I almost dropped my mug. "You did what?" I asked.

"This was supposed to be my big break. I don't want to work security at a hotel forever. I was going to use the gift to start a new life."

"Damn it, son," Paps said in frustration.

"Can you get it back?" I asked.

"I don't know. I'm supposed to be working my last two weeks." He looked at me. "But I don't want it back. I want for *something* Elias told me to be true." His head fell back again.

I knew the feeling.

Paps was staring at me, his mouth set in a hard line. He gave a hard, deliberate blink.

"What?" I mouthed.

"Will you tell him, or shall I?"

My heart stopped.

Ransom looked at him. "Tell me what?"

"You know?" I asked Paps.

"Why do you think I'm here? It's Sunday. I'm missing pickle ball."

"Know what?" Ransom's feet dropped from the table with a heavy *thud*.

Paps and I stared at each other.

"Someone had better start talking fast," Ransom said, his volume up a few decibels.

My feet felt like they weighed a thousand pounds as I crossed the living room toward my brother. I sat on the coffee table in front of him. "Ransom—" My voice cracked. I put my coffee down and rubbed my sweaty palms on the sides of my pants. "I don't think Elias lied. I think he was just wrong."

"What are you talking about?" he asked.

"Elias's power did transfer . . ." I swallowed hard. "To me."

Ransom's eyes glazed over as he stared straight through me. Neither of us moved, or breathed, for what felt like eternity.

"Please say something," I said, leaning forward and touching his knee.

He sat back, folding his hands in his lap as he shifted his stare to the ceiling. Still, nothing.

I turned to Paps for help.

"Ransom?" Paps asked.

Ransom finally met my eyes. "You?"

I nodded, bracing for the worst.

He stood and walked between the back of the loveseat and the patio door. He paced back and forth. "You?" he asked again.

"I didn't know. He told me the same as he'd always told you. The gift would be yours when he died. It was supposed to be you, not me."

"You don't even want it! You've called me stupid my whole life for wanting it."

I straightened. "I've never called you stupid."

He threw a hand toward me. "Well, you certainly made me feel stupid."

My insides twisted.

Suddenly, Ransom froze. Realization flickered on his face. "Wait a second. If the gift passes to the firstborn, was Elias even my father?"

About that, I really had no idea. I looked at Paps. "What do you know?"

"Elias told me this might happen," Paps said.

"When?" I asked.

"He sent a letter not too long ago, just after your grandmother died."

"Was he sick then?" I asked.

"Yes. They'd just found the *necrofecitis*—"

"Necrotizing fasciitis," I corrected.

He lifted his hands. "That's what I said. I think he knew he was in trouble then." Paps's face softened when he looked at Ransom. "Elias hoped it wasn't true, but someone from the Boundary told him to prepare for Nyx to be his heir."

"Does Mal know Ransom had a different father?" I asked.

Paps smirked. "Knowing your mother, probably, but she'd never admit it if she did."

He might have been our mother's father, but Paps would be the first to say he didn't like her any more than we did. As he put it, Ransom and I had only been dealing with her shit since she got out of prison. He and Gran had been dealing with it for Mal's whole life.

"She doesn't know," Ransom said.

"Have you talked to her?" I asked.

He shook his head. "Not recently, but I'm sure I'll hear from her as soon as she finds out Elias is gone."

"You won't have to wait long. My department is questioning her soon," I said as Ransom began wearing down my carpet again.

"Why?" Paps asked.

"Because hypnox is back on the streets."

Ransom stopped pacing. "Shit. Really?"

The fact that hypnox so quickly drowned out Ransom's existential crisis amplified my concern.

"The lab confirmed it was there the night Ryder Stone died," I said.

They both looked as worried as I felt.

"And I think whoever killed Elias tried to kill me yesterday."

"What happened?" Paps asked.

"A man attacked me. Put me to sleep somehow, and I woke up inside the Boundary. There was a fight."

"What man?" Ransom asked.

"I didn't know him."

"Are you all right?" Paps asked.

"I'm OK, for now, but I don't know what will happen if I can't keep myself from detaching."

We both looked at Ransom. "Can you help your sister?" Paps asked him.

Ransom pulled both hands through his hair.

I got up and went to my brother. "You know better than anyone this wasn't my choice. I don't want this. I never wanted it, and if I could figure out a way to give it back to you, I would. But I can't do this alone. I need your help."

Ransom stared at me a second, pain etched deep in his dark eyes. "I can't talk to you right now." He pushed by me.

I caught his arm. "Ransom, please. I'm sorry!"

"For stealing my gift or because my whole life has been a lie?" he snapped.

"Both," I said sadly.

"Whatever." He yanked his arm free and stormed through the kitchen.

"Let him go," Paps said.

Ransom slammed the front door behind him. Through the door, I heard him yell outside.

I collapsed on the sofa by my grandfather. He patted my knee when I rested my head on his shoulder. "Give him time, sweet pea. Ransom will come around. He always does."

"I need him. I have no idea what I'm doing."

"I'll talk to him."

I looked at Paps. "You've really known about this for months?"

With a sigh, he leaned his head against mine. "I didn't move to Reno for the showgirls, Saphera."

"You said you moved because you couldn't imagine life in Sapphire Lake without Gran."

"That's true too, but I was worried about your brother. I knew if this happened . . ."

"He might fall off the wagon?"

"You say *fall.* I say *swan dive.*" He shrugged. "I just knew he shouldn't be alone. It wouldn't be good for him or Milly."

I slumped. "What about for me?"

He squeezed my knee. "You, my sweet girl, have never had a problem taking care of yourself. You'll get through this too."

"I don't want it, Paps."

"Really? Not even a little bit?"

I shook my head.

"You know, your father once told me he could go anywhere in the world. That just that morning he'd been sitting on a beach in Tahiti. If I had that kind of power, you kids would never see my old ass awake again."

I laughed softly.

"What's it like?" he asked.

"You ever had a dream so real that you couldn't tell if you were awake or asleep?"

"No. I sleep like the dead. I don't dream, or at least I don't remember it if I do."

"Ever?"

He shook his head.

"Huh, well, it's weird. Like I'm a ghost or something."

"Boy, the things I would do if I could be invisible for a day."

"Yeah? Like what?"

He shrugged. "I might not have moved to Reno for the show-girls, but that doesn't mean I don't know where to find them."

I gagged.

A laugh erupted from deep in his belly. "I'm only joking."

"Are you?"

He winked and chuckled again. "You spy on anyone inter-esting yet?"

"No."

"Liar."

"My boss," I whispered, like Essex might be able to hear me through the atmosphere.

He turned toward me. "Oh really? Would this be the same boss you always swear you're not canoodling?"

"Paps!" I buried my face in a couch pillow. "Geez."

"What?"

"I'm not canoodling anybody."

"The shade of your face tells a different story."

"I don't blush."

"A grandfather can see it. Does he still live in Seneca Park?"

"Yeah. Not far from your place."

"I know the house. Your Gran and I checked him out a time or two. She'd approve of the canoodling too."

I pinched the bridge of my nose. "You know, most grandpar-ents don't talk like this."

"What'd I say?"

"We're not talking about my sex life, and we're not talking about my boss. Besides, I didn't mean to spy on him. I'm still figuring out how it works."

"Be careful." His voice switched to a suddenly serious tone.

I nodded. "I never thought I'd wish for Elias to be around to give me advice."

"Your father wasn't all bad."

"He was a professional con man."

"I think most of that was your mother's doing."

"He was a thief before he met Mal."

"Well, yeah, but he wasn't robbing *people* until he teamed up with her."

Before my mother, Elias had made a living through the stock market. I could see now how easy something like insider trading could be. He never made big enough trades to raise any eyebrows, but he did well enough to lure my mother away from his investment broker, Renzo Bianchi.

Renzo had the final laugh, however. Rumor has it, he was the one who tipped off the police about Elias and Mal.

"I can't believe you didn't tell me about Ransom," I said.

"I didn't want to tell either of you if it wasn't true. But even your Gran and I have wondered since before Ransom was born."

"Because Mal was still with Renzo when she got with Elias?"

"Partly, but even apart from Renzo, that woman has never had a faithful bone in her body."

My eyebrows rose. "Wow. Tell me how you really feel."

"OK." Paps took my hand. "The best thing your mother ever did was have you and Ransom."

Resting my forehead against his, I closed my eyes and let the moment sear into my memory. The slight hitch in his voice. The thin, soft skin of his warm hand around mine. The faint scent of menthol joint cream and peppermint candy.

He didn't pull away. "You kids have suffered enough because

of Malena. I didn't say anything because I didn't want to hurt your brother more if it wasn't true."

"I get that." I squeezed his fingers. "I love you, Paps."

"I love you too, sweet pea." He pointed at the television. "Now turn that thing on. They've got a marathon of *The Family Stones* on channel two."

Ten minutes later, Paps, Milly, and I were watching the now-deceased Ryder Stone dye his superstar father's beard bright blue. Had to say, the show was pretty funny, like a redneck spoof of the Kardashians. It explained the current media hullaballoo in Sapphire Lake.

My front door opened, and Ransom returned. I patted the seat beside me on the sofa.

He stared for a second and finally shook his head. "Paps, Milly, we need to get going."

"Not yet, Dad!" Milly protested.

My shoulders fell. "C'mon, Ransom. Please don't leave already."

He looked out the door.

I turned to Paps for help.

He was on the edge of his seat, ready to rock himself to standing. His eyes were serious. "Give him time," he whispered again.

Milly put her arms around my neck. "I'm gonna stay with Nyx."

"Not today, you're not," Ransom said.

"But *whyyyyyy*?"

"Amelia." He used his dad voice.

Milly's pouty mouth snapped closed, and she slid off my lap.

I tousled her hair. "I'll see you soon, all right, kiddo?"

She groaned. "All right."

I stood and took her hand to walk her to the door. "Will you call me later?" I asked my brother.

Ransom didn't answer. "Come on, Mills." He picked her up

and put her on his back. He paused long enough for me to kiss her goodbye, and then they started down the stairs.

Paps lingered behind and hugged me. "*I will call you later. Please be careful.*"

"I will be." I watched them leave. When they were gone, I closed the door and rested my forehead against it.

This wasn't my fault. Ransom was right—I didn't even want the gift. My heart ached for my brother. My mind worried about what he might do. And my temper flared against our parents. How could they not have told us?

To make matters worse, I got to lie around the house all day and stew on it. I turned to walk back to my bedroom and my eyes snagged on the whiteboard calendar.

Circled in red was my interview last Friday.

Elias had known about it. He hadn't been traipsing around Tahiti lately. He'd been in my condo. And the night he'd come to find me, who knows where else he'd been snooping? He'd been out searching for clues.

And answers.

Ransom wasn't the only one with information.

I looked at my dented refrigerator again, and my heart picked up its pace. The dangers of the Boundary aside, I needed to find Orion.

Elias had said he hoped Orion would help me, and despite all the ways Elias was a shitty father, he wouldn't put me in harm's way intentionally. Sooner or later, I'd have to face the uncertainties that came with this so-called *gift*.

I grabbed a notepad from the kitchen and scribbled a note to Bess.

Taking a nap.
Do NOT wake me up.

CHAPTER ELEVEN

I'm going to have to give up coffee was my last coherent thought before I slipped into REM sleep. I'd closed the blackout curtains. I'd meditated. I'd even counted sheep. When I finally detached a few miserable hours after lying down, I felt a strange new emotion—relief.

The shoes I'd worn to bed hadn't helped. Knowing this would be my first venture out, I had dressed smarter in drawstring lounge pants and a T-shirt. Aside from the sneakers, the outfit was still comfy enough for sleep, while decent enough to meet a strange man.

It was 4:27 p.m. I had less than three hours until sunset.

A manhunt in that time would be tricky, especially considering I had no idea how to get out of my condo. Or my bedroom, for that matter.

I tried the doorknob again. Nothing. I still couldn't turn it.

I'd purposely left the window curtains cracked open on the far side of the room. I slowly eased my head through the glass again. Looking around outside, I didn't see anyone, but there wasn't much open real estate between my building and the trees.

How to get down?

The balcony off the living room was almost within reach.

With enough speed, I should've been able to make the jump. If I missed, and if the Boundary worked like the real world, I'd probably only break my ankles. Could a spirit even break its ankles? Would my ankles break in my bed?

I stopped thinking.

Like a crazy lady, I swatted the drapes until the grommets scooted across the curtain rod, and I had a decent view of the porch. Then I backed all the way to the nightstand, nervously pumping my fists.

"This is stupid, Nyx."

With a deep breath, I took off running and jumped . . .

In the real world, the distance wouldn't have been a problem, but my hands barely caught the bottom rung of the iron rails. Thankfully, I could grip them as easily as if I were awake. I pulled myself up and over without a problem. Panting, I took a second to catch my breath.

Everything outside was amplified.

The sunlight.

The cold breeze.

The noise.

Closing my eyes, I listened. Flogging Molly played inside Delaney's, over the chatter and laughter and the sound of clinking glasses. A car somewhere nearby needed to have its brakes checked. And even from here, I could hear the lake's gentle waves lapping the community's dock.

A door inside my condo slammed, making me jump. I turned to see Bess twirl in the hallway as she walked to the kitchen. Her arms were full of paper grocery bags, and the pink note I'd stuck on the whiteboard calendar was pinched between her teeth. She put the bags on the counter, tossed the note in the trash, and opened the fridge.

Bess unloaded the bags. Milk, eggs, coffee creamer . . .

I hadn't been to the store in weeks, as evidenced by the sad state of my refrigerator. Maybe having a roommate wouldn't be so bad after all.

I wonder if I can get her attention.

I raised my hand to knock on the glass before remembering my hand would go straight through it. Slowly, I stepped inside. The cool energy of the glass tickled my senses as I crossed it.

Bess didn't notice as I walked up behind her to peek into the bags.

Ooo, cookies.

On the counter, her phone buzzed. Without thinking, I looked at the screen. *Who's David?*

She frowned when she picked up the phone, but she answered it and put it to her ear. "What do you want?"

I moved closer.

"Where are you?" David asked, his voice almost as clear as if he were standing in the kitchen with us.

Bess pinched the phone against her ear with her shoulder and pulled a loaf of bread out of a bag. "That's none of your business."

Or mine.

"It *is* my business, damn it. I care about you."

"Then you should have informed your penis before it found its way into somebody else."

I laughed and clamped my hand over my mouth, but there was no reason to. Bess couldn't hear me.

"Baby, I said I'm sorry."

As Bess launched into a rant, I mentally scolded myself for spying—*again.*

I was slowly backing out of the kitchen when Bess whirled around and stormed straight through me. It was a jarring sensation, cold and tingly, like all the molecules of my ethereal body had separated and come back together.

Bess froze, then spun all the way around, searching the empty space. Fear flashed across her face, and I flattened myself against the wall.

She had felt it too.

My throat thickened.

How many times had that same look been on *my* face? How many times had Elias spied on me when I'd felt that creepy chill?

"David?" She looked at her phone.

Shit. I hoped I hadn't destroyed it.

As she walked toward the front door, her phone buzzed again. Thank god because I was already down a phone myself. I couldn't afford one for Bess as well.

"No, I didn't hang up on you!" She threw open the front door, and I followed her through it.

In front of the garage, her car's trunk was standing open. She grabbed the last couple of grocery bags, slammed the lid, and turned to go back up. I stayed in the driveway a moment to make sure she got back inside.

When the door closed behind her, I walked down the hill to the main road. Across it, at Delaney's, the stone courtyard was dotted with groups huddled around firepits. None of them were inside the Boundary.

But someone waved from the stone wall surrounding it.

A boy, clear and in perfect focus, jumped down from the wall. He was about ten years old and four-and-a-half feet tall, judging by the wall behind him. He had a black buzz cut and skinny legs, partially hidden by long blue jogging shorts. His white hoodie had a troop of superheroes on the front.

He waved again.

I waved back.

He walked to the street and motioned me over as cars zoomed between us.

"You come here!" I called to him.

He shook his head.

Shit.

Snowshoe wasn't the busiest road in Sapphire Lake, but cars didn't slow for pedestrians they couldn't see. I wondered what would happen if I stepped in front of one. I *really* needed Ransom. He'd been preparing for this his whole life. And here I was, completely incapable of even crossing the street in the dream world.

Staggering to my feet, I braced to run.

Wait.

What if sprinting had the same sludge-like effect as jumping? A test run would probably be smart. I turned and raced up the narrow bike lane instead. Running was fine. Maybe the glass had slowed me down in my leap from the condo.

When I looked across the street again, the kid's hand was clamped over his mouth to cover his laughter.

My metaphorical insides melted with embarrassment. No. I refused to feel stupid. Better to be safe than wind up as a hood ornament, trapped in the front grill of a pickup.

After a semi barreled past, I ran to the center turning lane. A minivan flew by, followed closely by a convertible. At a break between the car and a delivery van, I bolted toward the side-walk. The van almost clipped my foot as I jumped onto the curb.

"You did it!" the boy cheered.

"No thanks to you."

"What'd you need me for? You practiced your running and everything." He snickered again.

My brow pinched.

"Watch." With a cocky smirk, he stepped into the road in front of a garbage truck. With a panicked gasp, my hand shot forward as the truck plowed through him. He turned around and looked at me as more cars sped through.

My mind drifted back to the accident. Essex had said the driver claimed he'd swerved to miss a man in the road. In the report, the driver said the man had vanished.

Like a ghost.

The boy hopped up onto the curb, jumping with both feet.

When his heels connected with the concrete, his shoes danced with lights.

"Hey, those are pretty neat," I said, pointing at them.

"Thanks. They were a birthday present."

I knelt for a better look as he showed them off. "Really? How old did you turn?"

"Forty-seven."

My spine straightened so quickly I toppled backward onto my ass.

His head tilted. "You OK?"

"I'm fine." I crossed my legs and took a few deep breaths. "You're forty-seven?"

He nodded.

My eyes squinted with doubt.

He patted the top of my head. "It's OK. You're new."

"Thanks," I said with a forced smile. "I'm Nyx."

"I know." He stuck out his hand. "I'm Flash."

"Flash, huh? That's quite a name." I pointed to his superhero shirt. "Like the guy who can run really fast?"

"Yeah. Flash Johnson."

My head snapped back. "Flash Johnson? The football player?"

"Not just a football player." He started counting on his fingers. "Three-time Super Bowl champ, Heisman Trophy winner, NFL Hall of Famer—"

I waved my hand to stop him. "I know who he is. You were named after him?"

He sat down and crossed his legs in front of me. "Well, my momma named me Aaron, but Orion said I can call myself anything I want."

My brow lifted. "You know Orion?"

"Of course I do." He jerked his thumb toward my building. "He's the one who told me to spy on you."

I folded my arms. "Oh really?"

He nodded. "Paying me a *lumin* a day to sit here and wait for you. You've got quite the view from your roof."

"You've been on my roof?"

"Yup."

"What's a lumin?"

Flash leaned forward, bracing his elbows on his knees and balancing his chin on his hands. "You've got a lot to learn, lady."

I sighed. "Tell me about it. You know, your spying almost got me killed the other night."

"What are you talking about?" His voice jumped up an octave with offense.

"The driver of the car that almost hit me said they swerved to miss someone in the road. That was you, wasn't it?"

"Oh no. That was Orion."

"It was, huh?" I asked, my jaw clenched.

"Yeah. That's past my bedtime."

"Did Orion attack me at home too?"

"What?" His eyes doubled, and he pointed at me. "Oh, you kicked him in the dingleberries!"

I blinked. "He choked me."

"Like this?" Flash put his left hand at the base of my throat, pressing his thumb into the notch at top of my sternum.

"Yeah."

"He just knocked you out so he could talk to you."

My head snapped back.

Flash chuckled. "You got him good though."

"Well, where can I find him?"

With a laugh, he shook his head. "Ain't no way you can see him today. He's busy."

"Busy with what?"

"Looking for hypnox. Duh."

"Do you know where he's looking?"

Flash lifted both shoulders all the way to his ears. "I just work here."

"When will he be back?"

"Soon. Maybe tomorrow. He really wants to see you."

"Why?"

"Because you're the great, great, great, great, great"—he paused for a breath—"great, great—"

"I get the idea."

"Great," he added quietly, "granddaughter of the Goddess of Night."

"What does that even mean?"

"You really don't know anything, do you?"

I glared at him.

"It means you have the power to go back and forth."

"Back and forth between here and—?"

"Your world. There are only a couple of you left who can do it."

"Who are the others?"

"I dunno. The Elders mostly care about you."

"Why?"

"I think because your bloodline's always making trouble."

Sounded like Elias.

"Did you know my father?"

He looked at me like I had three heads. "Of *course* I knew him, but I haven't seen him since it all went down."

"Since he went to prison?"

"Yup. He didn't detach much after they sent him to the big house. Only to see family, I think."

"Do you know why?"

"He was *your* daddy. Don't you know why?"

"We weren't close." That was an understatement. Not only didn't I talk to Elias, I refused to talk about him either. Something I was immensely regretting now.

"Somebody wanted him dead," Flash said.

"He killed a cop. Lots of people wanted him dead."

"Not people. The *gods*."

I lifted an eyebrow. "The gods. Like Zeus?"

"No, Zeus is dead."

My head pulled back. "Dead?"

"Yup, all those guys are gone."

"Poseidon? Hades? Athena?"

"All of 'em. And a few of the ones who are still around are stuck living like humans." He pointed at me. "We think they want your blood. It's a pretty big deal."

"Why?"

"Because it's so powerful."

"You think someone might be after me?"

"Orion's pretty worried about it. He told me to tell you not to go out much when you're detached until you see him."

"No argument there. If there was a pill I could take to keep from detaching, I would."

"I don't know about a pill, but there are some stones that will work."

"What kind of stones?"

He lifted his shoulders again. "Not my area of expertise. I'm permanently detached, you know."

"No, I don't know. How did that happen?" The spark went out of his eyes, and I immediately regretted the question. "I'm sorry. I shouldn't have asked."

The corners of Flash's mouth twisted up into a sad smile. "It's OK. They say I got a bad batch of twilight anesthesia and meperidine during an ear surgery. I remember seeing myself in the hospital bed, with my momma praying beside me. I was detached too long, so I got stuck here."

"I'm so sorry."

He shrugged. "It was a long time ago, and I like it in Imera."

"Imera?"

"It's where all the permanently detached spirits live."

"Is that in Nevada?"

Flash burst out laughing.

I frowned. "Are you about finished?"

His laugh died on a melodic slide. "No. Imera isn't on Earth. It isn't in the Boundary either. It's like a whole different world the gods created for spirits who get detached and can't return to Earth."

"How do you get there?"

He reached under the collar of his shirt and pulled out a necklace with a small glass vial attached. "You ever seen one of these?"

I shook my head.

"It's *oneiryte*. Watch." Flash bent over and poured a thin line of sand on the ground, stepped over it, and vanished in a burst of light and wind. My hand shielded my eyes, and when I looked again, the boy was gone. So was the line of sand.

I looked all around me.

"Over here!" he called.

I spotted him, waving from my rooftop. "Holy shit," I whispered.

He poured again, more carefully this time, on the roof. Then, with another explosion of light, Flash reappeared back in front of me. I recoiled. With jazz hands, he said, "Ta-da!"

I clapped. "Impressive."

He lifted the vial and shook it. The one-ounce bottle was nearly empty. "I'd better stop showing off. My stash is getting low."

"Can you get more?"

"Yeah, but only in Avalon. It's the sand on beaches there."

"And Avalon is . . . ?"

"In Imera. It's where I live."

"Is that where Orion lives?"

"No. Orion lives in Synora with the other guardians. Avalon and Synora are like different countries of Imera."

"Will that magic sand take me there?"

"Oh no." He plopped back down in front of me. "You're not allowed to go to Imera."

"Why not?"

"The Elders like to keep the citizens of Imera away from Earth. It makes a lot of 'em sad."

"But you can come here?"

"Only because I'm training to be a guardian, like Orion." His chest puffed out.

"Orion's a guardian?"

"Yup."

"What does he guard?"

"The Boundary. He makes sure people like *you* don't mess everything up!"

I put my hands up in defense. "Simmer down there, *flashlight*."

"Hey!" He pointed at me. "Don't call me flashlight."

I smiled. "How would I mess everything up?"

"Lot of ways." He counted on his fingers. "Letting one of the gods get your blood, detaching other people, getting tangled up with nightwalkers—" His eyes snapped toward the sky. "Speaking of, I'd really better get back. I'm supposed to check in long before sundown." He pushed himself off the ground, and I followed his lead.

"So what happens now?" I asked. "When do I get to go see Orion?"

"You don't. I told you, you can't go to Imera."

"Yeah, yeah."

"Don't worry. Orion *will* find you. I'll tell him you wanna see him too."

"Please do."

"Remember, don't go far from your body, and watch your back."

"I promise."

Flash stuck out his hand, and I accepted it. "It was nice to meet you, Nyx."

"Nice to meet you too, Flashlight."

His eyes narrowed. "That's how it's going to be, huh?"

"I only pick on the boys I like," I said with a wink.

He laughed as he drew another line of sand on the sidewalk. Then he stood, and with one step and a bright flash, he was gone.

CHAPTER TWELVE

*M*onday morning, Dr. Alina Pratts shined a penlight in my eyes. "Any lingering headache?"

A little. "No."

"Blurry vision?"

Not in this realm. "No."

"Any trouble sleeping?"

I almost laughed. "No."

She turned my head to the side and examined the staples and stitches. "These look like they're healing up nicely. Hopefully, they won't scar too much."

"They're starting to itch."

"That's a good sign." She opened a laptop on the small work desk. "Means they're healing."

"Can I go back to work?"

"Are you supposed to be at work now?"

I did some quick math in my head. We worked twelve-hour shifts that rotated to give us every other weekend off. "This is my long week. I'm only off Wednesday and Thursday."

She studied my face.

My eyes were pleading. I stopped short of clasping my hands

beneath my chin in full-on begging mode. "I really don't want to sit at home," I added.

"I'd rather you wait a few more days."

My whole body slumped.

"I'm sorry, Nyx, but that's a nasty head trauma, and you don't exactly have a desk job."

I nodded, but I wanted to kick my boots against the bottom of the exam table. "What about riding with someone? Can I go to work if I ride shotgun?"

"Light duty?"

"Sure." I could do light duty as long as I wasn't stuck in the office all day.

She considered it. "Fine, as long as you're staying hydrated and not having intense pain or light sensitivity."

I could have jumped off the table to hug her. But I didn't. "Thank you."

"But only light duty for two weeks. No foot pursuits and no fights." She pointed at me. "*Especially* no fights."

"It's not like I ask them to assume I'm a weak woman and attack me."

She scowled.

"OK. I promise. No fights," I said, crossing my heart. "When can I get the staples and stitches out?"

"Come back next week, and I'll take them out." She typed something into the computer, closed it, and then stood up. "Can I help you with anything else?"

I stood and picked up my keys and phone. "Nope. I'm all good." On the screen was a missed call from Essex. "Am I free to go?"

"Yes. I'll see you in a week."

"Thank you, Doctor."

"Bye, Nyx. Please be safe."

"Always."

When she left, I followed her and tapped Essex's name in my missed call list.

"Hey," he answered, his voice muffled. There was a lot of chatter in the background.

"Is this a bad time?"

"Yeah. Turn on the news. I'll call you back in a minute."

He hung up before I could explain that I was leaving the doctor's office. I stopped at the empty checkout desk. Odd. I leaned across it. "Hello?"

The nurse walked backward from the check-in window on the other side of the wall. "Hey. Sorry, Nyx. Need to schedule a follow up?"

"Yeah, Monday to get the staples out. And I need a note for work. She said I can return to light duty."

"You got it." She typed something into her computer while I tapped the news app on my phone.

The stock market was up, the president was meeting with Australia's prime minister, and the Yankees beat the Red Sox. Essex liked baseball, but not enough to hang up on me over it.

The printer hummed and spat out a sheet of a paper. She handed it to me. "Guess they really need you back at work now, huh?"

"Why? What's going on?"

"Drug thing, all over the news."

"What?"

She pointed to the door. "There's a TV in the lobby."

I walked out and found nurses and patients gathered around the waiting-room television. I joined them and saw a breaking-news story was in progress. Marianne Clarke was reporting live from the elementary school in Seneca Park. The tagline below her name read: *One child dead, two in critical condition after accidental drug overdose.*

"A first grader has died from what police believe to be a heroin overdose," Marianne said. "The six-year-old girl was airlifted to the children's hospital in Reno, but it was too late. Two other children are fighting for their lives in intensive care."

They were the same age as my niece, Milly.

I felt sick.

The camera cut to a K-9 unit searching the playground. "The school was immediately closed so police could thoroughly search the campus."

My phone rang. Essex. I tapped answer. "Hey."

"Did you see it?" he asked.

"Yeah." I turned away from the group. "Please don't tell me its heroin mixed with hypnox."

"OK. I won't tell you."

"Where'd they get it?"

"The only kids who know anything are in comas."

"Shit." I rubbed my forehead. "I'll head that way."

"Have you been cleared by medical?"

"For light duty. She said I could ride along. Can I still ride with you?"

"Yeah. Where are you now?"

"Leaving the doctor's office." I walked out the door. "Gonna run home and change. Meet you at the office?"

"I'll pick you up at home."

Here.

The text from Essex came exactly twenty-one minutes after I'd left the doctor's office. I walked out of my bedroom to find Bess packing a sandwich into a lunch sack printed with unicorns. I hadn't seen her when I'd gotten home.

She wiped her hands on a dishtowel as I fastened my weapons belt. "I figure you'd probably be going to work. Those poor kids. Was it really heroin?"

"It looks like it." I nodded toward the bag. "Heading to work?"

"Yeah, but I'll eat at the casino." She handed me the bag. "This is for you. Figured you might not have a chance to stop and eat."

My head snapped back. "Seriously?"

"Yeah." She thrust the bag closer. "It's the least I can do. Seriously."

I took it, eyed the unicorns and considered the shit I was going to get at work, then smiled. "Thank you. And I really appreciate you buying groceries. Let's split the cost, OK?"

"Just like real roomies?"

I laughed on my way to the door. "Yeah. Just like real roomies." When I opened it, I saw a box outside. It had "BESS" scrawled in all caps. "You've got a package."

"Great!"

I picked it up and handed it to her. "What is it?"

"A hard drive for the new computer I'm building."

"You can do that?" I asked, impressed.

"Sure. I bought this a while ago, and the mail service forwarded it to my ex's new apartment."

"I'm surprised David gave it back without showing his ass."

"Ha. Me too." She looked at me, puzzled. "Did I tell you his name was David?"

Shit.

"Yeah. How else would I know?"

It took a second for her puzzlement to fade to a smile. "I talk too much."

No argument from me. I lifted the bag. "Thanks again for the food."

"Be safe, Nyx."

"I will." I let the heavy door close behind me, and I took the steps two at a time to the bottom.

Essex had backed into the spot beside Bess's car. His eyes doubled when I opened the door and he spotted the unicorns. "You're really getting into this trip to the school, aren't ya?"

"Shut up," I said, getting inside.

"You got a juice box and everything?"

I scowled. "My roommate packed me something to eat."

"Did she put a motivational note in there?"

"No." *She probably had.* "Any news on the heroin?"

He put the SUV in drive, and we rolled toward the street. "No, but I got a call from O'Malley, who was at the hospital with the families. Looks like the boy is probably brain dead."

I closed my eyes and swore. "What about the other one?"

"She seems to be stable. Pupils are responsive, which is a good sign, but she can't breathe on her own."

I thought about what Elias had said about the woman, Norina Grumley, who'd been inside the Boundary. He'd said Orion had returned her to her body in time. I wondered what that meant for these kids. "They're still on life support?" I asked.

"Yeah."

The clock on the dash said 11:17. Luckily, the days were longer this time of year. Eight-ish hours of daylight remained. If one or both of those kids had detached . . .

I gulped.

It would be bad news for all of us. I hoped Orion, or *whoever* on the other side of the Boundary, was aware of what was happening. Maybe I should have stayed at home in bed.

"What are you thinking?" Essex asked.

I couldn't tell Essex what I was thinking. There was no way he'd believe me—at least not without a lot of convincing, which we didn't have time for.

"Just thinking about those poor kids. Where are we headed?"

"Bees Ferry Road. We got a call from an elderly resident who says she has information on a possible lead."

From Essex's tone, I could tell he didn't think the lead was credible. "The department has been flooded with calls, hasn't it?" I asked.

"Yeah, tsunami-type flooding. Everyone has a shady neighbor

or a nephew who's up to no good. They all think they know where the drugs came from."

"What's narcotics saying?"

"Gregg says hypnox has never been tied to mass-production operations, here or anywhere else in the world that we know of. In other words, there's no way to find the source until someone starts talking."

"Did the kids find the drugs at the school or did one of them bring it there?"

He turned his palm up on top of the steering wheel. "No clue, and aside from what we found in Ryder Stone's chalet, no one else has seen this stuff for a few decades."

Wait.

That wasn't true.

"Norina Grumley," I blurted out.

"Who?"

Shit. That wasn't public knowledge. "A CI told me she might know something about hypnox." That was sort of true. Elias was like a confidential informant.

"When have you been talking to CIs? You're supposed to be on medical leave."

"I made some calls. I wonder if she has any kids."

Essex either looked perturbed that I was working when I was supposed to be off, or he wasn't buying my lie. He nodded to the computer mounted on the dash between us. "See if you can find her."

I swiveled the laptop toward me and brought up our database. I started typing in the fields. "Norina Grumley, Seneca Park—"

"How do you know she lives in Seneca Park?"

Shit. "CI told me," I lied again.

Before he could speak, her name popped onto the screen. I read the record aloud. "Boom. Norina Grumley, thirty-one. Two priors for possession and a CPS case number. Address is incomplete though."

"How old's the kid?"

"It doesn't say. Who's leading the investigation?"

"Right now? Gregg."

"Call and ask if she's talked to Grumley."

Essex was clearly skeptical, but he pressed a button on the steering wheel, and the car chimed. "Call Sharon Gregg," he said.

The line rang over the speakers. "Gregg."

"Hey, it's Essex and Nyx. Random question, but did you interview a woman named Norina Grumley? She might be a parent of one of the kids at the—"

"Grumley, yeah. Her kid left early today. Went home sick. He's fine."

"So you actually talked to her?" I asked.

"Yes. Her kid was sick."

"Did you ask if her son brought anything to school with him?" I asked.

"What do you think this is, my first day? Of course I asked. She answered no."

"Did you run her?"

"Since I didn't have a reason to, no."

"Can you?"

Gregg sighed. "Look, Nyx, I'm in over my eyeballs right now with all the shit—"

"Can we question her?" I asked.

"Sure. Knock yourselves out."

"What's her address?"

With a huff, Gregg put us on hold.

"What CI have you been talking to?" Essex asked.

"You know I can't tell you that."

His brow crumpled. "Why not?"

Before he could squeeze an answer out of me, I was saved by Gregg with an address.

"It's 1708 Big Pine Way."

"Thanks, Gregg," Essex said and disconnected the call. He looked across the car at me. "I hope you're right about this."

I couldn't say the same. I didn't want to be right about anything I knew might be true.

Eight minutes later, Essex turned onto Big Pine. "Is that 1708?" He was looking at a wood-paneled, one-level home.

"Yeah."

He pulled into the short driveway, and we both got out. While he rang the doorbell, I walked to the front of the patrol car where I could see the angles of this side of the house. The door opened, and a painfully thin woman with straggly brown hair stood in the gap. "Hello, Officer."

"Ma'am, I'm Sergeant Tyler Essex with Sapphire Lake Police Department. Are you Norina Grumley?"

"Depends who's asking."

"I'd like to ask you some questions about—"

"If this is about what happened at the school, they already called. I told them Aiden's fine. He was picked up early today and doesn't know anything."

When Essex looked down at her track-marked arms, she quickly folded them. "You're not in trouble, but we would like to ask what you know about a drug called hypnox."

All the blood drained from her face.

Bingo.

"Is that what those kids got into?" Her voice was suddenly scratchy.

"We believe so. A dark residue was on their hands, consistent with hypnox. The packet found was branded with a crown. A child could have mistaken it as candy. Does any of this sound familiar?"

Guilt filled Norina's sunken eyes, but before she could speak, Essex's head flinched up as he looked beyond her. I checked the back yard again.

Essex pointed. "Is that Aiden?"

Norina looked back. "Aiden, come here!"

A young boy with a brown buzz cut and no shoes or shirt squeezed between his mother and the doorframe to stand in front of her. She put her hands on his shoulders. "Aiden, did you see any little packets at school today with a gold crown on them?"

Essex hadn't told her the crown on the packaging was gold.

When the boy looked at Essex again, he seemed ready to burst into tears. "Please, Officer, don't take my momma to jail."

Essex knelt down. "Hi, Aiden. I don't want to take anyone anywhere. Did you know some kids at your school got really sick today?"

The boy sniffed and wiped his nose as he nodded.

"Have you seen any little white packets about this big?" Essex held his finger and thumb two inches apart. "They have a picture of a crown, like kings wear, on them."

Aiden nodded again.

"Did you take some to school?"

"Aiden, don't answer that," the woman snapped.

Essex grabbed the radio on his shoulder. "Dispatch, this is Delta One. Need CPS at 1708 Big Pine Way—"

"Not CPS!" Norina cried, pushing Aiden back into the house.

I crossed the driveway and walked up on the short porch. I touched Essex's arm. "Go call Gregg. I've got this."

With a nod, he walked back toward the car.

"Norina?" I asked gently.

She stared at me, tears flooding her eyes.

"My name is Corporal Saphera Nyx. My partner is calling CPS to talk to your son. They have licensed people trained to talk to kids, that's all."

She relaxed a little.

"I want to help you, Norina, but I can't do that if you lie to me. Do you understand?"

Tears streamed down her cheeks. "Are you going to take my boy?"

I shook my head. "That's not my call, so I don't know. What I do know is someone else's child died today and two others are being kept alive by machines. I also believe the heroin they found came from here or someone you know, and I need you to tell me so—"

Aiden pushed through the doorway again and grabbed my pant leg. "It was me. Please don't take my momma. I didn't want her to get sick anymore, so I took that stuff and threw it in the woods."

Emotion bubbled up inside me as the boy started to cry. I knelt in front of him. "You must love your momma a lot."

He nodded and grabbed her legs.

"Thank you for telling the truth."

Norina held Aiden's head against her. "I've been off it for a few days. He must have found what was left."

I stood. "Where did you get it?"

She hesitated.

"They'll go easier on you if you cooperate, Norina."

"This guy I see. Lucas Costa." She lowered her voice. "He's a King."

"Nyx!"

I looked at Essex in the driveway.

"CPS and narcotics are on their way."

I nodded.

Norina sank onto the top porch step with Aiden in her lap. She sniffed and wiped snot on the back of her arm. "You promise I'm not going to jail?"

"That's another promise I can't make." I sat beside her. "But I'll do everything I can to help you if you're honest with me. I have some questions."

"Can Aiden go play on the swings?" The rickety swing set was in the side yard, in front of Essex's SUV.

"Sure."

"Go on," she said, patting his thigh.

When he was out of earshot, I checked to make sure Essex was still on the phone. He was.

"What do you know about the gold heroin?"

She hesitated.

"You took it, and it scared you off it. Am I right?"

She nodded. "They're calling it Kings' Gold. I ain't never been high like that. I was out of my body. Walked all around the house. All around the neighborhood. I even watched Aiden sleeping in his bed."

"That shit you're messing around with isn't normal heroin. It opens a door you don't want to walk through, you understand?"

"Hold up. You mean that was real?"

I nodded because that couldn't be seen or heard on my body camera.

"The man, was he real too?"

I straightened. "What man?"

She touched her forehead. "I thought I was hallucinating."

"What man are you talking about, Norina?"

"He was kinda like an angel." She licked her cracked lips. "Had the prettiest blue eyes I'd ever seen."

Blue eyes.

"Did he give you a name?"

"Orion." She pointed to the sky. "Like the constellation. Do you think he *was* an angel?"

"I don't know."

Sirens wailed in the distance.

"Norina, do you still have drugs in the house?"

She shook her head. "I flushed everything else I had." Tears flooded her cheeks. "Those kids died because of me."

"All you can do is cooperate now. That's the only way this gets any easier." I stood.

"Officer?"

I paused.

"Was that place heaven?"

I smiled. "God, I hope not. Do me a favor?"

"Anything."

"Whatever happens, get your shit together. That kid deserves a mom and a better life."

She wiped her nose again. "I promise."

I'd heard that a thousand times.

Essex was off the phone. "What were you talking to her about?" he asked as I walked over.

"She was just telling me about what she took. Said she had some kind of out-of-body experience. She flushed all the heroin she had. Think they'll work with her since she's being helpful?"

"Kids died today. I doubt it."

"Kids, plural?"

He held up his phone before snapping it back onto his weapons belt. "That was O'Malley. The boy didn't make it."

CHAPTER THIRTEEN

I wiped vomit off my chin with a wad of toilet paper before flushing. Slumping sideways onto my hip, I rested the back of my head against the toilet-stall door.

Silent tears drizzled off my cheeks.

Norina Grumley was booked in to jail for child endangerment. I suspected some form of murder charges would follow as well. The magistrate denied bail, so Norina wouldn't see the outside world—or her son—for a long, *long* time.

She'd cried as I'd led her by the elbow into booking. And people around us clapped.

I was crying now. Not because I didn't think she had endangered anyone—she absolutely had—but there were no winners in this situation.

And I certainly wasn't a hero.

All those letters I'd thrown in the trash. All the calls I'd sent to voicemail. If I'd actually talked to my father, maybe I could have prevented everything from happening.

Five people were now dead—far more than the number Elias was guilty of. Except these could very well have been all *my* fault.

Essex was in the hall chatting with Baker when I walked out.

Baker beamed when he saw me. "Nicely done, Nyx." He offered me a fist bump, and I knocked my knuckles with his, forcing my lips into an appreciative smile.

"What are you doing here?" I asked.

"Same as you, but not as successfully." Baker gripped his weapons belt. "You on tonight?"

"Riding with Sarge. I'm on light duty until next week."

"That reminds me, I need your doctor's note to turn in to HR," Essex said.

"Shit. It's at home."

"It's OK. We'll swing by and grab it."

"How's the head?" Baker leaned sideways for a better look at the gash in my skull.

I turned my head so he could see. "It's healing."

He sucked in a sharp breath through his teeth. "Damn, girl. That looks like a shark bite."

"I think I'd rather take on a shark." The three of us started down the hall toward the exit.

"You calling 10-8 early?" Essex asked him.

"Nah. I'm going home to crash for a few hours. You?" Baker replied.

"I don't know." Essex looked across him at me and smiled. "I hadn't planned on being done this early."

"You're welcome," I said with a wink as my heart twisted deep inside my chest.

When we walked out into the bright sunlight, Baker slipped on a pair of black sunglasses. "Well, I'll see you guys tonight. Shift briefing at five forty-five?"

"Yep. See you here," Essex said.

"Bye, man," I said as Baker walked out into the lot.

Essex turned toward me and put on his aviators. "What do you want to do?"

Part of me really wanted to go home and sleep. I could detach for a few hours while there was still daylight. Maybe find Orion and check on the one kid still living. Then again, with all the adrenaline pumping through my bloodstream, sleep wouldn't come easy. Perhaps not at all.

"You hungry?" Essex asked before I could sort my thoughts into an answer.

"Actually, yeah."

"Want to get something to eat at that pub across the street from your place? We can grab your paperwork when we're done."

"Sounds good." We started toward his SUV.

"Nice work today, Nyx!" a man called out as I reached for the passenger-side door handle.

I looked across the lot and saw Lieutenant Henley sitting in his squad car.

"Thanks, Lieutenant!" I replied with a wave.

"That's got to be a good sign," Essex said as he got in the driver's seat.

"Henley's opinion isn't everything. I still need the chief's approval." I buckled my seat belt.

"You've got the chief in the bag. I talked to him mys—" He turned his wide eyes toward me.

I shook my head. "I knew it was you."

He chuckled. "I put in a good word. There's nothing wrong with that."

"It shows special treatment."

"I'm your boss. They always ask our opinion."

"Did he ask your opinion?"

"Well, not in so many words . . . or in *any* words."

I backhanded his arm, and he laughed.

As he started the engine, I saw the lunch sack Bess had packed. I grabbed it and opened it on my lap. "Forgot about my lunch."

Smiling, he stretched his arm across my seatback to reverse

out of the parking space. "Gonna ditch me in favor of a PB&J and some fruit snacks?"

"Maybe." Inside was a sandwich, a bag of pretzels, a soda, and —I pulled out a piece of pink paper—a note decorated with smiley faces. I read it aloud. "Nyx, watch out for cars."

Essex chuckled. "I like her."

"She likes you too," I said, stuffing the paper back into the bag and dropping the whole thing by my feet. "She thinks you're hot."

"Well, of course she does. She's got eyes."

I laughed.

"How's that working out?"

"The roommate situation?"

"Yeah."

"I'm hoping it's more temporary than I offered."

"Driving you crazy?"

"She has her moments. She sings a lot."

"Oh no. Not *singing*."

"And god, she's messy." I laid my head back against the head-rest. "But she buys groceries and packs my lunch, so . . ."

He smiled. "As weird as it is, I think she might be good for you."

"Gran would have loved it. She hated that I lived alone." My phone rang. I pulled it off my belt and looked at the number. "Excuse me a sec. It's my brother." I put the phone to my ear. "Hey."

"Hey." Ransom's flat tone said he still wasn't over it. "Paps and I saw the news. Those kids are dead?"

"Two of them, yeah."

"Is it really hypnox?"

"Yes." I lowered my voice. "I could really use your help."

"OK." He cleared his throat on the other end of the line. "I have to work tonight, but I'll head that way when I get off in the morning."

I exhaled for what felt like the first time all day. "Thank you, Ransom."

"Mmm-hmm."

"I'll see you tomorrow."

"Nyx?"

"Yeah?"

"Don't detach at night."

"I won't." I was smiling when he ended the call.

"Everything OK?" Essex asked as he turned onto the highway.

I sighed, settling back into my seat. "It will be."

When we arrived at Delaney's, the lot close to the restaurant was full, so Essex pulled into a spot near the ice cream shop farther down the block. At one of its outdoor tables, a blond-headed man was playing air drums.

Essex nudged me. "There's Teek." He immediately began panning the area.

Teek had a part-time job stocking shelves at the grocery store in the village. He usually loitered somewhere close by, waiting on a ride home after his shift.

The last time we'd all been around this block together, Essex had lost a tooth.

I walked over. Teek was too busy jamming out to notice me at first. I waved my hand in front of his face. With a startled jerk, he smiled and plucked the earbud from his ear. "Hey, Nyx."

"Hi, Teek. What are you listening to?"

"The Freckled Misters."

"Never heard of them."

He offered me the earbud. "They're awesome. You wanna listen?"

I smiled. "Thanks, but I'll take your word for it. What are you doing here?"

"Waiting on Kush. He's late."

Kush, his brother. Not Kush, the cannabis strain. I hoped, anyway.

"You guys going to have some ice cream?" Essex asked.

Teek's face scrunched with confusion. "Why would we do that?"

Essex and I both looked at the ice cream parlor behind him. Essex chuckled and shook his head. "Never mind. Dumb question."

"Are you staying out of trouble, Teek?" I asked.

"Oh, yes, ma'am."

"No more zucchinis in your future?"

He shook his head. "Nah, I don't like zucchini."

"You're done being a lone wolf then?"

He howled toward the sky and laughed.

A car horn honked in the parking lot. "Teek!" a voice boomed. "Get in the truck!"

Essex spun before I did. When I looked, I saw why. It wasn't Kush. It was Borg Fleming in a wife beater, with a fresh new prison tattoo on the side of his neck. When he registered our faces, he smiled, showcasing the worst meth mouth in Sapphire Lake. "Tyler Essex."

"Mr. Fleming." Essex's glare was dark. I was surprised he didn't have a hand on his gun.

"He's out?" I whispered.

Teek stopped beside us. "I gotta go. You sure you don't wanna hear my beats?" He offered me the earbud one more time.

My eyes fell to the earbuds' cord dangling free in front of him, not plugged into anything. "No thanks, buddy." I patted his shoulder. "You'd better get going. Don't want to keep your dad waiting."

"Yeah." Teek waved as he walked into the parking lot. "I'll see you soon, Nyx!"

Neither Essex nor I moved until Borg's pickup squealed its tires pulling out of the parking lot. "Did you know he was out?" I asked, looking up at my boss.

He let out a breath like he'd been holding it for minutes.

"Yeah. I was notified that he finally made bail a couple of days ago."

I tugged on his arm. "Come on. I'll buy you a drink."

"We're on duty soon."

"Then I'll buy you a sweet tea and have them put it in a frosted mug."

He laughed and followed me toward the restaurant.

As usual, Delaney's had a wait when we arrived. Essex looked at his watch and shrugged. "We've got the time if you want to—"

"Oh god, it's the fuzz." Chael Delaney was smiling and holding his wrists together as he walked toward me. "I hope you're here to put me in handcuffs."

Essex's spine went rigid beside me.

Maybe this wasn't a great idea.

"Chael," I said.

The bar's owner hooked his arm around my shoulders and planted a loud smacking kiss against the good side of my forehead. "Where have you been all my life, gorgeous? You haven't been in lately."

"I popped in a couple of days ago, but you weren't here. Aside from that, I've been at home nursing my wounds." I turned to show off the side of my head.

Chael cringed, made a fist, and bit into his knuckles. "*Geeeezus.* What happened to you?"

"Hit by a car during a traffic stop. I'm surprised you didn't see it on the news."

"Damn, no. I never watch it. Too depressing. I'm glad you're OK though."

"Yeah, I'm fine." I turned toward Essex. "Chael, this is my boss, Tyler Essex. Essex, this is Chael Delaney. He runs this shithole."

Chael laughed. "You sure spend a lot of time here for it to be such a shithole." He offered Essex his hand. "Nice to meet you, man."

Essex gave a tense nod. "Mr. Delaney."

"Please, call me Chael." He slapped Essex's shoulder. "Come on back. I'll find you a table."

Had we not been in uniform, I might have hip checked Essex as we crossed the bar. He was stuck in full-blown cop mode: jaw set, glare fixed, fists ready to break shit.

I guess I shouldn't have been surprised. Chael always had that effect on other alpha males. He was confident and charming, built like a life-size action figure, and he had hazel eyes that seemed to change with his mood.

He led us to a round booth in the corner beyond the large mahogany bar. "Here you go," he said, swiping a couple of menus from behind the bar's cash register. "What are you drinking? In uniform, so no booze, correct?"

"Correct. I'll have a water," I said as I slid into the booth.

Essex didn't make eye contact. "Sweet tea."

Chael drummed his hands on the side of the table. "Coming right up," he said, spinning away from us.

"He seems fun." Essex didn't look up from his menu.

"Yeah, he is."

"Have you known him long?"

"Since I moved across the street last year."

It was cute that he was pumping me for information, but if he was concerned, there was really no need. Chael flirted with everyone; I certainly wasn't special.

Essex put down the menu, pulled his phone off his belt, and looked at the screen. "Looks like they've accounted for all the heroin the kid took to school. No one else should be in danger."

For now. I felt sick again.

"You all right?"

"I'm worried. We both know there's more of that shit on the streets."

Essex crossed his arms on the tabletop. "You're taking this really personally."

He was right. I was taking it personally. And I couldn't tell anyone—not even Essex—why.

"Maybe it's the head injury," I lied with a small smile.

"Is it because of your dad?"

I looked away.

"Nyx, I don't care about any of that. I just worry about you."

"Can I tell you something without you jumping to the worst conclusions?" I asked.

"Do I have a habit of jumping to conclusions?"

"No." And he really didn't. Essex was one of the most thorough cops I knew. He listened and watched, rarely acting before he understood all the angles of a case.

He leaned forward. "Your secrets are safe with me, Nyx."

But I wouldn't go that far.

"What if the cases are connected? Doesn't it seem odd that the last time hypnox was on the streets, my father burned a man alive? Now it's back the same week my father's murdered." I wanted to hear his opinion more than anything.

He nodded. "I know what you mean. The timing seems almost . . ."

"Otherworldly?"

"Something like that."

I picked at the peeling plastic on the corner of my menu. "I never dreamed I'd wish for Elias to be around."

Essex reached across the table and squeezed my hand. He jerked it back when Chael returned with our drinks.

"What can I get you guys to eat today?" Chael pointed at the shamrock-painted chalkboard tacked to the bar behind him. "The lunch special is the fish and chips."

I lifted an eyebrow. "Is it ever anything else?"

"Absolutely not."

"I'll take buffalo mac and cheese."

"Ooo, bad day?"

"What makes you ask?"

"Because you only order good food when you're stressed. Otherwise, it's grilled chicken and tree bark."

Even Essex chuckled.

"And for you, my man?" Chael asked him as he took my menu.

"The fish and chips, please."

"Coming right up."

"Thanks," Essex said as Chael walked away. When he was gone, Essex picked up his tea. "He knows you pretty well."

I squeezed the lemon slice from my glass's rim into my water. "Is there something you want to ask me, Sarge?"

Essex drowned a smile with sweet tea. "No."

"OK."

He put his glass down. "Actually, yes." He clicked off his body camera.

My brow lifted, and I did the same.

"How'd you know about Norina Grumley?"

My appetite vanished. "I told you."

"And you know I'm not buying it."

I took a deep breath. "Do you trust me?"

"With my life."

I leaned forward. "Then trust that I have an informant I need to keep quiet."

His eyes carefully studied mine. Finally, he nodded. "OK. For now."

When we finished lunch, we went across the street to my condo. He waited in the car while I ran inside to get my paperwork from the doctor's office. Bess was already gone, and she'd left a note on the whiteboard calendar saying she'd be in after midnight. I scribbled an addition saying I'd get off in the morning and that I'd need to sleep until after lunch.

I wondered how much good the note would do.

On the way back to the station, Essex and I stopped by his

house to let Karma out to potty. "You're coming in?" he asked when I opened my door to get out.

"Of course. Your dog loves me." I followed him to the front door.

He stepped really close to the electronic door lock and checked over his shoulder before punching in his unlock code.

I crossed my arms. "Are you afraid I'll see your code?"

"No."

"You just used your whole body as a shield."

"Did not."

The door swung open, and Karma charged down the hallway.

"Karma, *nein!*" Essex shouted.

To his credit, the dog tried to stop, but his momentum was too great. His nails scrambled on the slick hardwood, and he starfished on the floor in front of us. Embarrassed, Karma whimpered.

I dropped to my knees by his snout. "Come here, boy." He jumped up to lick my face.

Essex started straightening his living room. He closed his laptop and carried it, along with two shirts and pair of running shoes, down the hallway. "Can you take him out back?"

I stood, and Karma latched onto my leg, thrusting his hips against it. "Knock that off," I said, shaking him free.

"Karma!" Essex said with a groan.

"Come on." I started through the kitchen to the back door. When I opened it, Karma galloped outside.

In the yard, the dog lifted its leg on everything standing still, including a strange pile of chain-link fencing and metal poles shoved up against the side of the house.

The door slammed shut behind me, making me jump. I looked at the tree in the corner of the yard. Its leaves weren't moving, so it couldn't have been the wind. I opened the door and saw Essex hunched over the coffee table in the living room. "Damn it, Karma!" he shouted.

I glanced back as Karma ducked behind the shed.

"Everything OK in there?" I asked, inspecting the door for auto-close hinges.

"He ate the buttons off the remote control."

I snickered as Essex walked toward me, holding up the remote for me to see. It had teeth scrapes all over it, and more than half the keys were missing. "Hey, is something wrong with this door?" I asked.

"What?" Essex stopped and visually scanned it. "Did he chew on it too?"

"No. It just shut behind me."

"Oh. I thought it was you. Maybe the air-conditioning kicked on." He walked to the laundry room, and I returned to the yard.

Karma didn't come out from behind the shed until we both heard dog kibble clinking against his metal bowl. When the dog ran inside, I leaned in the doorway. Essex was at the sink filling a giant water bowl.

"What's with the scrap yard back here?" I asked.

"Since he won't stay in the fence, I'm building a big dog kennel onto the back of the house and adding a dog door to it from the laundry room." He carried the water bowl back to the mat near the garage door. Karma's nose was buried in the dog food. "I hate he's stuck inside when I'm running late."

I came in and locked the door behind me. "He's lucky to have you."

"He's lucky I haven't killed him yet. Did I show you the video of him climbing the fence?"

I leaned against the counter. "No."

He took his phone off his belt as he walked over to me. His holstered gun brushed my Taser as he leaned next to me and held up his phone. He scrolled through some photos until a video appeared. Karma was halfway up the backyard fence, with his paws over the top, glancing back like he knew he'd been caught.

"They can do that?" I looked up at Essex. My throat cinched when I realized how close his neck was to my face.

"Apparently so." His eyes met mine, and I watched the same realization flood his gaze.

God, he smelled tempting, like all my many months of abstinence soaked in Armani cologne and pheromones. My mind went blank, but I may have dragged my teeth across my lower lip because his eyes fell to my mouth.

Karma barked, snapping us both out of the danger zone. The dog was barking at the dining-room table. Confused, Essex looked at me, then back at Karma. "You weirdo."

Dread churned in my stomach as I remembered a couple of nights before when Karma had barked at me in the hallway. Then there was the door slamming on its own . . .

We weren't alone.

I stepped away from the counter. "You ready to head out?"

Visually noting the sudden distance between us, he seemed alarmed. "Nyx, I hope I didn't do anything to make you uncomfortable—"

I waved him off. "Not at all." Whoever was watching us was making me uncomfortable.

"OK."

Karma was still barking at the table.

"Karma, shut up," Essex said. He turned his back and opened the refrigerator. "Need anything for tonight? I've got energy drinks."

"No, thanks. They make me jittery." I walked to the front door.

Essex noticed. "You sure you're all right?"

"I'm great." I forced a smile as the dog trotted over to me. Suddenly, a chill washed over and through my body, taking my breath and flattening my back against the door.

Whoever it was . . . they were gone.

CHAPTER FOURTEEN

After handing in my doctor's note to admin, Essex and I were among the last members of our team to arrive at the weekly shift briefing. When we walked through the door, the room erupted in applause. I waved my hand, praying they'd stop. I slid into an empty seat at a table near the back of the room, and Eric Jones offered me a fist bump.

Essex carried his padded notebook to the front and sat at the table facing all of ours. "I'll try to make this fast. Obviously, congratulations to Corporal Nyx for finding the source of the heroin at the school today."

Everyone applauded again.

Essex lifted a hand and raised his voice. "This is still an evolving case, and our top priority at the present time is getting this shit off the streets, but I'll let Gregg talk about that in a second." He nodded to where Gregg was standing near the door before continuing.

"Same zones as last week. Nyx is on light duty, so she'll be riding with me."

Two tables ahead, I saw Baker and Rivera exchange a whisper. I didn't think much of it until Rivera glanced back and looked directly at me.

I lifted my eyebrows to ask, "What?"

He turned back around.

Essex was in the middle of reading out zone assignments. "Baker and Legieza are in zone two, Everly and Jones zone three, McCollum zone four, and Rivera will be roving. Friday is weapons and car inspection. Please get your shit cleaned up, so I don't have to hear about it." Essex glared at McCollum, the Pig-Pen of our shift.

The door opened, and we all turned to look as Valerie from admin walked in with a sheet of paper. "Hey, Valerie. You need something?"

She pointed at me. "I just need to speak with Corporal Nyx a second."

There were several "Ooos" around the room.

"Can I step out?" I asked Essex.

"Yeah, go ahead. I'll fill you in later."

Rivera and Baker exchanged another snicker. *What the hell?* God, sometimes the police department was worse than high school.

I stood and walked to the door. Valerie and I stepped outside. She grimaced and handed me the paper. It was my doctor's note. On it, she'd highlighted the date in yellow. "Sorry, Nyx. This says you can return to light duty tomorrow, not today."

I took it. "Are you serious? It's a mistake."

"Can you call and get them to change it?"

I looked at my watch. "No. The office is closed."

"Sorry. We have to abide by the paperwork. Too much liability."

I groaned. "I know. Damn it." I handed it back to her.

"You can keep that copy. I have the original in my file. I'm really sorry," she said again.

"It's not your fault. I should have read it."

"But you can work tomorrow," she said, feigning her usual chipper attitude.

"Thanks, Valerie." I was trying hard to mask my disappointment.

Chief Magnus rounded the corner. Valerie looked surprised. "Good evening, Chief. You need something?"

"I was hoping to catch Corporal Nyx."

"Then I'll get out of your way," Valerie said with a wave before exiting down the hallway.

"Good work today, Corporal," the chief said when she was out of earshot.

"Thank you, sir."

He crossed his arms. "Lieutenant Gregg is questioning your mother tomorrow. Did you know?"

"Yes, sir."

"Do you think she's tied up in this somehow?"

"Honestly? I doubt it." Without Elias, I wasn't sure how she could be. Part of me wished I could talk to my mother myself, without a body camera, but that would have to come later, if ever at all. "But whether she's involved or not, I wouldn't expect much cooperation from her."

"I figured as much. How's the head healing?"

"It's getting better."

"When are you back on regular duty?"

"The doctor said two weeks."

He nodded. "Good. The sooner the better, but not before you're a hundred percent."

"Yes, sir."

"Have a safe night. We'll talk soon."

I bowed my head, wondering what that meant. Talk soon about my mother? Talk soon about the new job? I didn't dare ask.

When I returned to the briefing room, Essex was against the wall near the door, and Gregg was at the front of the room showing a slide presentation. A picture of the heroin they'd confiscated was on the screen.

I gave Essex the sheet of paper. As he read it, I listened to the spiel about the drugs. "Melatryptophine has a few street names. Hypnox is the most common. Other names are sleeping beauty, pixie dust . . ."

"Damn, that sucks," Essex said, handing the paper back to me.

"I know." When I turned my attention back to the meeting, Rivera was looking at me again. I nudged Essex. "What's with Rivera and Baker? They keep whispering and looking at me."

"Everyone's looking at you. You made the most important arrest of the year today."

"No. This is something else."

"Want me to talk to them?"

"Nah, it would only make it worse."

Gregg was still talking. "Melatryptophine is one of the most dangerous drugs we've ever seen hit the streets. It's highly potent, and it absorbs quickly and easily through the skin. If you come across it in the field, call narcotics immediately."

Essex raised a hand to interrupt. "Until this stuff is eradicated, no one searches cars alone. If you suspect drugs, you call for backup."

"What good will backup do on a car search?" Jones asked with his hand in the air.

"If your skin comes in contact with it, you'll need someone to call an ambulance," Gregg said.

"Everyone carries extra Narcan," Essex said. "And no one field tests anything that looks like heroin. It all goes straight to the lab."

"The Kings are no strangers to violence, but everyone should be extra cautious when making arrests concerning Kings' Gold. Its markup is five hundred percent of their normal heroin, a price tag they won't let go of without a fight," Gregg warned.

"What junkie will be able to pay that kind of increase?" Legieza asked.

"One that's promised this drug will reset their neuroreceptors. Hypnox supposedly offers something even better than the 'first-time high' habitual users have been chasing since they became junkies. Any more questions?"

Baker crossed his bulky arms and leaned back in his chair. "Where did the hypnox come from?"

Everyone shut up and listened. Me too, but for a wildly different reason.

Gregg shrugged. "We don't know yet. It's so rare that it hasn't been seen since 1988."

I wanted to disappear into the wall as Gregg used a remote to flip through some slides on the screen. She stopped on a blurry photo of a patch of black flowers almost as tall as the privacy fence behind it.

The picture was taken in the courtyard of my parents' house.

"That looks like a poppy," Rivera said.

Jones clapped. "Look at you, Martha Stewart."

Gregg ignored them. "It is a member of the poppy family, and it's harvested the same way as the opium poppy. The seed pods in this photo were scored to drain the hypnox."

McCollum raised a hand. "Opium's where we get morphine and heroin?"

"That's correct," Gregg answered. "The difference is the raw hypnox derived from these plants requires no refinement or production. It can be deadly straight from the pod in any amount. And whereas an opium poppy produces only drops per plant, the hypnox poppy can produce ounces of liquid per pod."

"You think it's growing here in Sapphire Lake?" Baker asked.

"We don't know, but there is a chance."

A bigger chance than she knew.

"Where was that?" I asked, pointing to the photo.

"This photo was taken right here in Sapphire Lake by an

undercover officer. It's the only known photo of the plant in existence." Gregg's gaze landed on me just long enough for me to notice. "To complicate matters, the press has learned that the same drug that killed those kids also killed Ryder Stone at the Drexler Resort."

"Has there been any movement on the Stone case?" Jones asked.

"Not that I'm aware of. Any more questions?" Gregg asked. When no one replied, she turned toward Essex. "Do you have anything else?"

"If anyone is running low on gloves, masks, or Narcan, see me before you head out. Otherwise, everybody stay safe and vigilant tonight." When everyone got up and started milling around, Essex faced me. "Meet you outside?"

"Yeah."

Jones came up to us. "Sarge, I need another box of gloves."

"You don't need shit, Jonesy," Rivera said, walking up behind him and grabbing both his shoulders. "Leave the real police work to the pros."

"You're such a dick, Rivera," I said.

"Come on," Essex said to Jones. "I'll get you squared away."

When they were gone, I stepped toward Rivera. "What's your problem, man?"

"I'm just giving him shit, Nyx. Calm your tits."

I wanted to punch him. "What were you and Baker gabbing about during the meeting?"

"I don't know what you're—"

"Don't lie to me. You two hens were gossiping like a couple of mean girls. If you want to say something, man up and say it to my face."

Rivera hooked his thumbs in his weapons belt. "I just heard you and Sarge were getting pretty cozy. Thought it was cute you two are patrolling together now."

"You know what I heard?"

He lifted his brow in question.

"That you picked up a nasty case of crabs from a toothless hooker in Reno."

His smirk went slack.

"But you don't see me shoving my tongue down anyone's ear to tell them about it during shift briefing, do ya?"

"Fuck you, Nyx."

"You'd like that, wouldn't you?" I called as he stormed out the door.

Baker filled the spot Rivera had vacated. "What the hell did you say to him?" he asked, smiling.

"I could ask you the same question. What were you two talking about?"

Guilt flashed in his eyes. "Nothing really. He heard from a chick at Sin City that you and Sarge were together."

"The taco place?"

"Yeah."

The memory of the night-shift manager's boobs popped into my mind. "There's nothing going on."

"I know that. Hell, Rivera knows that too. Don't let him get to you. What did admin want?" Together, we walked out into the hall.

"To tell me to go home. My paperwork says I can't return to light duty until tomorrow."

"That blows."

"Yep. Be safe tonight, brother."

"You too. See ya, Nyx."

Essex came down the hall carrying a couple of boxes of latex gloves. He looked past me. "Is Rivera gone?"

"I hope so."

He put the boxes on the table in the hallway as Gregg walked out of the briefing room. "Nyx, glad I caught you."

For the first time ever, I was nervous to speak to her. "Hey. What's up?"

"I'm questioning your mother tomorrow."

I really wished people would stop calling her that. "So I heard. I'll apologize in advance."

"Think she'll cooperate?"

"I wouldn't pin too much hope on her. Helpful is not in Mal's skillset."

"Got any tips?"

"Yeah. Stock up on antacids, and make sure your Taser is charged."

She and Essex both chuckled.

"Hey, I really appreciate you not putting a spotlight on me in there," I said quietly to her.

"Don't thank me. That was self-preservation. I don't want you coming after my job once you make narcotics." She winked one of her dark-brown eyes.

I smiled.

"Nice work today, by the way."

"Thanks, but I literally did nothing. By the time we got there, the drugs were gone. Nobody else would have gotten hurt."

"Maybe, but you freed up a lot of resources," Essex said.

"And roped in another human who knows something about this shit," Gregg added.

"Is Grumley cooperating?" I asked.

Gregg nodded. "Even told us she OD'd on the stuff a few days ago."

"Really?" I lowered my voice. "What'd she say?"

She grinned like she knew what she was about to tell us would sound nuts. "She said she left her body."

"Left her body," Essex repeated slowly.

"Yep. Said she wandered the streets of Seneca Park. Even watched the sunset from the roof of the credit union."

Essex let out a low whistle and swirled his finger around his ear. "Sounds like some good shit."

My heart sank at his reaction.

Gregg laughed too. "Then she said some man dragged her home and forced her back into her body. When she woke up in a puddle of vomit and sweat, he was gone."

"Did she say anything else about him?" I asked.

"Who?" Gregg asked, confused.

"The man who dragged her home."

Gregg and Essex both looked at me like I was speaking another language. "Does it matter?" Gregg asked.

"She's a junkie having hallucinations." Essex's voice had a "duh" quality to it that turned my stomach.

I looked away. "Yeah, you're probably right."

If I'd wondered at all how any kind of revelation about my new ability might go over, I would wonder no more. "Sarge, you ready to go?" I asked, steeling my face and my heart as I turned back toward them.

"Yeah. Thanks for hanging around for briefing, Gregg," Essex said, shaking her hand.

"Call me if you need to tonight. I'll leave my phone on."

I walked a few steps ahead of Essex on our way out. He jogged to catch up with me. "The stolen car they impounded from the Drexler is here. Wanna see it?"

"Sure." I didn't look at him.

"You OK?"

"I'm fine."

"You're pissed about something."

I realized I could answer the charge without giving the *real* reason. "I found out Rivera is telling people there's something going on with us."

"What?"

I nodded. "Apparently, your busty girlfriend at Sin City Tacos has been running her mouth that we showed up there off duty together."

"So?"

"So it makes us a talking point. I don't need that right now."

He used a fob on his keys to open the gate. "Since when do you give a shit about what anyone thinks?"

"About my job? Since always. Essex, my whole life has been an uphill battle with trying to be taken seriously."

He held up his hands. "Whoa. Sorry I asked."

Sure, I cared about the shit Rivera was trying to start, but not as much as I cared about the possibility that Essex wouldn't believe me if I came clean about what I could do.

Or, even worse, if he did believe me, how it would change the way he looked at me.

He pulled on my arm to stop me. "Wait a second."

Facing him, I folded my arms and waited.

"I'm sorry. Screw Rivera. Let him talk. You and I both know nothing's going on here." His eyes lowered enough to convey his disappointment about that.

"Right. Nothing's going on."

With a deep breath and a clenched jaw, he looked awkwardly around the lot. Neither of us spoke for a moment. Then he pointed at something.

I followed the direction of his finger to a dark-blue hatchback.

"I think that's it," he said.

Like a lot of cops, Essex was skilled at diverting away from painful personal subjects using work.

So was I.

I walked toward the car. It had a Nevada tag about to expire. "If the car was stolen, where'd the tag come from?"

"It was stolen too. Can't remember the story behind it."

Using my flashlight, I peered in the windows. Oddly, it was spotless. "Doesn't look like it was driven much."

"No. It was freshly detailed."

"That's weird."

"Not if the driver was planning to use it to commit a crime."

True. I walked all the way around the car, not seeing anything until I reached the passenger's seat. In the floorboard was a sneaker.

A safety-yellow sneaker.

"Oh my god."

"What?" Essex asked.

"I know who was in this car." I looked at him. "Teek Fleming."

CHAPTER FIFTEEN

"What do you think you're doing?" Essex asked as I followed him out of the lot.

"I'm coming with you."

"No, you're not. Admin told you to go home."

"You're my boss. You can allow it."

"And then we'll both get written up."

"Teek trusts me. You need to let me bring him in."

Essex was torn. He stared past me.

I took a step closer. "You know I'm right."

"Damn it, Nyx." With a heavy sigh, he started walking again. "Come on."

It was a twenty-minute drive past my neighborhood, down the mountain pass, to the Boro, where the Fleming family lived. I'd heard it was once the premier place to live—back before a psychic and her husband burned a cop to death.

Essex slowed as we neared Borg's house. "If Borg is home, I'm calling another unit to come get Teek."

Fair enough. I'd sworn to my doctor no fights.

I strained my eyes at the road up ahead. "Looks like Gramma T's car in the driveway. I don't see Borg's truck."

Essex pulled to the side of the road. "I'll park here. Don't want to risk him blocking us in."

Smart.

The lights were on inside the mint-green single-wide. Essex studied the trailer. "You know what it means if Teek was in that car."

"It means Kush is probably our John Doe." I'd been trying *not* to think of it since we left the impound lot.

While Borg Fleming was notorious for smoking crystal meth and tearing up the neighborhood, his oldest son, Calvin "Kush" Fleming, was generally a harmless pothead. He had a record, like everyone else in his family, but he'd only been convicted of nonviolent crimes, like simple possession and loitering.

Teek and their grandmother would be lost without him.

We both got out, and I carefully checked the side yard as we approached the front door. Essex rang the doorbell, but it zapped his finger with electricity.

With a yelp, he jerked his hand back.

"You okay?" I asked, fighting to suppress a grin.

"No surprise they have this place booby-trapped," he grumbled, pounding his fist against the door.

I doubted the doorbell hazard was intentional. The joints of the walls were rusted, and the railing around the small stoop was missing more spindles than it had.

The door opened with a loud *creeeeeak*, and Gramma T filled the opening and then some. With her wrinkled face and boxy mouth and chin, she always reminded me of a bulldog in a shaggy brown wig. Her stumpy legs and round body didn't help.

Her brow furrowed. "Borg ain't here."

"Good evening, Tawny. We're not here for Borg," Essex said politely. "Is Teek home?"

"Depends. What'dya want with him?" She was staring at me, so I answered.

"We need to take him down to the station for some questioning. He isn't in trouble."

"Is that what you told him the other night when you hauled his ass to jail?"

"He held up a convenience store," I said.

"With a cucumber!"

"Technically, a zucchini, but that's beside the point. We need to ask him some questions about that night. Is Kush here?" I tried to look in over her shoulder, but she kept moving to block my view.

"I ain't seen Kush in about a week. What's this about?"

Next to Teek, Gramma T was the most passive of the Fleming bunch, but she wasn't exactly cooperative. No matter what they'd done, looking out for her own was top priority.

"You haven't seen him in a week? Did you report him missing?" Essex asked.

"No. Why would I? I don't live here. Besides, I figured he's been out burnin' up the highways now that he's got a car."

The sinking feeling in the pit of my stomach plunged deeper and deeper. "Kush got a car?"

"Yeah. An old piece of shit if you ask me."

"What kind is it?" Essex asked.

"I don't know. *Blue*," she said with a smirk.

Essex and I exchanged a look.

"Did you hear about the fire last week at the Drexler?" I asked.

"Of course. The news won't shut up about it."

"I believe our investigators found Kush's car there. Teek's missing sneaker was inside it," I said gently.

Gramma T's eyes narrowed, like she was trying to connect the dots but couldn't.

I lowered my voice. "Tawny, it might've been Kush who died in the fire."

She gripped the doorframe when her knees wobbled. Essex moved to help her, but she raised a hand to stop him.

"We don't have any proof yet, but we need to talk to Teek," Essex said. "Corporal Nyx found him down the road from the fire when it happened."

She held her stomach and took a deep, shaky breath. Then she stared at me for a long and hard moment before looking over her shoulder. "Teek! Get in here!"

Down the narrow hallway to the left, I saw Teek's head pop out of a doorway. Stretching on my toes, I waved.

He waved back. "Hi, Nyx."

Gramma T pushed the door all the way open and motioned us inside. It had been a while since we'd visited Borg's, but nothing had changed for the better. The brown shag carpet hadn't been vacuumed, maybe ever. Water stains spotted the ceiling, and the wood paneling was pulling away from the walls. It smelled of bacon grease, dog piss, and stale cigarettes.

I wondered what Gramma T thought of the place. Her home up the road was old, but it was tidy.

"Teek, the cops wanna talk to you about Kush," she said.

With a small skip, Teek started toward us. He wore red basketball shorts, an Iron Maiden shirt, and white socks.

"Have you seen your brother?" I asked.

"Sure!" Teek pointed to the only framed photo on the wall. A nineties throwback to when Teek and Kush were still toddlers, and to when Borg still had a wife and all his teeth. "There's Kush." He'd been a cute kid with an unfortunate bowl cut.

Now, in his midtwenties, Kush's blond hair had grown long and straggly, giving him a Woodstock-era flair, appropriate for his love of all things marijuana. He had light skin, a slender face, and a chin dimple just like Teek's.

"Have you seen Kush today, Teek?" Essex asked.

Teek shook his head.

"When was the last time you saw him?"

He pointed to the photo and laughed.

Frustrated, I tried a different angle. "Teek, do you remember the last time you saw me?"

Guilt lowered his eyes, and he nodded.

"Did Kush drive you to the Drexler that night?"

He nodded again.

"Why?" I asked.

"Kush told me to stay put, but he was gone a long time and I got hungry."

"Was he visiting someone at the hotel?" Essex asked.

"His friend," Teek answered. "I wasn't allowed to go inside. Kush told me to stay in the car."

"Have you seen Kush since that night?" I asked.

He thought for a moment, then shook his head. Gramma T covered her mouth.

I bent to look him in the eye. "Teek, do you mind coming down to the station to answer some questions for the detectives?"

"Sure, Nyx." He turned around and put his hands behind his back.

With a smile, I touched his elbow. "Handcuffs aren't necessary this time, buddy. Why don't you get some shoes on?"

His grandmother was pacing a small circle in the living room, her face flushed with panic. "How will we know if it was Kush burned up in that fire?"

"The detectives will let you know if they come across any forensic evidence. In the meantime, we need to find out if anyone else has seen Kush. If not, a missing-persons report should be filed," I explained.

"Borg came by earlier today. He mentioned Kush was slackin' at lookin' after his brother, so I don't think he's seen him."

I thought of us seeing Teek and Borg earlier at the ice cream shop.

"Do you know where Borg is?" Essex asked.

"Beats the shit outta me. I stopped by to make sure Teek got his dinner." She picked up her cell phone from the coffee table.

Essex's hand shot forward. "Who are you calling?"

"If you're worried about getting your ass kicked again, don't. I ain't callin' Borg."

A quiet snicker escaped my nose.

"I'm callin' Kush." She pressed the phone to her ear and immediately lowered it. "Voicemail."

"We need to search Kush's room," I said quietly to Essex.

"You know that's not happening without a warrant, missing person or not."

He was probably right.

Teek carried a pair of black boots out of his room. I gestured toward the camouflage-print sofa. "Put them on, Teek. We'll go in a minute."

Obediently, he sat in the chair.

A flash of headlights and the familiar grind of gravel under tires turned us both toward the door. "Shit," Essex whispered.

Borg.

"What the absolute hell is going on here?" Borg shouted, followed by the slam of a truck door.

Gramma T ran out the front door.

I grabbed Essex's sleeve. "Take Teek out the back and put him in the car. I'll deal with Borg."

Worry filled Essex's eyes as he searched mine.

"He won't hurt me. But if he walks in and finds you in his living room, he's liable to blow a gasket."

Essex didn't want to leave me, but he knew I was right. "You've got ninety seconds to meet me at the car before I bring every LE officer in the state down on this place."

I held his gaze for a second. "Ninety seconds."

With a nod, he hooked his arm through Teek's and pulled him off the sofa. Teek's untied boots flopped up and down on his feet as Essex dragged him out the back door.

Gramma T was crying outside. I needed to get out of the house and distract Borg as Essex took Teek to the car. I walked out with my hands raised. "Borg, I just need to talk to everyone. Nobody's under arrest. Nobody's—"

Borg jabbed his finger in the air toward me. "You need to get off my goddamn property if you don't have a warrant!"

I cautiously walked down the front steps. "Trust me, I'm not staying here a second longer than I have to. But before I can leave, I need to know if you've seen Kush. I'm afraid his life might be in danger."

Borg blinked with the slightest flash of concern for his eldest son. "I ain't seen Kush since I got out of jail."

"And when was that?"

His temper flared again. Borg didn't like being questioned. "I don't have to tell you—"

Gramma T shook his arm. "I swear to god, Borg Fleming, if you don't help them find my grandson, I'll bury you under that trailer and burn the whole shitpile to the ground."

Behind them, Essex peeked around the corner.

Glaring at his mother, Borg finally answered me. "I haven't seen Kush since he paid my bond on Thursday morning."

Kush paid his bond?

"Thank you, Borg," I said calmly. "Can you tell me if Kush knew Ryder Stone?"

All the emotion went out of Borg's face. "Why?"

"They think Kush might have died in that fire," Gramma T said.

Borg looked at me for confirmation.

"We think it's a possibility. We found his car in the parking lot outside."

Borg's sigh puffed out his cheeks. He put his hands on his head and began to pace. When he started to turn toward the road, where Essex and Teek had almost reached the SUV, I panicked.

"Heroin!" I blurted out.

Borg froze and looked at me. "What?"

I swallowed. "Do you know if Kush might have been using heroin, or if he's come into the possession of a substance similar to heroin?"

Borg crossed his arms. "So you're not really looking for my boy. You're looking for drugs."

Oops.

"We're looking for both, but the drug they found in Ryder Stone's safe was the same drug that poisoned—"

"Bitch, get off my property!" He pointed toward the road and saw Essex helping Teek into the back seat. "Teek?"

Teek waved. "Hi, Dad."

Borg whirled toward me then, and I jumped back out of swinging-distance. "What do you think you're doing with Teek?"

"Just taking him in for questions."

"The hell you are!"

I backed slowly toward the road. "He's a consenting adult, and he's not under arrest."

Snarling, Borg started toward me.

I pulled out my Taser. "Don't make me drop you like last time. I'll take you right back to jail."

When his eyes fell to the stun gun, he stopped. Couldn't blame him. Tasers hurt like hell. Like being attacked by electrified bees.

I kept backing toward the SUV.

"You can expect a call from my lawyer!" Borg hissed.

I wanted to remind him that public defenders don't get involved in other people's cases, especially when no one's been charged, but I didn't. No sense in poking the dragon when I just wanted out of there.

"Get in the car, Nyx," Essex said calmly behind me.

I jogged around the hood and got in the passenger's seat. My heart was pounding so hard my pulse thumped against my staples. "Teek, you all right?"

"I'm good, Nyx."

Essex pulled back out onto the road. "Well, that was almost a disaster."

"It certainly didn't go well." I turned around in my seat and grabbed the sliding window to the back seat. "Hey, Teek, I'm going to close this, OK?"

He held up two thumbs. "Can you put on some music?"

"Sure. What do you want to hear?" I asked.

"Got any Freckled Misters?"

I wasn't sure *anyone* had the Freckled Misters. "Sorry, bud. How about rock?"

"OK, Nyx."

Bon Jovi was on the radio. Teek gleefully bobbed his head behind the glass when I closed it. "His brother's dead," I said to Essex.

"I know."

"And we need to search that house for hypnox."

"How would Kush get hypnox? He's not exactly a botanist or an international drug lord."

True.

"What did Borg say about the heroin?" Essex asked.

"You heard that?"

"I think the whole town heard it."

"What do you think he said?" I asked with a smirk.

"Is that when he called you a bitch?"

"Yep." I shook my head. "People really need to get more creative. I should have a swear jar for how many times a day I get called a bitch or a whore."

"Don't forget the C-word."

I laughed. "The C-word? What are you? Twelve?"

"Oh no. Twelve-year-old-me would have totally said it."

Smiling, I looked out the window at the sun setting over the trees. Teek sang loud and off-key in the back seat. Essex turned off the main highway toward my neighborhood.

"What are you doing?" I asked.

"Dropping you off at home. I'll take Teek the rest of the way alone."

I started to argue, but he put up a hand. "Nyx, you're supposed to be off. I'm not pushing it by parading you around the station if I don't have to."

He was right, so I let it go and settled back in my seat and listened to Teek murder "Livin' on a Prayer."

"It doesn't make a difference if we're naked or not," he sang at the top of his lungs.

Essex cut his eyes at me. "Did he just say 'if we're naked or not'?"

I laughed. "I don't know, but I'm glad his window is shut."

When we reached my street, Essex slowed the car. "Want me to drop you here, or do you care if I pull in your driveway?"

We'd never be anywhere near my home if it were anyone other than Teek in the back seat. Teek was harmless, and he'd probably forget where I lived anyway.

"It's fine," I said, and he pulled through the gate.

He put the car in park.

"Am I still riding with you tomorrow?" I asked.

"If you still want to."

"Yeah. See you then." I reached for the door handle.

"Nyx?"

I paused and looked back.

"I'm sorry about Rivera. I do recognize that you have to work harder at this job than the rest of us."

My mouth smiled, but my eyes were somber. "Thanks. To be fair, I overreacted, so I'm sorry too."

"Don't be." He held my gaze for a second. "I'll see you tomorrow."

I got out and closed the door. I expected him to drive off, but he didn't. Instead, he waited in the driveway until I was safely inside my condo. Then I watched him leave from the kitchen window. I wilted over the sink, under the weight of my heart.

I hated leaving things so unsettled. I really wished I could tell him *everything.* Essex was my closest friend, and as my boss, my closest ally. If I couldn't trust him, who could I trust?

A ripple of cool air kissed the back of my neck, and I suddenly realized how alone I was. With a shudder, I remembered the bright blue eyes leaning over me and the pressure of the hand clamped around my throat.

But there was no time left for fear.

I straightened my spine and lifted my chin. "If you can hear me, I'm ready to talk."

And in response, the hallway light flickered.

CHAPTER SIXTEEN

"I don't want to hurt you."

The deep voice came from the silhouette backing slowly away from my bedside. In the moonlight from the window, I watched the man sit on the chair in the corner. Even in the shadows, his eyes were bright and topaz blue.

Something weighed on my chest. Looking down, I grabbed the handle of the heavy dagger laid between my breasts.

"It's a shadow blade, one of the only weapons in existence that can kill me. Call it a gesture of goodwill."

My spirit slowly sat up. "Goodwill exhibited by your choking me out the other day?"

"I didn't choke you. I simply disrupted the neural transmissions in your cerebral cortex. You fainted." Balancing his elbows on the armrests, he steepled his fingertips. "I only wanted to talk to you."

"So talk. Start with a name."

"You know my name."

"Orion?"

He nodded.

"Do you want me dead?"

"What?" He sounded genuinely confused.

"It was your fault I was almost creamed by a Tesla."

"That was an accident."

"You almost got me killed."

"Are you dead?"

I scowled.

"Then I didn't *almost* do anything." His eyes darkened. "If I'd wanted you dead, you would be."

"I'm not afraid of you."

"You don't even know who I am. Or what I'm capable of."

My eyes were still locked on his. "Neither do you."

Amusement tugged at the corners of his lips. "Good thing we're on the same side then."

I relaxed a bit. "How did you make me faint?"

"Every scion has a nerve here." He pressed two fingers between his clavicles. "It functions like an emergency off switch." He pointed to my broken alarm clock on the nightstand. "It's similar to the way I assume you shorted out your clock."

"So you've just been hanging around my condo, waiting to short-circuit my brain?"

"Yes."

I was surprised by his candor. "Who are you? Or *what* are you?"

"Human, same as you."

My brow pinched.

"Well, at least I *was* human, once upon a time." He stood and walked to the door, pulling something from his pocket. It was a black glove. He slipped it on and flipped the light switch.

Aside from the unearthly blue eyes, he looked human enough. Dark-brown crew cut, athletic build, strong and scruffy jaw. He wore dark blue jeans and a fitted white T-shirt. "Now I'm a guardian of the Boundary and Imera."

"OK, but why are you in my bedroom?"

"Because your world is at risk. The hypnox, have you found its origin yet?" he asked.

"I'd hoped you could tell me."

"Trust me. I wish I knew."

"I don't trust you."

"You don't have to trust me, but can we talk?"

I looked at my body open-mouth breathing on the bed. "Yes, but let's go somewhere else. This is creepy."

Using the glove, he opened my bedroom door. "Let's go outside. There's something I want to show you."

"OK." I took the dagger, just in case.

He followed me through the living room, and at the sliding-glass door, I reached for the handle. It didn't move. Orion walked straight through the glass, fighting a smile at me as he went.

I groaned. *This is going to take some getting used to.*

Outside, he sat on a patio chair. "I imagine you have lots of questions. I know you and Elias weren't close."

"You knew Elias?"

"Yes. I hated him."

Common ground already. I eased onto the chair across from him. "OK. Why can I move through glass but not through walls?"

"You only exist inside the Boundary because your consciousness has left your body. In the same way your brain tells your legs to move, your mind moves your spirit. You have to be able to see or envision where you're going in order to get there. Glass you can see and move through. Walls you can't."

"Why can I sit on this chair, but a semi-truck drove straight through your friend Flash?"

A quiet snort escaped his grin. "Oh yeah. I heard about your running."

I pointed at him. "Don't start."

He put his hands up in defense. "I wasn't going to say a word."

"Sure you weren't."

"You don't exist to your world in this form, so the truck can't hit you. But your mind sees the chair, allowing you to interact with it here without actually influencing it in your world."

"I moved a shoe."

"Congratulations."

I frowned. "You just said—"

"Yes. You can move objects with enough momentum or energy, but as I'm sure you've learned, it takes a lot of effort, unless you have one of these." He pulled out the glove again.

"What is that?"

"The fabric is called *ergane*. As long as it comes in contact with light, it can exist in both realms at once. So don't try to walk through windows with it out in the open."

"Can I get a glove?"

"I thought Elias left you some."

"Elias left nothing but a bad taste in my mouth for all this shit."

"I'll see what I can do."

"What about clothes?" I looked down at my uniform. I'd only removed my weapons belt and radio before lying down. "Am I doomed to wear whatever I slept in?"

"Yes, but the next time I come I'll bring some clothes you can put on here. What else?"

"Can I die here?"

"Yes, and if you die in the Boundary, your body dies on Earth. But only things of this world, like the dagger, can kill you here. I believe something like it was used to kill your father."

"Why was he killed?"

"I don't know, but you should be careful in case someone is hunting gods."

I laughed. "You think Elias was a god? Are you sure we're talking about the same person?"

Orion looked confused. "You do know who Nyx is, right, Saphera *Nyx*?"

"And *you* know my last name was supposed to be Charis,

right? Elias changed his name in 1982." A few times I'd considered changing my name to match Gran and Paps's, but in the state of Nevada, their family name, Marcotte, was just as notorious as the name Nyx.

Paps's mother was one of the only women ever executed in the state of Nevada. When he was a baby, she killed her husband and her mother before she died in the gas chamber.

In the end, I stuck with Nyx simply because it had a cooler ring to it.

"That doesn't mean he was wrong." Orion studied my smug face. "Are you telling me you're sitting here, *outside* your body, talking to a ghost, and you still doubt what he said he was?"

"No?" Even to my own ears, I didn't sound so sure.

"No?"

Closing my eyes, I took a deep breath. "I mean, I don't know. To be honest, I was really hoping that when Elias died, this disability of his would die with him, that my brother wouldn't inherit it, and that I'd never have to hear about the Boundary or Nyx or detaching ever again."

Orion stared at me a moment, a muscle working in his jaw. "I understand this is a bit of a personal crossroads, but can you please save that shit for later? Close by, a little girl and her parents don't give a damn about how you got here."

I blinked a few times. Had to give it to him, Orion was direct, a quality I respected. I jumped back on point. "Nyx was the Goddess of Night."

His face softened. "Yes, and her power now flows through you. It makes you a valuable target."

"Why do you care if I'm a target?"

"Because I don't want you to end up like your father."

That made two of us.

"Elias could have done great things to help others with his gift, but he was selfish. You have a chance to do better, for all of us."

"No offense, but I'd really just like to do my job. There's way too much shit happening in Sapphire Lake to worry about my whole world and yours right now."

He smiled. "And in this, our priorities are aligned."

I eyed him skeptically. "If we're going to be on the same side, there have to be some ground rules."

He reclined in his seat and folded his hands over his stomach. "OK?"

"No more of that shit." I pointed inside to my dented refrigerator. "If you need to talk to me, we have to figure out a different system, because I swear if you knock me out again, I'll—"

"You'll what?" He looked amused.

"I'll do worse than punch you in the nuts next time."

"Fair enough."

"And no more following me around."

He stared at me.

"You were at my boss's house today, weren't you?"

"I wanted to know how much progress you were making. None, I saw."

"If you want me to trust you, then no more lurking and spying."

"That's not going to happen."

"Then this"—I gestured between us—"whatever the hell this is, will never work."

Orion leaned forward, balancing his elbows on his knees. "I know this is all very new to you, but someday you'll understand the value of what I can do. Of what *you* are now able to do. I'm the eyes and ears where eyes and ears aren't allowed. I won't give that up, not even to make you trust me, because by comparison, *you* are expendable."

Well.

"Now, would you like to know what you're up against or not?"

I was still too dumbfounded to speak.

"Listen, kid, your father wasn't any help to me either. I have no problem leaving you to follow in his footsteps if you're going to be more hassle than you're worth." He sat back again as my mouth gaped. "But if you ask me, it would be a waste. Even Elias believed you could do what he never could."

"What's that?"

"Use the gift for good."

"So he knew I was his firstborn and not my brother?"

"He knew once I told him."

"You knew?"

He nodded. "Ever since the night you almost died."

I smirked. "Which time?"

"The only real time." His eyes softened. "The night your husband was killed."

"My fiancé," I corrected him.

He leaned forward again and lowered his voice. "Didn't I just tell you I have eyes and ears where you can't see them?"

"You know about that?"

"I know you had an impromptu wedding ceremony with your Army chaplain the night Josh died."

It felt like all the blood drained from my head and pooled around my ankles. Had I not already been unconscious, I might have passed out.

"You were on your way to Savannah to celebrate."

"H-how did you know that?" My throat suddenly felt like sandpaper.

Because it had been such a spontaneous thing, I hadn't told anyone about that small riverside wedding. Not even Ransom or Paps or Gran. Josh's death had been so crushing, I wouldn't have been able to bear the added devastation in anyone else's eyes.

"The guardians of Imera have watched over you and your brother, even before you were born."

I thought of whoever had been at my bedside in the hospital.

"One of you would someday become a new gateway, so for our safety and yours, we had to watch you both."

I bent forward, cradling my head in my hands. "There was a man in the hospital."

"Yes. I was with you that whole first night."

"No, it wasn't you."

"I was in your hospital room all night. No one else was there except for the medical staff."

I looked up at him. "I think it was Death. He looked like Josh, but it *wasn't* Josh."

He considered it, without judgment or amusement, which I never dreamed I'd find so comforting. "Could have been. I've heard Death comes as an old friend, usually in the form of a loved one who's passed on. You may have crossed to the other side."

"What other side?"

"The human body is a gate, a portal between worlds. When a human dies, Death takes the spirit to either Elysium or the Abyss. When a human spirit detaches *before* the body dies, the spirit is stuck here in the Boundary, hidden from Death, even when the body deteriorates."

"So Imera isn't heaven?" I asked.

"God, I hope not."

I wanted to smile, but I couldn't. "Did you see the accident?"

He shook his head. "Others were there right after it happened though."

"Did Josh . . ." The words I didn't want to ask hung in my throat.

"He didn't suffer."

A rogue tear slipped down my cheek. I brushed it away and nodded.

Orion pointed at me. "You must have been even closer to dying that night than we thought. Maybe that explains why your spirit was fighting so hard to detach. You wanted to die."

I swallowed hard. "Is that how you knew I might be the heir instead of Ransom?"

"Yes."

"Is there any way to get rid of it?"

"You don't want it?"

"No, never. It was supposed to be Ransom."

"If you ask me, the more capable sibling inherited it."

"I didn't ask you," I said defensively. "And you didn't answer the question I *did* ask. Can I get rid of it?"

Orion held my gaze a moment before finally nodding. "Yes."

I sat up like I'd been electrocuted.

"But it's a complicated process—"

"I don't care. I'll take it."

"Be careful what you ask for, Saphera."

The sound of my name on this stranger's lips was jarring. Few people knew my first name, even less used it, including my family.

But I didn't correct him. Elias had always called me Saphera. Somehow it made me feel reconnected—reconnected to something I'd never thought I wanted to be connected to in the first place.

"Can I give the power back to Ransom?" I asked.

"No. You can only pass it on to your heir."

"What if I don't have an heir?"

"You will."

My brow crumpled. "How do you know?"

"The spirit always finds a way."

There was no time to get too hung up on children who hadn't been—and probably never would be—born. I wasn't exactly the maternal type. "How do I get rid of it?"

"You must mix your spirit's blood with water from the River Lethe and drink it. The Lethe is the river of forgetfulness."

"Where's the river?"

"Imera."

"And I can't go to Imera, so I hear." I scowled.

"No, but I can. I'm allowed to travel as far as the Lethe, but no farther. I'll bring it when I return."

"You're not *allowed* to travel farther?"

"Guardians aren't permitted in Imera either. It's part of the vow we take to guard the Boundary."

"Why?"

"In the beginning, permanently detached spirits were able to visit Earth via the Boundary anytime they pleased. What it created was a land full of miserable inhabitants who longed to be elsewhere. The Order realized—"

"The Order?"

"The Order of Elders in Imera. They've been there longer than any of us. Some for thousands of years."

"In Imera for thousands of years?"

"Yes. They're our governing body. They realized the only way Imera would ever truly become a home was for its citizens to cut themselves off from Earth. Those who aren't ready to make that commitment live in Synora, across the Lethe from Imera's mainland. Most of us in Synora are guardians, and our minimum service commitment is twenty years."

"How long have you been a guardian?"

"Longer than you've been alive. My time is almost finished as a guardian. I had hoped to leave Earth better than it was before I took my post. Now I fear it will be exactly the same."

Something screeched in the distance. We both looked toward the sky.

"Was that what I think it was?" I asked.

Orion nodded. "Nightwalkers. They approach with the darkness, but we have a little time."

My spirit tingled with anxiety. "You sure this isn't dangerous?"

"It's not as dangerous as this conversation not happening." His face whipped toward me. "But don't make a habit of detaching this late in the day. Any time after sundown is dangerous."

I put my hands up. "I have no intention of being out of my body for one second longer than necessary."

He smiled. "You say that now."

"Why are you here?"

"After I found Norina Grumley inside the Boundary, I went to confront Elias. As I'm sure you know, it wouldn't have been the first time he'd been front and center in an outbreak of hypnox poisonings."

"No. He was my first assumption as well."

"And we were right. His blood created the hypnox poppy growing somewhere in this city."

"He told you that?"

"No. He was unconscious but not detached when I got to the prison. His injury told me what I needed to know. Only weapons forged by the gods can cause someone to rot from the inside out. I knew then he was stabbed inside the Boundary. I left a note, hoping he would lead me to the plant."

"It led him to me."

"What?"

"Elias found me the night of the fire at the resort."

Orion sat on the edge of his chair. "Did he tell you where the plant is?"

"No. I think he was about to when—" I lost my words, thinking of that conversation. Elias had urged me to stop arguing and to listen.

I wished I had.

"I think the nightwalker got to him before he could tell me where it was."

That was clearly not what Orion wanted to hear. He sat back hard in his seat.

"The hypnox really grew from his blood?"

"Yes. It grows where the blood from Nyx's line is spilled on fertile soil inside the Boundary. The hypnox poppy produces an opioid so powerful it can separate the spirit from the body."

"And you're sure one is growing here in Sapphire Lake?"

"Yes."

"Do you know who stabbed Elias?"

"No, and for that reason, you should be extra vigilant. Whoever killed your father will know he has an heir; it's only a matter of time until they figure out it's you instead of your brother."

"Is Ransom in danger?"

"You both are."

"Who knows about Elias?"

"Plenty of beings, human and gods alike."

"There are other gods beside Nyx out there?"

"Yes, but most of the old gods that humans are familiar with are dead."

"Flash said Zeus and the Olympians are dead." The corners of my mouth twitched as I tried to suppress my amusement.

"Yes." Orion wasn't smiling.

"How did they die?"

"Later. It's a long story, and it will not help us tonight." He must have registered my dissatisfaction because he continued. "I promise to tell you everything when we have more time."

I held up a hand. "But the goddess Nyx is alive?"

"Yes, or you wouldn't be here."

"Where is she?"

He gently pushed my hand down. "These questions will tumble like dominoes all night if we let them. We'll have plenty of time to answer everything later." He pointed to the darkening sky. "But we don't have it tonight."

With a reluctant huff, I nodded. "So if I assume all this shit is true, what other bloodlines might be responsible?"

"We fear it's Icelus, the God of Nightmares."

"Is he responsible for the nightwalkers?"

"Yes." Orion's eyes widened with surprise. "Did Flash tell you the nightwalkers are nightmares?"

I shook my head. "Elias. I think I was eight. It scarred me."

He finally smiled. "I'm sure."

Elias had also told me that soon I'd know the nightmares were real. I hated that he might be right.

"What did he tell you about Icelus?" Orion asked.

"Nothing. I think bloodsucking demons was enough for an eight-year-old. Who is he?"

"A son of Hypnos."

"I assume Hypnos created hypnox?"

"Correct. He sowed his blood into the earth to poison mankind. From that first crop, the seeds of the hypnox were replanted and replanted, harvest after harvest, diluting in potency to the opium poppy as we know it today."

"Why did he want to kill humans?"

"Anguish—at least at first. His mortal wife had died in child-birth, and he retaliated against everyone. It sparked the war that killed most of the gods."

"Damn," I said, forgetting for a moment that it all sounded nuts to me.

"For his deeds, Hypnos was sentenced to the Abyss. There, he fathered three more sons: Icelus, Morpheus, and Phantasos. The sons were allowed passage to Earth, which was a mistake. Icelus created the nightwalkers, and he and his brothers tried to destroy mankind and take Earth for themselves.

"As punishment, Chaos—the god of the gods—stripped their powers and sentenced them to live as humans, cursed to never-ending cycles of death and rebirth for all eternity."

"Reincarnation?"

"Yes."

"But the nightwalkers are still dangerous?"

"As long as they stay between worlds, they're mostly harm-less. They feed off fear, so they induce night terrors in humans and sometimes cause sleepwalking and sleep paralysis. But if they come here . . ." He looked toward the lake.

"Was that what happened at the Drexler the other night?"

"Yes."

"Did you start the fire to kill them?"

"There was only one, but yes."

"Why?"

"Because the more they feed, the stronger they become. It tears through the human completely, creating a gateway for other nightwalkers to come here, or even more worrisome, for Icelus to enter the Boundary."

"That would be bad?"

"Icelus could reclaim his stripped powers and dominate Earth, the Boundary, and Imera."

I doubted the creator of bloodthirsty monsters would be a benevolent leader. "Reclaim his powers how?"

"Drink the blood of a god."

I blinked. "My blood?"

"Yes, inside the Boundary."

"Which is why he can't come here."

Orion nodded.

With another dry and painful gulp, I stood and walked to the porch rail. "Did Elias die to kill another nightwalker in his cell?"

Orion stood next to me. "Like I said, I didn't speak to Elias before he was killed, but I do believe he spent a lot of years wanting to make amends for what happened in the Boro. I don't know that there's a better way to do that than to kill a nightwalker."

We were both quiet for a while. Orion leaned on the rail and looked over at me. "He also might have wanted you to understand the gravity of what you're up against. I know he didn't really understand it until he faced the demons himself."

"How do I find Icelus?" I asked.

"I only know of two certain ways."

My brow lifted.

"Let the nightwalkers come here and see where they gravitate."

"While they kill everything in their path?" I asked with a smirk.

His shoulders rose.

"And the second way?"

"Poison everyone you suspect with hypnox. The three sons of Hypnos can't detach."

"So it's impossible," I said with a sigh.

He straightened and gripped the metal railing. "If it were easy, we wouldn't be here, would we?"

"What do I do?"

"It's simple. Hypnox causes the human spirit to detach, and any human with a detached spirit is vulnerable to the nightwalkers after dark. You have to get that stuff off the streets."

"We're trying."

"You have to try harder. You must use your gift to find the plant."

"I don't know how."

He nudged his shoulder against mine. "That's why I'm here."

Worry fluttered in my chest. "And all I have to do is trust you."

"Yeah." He stepped back. "For now, I have to go, and you must assimilate. It's getting late."

I turned around. "But I still have so many questions."

"I'll be back."

"When?"

"In the morning."

"My brother's coming in the morning."

"Can you put him off?"

"No. I asked him to come." I sighed. "And if I'm going to actually do this, I need Ransom's support."

"OK. I'll be here when he leaves. Do I have your *permission* to put you to sleep?" His tone was mocking.

I thought for a moment. "I'll leave my bedroom door open when I go to lie down. Then you can come in and put me to sleep. Deal?"

"Deal." He stuck out his hand.

I shook it. When he moved to pull away, I held on and jerked him close. "But stay out of my bedroom until I invite you in. No doing any creepy shit like watching me change."

He appeared genuinely offended. "I wouldn't do that."

"Mmm-hmm."

"Remember to dress light. I'll bring clothes you can put on over what you wear to bed."

"OK."

"I'll see you tomorrow, Saphera. It was surprisingly nice to finally meet you."

I felt obligated to say the same, but I couldn't. "I'll see you tomorrow."

He pulled an oneiryte vial out from under his shirt. He held the vial between his index finger and thumb. "Do you know how to use this?"

I shook my head. "Flash only showed me how he uses his. Popped on and off my roof."

"I love that kid," he said with a smile. "I'll teach you when we have more time."

"Flash told me he's forty-seven. Is that true?"

Orion's smile faltered. "Unfortunately. He received a bad combination of drugs that caused his detachment."

"Is there anything that can *prevent* detaching?" I asked.

His head tilted in question.

"I could really use some peaceful sleep."

"Elias had a purple stone once that prevented detaching. He wore it set in a silver ring on his middle finger."

"I've seen pictures of a ring with a purple stone."

"If you can find it, you can wear it when you sleep. Someday, you should be able to control detaching without the stone, but that's why Elias had it. He never really mastered his abilities."

"Shocker."

More screeches, closer this time. "You should go back to your body," Orion said.

"They're almost here."

"Yes. Nightly, these days. They've tasted blood in Sapphire Lake, and they know there's a weakness in the Boundary."

I handed him the dagger.

He put up a hand to stop me. "It's a gift. I won't ask if you know how to handle a knife. I know you do. A shadow blade will work in either realm, on any adversary, human or spirit."

"Even nightwalkers?"

"Yes, but if you ever get close enough to a nightwalker to use it, you'll already be dead."

"Good to know."

He pulled up his pant leg and unfastened the knife holster around his calf. "Like with ergane, the blade is visible in your world even if you're detached, so keep it covered if you can."

"Thank you, Orion." After I accepted it, I started toward the door.

"Saphera?"

I stopped and lifted my brow in question.

"In the spirit of the newfound trust in our relationship, I feel it only right to confess something to you." His eyes fell just enough for me to notice before they quickly snapped back up to mine. "When you hear the news . . . it was me."

Then he stepped out of sight.

CHAPTER SEVENTEEN

Bess got home at a quarter past midnight. After a light workout, I'd showered and was letting my hair air dry as I flipped through the television stations. There was a new documentary online: *Who Killed Ryder Stone?*

I opted for *The Witcher* instead.

If only hunting monsters was so straightforward.

"Yo," Bess said, dropping her keys on the table by the door.

I lifted a hand. "How was work?"

"Good." She paused in the hallway. "You all right?"

"Yeah. Why?"

She jerked her thumb over her shoulder, toward the door. "There are cops in front of the building again."

"There are?" I checked my phone. Nothing.

"Two of them across from the driveway."

I got up and walked barefoot to the door. "I'll be back." As I opened the door, a marked squad car drove past, and Essex pulled into my driveway.

He parked and got out as I reached the bottom of the stairs. In the moonlight, his face was grim.

I stopped. "What's wrong?"

He took a deep breath, staring at the concrete. "The kid is dead."

"What?"

"The third child from the heroin poisoning."

I covered my mouth. "Oh my god."

Essex looked away. "They don't know what happened, but the machines keeping her alive—" His voice cracked, and he coughed to cover the emotion that choked him.

My hands fell to my sides in disbelief. "The machines shorted out."

His eyes snapped back to mine. "How did you know that?"

Because Orion had basically told me.

Ignoring the question, I walked out in front of my garage and turned to look at my roof. Of course, I couldn't see anything or anyone up there, but I glared and shook my head nonetheless. Tears I wouldn't dare let spill burned the corners of my eyes.

"Nyx?" Essex asked.

Hugging the slouchy sweatshirt around me, I walked back to him.

"How did you know that?" he asked again.

"Lucky guess."

"Bullshit." His voice echoed off the building.

I flinched.

"How did you know about the machines? And how did you know about Norina Grumley?"

I stared at the ground, my mind racing.

"What are you not telling me?"

I opened my mouth, hesitated, and shut it.

He closed the space between us. "Narcotics called a little while ago. They're digging into Teek, so they reviewed the body-cam footage from his arrest."

My stomach clenched. "Teek has nothing to do with all this."

"And I'm sure they'll prove that, but my question is, why did you turn off your in-car cameras when he was still in your back seat?"

Shit.

I looked down at the camera lens on his chest.

"It's off," he said, as if reading my mind.

"Are they investigating me?"

"No. They're waiting on a valid reason for why you shut it off."

"Is that why you're here?"

"Not officially."

"I didn't shut it off, I swear." And it was the honest-to-god truth. Elias had, but that would only raise more questions than it answered.

"Then I'll get IT to check the in-car setup."

I nodded as dread overwhelmed me. IT wouldn't find a damn thing wrong with my car cameras.

"But you're not off the hook that easy." Essex bent so we were eye level. "Why do you know so much about this case?"

I looked away. Across the street, a loud and drunken "Whiskey in the Jar" was blaring from the stage speakers.

He touched my side. "Look, you and I both know something's going on here. I can't help you if you don't tell me what that something is."

When I met his eyes again, he was standing *so* close. My heart thumped in my chest. I wanted to tell him. I hated having secrets between us. Hated all the uncertainty. Hated feeling so damn alone with him right here.

"Please talk to me," he urged gently, quietly. He put his hands on my hips. "Please."

My eyes fell to his lips, and without thinking, I stretched on my toes and kissed him. Stunned, he froze, and I realized what I'd done.

Horrified, I jerked back.

Only once before had I ever seen Essex so stunned. He'd literally been shot with a Taser in training.

What the hell did I just do?

Essex blinked a few times until his gaze sobered.

I wanted to crawl under the concrete and die. "Essex, I'm sorry. Fuck, I shouldn't have done that."

With a slight nod, he took a deep breath. "You're right." He fisted the front of my sweatshirt and pulled me back to him. "I should have."

His mouth collided with mine with all the unleashed force from three years of carefully bridled restraint. One hand slipped behind my neck as the other held my waist just off his weapons belt.

My arms melted around his shoulders, and I whimpered with relief as his tongue dragged deliciously across mine. Like it was exactly where it should have been all this time. Searing desire burned through me, and I scraped my teeth across his bottom lip.

It wasn't until my hands were on his chest, on the hard body armor beneath his black uniform, that I realized there was no way in hell this could happen.

He was on duty.

He was my boss.

And he was Essex.

I broke the kiss and released him, touching my fingers to my bottom lip. He raked his hand back through his dark hair, fear as clear in his eyes as it felt in my heart.

I backed toward the stairs. "I'm sorry." Then I took the steps two at a time to my front door and went inside without pausing to look back.

On the verge of hyperventilating, I slammed the door behind me and flattened my back against it. I heard a car door open and close outside, and I pressed my eyes shut.

Bess stuck her head out of the hallway bathroom. "Is it a standoff? Are we under siege?"

I forced a smile. "Everything's fine. They're gone."

"Everything is clearly *not* fine." She came out in her pajamas. "What happened?"

I walked to the kitchen. "Remember the three kids from the drug ordeal?"

"Yeah."

"They're all dead."

Bess gasped. "No."

"That's why the cops were here."

"They were so little."

"I know." I slumped over the bar.

She touched my shoulder. "I'm sorry, Nyx. Did you know them?"

"No." I raked a hand back through my hair as I straightened. "That's not all that happened."

When I turned, she was staring expectantly.

"I just kissed my boss."

Kissed was a stretch. I'd barely stopped short of humping him like Karma in front of my garage.

"Like, for the first time?" she asked with one eyebrow cocked.

"Of course."

"Oh boy. So which thing are you so upset about?"

"Both." My stomach was twisted in knots.

"OK," Bess said cautiously. "We can figure this out." Walking past me, she opened the refrigerator, retrieved two beers, and handed one to me. "You got a bottle opener?"

"The drawer by the stove."

She found it and opened our beers. After she passed me mine, I drained half of it before putting it down.

"What the hell am I going to do?"

Bess eyed the bottle. "Develop a drinking problem, apparently."

I groaned and cradled my forehead in my palm.

"Was it a good kiss?" she asked, leaning against the counter across from me.

It was the best kiss I'd had in *years.* Maybe ever if I was really being honest.

"It doesn't matter. He's my boss."

"Your smoking-hot boss, who is clearly crazy about you. I'm not sure I'm seeing the problem here."

"What would happen at your job if you hooked up with *your* boss?"

She paused and laughed with her beer halfway to her mouth. "I'd bathe in disinfectant before I checked myself into Sterling Heights. You've met my boss. We are *not* talking about that creep."

Fair enough.

I folded my arms on the countertop and laid my head facedown on top of them. "Shit. I have to spend twelve hours in a car with him tomorrow."

"Why?"

"I'm only allowed to ride along this week." I picked my head up and pointed to the staples in my head. My eyes widened with a thought. "Maybe I *do* have brain damage."

"The only evidence of brain damage is the fact that it's taken you this long to cram your tongue down that man's throat. I mean, have you seen him, Nyx?"

I took a few more deep gulps of beer, letting the fizz burn the back of my throat.

"Seriously, what's the worst that could happen?" she asked.

I let out a small burp. "I could be forced off my team and moved to day shift." Which was a much bigger problem than I could explain to her.

"That might suck, but you wouldn't be fired, right?"

I didn't think so, but I honestly didn't know. I hadn't read the section in our handbook about fraternization too closely. Until now, I'd never needed it. "I'm not sure."

She put a hand on my shoulder. "So let's have some perspective here. Worse things have absolutely happened today."

Bess was right. But instead of making me feel better, the thought of those kids dying made me feel infinitely worse—and furious. I couldn't wait to pummel Orion's crotch again.

I looked at the clock. It was at least six hours until sunrise.

"Did they ever find out how the drug got to the school?" she asked.

"Yeah. We took the woman into custody this afternoon."

"Well, thank goodness for that."

I wrapped both hands around the cold bottle. "It's not over, I'm afraid. The drug is still out there."

"Maybe that will keep you busy and distracted from jumping your boss's bones in the car tomorrow." She snickered quietly.

I glared at her.

"If you do, think you can snap a photo with your body camera? I'd love to see that man shirtless."

My body camera. I may have temporarily dodged the cameras question, but I needed to come up with an answer fast. I got up. "Excuse me."

"What? I mention him shirtless, and you need some alone time?" she asked as I walked into my bedroom.

I grabbed my work phone charging on the nightstand. I expected there to be a missed call or a text from Essex.

There wasn't.

I pulled up our chat history and typed out a reason. *Turning my car cameras off must have been an accident.*

Guilt came surging back, so I deleted the lie and laid the phone down. I sat on the edge of my bed and put my head in my hands.

I had to make a choice: either be honest with Essex or walk away. There was no middle of the road. No other option.

This wasn't just about worrying he'd think I was nuts. Telling Essex the truth would commit him to my lie. Rogue gods aside, I couldn't risk many humans finding out about me. It wasn't safe. Not only for me, but anyone I cared about.

Elias had named my brother *Ransom* after all. Who knows? Maybe this light-bulb moment was why.

I also couldn't involve Essex in something so dangerous without his full knowledge. And there was no way we could ever be together in a relationship built on a lie.

Walking away would be a kindness. Something I should have considered *before* inhaling his face in my driveway.

Closing my eyes, I could still feel the pressure of his lips on mine. Both sides of that kiss had been anything but casual. The attraction was too intense. The friendship far too deep.

And no matter my inner conflict, I knew the truth in my heart: walking away was no longer possible—for either of us.

For better or worse, I had to tell Essex the truth.

CHAPTER EIGHTEEN

Ransom showed up with fast-food breakfast and coffee at six fifteen a.m. Judging by the time and his black dress pants and button-up shirt, he'd come straight from the hotel. A backpack strap was slung over one shoulder.

He held up the food bag. "I brought a peace offering. I'm sorry I stormed out the other day."

"I'm sorry I stole your destiny."

At that, thankfully, he chuckled.

I pulled open the door, and he walked inside and handed me a cup of coffee. "It's decaf. Figured you'd be sleeping soon."

"Thanks."

He looked down the hall. "Is your roommate home?"

"Sleeping, so keep it down. And ground rule: you cannot date my roommate. I have enough drama these days as it is."

He put the food on the table and his backpack on the floor. "But she's cute. And spunky."

"And off-limits." I sat beside him, where I'd placed my brown leather journal in anticipation of our conversation.

"But you stole my destiny." He pulled a wrapped biscuit out of the bag and handed it to me.

"Trust me, if I could give it back, I would." When I unfolded the greasy wrapping, the smell of sausage overpowered my sleepy senses. "Thank you for breakfast."

"You're welcome. You on duty tonight?"

"Unfortunately."

"Why?"

"I've kinda complicated the shit out of some things at work."

"You finally screwed your boss."

I flinched. "I didn't screw anybody."

"Lies."

"I only kissed him."

Ransom laughed *really* hard.

"Shut up."

"Aren't you supposed to do that *before* you interview for a promotion?"

"You're such an ass."

"I know." His laughter finally faded. "If it's any consolation, you'll probably be more of an asset to them if you stay home and sleep."

"You think so?"

He nodded.

I picked up my coffee. "What made you change your mind?"

"Paps. That old man can lay on one hell of a guilt trip when he wants to. He's been glued to the news since they found those kids yesterday."

"I bet."

Ransom's face fell. "They were the same age as Milly."

"I thought the same thing."

"They all died, didn't they?"

I nodded. "A man from the Boundary named Orion shorted out the life support on the last one. She died sometime last night."

"Was it hypnox?"

"Yes."

He swore under his breath.

"Have you heard from Mal?" I took a bite of my biscuit.

"No. You?"

I shook my head and swallowed. "I wonder if she even knows Elias is dead."

He picked up his coffee. "She probably felt the universe shake along with all the other demons from hell."

We both chuckled.

"If she doesn't know already, she'll find out today. Narcotics is questioning her about the hypnox."

"Damn. Even though you cut her out of your life, she still manages to make shit difficult for you, huh?"

"Yeah." I rolled my eyes.

"I'll bet she shows up when she finds out." He curled both tattooed hands around his coffee cup. "She'll want to use you the way she used Elias."

"Yeah, but whoever she visits first will tell us if she really knew who your father was."

Ransom nodded but didn't comment. "Do you think Mal has anything to do with the hypnox now?"

I leaned back to doublecheck that there was no movement on Bess's side of the condo. There wasn't. Still, I kept my voice low. "No. Hypnox only grows when the spirit blood of someone like Elias is spilled in the Boundary."

"So someone like *you*." There was a bite to his statement.

"Yes," I said sadly.

"This makes you a target now too, doesn't it?"

"Possibly. Orion thinks someone might be hunting scions."

"You trust this Orion guy?"

I leaned my head on my hand. "Trust is a dangerous game."

Orion had murdered a child, but he had told me about it. Not that the latter outweighed the former by any stretch, but if I'd learned anything in my job, it's that honesty goes a long way, even among the most ruthless of criminals. In fact, the ones who unashamedly stated their intentions outright were usually the most trustworthy—they never failed to be the bad guy.

"The problem is, I've never felt more inept in my life, and Orion might be the only person who can help me."

Ransom bent to look me in the eye. "Nobody ever said you had to save the world, Nyx. God knows that's not what Elias did with the gift, and you can bet your ass I never thought beyond a new business venture to clean up some old debts and buy a boat."

"Business venture?"

He leaned to the side and pulled his wallet from his back pocket. "Had business cards made and everything." He handed me a sleek gray card with the word "Specter" across it, with his name and phone number. "Specter means ghost."

"I know what it means. What were you going to do?"

"Private-eye stuff. Like James Bond, but American."

Sadness filled my heart. I slid the card back toward him and put my hand on his. "You have no idea how sorry I am, Ransom."

He pulled away, the same way I do when I'm emotionally uncomfortable with others. Guess it runs in the family. "It's not your fault. I honestly don't know why I was so shocked. Our parents screwed up everything else for us. Why not this too?"

"What are you going to do about work?" I asked.

"I don't know yet. Everything changed so fast. I'm sure Harlan will let me stay at the Drexler if I want to, but I'm not sure I want to."

He stuffed the last massive bite into his mouth, wiped his crumb-covered lips with a napkin, then crumpled the napkin around the business card. With a perfectly arched shot, he tossed both into the kitchen garbage. "Maybe I'll try out for the NBA." He flashed me a million-dollar smile, but there was a lot of pain and worry behind it. "What do you need to know about the gift?"

I didn't want to change the subject, but it was clear Ransom wasn't ready to talk about whatever was going through that thick skull of his. "Everything."

Worried, he looked at his watch. "Not sure if we have time to cover *everything*." He lifted the backpack off his chair and *thunked* it down on the table.

"I know not to detach at night and that if I die in the Boundary, my body dies here."

"You can't walk through walls," he offered.

"Or closed doors," I added, the corner of my mouth tipping up into a smile. "I found that out the painful way."

"What did you do?"

My shoulders slumped. "Bounced off my bedroom door like a rubber ball."

"Hate I missed that."

"It hurt. Is that because pain is in the mind?"

"Yep."

I thought of Orion in the fetal position on my floor. After what he'd done since then, I smiled at the memory.

"You should be able to walk through clear glass," Ransom said.

I nodded. "I can. I have to be able to see where I'm going."

"You can also travel place to place the same way. You just have to see it here." He tapped the center of his forehead.

"Using oneiryte?" I asked.

His head pulled back with surprise. "Where'd you hear about that?"

"I met a kid from the Boundary who showed me his. Orion said he'd teach me how to use it."

Ransom pulled a wooden box from his backpack.

"What's that?" I asked.

"Some stuff Elias gave me."

I almost jumped out of my chair. "Are you serious?"

He slid the box across the table.

If I was a squealer . . .

I slid off the lid. Inside, on a pillow of blue velvet, was a glass vial halfway full of the same shimmering white sand Flash and

Orion had shown me. It was fixed to a long tarnished chain and had a cork stopper. "Oneiryte."

"Yep."

"How do I use it? Click my heels together three times?"

"Huh?"

My head tilted. "Dorothy? Ruby slippers?"

His eyes narrowed with confusion.

"*The Wizard of Oz.*"

"Oh, that munchkin movie you can watch in sync with Pink Floyd when you're stoned?"

My eyes widened. "Brother, you and I have led different lives. Never mind. How do I use it to travel? The kid poured some on the ground."

"Yeah. That's part of it. You pour a line on the ground, picture where you want to go, and step over the line. It creates a portal."

"That's it?"

"So I hear."

"Sounds too easy."

"Yeah, especially for a girl who walks into doors." I shot him the bird, and he laughed. We both did, and it felt so good. "Technically, you don't even need the sand to travel, but it makes it a lot easier."

"You don't?"

"No. Elias didn't have it most of the time while he was locked up, and he got around fine. It's just a concentration aid. He said it was a gift from someone who lived in the spirit land."

"Imera," I said.

"Yeah, that's it. Have you been there?"

"No. Apparently, I'm not allowed to go there."

"Why?"

"Orion said they keep Earth and Imera separate." I put the necklace back in the box.

"There's more stuff in there," Ransom said.

The blue velvet was a bag. I untied the strings holding it

closed and poured its contents into my palm. There were eight stones, each a different color, most with eight sides. One stone was larger than the rest, a long icy-white crystal wrapped in silver wire. It was beautiful, and a little creepy. "What's this?"

"Oh, this is very, very special." Ransom took it, holding the stone up to the light.

I clasped my hands beneath my chin. "Well?" I asked, wide eyed with excitement.

He laughed and gave it back. "I have no fucking clue." He picked up one of the smaller stones. "I don't know what any of these are."

I put the stones into the box and examined the bag. "I think this is ergane." I laid it on top of the stones.

In the box's corner was a man's silver ring with a diamond-shaped purple stone. "He was right," I muttered, taking the ring from the box.

"Who was right?" Ransom asked.

"Orion said Elias had a ring with a purple stone that would prevent detaching."

I slipped the ring on my right index finger and admired the colors sparkling in the light. Its sides were engraved with symbols I didn't recognize.

Ransom sat back and crossed his arms. "You want to *prevent* detaching?"

I caught the offense in his voice. "Not all the time." I put the ring back into the box.

"It would help if you didn't despise all this so much. I'll probably get my ass kicked for no longer having the power you keep reminding me you hate."

"Ass kicked by who?"

"Don't worry about it."

"Ransom, are you in some kind of trouble?"

The way he carefully studied my face was answer enough: yes, my brother was deep into something.

"It's not trouble exactly."

"Then what is it?"

His eyes fell, and he scratched at something invisible on my tabletop. "Remember when I was in Vegas?"

"Yes." How could I forget? Those awful days weren't long before my accident. Even though I'd been in the Army, Gran had called me every night worried sick.

"I got in pretty deep at the Nebula. Had a few markers I couldn't pay back after I lost my fighting contract. I was facing more jail time, and I would have lost Milly."

I rested my forehead in my hand. "What did you do?"

"I made a deal."

"With who?"

He looked away. "Mal."

"You did *what*?" The question was so loud it even startled me.

"Mal had just gotten out of prison. She paid my debt in exchange for my help after Elias died."

"What kind of help?"

"She promised it wouldn't be anything illegal."

"Says the woman who spent a few decades in prison. How much do you owe her?"

He paused. "I don't wanna tell you."

"How much?"

"A hundred and twenty thousand dollars."

I almost fell out of my chair. "Holy shit. Are you serious?"

"See?" He threw a hand toward me. "That's why I didn't want to tell you. Maybe I should start a swear jar and make some of that money off you."

I buried my face in my hands. "Damn it, Ransom."

"Would you rather me be in prison and lose custody of Milly?"

"Of course not. It's just that . . ." I wasn't even sure how to process this information. I sat back and looked at the ceiling. "Where did Mal even get that kinda money?"

"Where do you think?"

"The money she and Elias stole."

"That would be my guess. She heard about my arrest from Gran and came to the rescue."

"Smart way to get you in her pocket."

"And now she's screwed."

"Serves her right."

"She's going to make my life hell, Nyx."

"Probably, but at least we shouldn't have to worry about her putting a hit out on you over it." I sipped my coffee.

"I wouldn't be so sure about that."

I didn't like the way his eyes were avoiding mine. "Why?"

"Mal made some connections during her time *away*. The guy with her at Gran's funeral could easily be a mob boss."

I remembered him. Stocky build, expensive suit, more tattoos than Ransom and me combined. "What did she say his name was?"

"Beats me."

I hadn't paid much—or any—attention either.

"What does she want you to do?" I asked.

"I don't know the details, but it has something to do with making Renzo pay for what he did to her. She's had plenty of time to contemplate retribution."

"But now you can't help her."

"So I'll get to be the object of her retribution."

"She'll have to go through me," I reminded him.

He rolled his eyes. "Exactly what I've always wanted. My baby sister as my protector."

Another thought struck me. My simply possessing the power of Nyx was leverage over Mal. Leverage I'd lose if Orion was right about the Water of Lethe. I'd have a harder time protecting Ransom without it.

"Have you heard of the Water of Lethe?" I asked.

He shook his head. "What is it?"

"Something Orion mentioned. Not important." I knew it would only rub salt in a very open wound. "What else is here?" I lifted a key ring from the box. On it were four keys. Three were normal-sized; one was long and ornate, like it might fit a jewelry box or a really old lockbox.

Ransom took the key ring and singled that key out. "I don't know what this goes to. Maybe Orion or one of your other friends from . . . wherever it is, can tell you."

"Imera," I said.

"Yeah." Ransom pointed at me. "Don't go getting stuck there."

"Is that possible?"

"Oh yeah. The body can't survive without the spirit for longer than twenty-four hours."

"Twenty-four hours." I made a note in my journal.

"It *shouldn't* be a problem if you're only detached during daylight. Nightwalkers are the biggest danger."

"Orion told me, and they're about the only thing I can remember Elias saying about the Boundary."

"Scary shit if it's true."

"I heard them last night. They sounded real enough, and I'm ninety-nine percent certain it's what killed Elias in his cell."

"This should help protect you." He reached into the box I'd emptied. Pulling it to him, he searched all four corners and even turned it over to look at the bottom.

"What's wrong?" I asked.

"The knife. It's missing."

"Knife?"

"Yeah. This fancy thing, like a long skinny—"

"Like this?" I pulled the dagger from my calf.

"Kind of." He took it from me. "The one Elias had was smaller. Where'd you get this?"

"Orion."

Ransom gave me the dagger back and looked in the box again. "It's gone."

"Where'd it go?"

"I don't know, Nyx. Let me just grab my crystal ball and ask."

I held up my middle finger.

"Maybe it's in my safe. I'll look when I get home. What else do you need to know?"

I looked at the journal again. "Mirrors. I know they're a problem, but I can't remember why. And they freak me the hell out because I don't have a reflection."

"No, but you can see the reflection of the space surrounding you. If you pass through one, you're in danger of getting trapped in a loop between what is real and what is reflected."

"Damn," I said, taking notes.

"Yeah, don't mess around with mirrors. Oh, and don't get fucked up and try to detach. Elias told me that a lot, though now I wonder if it wasn't a ploy to try to keep me sober."

I hesitated. "How are you doing with all that?"

"I'm fine." He took a deep gulp of coffee.

"You sure? I've been worried about you with all—"

"Nyx, I said I'm fine."

It wasn't an angry, defensive snap, like we'd seen a lot when he was clearly *not* fine, so I changed the subject. "How did Elias animate bodies?"

"Through touch. I assume you've been able to return to your body when you're detached."

I nodded.

"It's supposed to work the same way, but it's a lot more difficult because bodies are not meant to house more than one spirit. It took Elias years of practice. He said it's easier to invade the minds of people who are unconscious."

"I don't plan on trying that *at all*. God, I hated it when he did that to me."

The light flickered in the kitchen. We both turned to look. "We're not alone," I announced.

"We're not?" Ransom asked, a little worried.

I looked around the room. "Orion?"

The light flickered again.

Ransom's eyes doubled. "He's here right now?"

"Yeah." I raised my voice, but not enough to wake Bess down the hall. "And he has a hell of a lot of explaining to do."

Ransom stood. "On that note, I'm out. I need to get home anyway. I'd like to get some sleep before Milly gets out of school. I promised to take her to Fun Zone today."

"Oh, I wish I could come."

"She would love that. You're welcome to if you're not busy."

"I'm afraid I am."

The lights flickered again.

"Oh," Ransom said, understanding.

I followed him to the kitchen. "Next time though."

"Of course." He stopped and pointed to my dented refrigerator. "What happened?"

"Orion. The night I thought he attacked me, I punched him in the balls."

Ransom chuckled. "I guess that hurts in any dimension."

"I guess. Listen, I really appreciate your help."

"And you appreciate your greasy biscuit and coffee," he added, taking my trash and tossing it in the can.

"And that."

He turned toward the door, and I took his arm. "I love you, Ransom."

He put his arms around me and kissed the top of my head. "I love you too."

We walked to the front door, and when I pulled it open, Essex was standing on the other side, his fist poised to knock.

I blinked. "Oh, hello."

Essex, still in uniform, slowly lowered his hand as he looked at Ransom. "Hey. Sorry, you're busy."

"Not at all. Essex, you remember my brother, Ransom."

The two men shook hands. "Of course. Good to see you again."

"It's good to see you too, Sergeant," Ransom said, flashing a wink in my direction.

I wanted to kill him. "Ransom was just leaving." Grabbing his sleeve, I pushed him out the door as he laughed.

"I hope we'll be seeing a lot more of each other." Ransom slapped the back of Essex's shoulder as he passed him, pausing behind his back to make kissy faces.

My jaw clenched. "Goodbye, Ransom."

"Bye, sis." He chuckled as he plodded down the stairs.

"Sorry about that. What's up?" I asked Essex, trying—and failing—to casually lean against the door. It slammed backward into the wall, and I stumbled trying to catch myself.

Essex stepped inside as I ungracefully recovered, pushing my hair out of my face. When I looked at him, I expected him to be laughing, or at least trying not to.

He wasn't.

For the first time since I'd known him, he looked like he might run back outside.

"Sarge?" I straightened my shirt, wondering if maybe I should snap my fingers in front of his bewildered eyes. "Are you—"

With one step, he cupped my face and pressed his mouth hard and steady against mine. When my stunned arms relaxed, and my hands settled on his biceps, his lips softened, then parted. His fingers trailed down the sides of my neck. Then he wrapped one strong arm around my waist, pulling my hips against him until the spare magazines on his belt dug into the sensitive flesh beneath my belly button.

I threaded my fingers into his hair as he kissed me, slow and deep. The kind of kiss that made me forget all the complications.

Forget he was my boss.

Forget the massive secrets I was hiding.

Forget an invisible man was watching us inside my condo.

I froze.

He didn't. His hand gripped my chin, and he teased my mouth with his tongue, licking and prodding in ways that spun my mind toward dangerous thoughts of him repeating those moves *elsewhere.*

"Tyler." I panted, pulling back.

His eyes closed, and he leaned his forehead against mine, slowly rocking his head side to side. "Don't tell me to stop."

My hands slipped to his shoulders. "We're not alone," I whispered.

His eyes popped open, but his alarm quickly faded into a smile. "I keep forgetting you have a roommate now."

I'd forgotten her too.

He bent toward my neck and kissed a path to the delicate spot beneath my ear. "She's not in your bedroom, is she?"

No, but another man might be.

My head fell back, and he kissed the center of my throat before finding my lips again. A strong hand curled around my breast, taking my breath. Before I lost my good sense completely, I broke the kiss. "I can't."

A muscle worked in his jaw, but after a tense second, he released me and looked away. "Is it because of work?" Before I could answer, he met my eyes again. "Because I'll switch shifts. Hell, I'll quit."

"You won't quit."

His eyes closed again. "I've wanted you for years."

Goose bumps prickled my skin. This wasn't exactly news, but hearing the admission aloud, so vulnerably, so desperately, sent a flutter through my stomach.

I put my hands on his cheeks, and he turned his face, pressing a kiss against my palm. Everything inside me wanted to forget Orion and drag this man—this painfully perfect man—to my bed.

But I couldn't. Not like this, anyway.

If Essex had started to wonder about my suspicious entanglement with the hypnox case, others might too. There was a very real possibility that work might open an investigation if any more leads ended at my door.

Never mind my whole family history. The events so far that week had the Nyx family all over it: Ransom and I both on scene at the Drexler; I'd found Norina Grumley; and now the missing video feed from my patrol car.

And if I found any leads from inside the Boundary, I wouldn't have an explanation for *any* of them.

I couldn't drag Essex into all that. Especially not without an explanation first and letting him decide for himself. That conversation would have to come, but not while Orion was eavesdropping in my condo.

"I'm sorry," I said quietly.

With a sigh, he turned toward the door, still wide open behind him.

"Please don't leave like this."

He stopped and curled his arms over the top of his head in frustration. "What do you want from me, Nyx?"

I stood at his back, twisting my fingers together to keep from touching him. "I want to talk later, when we've both calmed down, had some rest, and are thinking clearly again."

He slowly turned and lowered his arms to his sides. "We'll have to. We're riding together tonight, remember?"

"Maybe I shouldn't."

His jaw went slack. Then his face flushed with anger. "You know what? Do whatever you want."

As he started to turn, I bolted forward and grabbed his neck. I kissed him again, but then pulled back. "You *are* what I want." My gaze fell to his mouth. "But I need it to be right."

He searched my eyes, then kissed me again. I threaded my fingers through the soft hair at his neckline, and when I broke the kiss, I held him close. "Please," I whispered.

He nodded, seemingly satisfied with that answer, at least for the moment. "We'll talk later," he said quietly.

I walked him to the door. "Give Karma my love."

He finally smiled. "I will." I leaned against the door, and he turned around in the breezeway. "Ride with me. It'll be all business. I swear."

"OK," I said. "Call me when you wake up."

When he was gone, I closed and locked the door. Then I carried the wooden box to my bedroom and flopped across the bed. "Orion, you'd better make this shit worth what I just gave up."

I closed my eyes.

And nothing happened.

CHAPTER NINETEEN

I was about to give up when I suddenly detached. Orion was backing away from my bed with his hands raised in surrender. I shot upright.

"Now, Saphera, calm down."

I moved away from my body and got up on my knees. "Don't tell me to calm down. You murdered a child."

"I did no such thing." He sounded offended. "Her body was already dead. There was no way to assimilate her."

"Wait. Is she here?" I looked around like the little girl might be standing in my bedroom.

He slowly walked forward with his hands still raised. "She's safe in Imera. All I did was neutralize the threat of leaving her body vulnerable."

I sat back on my heels. "You promise?"

He held up his little finger. "I pinky swear."

I hooked my finger around his. "You should have told me."

"I did tell you. In the safest way possible." He sat next to me on the bed. "If I'd told you what I was going to do, you would have tried to stop me."

That was true.

"Sometimes the choices we make aren't easy. You're no stranger to that."

I thought of Norina Grumley's tearful little boy when I put her into the back of my patrol car.

But I didn't want to tell Orion he was right. That seemed like a dangerous precedent to set this early on. "Where have you been? I thought you'd left."

"I did leave."

My head pulled back with surprise.

"What? I'm not a voyeur. I stepped outside while you were . . ." He wafted his hand toward the front of the condo.

"I know what I was doing."

"I waited out front, but then the guy left. Isn't he your sergeant?"

"Yeah," I said with a sigh.

He smiled. "Getting kinky with the department handcuffs, huh?"

"No!" *Maybe.* I sighed and ran my hands through my hair. "It's complicated."

"I bet." He stood. "Well, do you want to sit here and talk about your love life, or do you want to hunt down some bad guys?"

I got up so fast it would have given me a head rush if I was still inside my damaged skull. "What do you think?"

With a smile, his eyes dropped to my outfit. "You should have dressed light." I was still wearing my slouchy sweatshirt and lounge pants. And I was barefoot.

"I forgot."

"You certainly had a whole lot going on when I got here," he said with a chuckle. He pointed to the overstuffed chair in the corner of the room. On it was a neat stack of what I assumed were clothes. "Grab your shoes."

"How did you know my size?" I walked over and picked up the black shoe.

"I didn't. You'll find some things are *infinitely* better in the Boundary."

I put them on. "These weren't what Flash was wearing. He had on light-up sneakers. Like the kind they sell in shoe stores here."

"That's because they are. Those shoes were a gift, brought from Earth."

"How?"

"We have our ways to transport small things."

"Ergane," I said.

He nodded. "Correct. Do you have your dagger?"

I patted my calf.

"Good. Here." He pulled something from his pocket. A pair of ergane gloves.

"For me?" I asked.

"Yes." When I moved to take them, he held on. "Keep them with you."

"Yes, sir."

He released them. "And keep them hidden when you're moving around. Humans get all freaked out by shit floating around."

I laughed as I pulled them on. "Noted."

"Do you have a backpack or something?"

"Yeah."

"Pack your Boundary clothes and items into it. Think of it as your spiritual-emergency go bag."

"I have an *actual* go bag from the Army."

"That's even better."

I retrieved the tan tactical backpack from my closet. Most of its emergency supplies had been removed over the years, but a few staples remained: an MRE, an empty bottle, a first-aid kit, and a flashlight. "Will this work?" I asked, plopping it onto my bed.

"Perfect." He brought me the clothes. "Pack these into it, and tuck your gloves in here." He hooked two fingers inside the outer mesh pocket on the side. "That way, if you're detached, you can still get to them to open the zipper."

"Smart."

"Keep the bag with you. You never know when you might need it."

"OK."

"Did your brother bring you oneiryte?"

"Yes." Using my glove, I opened the box on the foot of my bed. I reached inside and found the vial. "This?"

"Yes. What do you notice about it?" He crossed his arms.

"It's fuzzy."

He pointed at me. "It's in Earth's realm, not inside the Boundary. So how do you put it on and use it?"

"I need to bring it inside the Boundary."

"And how do you do that?"

I lifted the ergane bag from the box.

He clapped. "You're getting the hang of it."

I put the necklace and vial into the bag and closed it. When I reopened it, both were inside the Boundary. "That's pretty cool." I put the necklace over my head.

"You don't even need to take the necklace off. Ever. It won't be seen when you're in your body, and it will always be there when you detach."

"What about the clothes and shoes?"

"I guess technically you can leave them on, but you don't have to. The necklace, however, is essential."

"Ransom said Elias could detach and travel without oneiryte."

"That's true, but he only learned to do that over the years he was incarcerated. Desperate times, you know?"

"So he couldn't always do it?"

"He was never disciplined enough to master it, but it is possible, at least for you."

"But not for you?"

"No magic runs in me. Permission to use the sand is given by the Order, and only for use outside Imera."

I held up the sand now dangling from my neck. "It doesn't work in Imera?"

"Sure it does, but we're not allowed to use it. Too many of us were getting hurt."

"Hurt?"

"Imagine people suddenly appearing in occupied spaces. From what I understand, it sounded a lot like human bowling pins."

I wanted to laugh but I didn't.

"Come on. I'll show you."

"You're taking me to Imera?"

"No." He crouched and drew a long line in front of us. When he straightened, he held out his hand.

With a deep breath, I took it.

"Hang on," he said with a smile.

My other hand sandwiched his, and we stepped—off a damn cliff, it felt like. The world was ripped from under my feet, and we fell straight down at a million miles per hour. I struggled to hold onto Orion's hand, and I crossed my legs to keep from peeing.

The ground reappeared beneath me so quickly and solidly that I landed in a heap on a familiar orange-and-brown tile floor. We were at the Sizzling Chicken all-you-can-eat breakfast buffet. A pair of tanned legs flew through my face, and I curled into a ball.

Laughing, Orion pulled me up by the arm as humans passed *through* us to pile their plates full of eggs and bacon. I latched onto Orion's chest, overwhelmed with the cold energy zinging through my body.

"You all right?" Orion instinctively and *uselessly* shielded me with his arms.

"Mmm-hmm," I lied.

He pulled back enough to look at me. "Now imagine if we were tangible."

My chin quivered. "We'd be the bowling ball."

"Exactly." He took my hand and wrapped it around my vial of magic dust. "Now, you have to get us out of here."

"I don't know how."

"Where was Ryder Stone?"

"At the Drexler. Chalet One-Ten, overlooking the lake."

He squeezed my hand around the tiny bottle. "Don't tell me. *See it.*"

Closing my eyes, I pictured the chalet.

"Got it?" he asked.

I nodded.

Guiding my hand, together we poured a line on the floor. "Keep that image," he said as we stepped. A jolt from my hand traveled through every nerve ending before the floor dropped out again. I fought through the fear and terrifying exhilaration to hold the image of the chalet in my mind.

With a jerk, my feet landed on asphalt, and when I opened my eyes, the chalet was in front of us. Orion gave me a squeeze. "Well done."

I felt too disoriented to be proud.

"Think you can stand if I let you go?" he asked against my ear.

I nodded, almost sure I meant it.

When he released my hand, I only wobbled once before my legs felt sturdy beneath me. "Whoa. We just went all the way across town in less than a second."

"Farther than that. We came all the way from Vegas." He started toward the chalet. "That was the Sizzlin Chicken near the Strip."

I stumbled when I started after him. He didn't notice. "So how do you get around in Imera?"

"Each city center has a channel hub, where we're allowed to

channel from place to place. Otherwise, we get around mostly on foot, with a few exceptions."

"Exceptions?"

"Other modes of transportation."

"Like what?"

"You wouldn't believe me if I told you." With a smile, he continued to the police-taped entrance of what remained of Chalet 110.

"What are we doing here?" I asked.

"We need to find where the hypnox came from. We'll trace the steps back to its source. So tell me what happened that night."

"It's still under investigation," I replied.

"I'm not the media. What *really* happened? Tell me everything."

"The Drexler sits on the line between two of the biggest patrol zones in Sapphire Lake. So the Mini Market next door is a common place my team and I meet up to talk about cases and work on reports—"

"And shoot the shit while you eat trash food that burns through your internal organs. Don't bullshit me."

I flinched. "Fine. When we're not busy, we shoot the shit and eat trash for dinner. While we were there, one of the city's regular offenders stole some stuff from the shop."

Orion's brow crumpled. "With a bunch of cops outside? Is he crazy?"

"Certifiably, I believe. Anyway, I was chasing him through the woods when a call came in about a noise disturbance here in one of the chalets. My boss—"

"The boss you just made out with?"

I rolled my eyes. "Yes, and two of the other guys on my team responded. One of them knocked on the door while my boss looked in the front window."

"Did he see anything?"

"No. As soon as he looked inside, an explosion detonated. That was you, right?"

"Right."

"That's when the rest of us hauled ass over here."

He walked inside the ruins of the chalet, and I followed close behind. I hadn't been inside the night it happened, but I didn't need anyone to point out where the blood spatter was. Even with the damage, it looked like someone had flung a paintbrush full of red paint at the remnants of the wall.

Orion walked to the bedroom, where the fire had started. In what used to be the bathroom doorway, he knelt and crooked his fingers over his shoulder, beckoning me to do the same. I crouched next to him as he scooped up a handful of shiny black rubble.

"That's inside the Boundary?" I asked, surprised.

"No, but many things of my world will always be tangible here."

"Like the shadow blade?"

"Exactly." He let the pieces sift through his fingers. "This is what remains of the demon. Nightwalkers are highly flammable. Daylight alone can cause them to ignite. That's why they stick to the shadows."

"So they're combustible with daylight, and they drink blood. Are they vampires?"

Grinning, he shook his head. "Not nearly so neat. I'm sure you heard what the bodies looked like."

"They couldn't tell much from the male victims. They were burned pretty badly, but the female was torn in half."

"See? Not nearly as neat as two puncture wounds on a jugular." He stood and looked around the room. "Do they have any leads on the identity of the John Doe?"

"The guy I arrested that night, I believe John Doe was his brother, Kush Fleming."

"Kush? That's his name?"

I smiled. "Yeah."

"Is he into heroin?"

"Not sure, but I wouldn't be surprised if he was. How did you know something was going on here?"

"Detaching causes a ripple through the Boundary. If it happens close to or past nightfall, the guardians always investigate. By the time I arrived, the woman was already dead in the first room. I assume she wasn't much of a heroin user. It's the rookies who usually die first."

"Why?"

"They have no tolerance at all. They detach for long periods of time, making it easier for the nightwalkers to get to them. Habitual heroin users will detach but usually not completely. All it takes is skin contact with hypnox for a non-user to detach and die from it."

I felt sick.

He pointed left toward the window where Essex had been looking inside. "A man with long brown hair was unconscious on the bed over there, high on hypnox, I'm sure."

"That was Ryder Stone."

"Who?"

"A celebrity."

"Huh. That explains all the media."

"Yep."

"Here in this doorway is where the nightwalker was feasting on John Doe."

"What did he look like?"

"I don't know. All I could see were lifeless, jean-clad legs. He must have been in the bathroom when the beast entered your realm through the girl's body."

"They believe John Doe—Kush—brought heroin and hypnox to the room."

"This?" Orion reached into his back pocket and pulled out a small velvet bag, much like the one in the box I'd gotten from

Ransom. He dumped its contents into his palm: a glassine bag stamped with 7K and a gold crown.

My eyes doubled. "Where did you find that?"

"The state crime lab."

"You stole it?"

He looked surprised. "You didn't think I'd let them keep it, did you?"

"Oh my god."

"What?"

"Eyebrows are already being raised in my direction. If you start stealing evidence—"

He held up a hand to stop me. "It won't blow back on you. I only took this. The rest I put in the incinerator."

"So you *destroyed* evidence?"

"The cops got what they needed from the reports. Do you want to keep piecing facts together or not?"

I sighed and gestured for him to continue.

"Did anyone else come or go from this room before the explosion?"

"I haven't heard about it if they did."

"Then that must have been Kush." He pointed to the sparkly black ash near the bathroom.

Unexpected sadness crept over me. Whatever happened that night, Kush didn't deserve to die, especially like this.

"Think he figured out a way to grow it?" Orion asked.

"He named himself after a strain of marijuana, and you think there's a chance that he's some ancient-magic specialist?"

Orion chuckled. "Probably not, but I have known some seriously resourceful potheads, so let's assume he's in on it. Where could it be?"

"I was at Kush's home last night. We brought his brother in for questioning. I didn't see any poppies, but it was dark, and I wasn't looking."

"There weren't any poppies there."

My head pulled back. "How do you know—" I crossed my arms. "You were following me."

"You knew I was. You bitched about it last night."

I huffed and shook my head.

He held up a hand. "Before you get all sidetracked on the injustice of it all, where else does Kush hang out?"

"His grandmother's. Tawny Fleming. She lives about a mile up the road from Kush and Teek."

"Anywhere else?"

"Not that I can think of offhand. We weren't exactly chummy."

I folded my arms and looked around at the mess. "Is it possible Elias lied about all this? That he was behind the hypnox on purpose?"

"Why would he be?"

"I don't know. Because he was an awful person?"

Orion smiled. "Maybe, but I'd say he learned his lesson the last time he dealt with hypnox."

"Were you there?"

"Yes."

"So he did create the hypnox last time."

"Was there a question?" Orion seemed surprised.

"Not from me. Our chief back then wasn't so sure it was an intentional murder."

"Elias may not have started the fire, but he certainly—"

I held up a hand. "Wait a second. Elias *didn't* start the fire?"

"No."

"Who did?"

Orion stared at me. "I did."

The admission plowed through me like a freight train. Everything I'd believed my whole life, all the anger and resentment that had shaped me, was all a lie.

"He didn't do it," I mumbled, staring across the room.

Orion put his hands on my shoulders. "He might not have struck the match, but it was absolutely his fault."

"I know, but still."

He leaned closer. "More than just your family was torn apart that night. Even Elias understood his guilt in what he did." Signaling the end of the discussion, Orion walked away. He paused in the doorway. "You coming?"

My legs felt like they were filled with concrete as I followed him. "Where are we going?"

"To pay a visit to the one party clearly identified in all this who is still alive." He held up the heroin stamp bag.

The 7 Kings.

CHAPTER TWENTY

Quick Fix Auto Repair, on the eastern edge of Sapphire Lake, offered more than just oil changes and brake pads to its questionable clientele.

Our department was currently working with the DEA in a months-long sting operation, with at least one undercover agent inside the 7 Kings-run establishment. For this reason, I was sure our narcotics division was treading lightly on the business—at least for the time being.

The shop was open when Orion and I appeared on the curb across the street. He gave me an encouraging smile. "I think you're getting the hang of this."

"Thanks," I said, my eyes glued on the repair shop.

From across the street, it was clear the auto shop was sketchy. The brick exterior had been painted white in another lifetime, and half of the pane-glass front window was boarded shut. Above the two open garage-bay doors, its hand-painted plywood sign barely clung to the brick wall at an angle.

Patches of grass sprouted through the cracks in the concrete driveway, and shoddy tires were stacked by the front door. It was a wonder this place had stayed in business as long as it had. Not because the Kings' clientele cared so much about aesthetics, but because the whole thing hadn't come crumbling down.

We were about to enter without cause and without a warrant. "This feels wrong," I said.

"Are you kidding? Your colleagues put their lives on the line to get a fraction of the access you're about to experience."

"Maybe, but at least what they find, they have a good explanation for in court."

"This is a whole lot bigger than admissible-evidence procedures."

"I know, but I've had those procedures beaten into my skull for the past few years."

"I understand that, but we aren't taking anyone to jail or killing anybody. No one will even know we're here, and we're sure as hell not going to court. The only thing that matters is finding that plant before anyone else dies."

I nodded nervously.

"Speaking of things beaten into your skull, how's the head?"

"It's to the itchy stage now. The doctor said the hardware should be able to come out next week."

"That's good news." He nudged my arm with his elbow. "Hey, I am sorry about the accident. I guess I've gotten used to being undetectable in your world."

"How did that driver see you?"

"Our presence disrupts the energy fields on Earth—not much, but enough that we're detectable when combined with the right elements, i.e. the mist from the rain and the beams from headlights. I must have refracted the light enough for him to make out a body outline. Again, I am sorry."

"Well, as you said, I didn't die."

He chuckled. "No, you didn't."

"Can I ask you a question?"

"Go for it."

I touched the side of my head where the staples should've

started. "Why isn't there so much as a scratch from the accident on Friday, but I can still see the scars on my body that are three years old?" I held out my left arm to show that, even in the spirit world, the tattoos barely covered the scars from the motorcycle wreck.

Orion turned to face me and looked at my scalp. "As bad as it was, this wound was superficial." He gently held my wrist and ran his finger along my forearm. "This was a lot more than just road rash."

"Josh."

He released my arm. "Scars fade some with time, but the truly deep wounds never leave us completely."

"I never talk about him." My eyes fell to the pavement between us.

"You really loved him."

I nodded and took a shaky breath. "When Josh died, I asked the chaplain not to file the marriage license with the court. Because it was never made legal, to this day, no one but you and the chaplain ever knew we were married."

Silence hung between us for a moment.

"Elias knew," Orion finally said.

My face shot up. "Really?"

"He was there."

I looked away, maybe to keep from crying. A week ago, this news would have enraged me. But now, my heart wasn't so sure.

"As shitty as he was as a person and a father, for what it's worth, I do think he felt genuinely terrible for being such a loser dad. The older he got, the more clear that became."

I sniffed and swiped away one lone confused tear that dripped down my cheek. "Time away from my crazy-ass mother helped, I'm sure."

"She is a piece of work." He cocked an eyebrow. "Kinda makes me wonder how you came out semi-normal."

"Semi-normal?"

"Don't worry. It's a compliment. Your umbilical cord was clearly filled with crazy juice."

My laughter eased the pain in my heart.

He jerked his head toward the auto shop. "Ready?"

"Let's do it."

Orion crossed the street without looking. I followed, stopping once without him to let a motorcycle pass. I jogged to catch up before he could laugh at me.

Without hesitation, he walked through the open bay door on the left. A gray coupe was on a short manual lift, and a heavily tattooed man lay on a rolling workbench beneath it. Metal clanged against the concrete floor when he dropped a tool.

"From what I've heard about the place, I'm a little surprised they actually fix cars in here," I said quietly.

"Most front companies like this usually have at least a few guys who are legit. Otherwise, they wouldn't be able to keep the doors open at all for the police busting them down. How long has your department been watching this place?"

"The past couple of months."

"Los Siete Reyes," he said with a wisp of nostalgia.

"You know them?"

"Yeah. I've been doing this a long time."

Made sense he'd be interested in any major players in the heroin trade.

"How much do you know about them?" he asked, looking behind an old bookshelf full of tools that was pulled away from the wall.

"I know they originated in Vegas, and they deal mostly in heroin, cocaine, and guns."

Orion nodded as he knelt beside the car the man was working on. "That's true." When I crouched beside him, he pointed to the man's forearm as he twisted a socket wrench. It was a tattoo of the Kings' official trademark: a crown with seven points. "Know why they're called the Seven Kings?"

I shook my head.

"In the late seventies, Los Siete Reyes began in a public-housing neighborhood on the south side of the city. Most of its residents were immigrants from seven countries: Brazil, Colombia, El Salvador, Honduras, Guatemala, Mexico, and Venezuela.

"The community was plagued by outside gang violence, and seven members of the neighborhood, one representing each nation, joined together to protect its citizens. They even tried to work with local law enforcement to help keep their neighborhood safe."

"Sounds like a neighborhood watch."

"It kind of was. Sadly, it didn't last. As the parents worked long hours to support their families, the kids spent a lot of time alone. And while the violence against the community had lessened, the kids were still targeted at school and on the streets. They finally got sick of it, and started fighting back. Bullies bred more bullies, and over the years, the Seven Kings evolved into what it is today."

"That's sad."

We both stood, and he continued his search around the shop. "It is. Sometimes I wonder what those original Kings think about what their good intentions created."

"At least one of them was in prison with Elias."

"I know. A few of them are still involved. A few more are dead. It's hard to believe that was forty years ago."

Muffled voices came from a door beyond the other garage bay. We walked toward it. Two men and a woman were talking about their weekends. The woman laughed a lot. One man was hungry.

"This is pointless," I whispered, like they might be able to hear me.

"We just need to direct the conversation."

"How do you propose to do that from a different dimension?"

"Easy." He walked over to the lift, stepped on top of it, and climbed onto the trunk of the car. Nothing in the real world moved under his weight. He stood and pulled on his ergane glove.

Overhead, he reached for the release handle on the garage-door opener. With a solid yank, the heavy door slid down its tracks, landing with a thundering *bang!* against the concrete floor.

The mechanic screamed.

"That oughtta get their attention," Orion said, smiling as he watched the door.

It flew open, and two men rushed into the garage, guns drawn. One of them had tattoos on his face and "Jesus" embroidered on the front of his Quick Fix work shirt. "What the fuck was that?" he shouted.

The mechanic slid sideways out from under the car. "Who shut the door?"

Orion got down and rejoined me. "This should get interesting quickly."

"It closed?" the second man asked, quickly walking to the front of the garage to inspect the door.

The first man jogged to the other open garage door and looked outside, carefully hiding his weapon behind his back. "I don't see anyone out here."

"Danny, check all the way around the building." Jesus waved his gun like it was a pointing device.

With a nod, Danny tucked his gun into his waistband and walked outside.

The mechanic wiped the grease off his hands with a towel that had been tucked into his back pocket.

"It wasn't you?" Jesus asked him.

"Man, my ass was under the car. Nobody else was in here. It just fell." The mechanic wasn't wearing a uniform. Neither was Danny, who'd run outside.

Behind Jesus, a woman with silky long black hair looked out the doorway. "I told you this place was falling apart, Jesus."

He shoved her back a few steps. "And I told you to shut the fuck up, bitch."

My metaphorical blood was boiling. Orion must have noticed because his arm shot across the front of my shoulders to hold me back. "Hang on," he said.

Danny returned. "I didn't see nothing."

The three men stood by the car, still looking for anything out of place. "Has that thing ever fallen before?" Jesus asked.

"I've never seen it," the mechanic answered.

"Me neither," Danny agreed.

Beside me, Orion pulled out the drugs.

"What are you going to do?" I asked.

"Incite an argument."

He put the stamp bag of heroin into the glove, then tossed it onto the floor between the men. The mechanic and Jesus saw it fall, and the mechanic's eyes popped with fear.

Jesus picked it up. "Where the fuck did this come from?" He held the baggie between two fingers, toward the mechanic.

The mechanic lifted both hands. "I don't know, *primo*. I haven't seen that shit since Costa left here. Same as you!"

"Nobody else has been in here today," Danny said, ripping his gun from his waistband. "You skimming Kings' Gold?"

"I swear I didn't. Jesus, you and I both saw that shit fall. I ain't got nothing on me." The mechanic turned his pockets inside out.

Jesus didn't look convinced.

"Watch the camera! I didn't even move." The mechanic pointed to the corner of the room. A tiny green light glowed on a black camera mounted to the wall.

"Maybe I will." Jesus did a quick lunge toward the mechanic, making him flinch. "You best believe I'm gonna be watching you." He snarled as he walked back to the office. Danny followed him. So did we.

Inside the messy office, papers littered the computer desk, a large safe was shoved into the corner, and one whole wall was covered in license tags—some with current registration dates. *Wow.* The only thing that looked legit about the space was the appointment calendar tacked to the wall, by the door.

The woman sat across from the desk on a folding chair. She couldn't have been older than twenty, and I noticed she was scrolling through a dating app on her phone.

I took a closer look at the tags. "Wonder where these came from," I whispered.

"Or what they're used for." Orion pointed to a few empty spaces. "And you don't have to whisper. They can't hear us."

"Ever?"

"Not when they're awake."

"But when they're asleep?"

"Sometimes."

"Interesting."

Jesus sat in the rolling office chair behind the desk. "Marla."

The woman looked up. Her lips were painted a dark plum, she wore fake eyelashes, and had a nose stud. Her gold hoop earrings were so large they could fit around my ankle.

"Get out," he said, not even bothering to look at her.

Marla stood, pushing her chair back so hard it smacked the wall behind her. Her heels *clacked* against the concrete floor as she stormed out.

Jesus tossed the drugs onto the desk, swiveling his chair back and forth as he stared at it. "Wonder if Costa knows he's missing some of the stash."

Danny sat on the corner of the desk and pulled a cell phone from his pocket. "Want me to call him?"

"Yes."

A second later, Danny held his phone to his ear.

"And ask him when I can expect to see my money."

Danny nodded. Finally, he put the phone down. "No answer."

Jesus swore.

Danny looked at his phone. "It's still early for Costa."

Jesus pointed at him. "Don't stop trying until you get him."

"I won't."

"And find out when more hypnox will be ready."

Orion and I exchanged a look.

"Costa said yesterday nobody's heard from Kush in days," Danny said.

I grabbed Orion's arm. "Did you hear that?"

"Shh."

"Motherfucker's probably hiding from us," Jesus said.

Danny nodded. "I knew we shouldn't have given him that car before he delivered the second batch of hypnox."

"I'll bet that dipshit brother of his has seen him. Go beat the shit out of Teek until he either talks or bleeds to death," Jesus said.

"Oh, hell no." I started forward. To do what, I wasn't sure, but Orion held me back.

"You can protect the brother later. For now, we listen." His grip eased on my arm. "Knowledge is your superpower."

"Do you know where he is?" Jesus asked.

"Nah, man, but I can find out," Danny said.

"Maybe you should give him a taste of this to loosen his lips." Jesus picked up the stamp bag of heroin and hypnox.

I dug my short black nails into Orion's forearm. "If you let them kill another innocent person, I swear to God I'll—"

Orion reached into his pocket as Danny reached for the bag. Faster than even my eyes could follow, Orion snatched the drugs from Jesus's fingertips with the glove.

Jesus slid his chair back against the desk.

Danny jumped, dropping his phone with a loud clatter, onto the floor. "What was that?"

"Where the fuck did it go?" Jesus asked.

Danny turned all the way around. "Did you see another hand?"

"Man, you're trippin'. Another hand from where?" Jesus asked.

Danny looked all around the room. "I don't know, but I swear to god, I saw another hand."

The two men uselessly searched the floor, the desk, and under the desk while we looked on, smiling.

Danny's eyes wandered all around the room. "What if there's a ghost in here?"

Orion chuckled as he put the drugs in his pocket. "That never gets old."

"A ghost?" Jesus got up and shoved Danny's shoulder. "Man, I think you're on drugs *right now*."

"Watch the tape," Danny said.

"Is that going to be our answer for everything? Watch the tape?" The last part he said in a mimicking voice.

Danny just stared at him.

With a huff, Jesus turned to his computer, grabbed the mouse, and clicked open a camera icon on the desktop. The two men watched the video feed from the office camera. So did we. It showed movement, but Orion's hand moved too fast for me to see.

Shaking his head, Jesus got up again. "I'm going to get some dinner. By the time I get back, you'd better have found those drugs."

"What do you want to do about Teek?"

Jesus grabbed the front of Danny's shirt. "Find him too."

After memorizing the tag numbers of the two cars in the parking lot, Orion and I returned to my condo. Together, we reappeared in my bedroom.

I sat on the edge of the bed, next to my body. "At least if it was Kush who died in that fire with Ryder Stone, plenty of eyes will be on the Fleming family. The Kings won't be able to get close enough to hurt Teek."

"Teek? Are these legal names?"

"No." My smile faded. "I wish I could get more patrols on the place, just to be safe."

"People ask for extra patrols all the time," he said with a shrug.

"But cops don't ask for them without a reason. What the hell am I supposed to say?"

"I can visit the home when they're asleep and make a suggestion. That is *if* anyone there has enough brain cells left to pick up the message."

"People can really hear you when they're asleep?"

With a nod, he sat beside me. "Somehow the soul and the subconscious are tied together. Not exactly sure of the mechanics behind it, but it works. People can hear you too, but the majority of them will be sleeping while you are unable to detach."

"Yet another curse of being a day sleeper."

"Yeah, graveyard sucks."

Graveyard. Paps was the only person I knew who called night shift that.

I wanted to ask Orion if he'd ever worked nights, but it felt too personal. Too soon. In addition to what his life had been like as a human, I had a million other questions.

Did spirits still need to sleep?

Did he, like Flash, like it in Imera?

Did he have balls?

He leaned toward me. "What are you so lost in thought about?"

"There are so many things I want to know. I'm not sure we'll ever cover them all."

"I think we have time." He grinned. "Does this mean you're more interested than you'd originally let on?"

I didn't meet his eyes. "Maybe."

"Well, one thing is for damn sure." He stood, and I looked up at him. "You're definitely not like your father."

No one outside my small family had ever known me or Elias well enough to make that statement. "Thank you," I said, meaning it more than he would ever understand.

"You should get some rest."

I looked at my body. "Am I not sleeping now?"

"Of course you are, but how many times have you really felt rested after a night of fitful dreams?"

He had a point.

"Multiply that exponentially," he said.

I nodded.

"Are you working tonight?"

"Yeah. With my boss."

"The boss you made out with?" he asked again.

"Shut up."

He laughed softly. "I need you to do some recon when you have access to a work computer."

"What recon work?"

"All the known associates, addresses, places of work, whatever you can get on Kush Fleming. He knew where that plant was before he died."

"OK." I pulled off my Boundary shoes. "What will you do?"

"Tonight, I'll drop in on the Flemings. Until then, my mission is to find Lucas Costa. He's the immediate danger, second only to finding the plant. It will continue to bloom until winter, producing enough melatryptophine to kill this whole city a few times over."

"Are you sure it's here? Couldn't it have been brought here from somewhere else? Kush just got a car."

"No, it's here. The nightwalkers are too fixated on Sapphire Lake for it to be anywhere else."

"What will you do if you find it?"

"Burn it. That's the only way to keep it from growing back."

"How do you do that?" I asked.

"Create fire?"

I nodded.

He wiggled his fingers. "Magic." I scowled, and he laughed. "Someday, I'll teach you. Fire is of my world. A long time ago, it was stolen from the gods and brought to Earth."

Skepticism was creeping back into my mind, but I kept my thoughts to myself. "We didn't accomplish much today. We still don't have any leads on where the plant might be."

"No, but we're not the only ones looking for it. It will turn up." He was quiet for a moment. "I need to talk to you about something else."

"Shoot."

"You need to watch your back. Whoever stabbed Elias is still out there. They won't have good intentions for you either."

"Do you think they know who I am?"

"I'm sure of it. They obviously knew what Elias was and how to kill him. They would also know he had an heir. Hell, Elias might have been murdered to get to you or Ransom."

"Why?"

"Because Elias's gift wasn't nearly so impressive with him behind bars."

"Great," I mumbled.

"I have some more things for you." He leaned to the side and pulled something from his pocket. In his palm was a small clear bottle, like something from a minibar, filled with clear liquid.

"Vodka?" I asked with a smile.

"The Water of Lethe."

My eyes widened. "My way out?"

"Yes."

I reached for it, but Orion held it out of my grasp. "Not so fast."

I frowned.

"You need to understand what this means."

"It means I'll get my life back." I reached again, and he moved the bottle farther away.

"Hear me out?"

I dropped my hands into my lap.

Orion balanced the bottle between his thumb and index finger. "If you drink this, your tether to the spiritual world will be severed. You will no longer detach, you will no longer dream—"

"I won't dream at all?" I asked.

"Not at all. Dreams are of the spirit, not of the body. You will be completely cut off from the Boundary, and every memory of it—and those connected to it—will be erased."

"I won't even remember Elias anymore?"

He shook his head.

"If you're trying to talk me out of this, it isn't working," I said.

"Consider it carefully. Once it's done, there's no undoing it."

"But the power will be gone?" I wiggled my fingers. "Like *poof*, gone?"

"The spirit of Nyx will pass to the next scion."

"The child I may never have."

The corner of his mouth twitched up. "Something like that."

"How does it work?"

"Can I see your shadow blade?"

I pulled the knife from beneath my pant leg and handed it to him. With its sharp tip, he pierced his index finger. Silvery white liquid oozed from the wound. When I leaned in for a closer look, he stretched his finger toward me.

I recoiled. "First rule of police work: if it's ooey, gooey, or sticky, and not yours, don't touch it."

With a chuckle, he held the finger over the bottle. "A few drops of your life blood will do. Mix it well and drink it."

"Give me the blade. I'll stick myself right now." I held out my hand.

Reluctantly, he handed it to me and wiped the blood—if that's what you could call it—on his shirt sleeve. I pricked my finger and watched mesmerized as the silver liquid drizzled down to my palm.

"Wicked," I whispered.

"Want some help?" he asked.

I handed him the bottle, and he unstoppered it. I turned my hand sideways above the narrow rim and squeezed. *Drip. Drip. Drip.*

"Is that enough?"

Orion nodded and put the cork back into the bottle. He shook it, and the blood sparkled like glitter as it mixed with the crystal-clear water.

"Will only my spirit blood work?" I asked.

"The blood is the power of Nyx, so any scion's will work—"

"Nyx has more scions than me?"

"A few, but don't count on their help." He balanced the vial between his thumb and finger. "Each scion's blood will only work once. Once this is used, and the magic activates, you'll never be able to create more."

"We can't just get more water?"

"No. It's a one-and-done shot."

"Do I drink it while I'm in my body or while I'm detached?"

His brow crumpled. "Your physical body must ingest it."

"Got it." I held out my hand.

"I have a request," he said, placing it in my open palm.

"OK?"

His hand lingered on mine. "I need your help to find the plant. You owe me nothing, but I would like to ask that you wait to drink this until after the threat is neutralized."

I swirled my free finger toward the ceiling. "Aren't there other guardians who can help you?"

"Yes, but with your knowledge of the area and your direct connection to an entire police force looking for this thing, you're our best hope to find it." His grip tightened. "Please?"

I took a deep breath and blew it out slowly. "Since you asked nicely."

He smiled. "Thank you, Saphera."

With a nod, I slipped the bottle into the ergane bag on the side of my go bag. My finger was still dripping, thankfully onto my knee and not onto fertile ground. "How do I make it stop?"

He wrapped his fist around my finger. "A little pressure will do." While he held it, he met my eyes. "Don't forget: this blood is very powerful. A god can never capture you in this form. And you can never allow them to use it to enter the Boundary."

"Tell me about Nyx. You said you would when we had more time."

The corner of his mouth tipped up. "For someone who wants out of this life, you certainly are curious."

I scowled.

"Tell you what. If you stick around after we've found the plant, then I'll tell you."

"That's blackmail."

"Yes, it is." He smiled.

I stood. "Never mind. I don't need to know because I'll forget it anyway."

The amusement faded from his eyes. He stood beside me and pulled out his oneiryte necklace. On the chain with the bottle was an icy-white stone, long and slender and wrapped in wire, very similar to the one Elias had given Ransom. "Keep this with you too."

"What is it?"

"The light of Imera."

I cocked a skeptical eyebrow. "The what?"

"Think of it as a homing beacon. I hope you'll never need it, but wear it always, and if you're ever in trouble, I'll be able to find you." He slipped it off the chain and gave it to me.

"Thank you."

There was a light knock at my bedroom door.

"You expecting company?" Orion asked.

Another knock. "Nyx, are you awake? Sorry to bother, but you have a package to sign for." It was Bess.

"That's my roommate. My new phone is probably here. So much for getting some rest," I said. "When will I see you again?"

"Tomorrow. Same time and place?"

"Sounds good." I put my hand on my forehead.

"Hey," Orion said.

I paused.

"You did well today."

"I have a decent teacher."

His dimpled grin was the last thing I saw before I disappeared back into my body. When I sat up, Orion was gone.

"We have to get a few things straight," Essex said when I opened my front door to him that evening.

My brow lifted with surprise. "OK?"

"We are not talking about what happened this morning."

I held up my hands in surrender. "I couldn't agree more."

"We both need to keep our heads clear tonight. We'll deal with"—he gestured between us—"*this* when we're not in uniform. No talking. Deal?"

"It's going to be a long, quiet night."

"You know what I mean."

I gave him the side eye as I walked out of my condo carrying my Boundary go bag. "Do I strike you as the kinda girl that likes to talk about feelings?"

With a laugh, he started down the stairs while I locked up.

"Got any leads?" I asked when I got in his passenger's seat. I put the backpack in the floorboard, by my feet.

"I think we should sniff around Quick Fix Auto."

"That's a solid place to start." More solid than he knew. "What have I missed?"

My replacement phone had been flooded with missed group-chat messages that would have taken days to catch up on. Most of it was the usual crap the guys post, memes and inappropriate jokes.

He pulled away from my building. "Last night was pretty quiet other than the news from the hospital. No signs of heroin or hypnox. Just a couple of MVCs; no fatalities. I also wrangled two loose cows back into John Larson's fence."

"You wrangled them?" I made a lasso gesture overhead.

"OK, I shooed them." He stared straight ahead, trying to keep a serious cop-like face. "Begged and pleaded and pushed a little."

I laughed. "You pushed?"

"Yeah. And I'm calling bullshit on cow tipping. Those suckers don't move." At the exit of my neighborhood, he turned toward the highway. "I did get to take a picture with a llama though."

"A llama?"

"Yep." He handed me his phone. "I made our selfie my new lockscreen."

I laughed. On his phone's screen was a picture of an alpaca licking his eyeball. "That's an alpaca."

"Same thing."

I returned his phone. "Any word from Gregg about Mal?"

"Not yet. Have you seen Mal at all since she got out of prison?"

"Only a few times, most recently at Gran's funeral. I'm lucky though. My brother's had it worse."

"How come?"

"He's the firstborn." Which was way more complicated in our family than most.

"I'm thankful to be an only child. No competing with siblings."

"Trust me, it's a competition I was happy for Ransom to win."

"Is she really that bad?"

"Well, if she collected puppies or trapped souls in a garden, she'd make one hell of a Disney villain."

Essex laughed.

"Seriously, Paps said she's even worse now that she's out. Like she's always been selfish and conniving, and now she's hateful and bitter too."

"Gregg says she got married again."

"Not surprised. She's made a career out of marrying for financial gain. I don't even know her last name anymore. Nor do I care. How's Karma?"

"Lonely today. My dog walker is out of town, so I'll have to stop by later to let him out. I can't wait to have the new kennel done."

"Have you had any time to work on it?"

"I framed the dog door from the laundry today. All that's left is to paint it and finish the fencing outside."

"Didn't you sleep today?"

"Not much."

I started to ask why, but my mouth snapped closed. After our morning exchange, he'd probably had too much on his mind for sleep. My cheeks warmed at the thought.

God, I needed to tell him the truth. We had a twelve-hour shift ahead of us, and we still had some time before calling 10-8 . . .

My heart pounded in my chest. I closed my eyes, took a deep breath, and blew it out slowly.

Was I really going to tell him?

What would he say?

What would he *think*?

I wasn't just jeopardizing our friendship and whatever more could be between us. If Essex thought I was a lunatic, I could lose my job.

But . . . what if he *did* believe me?

For once in my life, I could have a true ally, and at least one person in the world who knew absolutely everything about me and stood by me anyway. Aside from Ransom and Paps, I'd only ever had that with Josh, and even he hadn't known *everything* about Elias and all the craziness that came with him.

"Nyx?"

My face whipped toward him.

"You all right?" he asked with an amused grin.

I turned in my seat and tapped my chest, the universal signal across the force to disable your body camera.

"All my cameras are off." He raised an eyebrow. "Why do they need to be?"

I sighed and rubbed my forehead. "Call it damage control. What I'm about to say is going to sound completely nuts to whoever hears it."

"OK," he said slowly.

"Delta One." A woman's voice came over the radio, startling us both.

"Geez, we're not even technically on duty." Essex shook his head as he grabbed the radio off its cradle. "Delta One."

"We're getting calls about a car heading the wrong direction on Highway Fifty close to your location."

"I'm heading eastbound, just past Overlook Road." He lowered the radio. "Nyx, cameras back on."

"Roger that." Our conversation would have to wait.

Dispatch started again. "It should be right on top of you. Gray four-door sedan—"

"Essex, look out!" I grabbed the handle above my window.

The truck ahead of us swerved, side-swiping the concrete wall dividing the highway. Essex hit his blue lights, but the oncoming car didn't slow.

It was heading straight for us.

At the last second, the car swerved and slammed head-on

into the green road sign. It impacted with so much force that the stakes holding the sign were ripped from the ground and the whole thing was flung into the ravine.

Essex cut sideways onto the shoulder, and I was out of my seat before the tires stopped rolling. When I reached the car, I saw the driver slumped over the wheel.

Essex radioed for EMS.

The driver's window was closed, and there were no sudden movements inside the vehicle. I looked into the back seat and froze. On the floorboard was a handgun and a *huge* bag of drugs.

What the hell?

I pulled my gun from its holster. "We've got drugs and a weapon in plain view!"

The man in the driver's seat had a shaved head, black scruff on his chin, and tattoos on his face.

My biggest concern was the firearm. Essex covered me as I opened the back door—thank god it was unlocked—and grabbed the gun off the floor. I jogged back to the SUV, unloaded the weapon, and put it in the center console.

Essex inched toward the car. "Delta One, I have an unresponsive Hispanic male . . ."

As I got closer, I realized the man might not be so unresponsive. He stirred in the driver's seat, slowly lifting his head off the spot where it landed on the wheel.

When he straightened, I saw the number seven inked in a chillingly familiar font on the side of his neck.

"Seven Kings," I said, glancing at the back seat again. "Looks like fifty bricks or more of heroin back here."

"You've got to be shitting me." Essex looked inside. "If that's what I think it is, I'm taking your ass to Vegas."

Essex tapped on the window. When the man's bloodshot eyes registered us, he flinched, then frantically searched inside the car.

"Hands where I can see them!" I shouted.

The man looked at us again, clearly weighing options: fight, flee, or give up. God, I hoped we hadn't used up all our luck finding the gun and the drugs in plain view of my body camera.

One of his hands gripped the steering wheel; the other reached for the keys in the ignition. He didn't find them.

"Step out of the car with your hands up!" Essex screamed.

In the distance, sirens wailed.

With an angry huff, the man pushed open the door and got out, stumbling a step. He outweighed me by at least sixty pounds of muscle. "What the fuck am I doing here?" he asked, squinting.

My head snapped back. *Not what I expected. At. All.*

"Put your hands on your head," Essex ordered calmly.

"Fuck you. What'd you do to me?" The man staggered sideways and bumped into his open back door. When he grabbed onto it, he saw what I'd seen in the back floorboard. "Holy shit. What the fuck is going on?"

"Get on the ground and keep your hands where I can see them," Essex demanded.

"I said—" He started toward me, but his legs wouldn't hold, and he stumbled again.

"Get on the ground!" I repeated.

The man shook his head as if to clear it, then charged forward again. At the same time, a patrol car pulled in behind Essex's SUV. The man looked toward the noise, and I took the opening.

Holstering my gun, I darted forward, hooking my arm through his and wrenching it behind his back as I tried to take him to the ground.

He jerked free and spun, and his giant hands closed around my throat.

Raising my right arm, I turned and sliced downward with my elbow, using all the power of my torso to trap his arm against my chest. The force pitched him forward, and his forehead slammed directly into my staples.

As my knees crumpled, I angled my elbow straight back into nose.

Crunch!

Over my head, Essex clotheslined the man with his arm, tackling him onto the grass.

Dazed, I slumped onto my side as Baker ran to help.

Blood poured into the gangster's mouth and down his neck. "Stupid bitch." He spat, showering Essex's face with red spittle.

Essex pushed his face to the side. "Congratulations, asshole. That's an assault charge. Try it again, and you'll have a broken jaw to match that nose."

Baker grabbed the man's wrist, and they flipped him over.

Something warm oozed into my ear. I gently touched it and pulled back fingers dripping with blood. "Damn it."

"You all right?" Essex asked, his dark hair falling into his eyes as he clamped the steel handcuffs around the man's wrists.

"I'm fine." Fighting the burning pain, I pressed the button on my radio. "Delta Three."

"Go ahead Delta Three."

"We have an unidentified male in custody, bleeding from the nose. Need EMS to evaluate."

"EMS is already en route."

Baker put a see-through mesh fabric hood over the guy's head to prevent any more spitting, then I stepped back to let the guys hoist him up onto his feet. Another patrol car pulled up, and Jones got out.

"Jones, got any clean towels?" I called.

He went to his trunk and opened it.

With blood still oozing into my ear, I walked toward the man. "What's your name?"

"Fucking cunt," he grumbled.

"Bet that looks pretty on your birth certificate. Wanna try again?"

"I'm not telling you shit."

"What about the bag of drugs in your car? Want to tell us about those?" Essex asked.

"You assholes planted it."

I tapped the circular lens next to my chest pocket. "Pretty sure all our cameras will tell a very different story. It was in plain view on the back seat."

"Fucking liar! I put that shit in the trunk—" The man's mouth snapped shut as mine fell open.

Baker laughed. "You put it in the trunk, huh?"

Essex laughed too, shaking his head with disbelief. "Maybe you were so high you only thought you put it in the trunk. Instead, you left it with a loaded forty cal on the floorboard."

"Gun too?" Baker asked.

"Yep," I said.

Essex pulled on gloves and turned the man around. "Do you have anything on you that will poke me, cut me, or stick me?"

"I don't even know how the fuck I got here!" he shouted at my boss.

"I'm going to search the car," I said.

"Take care of your head first," Essex said.

Jones carried over a white towel. He handed it to me, looking at my head. "Geez, Nyx."

"Care if I ruin it?" I asked.

"My wife might, but go ahead. Shit. I think I see your skull."

I pressed the towel against the side of my head. "Thanks for the backup."

"What have you got?" he asked, following me to the crashed sedan.

"Heroin, pretty sure."

"You're shitting me?"

"No, I'm not." At the back door of the car, I draped the bloody towel over my shoulder and pulled a pair of thick leather gloves from my pants' cargo pocket.

"Why don't you let me do that? That gash needs pressure," Jones said.

"I appreciate the offer, but I've got it." If it was hypnox, I had a better chance of surviving it than Jones. At least I'd understand what the hell was happening to me if I detached. "Stay back."

I carefully lifted the bag and carried it to the hood of the car. Jones and Baker joined me as I slowly removed one of the bricks, a tight bundle of heroin packets. I peeled back the tape and unrolled the paper. Inside were glassine bags stamped with "7K" and a gold crown.

Jones and Baker took a step back.

"Be careful with that shit," Baker said.

"I know," I replied. "We have Kings' Gold."

"Don't touch it!" Essex yelled back.

"This guy was driving the wrong way on the highway?" Baker asked. "Big mistake for such a huge haul."

I'd thought the same thing. Serious drug dealers were usually more careful. "Baker, can you finish searching the car?"

"Sure thing."

I pressed the towel against my bleeding head with one hand and pulled out my phone with the other. I tapped the number for narcotics in my phone book.

"Gregg," she answered.

"Hey, it's Nyx. I'm on fifty, eastbound just before Clear Creek. You won't believe what I've got in front of me."

"Try me."

"One of the Kings and a huge bag of Kings' Gold."

"Are you kidding?"

"No, I'm not."

"Shit. I'm close. Be right there."

"Cash," Jones announced, laying a roll of money on the car's roof.

Baker let out a low whistle. "Damn. Thick wad."

"Got a name!" Essex called. He held up a driver's license. "You won't believe it."

We all looked over.

"Lucas Costa, thirty-one, of Las Vegas."

My stomach clenched. *Lucas Costa.* The man we were *all* looking for, on both sides of the Boundary. Costa didn't wind up on this highway by accident; Orion brought him here.

"Nicely done," I whispered if Orion was listening.

A cold, invisible hand lighted on the back of my neck.

I walked over to the man in handcuffs. "You're Norina Grumley's boyfriend."

"I don't know that bitch," Costa growled.

"Mmm-hmm."

"He says he borrowed the car from a friend," Essex added.

"Did you *borrow* the gun too?" I asked.

Costa glared at me.

I walked back to Essex's SUV to get the weapon. Of course its serial number had been filed off. I put it with everything else on the hood of the sedan.

An ambulance with red lights flashing pulled up beside us. "What have you got?" Dani Lunn asked, pulling on gloves as she got out of the passenger's side. She stopped when she saw me. "Jesus, Nyx."

"Hi, Dani."

"What the hell happened to you?" She looked over her shoulder as she approached. "Bring my bag!"

"It's OK. Just split some staples. We've got a bloody nose over there for you to check too."

She looked over at Costa, then flashed me a smile as she checked my head. "You have something to do with that?"

Baker smirked. "Oh, he deserved it."

"No doubt." Dani's face sobered. "Nyx, I can't fix this here. You have to go to the ER."

I groaned.

"Sorry. You want to ride with us? I don't recommend driving."

"I'm not driving. I'm already on light duty, riding with Essex."

"Light duty, right." She laughed as she pressed a wad of gauze to my head. "Hold this here. How's your head feel?"

"It hurts."

"Any spots in your vision or dizziness?"

"Nothing like that. I don't think he hit me hard enough for another concussion. Just in the right spot to split open the gash."

"Better be glad."

While Dani wrapped my head in gauze, her partner went over to where Costa was now sitting behind his car. The male paramedic examined Costa's bloody face. When he finally rejoined us, he shook his head as he pulled off his gloves. "It's broken."

"Damn it." I clenched my jaw and sucked in an angry breath. "I should have kneed him in the nuts. That wouldn't have required a hospital visit."

"What'd he do?" Dani asked.

"Tried to choke me."

"Then he's lucky he didn't get worse."

Essex walked over.

"You've got two who need to go to the hospital, Sarge," Dani said.

"Thanks, Dani." His eyes flashed toward me. "She OK?"

"Staples have to be redone, but yeah. She'll be fine. Want us to take anybody?"

"Better let us." Essex looked back at Costa. "He's a fighter. Nyx, you want a flashy ride to the hospital?"

"God, no. No offense, Dani."

She smiled. "You guys stay safe."

"Thank you," I said.

An SUV flashed its lights as it pulled up behind my car. "Gregg," Essex said as he took Costa to his SUV.

Sergeant Gregg got out of the driver's seat, carrying a black backpack. "What the hell happened out here?"

"What do you think the odds are that we found a King with a back seat full of hypnox heroin, driving the wrong way down the highway?" Essex asked.

"The wrong way?"

"Yeah. Like he wanted to get caught," Essex said.

Gregg looked at me. "You OK?"

"It's just blood. The drugs are on the hood." I led her toward Costa's car.

Gregg pulled on a pair of rubber gloves. She shook her head in disbelief when she saw it. "What are the odds, indeed."

She put on a paper mask and pulled an extra-large, double-seal evidence bag out of her backpack. The guys and I kept a safe distance while she put the heroin into it.

"Costa's got warrants out of Vegas and Reno. Assault and a couple of FTAs," Essex said, standing beside me.

"Think he's here hiding out?" I asked, watching Costa snarling through his mesh hood sitting at Baker's feet.

"Maybe."

"Or maybe he's permanently relocated with so many of his other buddies," Gregg said as she sealed the bag. "I'm going to put a rush on this at the lab, but I'm sure it's the same shit. Nicely done." She smiled at me. "Two huge arrests and it's only Tuesday? It's like she's going for a big promotion or something."

I laughed and shook my head.

"You in on that pot too, Gregg?" Baker asked.

"Fifty bucks on Nyx." Gregg smiled and carried the drugs to her car. "I'll probably see you guys back at the station."

"We have to stop at the ER first," Essex said as we followed her.

Gregg looked around to see who was in earshot and lowered

her voice. "You were right about your mother. She said she didn't know anything about hypnox. It was a total waste of time."

"Hate to say I told you so," I said.

"You did. She's a real piece of work."

"I know. I'm sorry."

"Not your fault. You're nothing alike."

My nerves calmed. "Thanks."

Gregg got in her driver's seat. "Good luck with the head, Nyx."

I waved to her. Then Essex and I returned to our team. "Thanks for getting here so fast," I said to Baker.

"Shit. I came to make sure the perp wasn't dead." He winked.

"Jonesy, you want your towel back?" I offered it to him. It was soaked in red.

"I don't know. Will some of your luck rub off on me if I take it?"

"Only if you wrap it around your waist and wear it like a skirt," Baker said.

Jones opened his car door. "Hell, it'd be worth a shot."

"We'll see you guys later," Essex said, pulling Costa back up to his feet. "Thanks for backing us up."

"No prob. Try to leave some bad guys for the rest of us," Baker said, getting in his car.

When we reached the emergency room, Celise took one look at Costa's face and grinned at me. "Wonder how this happened."

"He went for her throat," Essex said, clearly not appreciating the joke.

"Then I guess he's lucky he isn't dead." Celise opened the electric doors behind her. "You bust open your stitches?"

"The staples," I said.

She led us to the open emergency room. "Nyx, over here.

Sarge, put the big guy in here." She pulled the curtain closed between Costa's bed and mine. I pushed it back to the wall before sitting on the bed.

Essex cuffed both of Costa's arms to the bed rails. "Be careful. He's a spitter."

"I'd better grab a face shield." Celise stopped on her way out. "Do you still see Dr. Pratts?"

"Yeah. Why?"

Celise jerked her head to the side. "She's here with a patient."

"Shit." My personal phone rang. It was the station. "Thanks for the heads-up."

She winked and left the cubicle.

I put the phone to my ear. "This is Nyx."

"Hey, it's McCormick. You bringing in one of the Kings?" Rick McCormick worked gang division.

"As soon as we get him cleared from the hospital. I broke his nose when he got handsy."

"Good. How long before you're at the station?"

I looked at my watch. "I dunno. An hour or two maybe."

"All right. I'll head that way soon."

"It's not too late?"

"Can't risk him bonding out before morning. Let me know if something changes."

"Will do."

Dr. Pratts walked around the corner and froze when she saw me. Her face melted into a frown as she crossed the tile floor. "Corporal Nyx, what don't you understand about light duty? I said no fights."

I pointed at Costa. "This one's not my fault."

"It never is." She put on a pair of rubber gloves. "What happened?"

"He headbutted me," I said. "Dani looked at it on scene. Said the staples busted open."

She carefully unwrapped my head. "Have you ever heard of second-impact syndrome?"

"No," I lied.

"Well, it can kill you. Second concussions are serious. Deadly serious. Hence"—she looked me square in the face—"the light-duty order."

"I'm sorry."

"Not as sorry as you're gonna be when you're on a medical vacation for the next couple of weeks."

"You're kidding?"

She scowled as she dropped the bloody bandages into the red hazmat bin. "Do I look like I'm kidding?"

Essex was fighting a grin.

The doctor shined a penlight in my eyes. "Any problems with your vision or dizziness?"

"No."

"Any numbness or tingling in your limbs?"

"No."

She leveled her gaze at me. "Are you telling me the truth?"

"Yes." I held up my pinky finger. "I swear."

"I'm ordering another head CT to be safe."

"That really isn't necessary—"

She held up a finger to cut me off. "You don't get an opinion."

Essex snickered as my doctor slammed her dirty gloves into the bin with more force than necessary before stalking out of the room.

The ER doctor fixed Costa's nose, and Essex took him to jail while I waited for my head to be restapled. Essex returned an hour later to pick me up. "You still in the doghouse?" he asked as I dragged myself from the gurney.

With a groan, I handed him my paperwork. In bright red ink the doctor had written, *No return to work until staples removed.* "I'm going to have to find another emergency room. Bye, Celise!" I called to the nurse's station.

"See you later, Nyx," she replied with a chuckle.

Essex held the door for me. "How's it feel?"

"Thankfully, not as bad as the first time."

"What did the CT show?"

I tapped my temple. "All cobwebs and dust, if you believe Dr. Pratts."

As we walked out, the television in the waiting room caught my attention. Our courthouse was on the news. I stopped. "What's going on downtown?"

"It's a replay. While you were getting patched up, there was an impromptu press conference. Apparently, Shooter Stone flew into town and led a march on the courthouse, demanding justice for his son."

Mayor Hector Navarro was at the podium, and Shooter Stone stood beside him. Shooter wore dark sunglasses with the brim of his worn-out cowboy hat pulled low to meet them. His gray beard brushed his barrel chest, clad in a bright red shirt with a snakeskin vest.

Navarro had heavy bags under his eyes. "Our detectives have found a strong suspect lead in the past twenty-four hours, based on another incident in the area, which occurred within minutes of the explosion. I'd like to invite District Attorney Harrison Birch to brief you on how this lead came together and on the next steps in our investigation."

I looked at Essex. "There's a lead?"

He lifted his shoulders.

Harrison Birch was visibly shaking. He cleared his throat at the microphone, sending a shrill wave of feedback through the speaker. "Good evening. I, too, would like to extend my deepest sympathies to the Stone family"—he turned toward Shooter —"and the Stevens family. I would like to announce that dental records confirmed today the identity of the third victim as Calvin Fleming, age twenty-five, of Sapphire Lake."

This wasn't news to me, but a small squeak still erupted from my throat.

"Also . . ." Birch swallowed. "We have a suspect in custody."

The crowd erupted into thunderous applause.

"The suspect we have apprehended was in the area, with motive and opportunity to commit these heinous acts. Charges and more information are forthcoming, and we appreciate the patience and support of the—"

The crowd shouted over him. "Let him burn!" "We want a name!" "Justice for Ryder!"

Birch shouted into the microphone. "We appreciate the patience and support of the community as we move forward with the investigation."

The scene cut back to Marianne Clarke, who was still reporting live from the courthouse. Most of the crowd had dispersed.

"That's it? What the hell?" I looked at Essex. "Who's the suspect?"

"No idea. They haven't told us anything yet."

"That's weird."

"I think so too."

As we walked outside, I looked at my phone. "This message makes more sense now." I showed him the text I'd gotten from Paps while waiting for my staples. *GET ME AN AUTOGRAPH!!!*

"That's funny."

Across the lot, Essex had backed into a space near a row of hemlocks. He walked all the way around his car to open the passenger-side door for me. My first instinct was to bristle at the chivalry, but I didn't. When I walked past him, he palmed my stomach to stop me.

"No argument this time?" he asked with a smile.

"Argument about what?"

"My driving you home."

"Not this time."

He looked carefully around, then closed the space between us. "You were done a lot sooner than I expected. I told Baker I wouldn't be back on the road for another couple of hours."

My heart thumped against my body armor. "What did you have in mind?"

He lowered his voice. "Absolutely nothing honorable."

A zing of excitement fluttered through me. "Let's go."

CHAPTER TWENTY-TWO

*D*elicious excitement was pulsing through me when we pulled up to my building and found a large, blacked-out SUV waiting in front of my garage. Only one vehicle like it existed in Sapphire Lake.

"What the hell is Magnus doing here?" Essex asked, shifting to park at the end of the driveway.

"I have no idea."

The chief got out and walked to his back bumper. The brass on his chest and the silver flecks in his hair reflected the moonlight. "Corporal Nyx," he said with a polite nod when I opened the passenger door.

"Hello, Chief. This is a surprise," I said, grabbing my backpack and closing the door behind me.

Essex got out too. "Chief."

"Good evening, Sergeant. Nyx, I heard about your ordeal tonight. Everything OK?"

"Had to have my head stapled again, but I'm fine. Unfortunately, I'll be out of work for a while. Essex has the paperwork."

"Well, we hate to lose you, even temporarily, but I want you back at a hundred percent. Not a day sooner."

"Yes, sir."

"Sergeant, are you on duty tonight?" Magnus asked.

Essex looked caught. "Uh, yes, sir. Reporting in as soon as I run home to let out my dog. Baker's covering the shift."

"Excellent. If you'll excuse us, I have business with Corporal Nyx."

I looked at Essex. His mouth opened, but no sound came out. The chief just stared at him. Finally, Essex gave a curt nod. "That's fine. You have a good night."

Every instinct in me wanted to ask him to stay, but there was no way in hell I could do that in front of the chief. The *chief*. What was he doing here?

Essex backed out onto the street, and Chief Magnus cleared his throat. It was then, I realized I was staring at my boss as he left.

I turned back around.

"I'm sorry to show up unannounced like this, Corporal."

I gestured toward the condo. "Would you like to come inside?"

"No, thank you. What I have to say won't take long. Gregg questioned Malena Nyx today. She wasn't very helpful."

"I heard. I'm not surprised, sir. And I apologize on behalf of my whole gene pool."

Magnus smiled. "No need. There are a few bad apples on my family tree as well. "

This small talk was nothing but awkward procrastination. A filler until he worked up the nerve to tell me what he really wanted.

"Chief, why are you here?"

He crossed his arms and walked toward me. A foot away, he stopped and stared over my shoulder. "An email is going out tomorrow morning with official word, but I wanted you to hear it from me." He met my eyes. "We're giving the narcotics position to Morris."

It was like a punch to the gut.

"And it was my call," he added.

Well, damn.

"Have I done something to—"

"No, no, which is why I'm telling you in person. Nyx, I denied you the position because I need you in investigations."

Um . . . what?

"With all due respect, sir, I have zero interest in becoming a detective. I thought I made my goals crystal clear in our final interview."

"You did, but my job as chief is to make the best use of our resources. And I know the best fit for all of us is with you doing investigations."

My head ached. I couldn't make sense of what my ears were hearing. "Why?"

"Because I knew your father."

My head snapped back so quickly it made me dizzy. "Excuse me?"

"I knew Elias Nyx. I knew what he could do, and I know what you can do now that he's dead."

I really needed to sit down. "How?"

"I was on the force when your father was arrested. I met with him several times after his conviction."

My brain scrambled. I'd never been confronted by anyone in law enforcement who *really* knew about Elias.

"I know you can see things the rest of us can't, and right now, this whole city needs the kind of help only you can give."

"Who else knows about me?" I asked.

"I haven't told a soul. Have you?"

I shook my head.

"Good. Others might take advantage of your ability."

He certainly sounded like Elias. The back of my neck prickled.

Chief Magnus stepped closer. "We need you in investigations,

Nyx. I can make it so you report directly to me, and no one else has to know about what you can do. You'll never have to worry about explaining yourself to anyone."

I backed up. "I'll consider it, but I can't give you an answer tonight." I started past him toward my building.

He grabbed my wrist. "If you won't do it for me, maybe you'll do it for Teek Fleming."

I wrenched my arm free. "What?"

"Tomorrow, the DA is charging Teek with the murders of his brother, Ryder Stone, and Stone's girlfriend."

"That's ridiculous. With what evidence?"

"Both Fleming brothers have records as long as my arm—"

"Teek's been clean for the past two years."

"Irrelevant. They're going to say it was a drug deal gone bad. That Fleming killed them, then rigged the place to blow up and destroy the evidence. They'll say he ran on foot and held up the convenience store as part of his getaway."

"No one will ever believe it."

"Not anyone who personally knows Teek, but none of them would make his jury. And they have the surveillance tape of Fleming robbing the Mini Market at gunpoint."

"It was a zucchini!"

"It doesn't look like it on tape. It's quite damning."

I grasped my aching skull and paced the driveway, staring up at the stars.

Chief watched me. "There's a lot of pressure from the media to make an arrest, so they're going to hang this on someone. And you and I both know they won't come up with another suspect."

I dropped my arms and faced him. "How do you and I both know that?"

"Because a nightwalker killed those people, and whoever set that chalet on fire did us all a favor."

I pinched the bridge of my nose. "I'll talk to Birch. Surely, he'll need my testimony since I was Teek's arresting officer the night of the fire."

"That's all well and good, but don't be surprised if that raises more questions. There was some talk about why the video feed was missing from your car when you transported him to jail."

My mouth gaped. "Do they think I did it on purpose?"

"No. After speaking to Sergeant Essex, I vouched for you and told them it could only be a system malfunction."

Part of me wanted to thank him, but the other part sensed manipulation in even his protection.

"Was it a malfunction?" he asked.

"No. It was Elias. He could mess with electronics when he was detached. Where is Teek now?" I asked, anxious to change the subject.

"Locked up."

"He's already been charged?"

"The judge ordered a psych evaluation. He's at Sterling Heights."

Sterling Frights, Teek had called it.

"That's bullshit!" My voice was louder than I intended, but the pressure rising inside me had to vent somewhere, so it came out my mouth.

A neighbor turned on their bedroom light.

The chief spoke quietly. "Tell me about it. But this is all the more reason we need someone like you. Even if we aren't able to save Teek, innocent people go to prison or are killed every day. You can help me put the right ones behind bars."

The chief's words sounded good, but unease burned in the back of my mind.

Elias's warning: "You must be vigilant."

Orion's too: "Watch your back."

I wondered if Orion was here, watching, now. My mind shifted to the shadow blade strapped to my leg.

"What if I refuse?" I asked.

"Then I'll be forced to make a tough decision. I'm not sure how you can continue on with the department."

"Why? I've done nothing wrong."

"No, but I can't *unknow* what you are, which will be problematic anytime you get caught up in a serious case that goes to court." He gave me a knowing look. "I'll never be able to truthfully defend you from the Norina Grumley cases of this world. Was Orion your so-called CI?"

My heart fell. "Elias told me Orion found her."

Magnus nodded. "That's going to be a problem in the future. You know as well as I do, plausible deniability can be everything in the chain of command."

In other words, if I screwed up somehow, he'd never be able to claim ignorance of my activities.

"If you worked *with* me, we could take measures to ensure the information you gather is admissible in court. You could be a real asset to our department and the whole city."

A knot rose in my throat.

"Think about it, Nyx." Chief Magnus walked to his SUV and opened the driver's door. "You know how to reach me."

When he was gone, I took the steps two at a time up to my condo. I went inside and locked the door, then dialed Essex's phone number.

He didn't answer.

Swearing under my breath, I unbuckled my weapons belt as I walked to the bedroom. I changed quickly into a pair of black leggings with a built-in holster, a tank top, and a button-up gray-and-black flannel.

I swapped my duty weapon for my compact 9mm and replaced the blade on my right calf. After I cleaned the blood off my face and neck, I grabbed the Boundary go bag, a jacket, and the keys to my Jeep.

CHAPTER TWENTY-THREE

I called Essex again on the drive. Still no answer.

What the hell?

Was he mad at me over Magnus?

When I pulled into his driveway, I parked behind his SUV and got out. At the front door, I started to knock and realized it was cracked open. I stepped back and looked around again. Nothing seemed amiss. His personal truck was in its spot, and a light was on in the living room.

Panic crept up my spine as I pushed it open. "Sarge?"

Dark-red blood was smeared across the tiles. I ripped my gun from the back of my hip and pushed the door all the way open. A blood trail, dotted with paw prints, stretched from the laundry room to the sofa, down the hall, and around the kitchen island.

"Essex!" I screamed, not seeing his body or Karma's in the carnage. My heart pounding, I tiptoed into the room and around the blood as best I could, but it was *everywhere.*

That was when the smell hit me.

Paint.

Kneeling down, I touched my fingers to a red puddle, then breathed a *huge* sigh of relief. "Oh my god."

There was a crash down the hall, followed by swearing. "Stop it now!" Essex yelled over a lot of sloshing.

I tiptoed my way across the living room. "Essex?" I called.

"In the bathroom!"

Exhaling the breath I'd been holding, I sidestepped down the hallway to the bathroom. I peeked inside, keeping my face toward the hallway . . .

Wait.

I lowered my gun.

"Lass das sein!" Essex yelled at Karma, wrestling the dog back into the tub. The walls that had once been white were splattered with red.

"What happened?" I asked.

He looked back; his face matched the walls. "Oh, good, you have a gun."

"Are you all right?"

"It's paint."

I bit down on the insides of my lips to keep from laughing.

"I was going to paint the dog door to match the trim of the house. Guess who knocked the can over while I was at work?"

A snicker escaped, and I covered my mouth. "I thought someone was dead."

"Not *yet*." He was holding Karma by the collar with one hand and spraying him with the detachable shower head with the other. The dog kept fighting to get out of the tub.

Essex had stripped down to his white T-shirt, but he still wore his black work pants. I pulled off my jacket and flannel and carried them with my gun to his bedroom. Even the comforter was slathered with red paint. Laughing, I put my stuff on the bed and pulled off my boots before returning to help.

In the bathroom, I tugged up my pants legs and held onto Essex's shoulder as I stepped over him into the tub.

"What are you doing?" he asked.

"I'll hold him still. You wash." I grabbed Karma's collar and straddled his back as my free hand stroked his chest. "Good boy, calm down. The torture will be over soon."

Essex sprayed us both with warm water. Then he laughed and shook his head. "I was searching for bodies when I found the paint can in the laundry room."

"I was too when you yelled." We both laughed really hard. I looked at the red covering my hand. "Think it could be toxic to dogs?"

"I called the vet when I realized it wasn't a homicide. They said it should be fine, and the knucklehead doesn't seem to have eaten any. Maybe sniffed it a little bit." Essex tapped Karma on his red nose.

"What are you going to do about the house?"

"I dunno. Burn it down?"

I laughed again.

He lathered Karma's body with shampoo. "What did the chief want?"

"The DA is charging Teek with the murders and the fire."

"What?"

"You heard me."

"But Teek wasn't there."

"I know. So does everyone else. They even have the gas-station video footage proving he wasn't."

"I wouldn't lose too much sleep over it. There's no way those charges will stick."

"I don't know. Magnus seemed pretty worried about it."

"Why did he come to your house to tell you?" He hosed Karma down again, soaking my pants as he washed off the pink suds.

"He also came to tell me Morris is getting the narcotics position."

Essex stopped spraying. "That's ridiculous. Everyone knew you were going to get it."

"Apparently, not everyone. He wants me in investigations."

"Not a bad move. Did he say why?"

"Yes. I need to talk to you about that."

"That sounds ominous."

"I need to talk to you about a lot of things."

He held my gaze until Karma squirmed to get free of my legs. "Let's get him out of here." He reached for a towel on the rack behind him, and I cloaked the dog with it. Essex examined his paws as he dried them. He showed me one. Still red.

I smiled. "I hope you like that color."

"Right?" He got up. His T-shirt was ruined. "I'm going to grab him and carry him to the backyard." He handed me another clean towel. "On the count of three? One . . . two . . . three."

I lifted my outside leg over Karma's back, and like a rodeo bull being released from its pen, the dog scrambled out of the tub. I caught myself against the wall to keep from falling. Before Essex could grab him, Karma shook out his brown coat, showering us with bathwater.

Essex lifted him off the floor. "Be right back."

I was completely soaked. I dried off with a towel and stepped carefully onto the paint-speckled floor, then I tried to sop up as much of the mess as possible. It was pointless. The entire room looked like a speckled egg, and the paint was there to stay.

As I pulled down my wet ponytail, I heard Essex swearing in the kitchen. I hung the towel on the rack and joined him. He put the open paint can into a bag then washed his hands at the sink. "What a mess."

"What are you going to do about work?"

"Baker's covering for me. Right before I wrestled Karma into the tub I sent a photo to the lieutenant and to the group chat. Enough said."

"In that case . . ." I retrieved two beers from the fridge, twisted the top off one, and handed it to him. "Here."

He sighed, looking around at the disaster. "Thanks."

There were even paw prints on the coffee table. "Seriously, what are you going to do?" I asked.

He tilted his beer toward the living room. "Buy a new couch and repaint the walls." He looked at the floor. "I'll pick up some paint thinner in the morning and try to save the tiles."

I grimaced. "You should replace the tiles. You should have replaced them years ago."

"What's wrong with the tiles? They match the rest of the place."

"Exactly." I took another swig of beer. "There is a reason you're still single."

A grin crept across his face. "You think the tiles are why I'm still single?" He came over and stood in front of me.

I used my bottleneck to gesture around the room. "I'm saying it's the whole damn package."

Laughing softly, he closed the gap between us. I backed up until my tailbone connected with the Formica countertop. He came even closer, shooting my heart rate through the stratosphere.

He took my beer bottle and his and put them on the counter behind me. "This shitty house"—he pressed his body against mine—"has nothing to do with me being alone."

"No?"

His arms slid around me, and he slowly shook his head. "No."

When he touched his lips to mine, the rest of the world went away, and his damp warmth against my cold, wet clothes sent a chill through me. I shuddered with excitement in his arms as he parted my lips and dragged his tongue across mine.

He smiled against my mouth. "Cold?"

"Not even a little bit."

"You're wet."

I dug my fingertips into his hips. "And you are doing nothing to help that."

A quiet growl rumbled deep in his chest, and he grasped the

hem of my tank top. As he peeled it up and away from my skin, I stopped his hands. "We need to talk first."

He bent so we were nose-to-nose. "If you wanted to talk, we should have done that before all the blood vacated my brain. Right now, all I care about is being inside you."

Smiling, I bit my lower lip.

"There is nothing you can say that will make me want you any less. If I'm wrong, you have my full blessing to say I told you so."

"What about work tonight?"

He glanced around the room. "If this mess doesn't qualify for an emergency night off, I don't know what could."

I laughed and bit my lower lip.

His eyes fell to my mouth. "Anything else? Because I've waited *years* to fuck you, woman. I don't plan on stopping once I get started."

I took a deep breath and blew it out slowly.

He cupped my chin and dragged my lower lip down with his thumb. "You nervous?"

"It's been a while."

"Want me to be gentle?"

"What the hell do you think?" Keeping my eyes locked on his, I lifted my foot and reached for the ergane holster on my calf. His gaze fell to my hands as I unsheathed the dagger and carefully and slowly trailed its deadly tip up the center of his chest.

Near the base of his throat, his breath hitched as I slipped the blade through the thin fabric of his T-shirt. He didn't exhale again until I sliced through the collar and put the dagger safely away.

"Holy shit." He panted.

Stretching onto my toes, I kissed him. While my lips worked his, I grabbed each side of the slit in his shirt and pulled the fabric apart. I pushed the sleeves back off his shoulders, trapping his arms behind him as I kissed a path down his throat.

"Fuck, Nyx." His rough voice was barely above a whisper. He pulled his arms free from the shirt and grabbed my waist. Taking a step back, he hooked both index fingers around the spaghetti straps of my shirt.

Slowly, he pulled them down my arms, enjoying the unhurried exposure of my cold, wet skin. Only he didn't stop when the tank top was bunched around my waist. He gathered the fabric of my waistband and pushed the entire outfit down past my hips.

His hands cautiously slowed as he leaned for a closer look at the purple-and-red splotches from my accident. "Spectacular ass bruise indeed. Does it hurt?" He pressed an open-mouthed kiss to the sensitive flesh where my hip bone met my thigh.

I took a sharp, flustered breath. "I can't feel anything right now."

"Let's see if I can't change that."

My clothes bunched around my ankles. As I stepped free of them, he kissed the inside of my thigh. Then his tongue teased and tasted its way back up the length of my body. Stars twinkled around my dazed vision by the time he made it upright again.

There was no pause.

No hesitation.

His strong hands slid lightly over my bruised ass until they settled behind my thighs. When he lifted me, I wrapped my legs around his hips, and he carried me to his bed.

Sometime later, I awoke to a finger tracing the inked lines on the back of my shoulder that covered the jagged edges of my scars. Leaning over my back, Essex replaced his finger with his lips.

I moaned as his hand slid down my bare back. "How long have I been asleep?"

"Not long. I didn't mean to wake you, but when I came back

to bed, I couldn't keep my hands to myself." He kissed my shoulder again and smiled against my skin.

"You were up?"

"I had to take care of Karma. I put his bed in the other bedroom, since it's the only space in this whole house without paint."

I hugged the pillow and laughed.

Looking down the length of my body, he sighed. "I can't believe you're finally here." His warm hand drifted over my ass and dipped between my thighs. Then he took a deep breath, setting his jaw with determination before pulling the sheet up over me. "You wanted to talk."

I *really* didn't.

"Yeah." I turned onto my side, pulling the sheet up over my breasts as I sat up against the headboard. Essex bent his arm and propped his head up with his hand.

My pulse throbbed in my ears, and I took a deep breath.

His hand rested on my stomach. "Whatever it is, I'm not going anywhere."

We'll see.

"Would it help if I made an admission first?"

My brow rose.

"I talked to the chief and pushed you so hard for narcotics because I wanted you off patrol."

I blinked. "What?"

"I was determined to help you get what you wanted, but my motivation was purely selfish. I knew there was no way you and I would keep things platonic once I took over your shift, and this"—he gestured between us—"can't happen while we work together."

"So what are we going to do?"

"I've already talked to the third-shift sergeant with Washoe County. He's going to help me get on there. It won't be as a sergeant, but you and I will still be working the same hours."

"You would do that for me?"

"Of course I would." He covered my hand with his. "I can be a cop anywhere, but there's only one of you."

I sank down in the bed, resting my head against the headboard as I closed my eyes.

"What's the matter? Did I say something wrong?"

I slipped my fingers between his. "No. You said everything right." Too bad nothing about his admission made mine any easier.

"Then what is it?"

How the hell do I even begin? "How long have we known each other?"

He didn't even have to think about it. "Two years, nine months, and a few days." My face must have shown my surprise because he laughed. "We met around Christmas. The math isn't that hard."

"OK. In that time, we've gotten to know each other pretty well, right?" I asked.

"Yes." He moved his hand down to my thigh and squeezed. "And even better in the past couple of hours."

"Focus, please. This is serious."

He bit down on the insides of his lips to rein in his smile. "Sorry. Serious."

"Is it safe to say you believe me to be an honest and level-headed person?"

"Absolutely."

"Please remember that with what I'm about to tell you."

He laughed. "Enough with the suspense already."

"I am the direct descendant of the Goddess of Night, Nyx."

Essex stared at me, his jaw slack.

"My father was before me, and since he died, I inherited the power that comes with our bloodline. When I sleep, my spirit can detach. I can leave my body and roam around."

I expected laughter. Or a snarky comment. Instead, without

remark, Essex lay on his back, draped his arm across his forehead, and stared at the ceiling.

I scooted toward him and put my hand on his chest. "I'm not crazy."

"I know," he said, easing the panic in my heart.

"You asked the other night why I knew so much about the hypnox case. I know because my father created hypnox."

He looked at me. "What?"

"He didn't do it on purpose. Hypnox grows where magic like mine, when I'm out of my body, has spilled on the ground. Elias was stabbed, and the poison from the wound is what made him so sick."

"Who stabbed him?"

"I don't know, but I could be in danger too. For now, we must find that plant, or a lot more people will die." Perhaps the whole world as we knew it, if the gods had their way.

"You don't know where it is?"

"No, but once it's found, it must be destroyed."

"Destroyed how?"

"Fire is the only way."

"It's that serious?"

I nodded. "The drug is every bit as powerful as narcotics warned us, but what they don't know is that it can cause a spirit to detach. Do you remember what Gregg told us about what happened to Norina Grumley when she was high on hypnox?"

"She said she left her body."

"Correct, and her vacant body created a doorway to another world. That's exactly what happened the night of the fire at the Drexler. The three victims weren't murdered by a human. They were killed by a nightwalker, a demon from a place called the Boundary. It used one of their vacant bodies like a portal to come here."

"Nightwalkers?" he asked, clearly unsure if he'd heard me correctly.

"Yes. And the more lives they take, the stronger they become. It's what killed my father in his prison cell."

"The thing that ripped him apart?"

"Exactly. They're combustible with sunlight, so he trapped it in that daylight cell to kill it. It's why I can't detach at night. They only come out in the dark."

"But there was no daylight at the Drexler."

"No, but there was fire."

"Who started it?"

"A guardian spirit from the Boundary who's also looking for the plant."

Essex let his eyes drift back to the ceiling, like he was trying to make sense of all the shit I'd just spewed from my mouth.

I touched his arm. "Please don't think I'm crazy."

"Never." He reached up and cradled my jaw. "It's a lot to take in, but I know you're not crazy, and I know you wouldn't lie to me."

The weight of everything lifted off me. Had I been a crier, I might have unleashed a river of tears. Instead, I collapsed over him, pressing my lips, and my naked body, against his.

He immediately responded, rolling on top of me and settling between my legs. After a deep and earnest kiss, he pulled back and rested his forehead against mine. "I don't suppose this guardian spirit could testify in court to get Teek set free?"

"Unfortunately not. Do you know what they could possibly have on him?"

Essex leaned onto his arm on the mattress. "Only the tape from the gas station as far as I know."

"What about the security footage from the Drexler? Surely they have cameras on those chalets."

"They do."

"Did you see the footage?"

"I saw it right after the fire. It clearly shows Ryder Stone, his girlfriend, and a person wearing a hood entering through the front door. That's where I stopped watching. I don't know what else is on it."

"If Teek didn't even enter the place, there's no way he could have committed the murders."

"That's true. They should also have the tapes from the main parking lot where Kush's car was found. I'll bet it shows Teek *leaving* the property."

"I wonder where those tapes wound up."

"The DA should have them. I hope they aren't locked in a drawer somewhere."

"Is Birch dirty?"

"Desperation can make anyone dirty. He's up for reelection this year."

"Stupid fucking politics." I looked toward the window. "In the morning, I might drop by Birch's office and see what I can find."

"After all the chaos of that press conference, you should probably call and make an appointment—" He stopped when he realized I was staring at him. "Oh. You mean . . ." He couldn't even say it aloud. "Who else knows you can do this?"

I dragged my fingertips down his neck. "I haven't trusted anyone but you enough to tell."

He pushed his hips into me, and he kissed me again. Before we got too carried away, I turned my face to add, "But my family knows, and Magnus knows."

"How the hell did Magnus find out?"

"No clue. It worries me though. Someone murdered my father. Until I know who, I'll have a hard time trusting anyone. What do you know about him?"

"I don't know him well, but he seems like a good guy. Although, come to think of it, he did approach me to talk about you. It wasn't the other way around."

"The goddess Nyx had several immortal children. One of her sons, Hypnos, fathered Icelus, the God of Nightmares. He could be responsible for all that's happening now. He created the nightwalkers, and they've been here in Nevada since my parents started messing with hypnox the last time."

"Where is this God of Nightmares?"

I lifted my shoulders. "I'm starting to worry the chief might know . . . or worse."

"You think it could be him?"

"All I know is everything I didn't want to be true has come to pass lately, so I'm not ruling out anything. He said if I don't take the job in investigations, he'll have to fire me."

"Why?" His question was *way* louder than necessary. "Seems like what you can do would be very valuable to the department in any capacity."

"He agrees with that much, but I guess my doing it in another role doesn't fit his plan of how to make the information I can come up with admissible in court."

"Huh. I can see how that could be problematic, but I can't believe he'd really fire you."

"I didn't imagine the conversation."

"I know. Want me to talk to him?"

"Why bother? It's not like you did any good the last time."

He tickled my side, and I laughed and caught his wrist. He turned over, pulling me on top of his hips, and my black hair fell into his face as I bent for a kiss. His hands gripped my thighs. I sat back up and gathered my hair over one shoulder.

"God, you're beautiful."

I scraped my nails down his bare chest. "Beautiful, even if a bit crazy?"

"I don't think you're crazy at all. I think you're perfect. I've *always* thought you were perfect."

I squeezed his torso between my knees. "Scars and all?"

"You know I think scars are sexy." His hand slid along my bumpy thigh. "How do we find the hypnox?"

I opened my mouth to answer, but before I could speak, he said, "Wait." He handed me the pillow he'd playfully hit me with, pressing it against my bare breasts. "I can't hear you with those things in my face."

I laughed and held the pillow against my chest. "We're getting closer. Orion is the reason Lucas Costa almost drove his car straight into us."

"Who's Orion?"

"The guardian from the Boundary. He's been helping me from *the other side.*"

Essex sat up on his elbows with sudden realization. "Is he the ghost?"

"Huh?"

"Is he the reason you were almost killed by the car?"

"Oh. Yes."

Anger flashed in his eyes.

"I punched him in the junk."

"You should've broken his neck."

One side of my face screwed up. "I'm not really sure that's possible."

"What did he do to Lucas Costa?"

"Spirits in the Boundary can animate bodies."

It was the most surprised Essex had looked during the whole confession.

"Elias could too. He did it all my life, randomly dropping in on me through my friends and coworkers, until I finally begged him to stop. He disabled my car cameras the night I took Teek to jail and used Teek's body to communicate with me."

"Damn. That explains a lot."

"I know."

"So this Orion guy drove Costa to us?"

I nodded.

"And you trust him more than the chief who signs your paychecks?"

"Honestly, I don't trust anyone at the moment."

His hands slid up to my hips. "Even me? Because given your compromising position right now, you seem pretty trusting."

I rocked forward against him, causing his head to roll back on the pillow with a soft moan. "*I'm* in a compromising position?"

He laughed softly. "Point taken. Damn, you feel amazing."

"Now, focus please. This is serious."

"Focus? Really?" He arched his hips between my legs. "You just sent all the blood rushing from my brain, and now you want me to pay attention?"

I felt the blood flow in question rising beneath me. I let the pillow fall to the mattress and bent to kiss him.

He broke the kiss and pushed my hair behind my good ear. "How can I help you?"

I rubbed my nose against his. "Not thinking I'm a lunatic is a damn good start."

"Look at me."

I pulled back to look at him.

His face was stone serious. "Saphera Nyx, you're the fiercest and bravest woman I've ever known. If you're a lunatic, it's only because you're here with a loser like me."

I kissed him again. With a smooth and fluid flip, I was beneath him. He slipped on another condom and pulled my knee along the side of his hip. Then his dark eyes locked on mine before he entered me.

My spine arched, and he kissed my throat, then my chin, then my lips again. "Tell me what you want, Nyx," he said in a deep, throaty whisper as he pushed deeper inside.

Then I did.

CHAPTER TWENTY-FOUR

*I*t was daylight outside when my spirit snapped free. Essex was asleep on his stomach with one arm under his pillow and the other across my naked back. His nose was nuzzled against my shoulder.

I hated to leave, but every second I spent warm in bed with Essex, Teek was spending in a padded jail cell at Sterling Frights.

The bedside clock said it was 8:47 a.m.

My go bag was on the floor. I jammed my fingers into its side pocket and pinched the ergane gloves between my fingertips. I pulled them out and slipped them on before quietly lifting the bag and swiping my dagger off the nightstand. I crept out of the bedroom and down the hall, taking care not to disturb Karma in the guest room.

I unzipped the bag in the kitchen and found the Boundary clothes and shoes Orion had brought me. As I pulled them out, I wondered what a man like Orion might pick out for me to wear. "This should be interesting."

I held up the pants first. They looked like plain black leggings. "Not bad," I said, slipping them on. Like the shoes, they molded to my legs, and they had pockets that were much roomier than those in any of my regular workout pants.

There was much less fabric to the shirt.

I put it on and rolled my eyes. It was a Lara-Croft style tank top that completely showed my stomach and fit like I'd been dipped into it. "Fucking men," I muttered, shoving my feet into the shoes.

Finally, I put on the oneiryte necklace and light stone. I uncorked the vial, poured a line on the floor, and closed my eyes. Concentrating hard, I pictured my driveway at home.

The floor disappeared beneath my foot when I stepped forward. A half second later, I was jolted to a stop when I collided with the asphalt in front of my garage.

I stumbled a few steps until I regained my balance. Then I looked around the building. On the stairs. Up on the roof. Down the street.

"Orion?" I called out.

Nothing.

I waited. Still nothing.

I guess I'm on my own.

With a deep breath, I opened the vial again and poured, this time picturing the courthouse. When I stepped, the falling journey was longer, but by only a fraction of a second.

My feet landed hard, and I collapsed to my knees in front of the courthouse's stone steps. Last night's press briefing had been right here. Swearing, I rolled onto my hip to inspect the damage. My kneecaps were pristine, but they felt like they'd been split open.

I limped as I stood.

"It's all in your mind, Nyx," I reminded myself as I hobbled up the steps.

The square was bustling with activity per usual for the morning rush hour. The press was still camped out front of the building, and several extra officers patrolled the area. The heavy wooden doors to the courthouse were roped off with a sign: "All visitors and staff, please use the office entrance through the parking garage."

I walked around the side of the building. Cars were rolling into the garage off Church Street, but entering that way meant immersing myself in a sea of office workers. I thought back to being metaphysically trampled at the Sizzling Chicken and shuddered.

Down the side of the building was a row of windows I'd never paid much attention to before. They were well off the ground, but thanks to the building's stone exterior, the walls appeared scalable.

I wiped my palms on my pants and shook my head. "I really hope no one can see this."

Stretching on my toes as far as I could reach, I stuck my fingers between the blocks. My foot narrowly fit on the lowest ledge made from the façade's ornate trim. Clinging tight with my fingers, I shimmied sideways across the wall, out over the hedges, and toward the first window. When I was directly beneath it, I slowly began to climb.

Every other row of blocks jutted out just enough to fit my inside arch.

Like Stallone in *Cliffhanger*, I passed the second row of blocks with shocking precision. The third was even easier. But when I reached for the fourth, my left foot slipped, and with a scream that certainly pierced the dimensions, I fell backward, shoulders-first, into the holly bushes.

The berries didn't even shake, but I felt the sharp thorns of the leaves slice through my skin as I plowed feet-over-head onto the ground. I landed hard on the grass and immediately checked my skin for blood.

There wasn't any.

I cursed again. Then I got up and instinctively brushed off leaves and dirt that *weren't* on me. "Whatever happened to flying in dreams?" I muttered as I walked off the invisible pain. "Why the hell isn't that a thing?"

Then like a lunatic, I tried the whole damn thing again.

For my second attempt, I didn't even make it past the second row of blocks before I crashed into the bushes. The pain was less —score one for my subconscious learning better—but this time, there was laughter.

I recognized the giggle and looked around for its source.

Flash was sitting cross-legged on top of a retaining wall. His elbows were balanced on his knees, his chin securely perched in his palms as he watched me.

"Where did you come from?" I shouted, though it really wasn't necessary.

"Macon, originally, but we moved to Savannah when I was—"

"Not where you were born. Where did you come from *right now*?" I searched the sky, wondering who else might be watching me.

"Orion sensed you were out and about." Flash pointed to the white crystal around my neck. "He sent me to find out why."

"A friend is in trouble."

"And you're helping this friend by falling off buildings?"

I cut my eyes at him. "Did you only show up to make fun of me?"

"Nope. This is entirely a bonus."

I would have flipped him off, but forty-seven or not, Flash was still a kid. "Can you please help me? I don't have much time."

With a huff, he pushed himself off the wall and walked over. "You haven't been inside before?"

Shit.

I looked at the building.

"You *have* been in there before. Why didn't you try your oneiryte, then?"

"I didn't think about it."

Flash shook his head sadly. "And Orion said you were a fast

learner."

"Hey!"

He offered his hand. "Come on. I'll go with you."

I took it.

"You know where you're going now?"

"I think so."

I'd been in the DA's office many times, but it had been a few weeks. Flash poured a line of sand on the ground, and I closed my eyes and pictured it as best I could recall. Mahogany furniture, lots of loaded bookshelves, a painting of Lake Tahoe on the wall . . .

"Any day now," Flash mumbled beside me.

"You're not helping."

"I'm just here for the show, lady."

I pressed my eyes closed harder and stepped. The ground dropped away, and we fell, landing hard inside the office.

Flash grabbed my arm as he toppled sideways. "Whoa! That was rough."

"I got us here, didn't I?" I asked, looking around the room.

"Miracles do happen."

"Oh, just hush." I dropped his hand and began to search the room. The office was empty, but the door was open, meaning Birch would be back.

"What are we doing here anyway?" Flash asked.

"I'm not exactly sure. I haven't had a whole lot of time to think this through."

"Surprise, surprise."

Putting the glove back on, I moved behind the desk and began trying drawer handles. The filing drawers were locked. So were the cabinets along the wall. I opened the pencil drawer and rummaged through it.

"What are you looking for?" Flash asked.

"Video storage."

"Like a VHS tape?"

My eyes narrowed before remembering that VHS had probably still been king when Flash was on Earth. "No. Like a flash drive or a—"

"A *me* drive?" His eyes bugged out.

I chuckled. "A flash drive. Like a little plastic and metal stick about this big." I held up my fingers a couple of inches apart.

"*Flash* drive; I like it."

I searched the high surfaces. Flash searched the lower ones.

I looked up above a row of thick law books and froze. "Shit." A green light on a security camera glowed from the bookshelf. It was exactly like the cameras I'd seen in the 7 Kings shop.

"What's the matter?" Flash asked.

"A camera."

"Want me to short it out?"

Voices echoed down the hallway. I recognized one of them as Birch.

"Someone's coming," I said, flattening my back against the wall.

"So? We're *invisible.*"

Birch and Mayor Navarro walked in. "You can't rush these things, Hector," Birch was saying as he carried file folders behind his desk.

I backed into the corner to listen.

Navarro closed the office door most of the way. "You need to find a way."

"I can't announce to the press that we're charging someone with murder until they've actually been charged with murder, and I can't do that without Judge Hill's signature. So if you want to hurry somebody, go visit his office."

The mayor pointed at Birch. "I'm checking into a houseboat on Lake Tahoe at this time tomorrow. I want the press off my front lawn before I leave."

I could have smacked him.

"I'm sure they will be. The announcement will be made as

soon as the paperwork comes across my desk."

"You don't leave here until it does. I don't care if it takes all night."

A muscle worked in Birch's jaw. "I won't, sir."

"What's taking so long? You assured me yesterday you had a conviction in the bag."

"We do have a conviction in the bag. It just takes time."

"You'd better be right, Birch, or both of us will be out of a job come November." Navarro stormed out, slamming the door behind him.

Birch leaned his elbows on the desk and cradled his head in his hands.

"What was that about?" Flash asked.

"My friend," I said quietly. "They were talking about—" *Wait.* I looked at the green light on the camera again.

They were *talking* about it.

"Bingo," I whispered.

"What are you thinking?" Flash asked, watching me.

I pointed to the camera. "I need *that* tape."

When Birch finally straightened, he stretched his neck and turned to his computer. I ran over and stood behind him.

He clicked on the password field.

"Flash, help me remember this. B-three-three-f-c-a-k-three."

Flash repeated it. "B-three-three-f-c-a-k-three."

With a quick look at the desktop, I saw the camera icon on the toolbar.

The phone beeped. "Birch?" a male voice asked over the speaker.

"Yes, Judge?"

"Can you come to my chambers?"

"Uh, yes, sir. Be right there." Birch pressed the sleep button, and the computer's screen went black. He hurried from the office, this time closing the door.

I quickly pulled on the ergane glove and tapped the keyboard to wake the computer. "What was that password?"

"B-three-three-f-c-a-k-three."

As I typed it in, I shook my head. "Beefcake."

"What?"

"The asshole's password is beefcake." I clicked on the camera icon. Then clicked "Export" in the menu. But export it to what? "We have to find a flash drive."

We began searching the office again.

Across the room, at a cabinet beneath the painting of the blue lake, Flash's arm shot into the air. "Is this a *me* drive?"

I looked. "Yes! Nicely done, Flashlight. Keep those investigative skills up, and Orion will have to make you a guardian."

He beamed.

I jammed the drive into the USB port and clicked "Download Seven-Day History" on the menu. An error message popped up. "Not enough storage."

Five-day. "Not enough storage."

Three-day. "Not enough storage."

Two-day. "Downloading . . ."

I turned and offered Flash a high five. He slapped my palm. "I just hope it turns up something."

"What did this guy do to your friend?"

"He's charging an innocent man with murder so everyone else can be less inconvenienced."

"So the guy in the suit can go to his houseboat?"

"Yep."

"That's mean."

"Yeah. Humans suck sometimes."

When the download hit 70 percent, the office door opened. Birch was on his cell phone. "Yes. I got the paperwork."

Shit.

I looked at the screen. 77 percent.

"That would be great, Marianne."

Marianne Clarke. I should've known.

"Sure. Press conference in"—he looked at his watch—"fifteen minutes?"

84 percent.

"Now, you know I can't promise exclusivity. News vans from all over have been parked all around the courthouse for days."

89 percent.

"Come on, come on, come on," I chanted. "Flash, get ready to take us home."

He unstoppered his oneiryte vial. "You got it, Nyx."

92 percent.

"I'll do my best. Thanks, Marianne. I owe you one."

94 percent.

Birch laughed. It was so fake. "You know I'm good for it."

Liar.

98 percent.

He walked toward the desk. "OK. I'll see you in a few minutes. Bye."

100 percent.

I grabbed the flash drive and slipped off the glove, enclosing the drive inside it. Then I took Flash's hand, and we channeled out of the office.

Flash was laughing when we appeared in front of my condo. "OK. That was fun. We're like Starsky and Hutch."

"More like Mulder and Scully."

"Who?" he asked.

"Never mind."

"What are you gonna do now?"

"Get back to my body." I pointed at my building. "I'm not here."

"Huh?"

"My body isn't here. I stayed at a friend's house last night."

"A sleepover?"

I grinned. "Sort of. When you see him, can you tell Orion I need to talk to him soon?"

"Sure." He looked up at me and smiled. "You're gonna be all right, Nyx."

"What do you mean?"

"You're gonna make a great scion."

I thought of the Water of Lethe inside my safe. "You know I might not be a scion forever."

He looked at me like I'd expected Essex to the night before—like I was crazy. "Why?"

"Because I want my old life back."

His brow pinched. "But you can go back to your old life anytime you want. It's not like you're stuck here."

Guilt rushed through me.

"That is true."

"Well, for what it's worth, I like you."

I smiled. "I like you too, Flash." I put a hand on his shoulder. "And I think you'll make an excellent guardian."

His chest puffed out. "Will you come to the ceremony if it happens?"

"There's a ceremony?"

"Yeah. Becoming a guardian is a *big* deal." He spread his arms wide.

I smiled. "Am I allowed to come?"

"Oh, yeah. It's in Synora, not Imera."

"Then I wouldn't miss it." I offered him a fist bump.

He just stared at it. "What are you doing?"

"It's kind of like how we give high fives these days."

"Oh!" He held up a fist. "Like this?"

I bumped my knuckles against his, and he giggled.

"I'll see you soon?"

"Yeah. Good luck with your friend."

"Thanks. I'm going to need it."

CHAPTER TWENTY-FIVE

The next time I awoke, I was alone and covered with two heavy blankets. On the pillow beside me was a sheet of torn notebook paper.

Gone to rid the city of paint thinner. Please don't leave before I come back. I'll bring food.

The clock on the nightstand said 2:48 p.m. It had been just after one when I'd hidden the ergane bag and flash drive in my backpack and had slipped back into my body. Essex was already gone, and I'd intended to get up and look for him then. Apparently, my body had other plans. With a satiated moan, I stretched my arms and legs across the bed. I hadn't slept that long or well in weeks.

Karma whimpered beside the bed. I sat up. "Morning, Picasso."

The dog's head fell to the side.

"Wanna go out?"

His tail wagged against the floor—the red-paw-printed floor.

"All right." I swung my legs off the bed and reached for the discarded white-and-red-streaked T-shirt beside the dog. It still smelled like Essex when I put it on.

There were zero bottoms anywhere. My clothes from the night before had been left in the kitchen. I grabbed my phone off the nightstand; Essex had plugged it in to charge.

"Come on, Karma," I said, forgetting the German command. He trotted beside me down the hallway, and I let him out the back door.

After going to the bathroom myself and giving my teeth a good scrub, I returned to the kitchen. Essex had made a pot of coffee. Bless him. I poured a cup and sat at the bar, as the stools were the only seats paint free.

There was one voicemail and eleven missed texts on my phone. Most were from the group chat. The newest one was from Bess. *Saw your car was gone. Just checking in.*

Another was from Paps. *DID YOU MEET SHOOTER???*

I messaged him back first. *Not this time, but I think he's still in town. I'll keep an autographing pen and paper handy.*

Then I messaged Bess. *All good. Be home later. Maybe.*

The group chat could wait. I checked my voicemail. "Good morning, Corporal Nyx. This is Warden McCain at the Nevada State Penitentiary. Please give me a call as soon as you're available. Thank you." He left a phone number.

I returned the call. "Warden McCain," he answered.

"Hello, Warden. It's Saphera Nyx. I'm sorry I missed your call earlier."

"Oh, hi, Corporal. I was calling to let you know that your father's autopsy was completed."

This should be good. "Anything turn up?"

"The medical examiner said Elias's injuries were consistent with a possible animal attack, but I assure you, no signs of an animal have been present in the prison and no—"

"Warden, you don't need to worry. My family won't be suing the prison."

There was a pause.

"I hope I don't come across as only caring about a lawsuit, Corporal."

"Not at all, sir."

"We all want to know what happened to your father."

I believed him. I also knew that wasn't possible. "Try not to lose too much sleep over it. My father was an eccentric man. I'm not surprised that his death would be unusual as well."

It was clear from the silence that Warden McCain was unsure how to digest that statement. After all, how could any sane person not at least be curious about what had happened in that cell?

"Well, the body has been released to be cremated. It's scheduled for this afternoon, if you'd like to come pick up his remains."

A lot had changed in the few days since I'd seen the warden, but I still had no desire to keep Elias—in any form—in my condo. "What will happen to him if I don't?"

"The ashes will be interred here in the prison cemetery."

"OK. That's fine with me."

"All right."

"Thanks for letting me know."

"You're welcome. If you change your mind, let me know."

"OK. Goodbye, Warden."

"Goodbye, Corporal."

When I ended the call, I stared at the screen for a moment. Elias really wasn't coming back. The corners of my eyes burned, but another message from the group chat popped up before any tears fell.

Legeiza: *Taking my day off to spend with the fam. You jokers be careful out there.*

Jones: *I'm in. Hell, can I come in now? LOL*

McCollum: *I'm out. I plan on getting 100% of my Vitamin Beer intake later today.*

Everly: *Count me in!*

Baker sent a photo of a wild-eyed man with the words, "Work overtime, they said. It'll be fun, they said."

Blinking hard a few times to dry my eyes, I scrolled back to the beginning of the messages I'd missed in the group chat. Baker, Jones, and Everly were working overtime. Rivera, per usual, was being a dick.

Rivera: *You're all a bunch of bitches. Don't you know we're off today?*

Baker: *OT, baby.*

Rivera: *Why? You saving up to buy a better personality?*

Baker sent a meme. It was a picture of the old lady from *Titanic* with the caption, "It's been 84 years since I worked a 40-hour workweek."

Essex: *Don't you assholes ever sleep?*

The time stamp on his message was two hours ago.

Jones: *On a cop's salary? You can afford to sleep when you're dead.*

Everly: *Welcome to night shift, Sarge.*

Rivera sent a picture of a skeleton behind the wheel of a patrol car, captioned, "A healthy work-life balance."

McCollum sent a news article that made my heart plummet again.

Suspect in the Death of Ryder Stone in Custody.

The front door opened and Essex walked in. In one hand he had a paint can. In the other was a to-go box from Sugar Pine Bakery, the best bakery on the planet. Originally from South Lake Tahoe, it was one of my favorite transplants to Sapphire Lake.

My eyes widened. "Is that what I think it is?"

He pushed the front door closed with his boot. "If you think it's cinnamon rolls for me and a bran muffin for you, then you're way more excited than you should be."

I scowled and put down my phone.

He leaned over for a kiss. An inch away from my mouth, he

paused. "I'm lying. It's two cinnamon rolls with extra cream cheese frosting."

"Sarge, you might never get rid of me."

He kissed me long and slow. "That *is* my plan."

I opened the box and took a deep and delicious inhale as he carried the paint to the counter by the sink. It clanged against the countertop when he set it down.

"What else did you buy?" I asked, pulling out a fat and gooey cinnamon roll. It was covered in fluffy white frosting so thick it could almost be measured with a snowfall gauge.

"The guy at the paint store said if anything will get the paint up, it's this stuff."

I stuck my finger into the heap of cream cheese frosting. "Does it contain a magic potion?"

"Hey, bigger miracles have happened to me in the past twenty-four hours." He opened the back door for Karma.

I offered Essex my finger, still loaded with frosting.

He smiled as he walked back to me. Then he bent and sucked the creamy goodness off my fingertip, scraping his teeth across my skin. "Mmm." He kissed me again, and his eyes fell to my bare legs. "You know what? Screw the floors. Screw breakfast. Let's just take that frosting back to bed."

I laughed and pinched off a hunk of the roll. "We can save some, but I need sustenance. I haven't worked out that hard all week."

"Hell, me either." He poured himself a cup of coffee and sat beside me.

I stuffed the bite into my mouth, and my eyes nearly rolled back into my head. "God, that's amazing."

He watched me lick my lips.

A text message lit up my phone's screen. I checked the screen to see if it was Ransom. It was Rivera. I ignored it, but Essex pulled his phone from his pocket.

"Does this group chat ever stop?" He showed me his screen. It was another meme from Rivera. This one had a picture of a cop and a dentist side by side with the caption, *"They all hate us until they need us."*

I laughed and almost sucked cinnamon roll down my wind-pipe. "OK. That's funny." I wiped my mouth. "And to answer your question, no. It never stops, it's rarely ever anything impor-tant, and it's often offensive."

"I've noticed."

"We're a good team though. If any of us are ever in trouble, everyone comes running."

"That's good to hear."

"Did they wake you this morning?" I asked.

"*You* did."

"Me?" I asked.

"Yeah. You were ice cold. I got up and loaded you down with blankets," he said.

"You could have stayed in bed and kept me warm."

"I definitely considered it." He picked up his roll. "Did you see the article McCollum sent?"

My shoulder's fell. "I saw it right as you were coming in, but I didn't read it. Does it name Teek?"

"No, but charges are coming faster than I thought." He took a bite, and his eyes closed in ecstasy. "Damn, that's good." He got up to get napkins and handed me one. "I made a call today."

"About what?"

"I got permission for us to visit Teek at Sterling Heights this afternoon if you want to go."

"Really? I'd love to go. He hates that place, and god knows, nobody but Gramma T will visit him."

"Figured you'd say that." He took another bite.

"It pisses me off that he's there. Even if he isn't all right upstairs, he doesn't deserve to be locked up in that awful place."

He wiped his mouth. "I know. I've been racking my brain all morning, trying to think of some way to clear him. The courthouse is on the way to Sterling Heights. We'll stop by and talk to Birch."

I couldn't look him in the eye. "I've already seen Birch today."

"You left while I was gone?" he asked without thinking.

"I left while you were still here."

"That's right." Essex looked like he was having a brain cramp. "You said you would." He put down his roll. "How'd it go?"

I told him everything Flash and I had overheard.

Essex shook his head. "Like you said last night, stupid fucking politics."

"That's not all."

His brow rose in question.

I got up and walked to my backpack on the other side of the island. Then I returned with the ergane bag and flash drive. I took it out and placed it in front of him. "Got a computer handy?"

"What's this?" he asked.

"I didn't have any luck finding the surveillance tapes from the Drexler, but I was able to download the video feed from Birch's office for the past two days."

"Damn," he said, impressed.

"If they were blabbering that much about it today, I guarantee there's been specific talk about Teek and what happened to those tapes."

"Only one problem," he said.

I knew it before he could say it. "I'll make some enemies if anyone knows I have it."

"Big enemies. You throw the mayor and the DA under the bus, and you won't have to worry about Magnus firing you."

"I know."

"What are you going to do?" He took another bite of cinnamon roll.

"Find out what's on the video and then decide. I can't let them keep an innocent man in jail for the sake of my job."

"I agree, but"—Essex licked some icing off his thumb—"as the arresting officer, you still should talk to Birch before you call him out. He should hear your opinion of Teek, and he might listen to it."

"I don't think Magnus wants me to talk to Birch."

"Why not?"

"I don't know, but he brought up the missing video feed from my car. He made it a point to tell me he had defended me, kinda like he was holding it over my head."

"You really don't trust him, do you?"

"Without all this shit, I don't know the guy enough to trust him. And if he is Icelus, then he's even worse a villain than I ever accused my father of being."

"That's a big statement. You think he could be that bad?"

"I hope I'm wrong, but something is off with that guy."

"He would have a cool supervillain name if it was him. *Magnus*," he said dramatically.

With a laugh, I pushed the box and what was left of my pastry toward him. "I'm hoping Orion can check him out."

"What do you know about this Orion guy?"

"Not much, but he's been helping me, so I think he's on the right side of all this."

"Could he be building your trust to burn you later?"

"Possibly, but if he wanted to kill me, he's had a few chances to."

Essex scowled. "Like with the car."

"Yes, but I wasn't detached when that happened, so it wouldn't have done him any good. Only the blood of my spirit is valuable."

"Valuable how?"

"Orion says if a fallen god drinks my blood, they'll be immortal again."

"Where did he learn that?"

"Imera, I guess."

"Huh?"

"Imera. It's where all detached human souls go to live."

His head pulled way back. "There are more of them?"

"Apparently, a lot more."

"What's it like?"

I shrugged. "No idea. I'm not allowed to go there."

His eyebrows pulled together. "So some strange ghost-man has appeared in your life out of the blue, from a place you're not allowed to visit, and you're convinced he's not a suspect?"

"I'm not saying he isn't a suspect, but I don't think it's him. He gave me the blade to protect myself."

"The blade on my nightstand?"

"Yeah. It's a poisoned magical dagger."

"You mean, the dagger you held at *my throat* last night?"

I bit down on the insides of my lips.

"Wow." He shook his head in disbelief. "It's a good thing you're hot, Nyx."

I turned toward him on my stool, letting my knees drift apart. With a smile, I leaned toward his ear and lowered my voice. "You didn't seem to mind so much last night."

His eyes fell to my bare thighs, or maybe to his shirttail barely covering the space between them. After a second, he jerked his head up and laughed. "Woman, do you want me to help figure this out or what?"

"Feeling flustered, Essex?"

He ignored my teasing. "We've learned talk like that is not the way to make my brain function at its best." He held up what was left of my cinnamon roll. "Pastries are the key." He took another big bite.

"Or tacos."

"Or tacos," he said around the food in his mouth.

I closed my legs and faced forward again. "Fine. Who else could it be?"

"What about your new roommate? Odd timing for her to show up with all this going on."

"Bess? That was a random traffic stop."

"Or so she would have you believe."

I laughed. "She's not organized enough to be diabolical."

He pointed at me. "What about that guy, Delaney, from the Irish bar? You haven't known him very long."

I folded my arms over my chest and laughed. "You are totally jealous of Delaney."

"Duh." He closed the bakery box. "Wouldn't you be jealous if some attractive woman was sniffing around the goods?" He gestured to himself.

I leaned toward him. "Do you not remember what's-her-face from Sin City Tacos?" I squished my boobs together.

"Oh, Carly," he said with a devious smile.

"Yeah. Maybe the demon is her."

He shook his head. "I think it's Delaney."

"Could be, I guess. He definitely has the body of a supervillain."

"Hey!" Essex playfully shoved me sideways.

I caught myself on the bar, laughing. "This is going to be fun."

"Don't make me go kick his ass, because I will."

"I'd love to watch that fight." I stood and put my arms around his neck from behind. "If you don't mind, I need a shower."

"Of course not. Use my bathroom, since it's the only one paint free."

"What's your plan?"

He nodded toward the can of paint thinner. "Gonna see if this shit works."

"Want some help?"

"Nah. I don't have enough faith in the experiment to require assistance." He spun around to face me, then pulled me forward onto his lap. "I like you being here."

"I like being here too." I kissed the tip of his nose. "What happens when we go back to work?"

"We lie our asses off," he said with a laugh.

I squeezed his hips between my thighs. "Seriously."

"Seriously, we play it cool for a while. I'll get the ball rolling with the city. Hopefully, by then, all the shit swirling around Sapphire Lake will have died down, and I can transition smoothly over."

"Are you sure you want to do that?" I rested my forehead against his.

"I'm sure I want you. I've been certain of that for a long time."

I kissed him. After a hot second, he came up for air. "If you want a shower, that's not the way to get there."

I licked my lips. "But you taste like frosting."

With a smile, he pulled my hips against his. "Yeah, screw the paint. I'll deal with the red."

It was another hour before I made it to the shower and Essex made it back to the paint thinner. I was lathering my hair with men's shampoo when I heard him swearing in the bedroom.

"No luck?" I called out.

He replied, but over the noise of the water, I couldn't understand him.

"What?" I yelled.

The door creaked open. "It's hopeless. I might as well—"

"Might as well what?" I peeked around the blue-striped shower curtain to see him frozen in the doorway. "What's wrong?"

He was staring at the mirror over the double sinks. In the fog on the glass was a message.

Nyx, meet me at home. — Orion

"**W**ell, this isn't how I wanted to spend today," Essex said, standing beside the open driver's door to my Jeep. He'd dressed in a loose plaid button-up over a white tee and jeans.

I slipped on my sunglasses. "I know. Me neither, but I knew all this shit wouldn't wait for long."

"Can I ask you a question?"

"Sure."

"What's it like when you're detached?"

"It's a lot like being here. I mean, it's exactly like being here because I *am* here. I'm just invisible to all you mere mortals."

I was trying to make light, but Essex didn't crack a smile. "So you'd be able to see me standing right here?"

"Sure. Why?"

"That Orion guy . . ." He looked toward the street.

I leaned against my door. "I don't think he's a Peeping Tom, if that's what you're getting at."

"You were in the shower. The writing was on the mirror. Where else could he have been?"

"He promised me he wouldn't do creepy shit."

"And I'll bet you promised your doctor you'd take it easy."

I linked my fingers behind his neck. "Don't worry. What are you going to do today without me?"

He looked at his watch. "Since it's almost five, meeting with the DA will have to wait. I'll probably still see Teek. Maybe take him some comic books or something."

"You're a saint, you know that?"

He pulled my hips against his. "That's not what you thought last night."

"No, it's not." I kissed him, letting my tongue slowly drag across his.

He pulled back. "Do you want me to take you back inside?"

"Yes, but there's no time. Can you do me a favor today?"

"Sure."

"Can you dig into Kush? Orion and I need to know all the places we should look for that poppy."

"Yeah, I can do that."

"Thanks. Are you working tonight?"

"For the city? No. For you?" He dropped his head back. "God, I hope so."

"Should I come back over when I'm finished?"

A deep growl rumbled in his throat. "I'd hate to have to be quiet for your roommate."

I bit my lower lip. "I'll come running when I'm done."

"If you beat me back, you can use the code to get in."

My head snapped back. "Really? You trust me with it now?"

Smiling, he looked away. "I guess you could say that."

I was confused. "Why?"

"The code is zero-five-two-nine."

"Zero-five-two-nine," I repeated. My eyes narrowed. Those numbers sounded familiar. I had to say them again before the lightbulb clicked on. "Oh."

His cheeks flushed. "Yeah."

I didn't have to ask why he'd hidden it before. "My birthday."

"Pretty cheesy, huh?"

"Not at all." It told me more about where we stood than anything words could articulate.

I kissed him again, threading my fingers through the soft hair at the back of his neck. It was a gentle kiss, deeper in so many more ways than any I'd ever tasted before.

This time, when he broke the kiss, his face sweetly nuzzled mine. "You'd better go," he whispered.

I took a difficult step back, my heart straining to stay with all the pull of a magnetic forcefield. "There's not much daylight left, so my phone will be silenced for a little while. I'll call you when I wake up."

"Oh, right. You'll be asleep."

"Yes," I said, bracing to hear something like, *"That's so weird."*

"Then sleep well."

I smiled. "Thanks. Bye, Essex."

"Nyx?"

"Yeah?"

"Call me Tyler."

At home, I parked behind Bess's car, as it was blocking my garage. I opened the door quietly, hoping to sneak in unseen and unheard. There was no time to get chatty with Bess if Orion was waiting with news.

The hallway was clear when I tiptoed inside. Her bedroom door was open, and the light was on. I crept quietly to my room and locked my door behind me. "Give me five minutes to change," I said quietly to Orion, if he was there listening.

In the bathroom, I changed into a pair of stretchy shorts and a black sports bra. I flopped onto my bed, settled back against the pillows, and crossed my ankles. "All right, let's do this."

Nothing happened.

"Orion?"

Nothing.

"Damn it," I muttered.

Conventional sleep was going to be impossible. With a frustrated groan, I got up and went to the kitchen. Once upon a time, when I'd first moved to night shift, I'd bought a box of chamomile tea. I opened and closed all the kitchen cabinets, looking for it to no avail.

Instead, I found a bottle of ibuprofen "PM" in the medicine cabinet. I pulled it down. "Hey, Bess?" I called down the hallway.

"Nyx? I didn't hear you come in."

I carried the bottle down the hallway. "Mind if I take a couple of these?" I asked when I reached her door.

She was behind her computer, wearing a pair of glasses I didn't know she had. "Not at all. You feeling OK?"

"Just a bit of a headache." Which wasn't a lie. My head hadn't been one hundred percent since the accident. "I'm all right though."

"Is PM stuff OK to take with a head injury?"

"I'm sure it's not half as strong as the prescription I didn't fill."

She smiled. "I guess you're right."

"Thanks." I poured two into my hand and swallowed them without water.

She looked down at my lack of real clothes, and her brow rose. "How long have you been home?"

"A few minutes."

"Did you work last night?"

"For a while, until I got into a fight with a suspect and wound up in the ER again."

"Are you OK?" she asked, alarmed.

"Had to have some staples replaced, but I'm fine. I'll be out of work for a while." I gestured toward the computer. "What are you doing?"

Looking up at me, she pressed her lips together. Guilt was all over her face.

"Bess?"

"I don't want to tell you."

I crossed my arms. "Now you have to tell me. It'd better not be anything illegal."

"It's not. Well, I guess technically . . ." Her head leaned from side to side.

"Excuse me?"

"I hacked into my ex-boyfriend's server, and I'm erasing all the shit off his computer that I paid for." She pointed at her wide computer screen, inviting me to look for myself.

I laughed and walked around behind her. "Seriously?"

"Yeah. Movies and games and stuff. He's going to be pissed when he realizes World of Warcraft is gone." On the screen, files were moving into the trash can. "I warned him to change the billing credit cards, or else."

"That's hilarious."

Her computer setup was impressive. The computer's brain—beats the shit out of me what it was really called—was encased in clear glass, with swirling colorful lights inside. "You're really good at this stuff, aren't you?"

She shrugged. "I'm all right."

"So why are you bartending?"

"It wasn't my first choice, but no one in Sapphire Lake or Reno is hiring in computers without a degree. Someday, I'll finish mine, but that takes money I don't have, so bartending is paying the bills for now."

"Have you had any more trouble with your boss?"

She laughed. "Oh, hell no. I think he's actually afraid of me because of you."

"Have you talked to Harlan yet?"

She beamed proudly. "I have a meeting with him Monday."

"Good for you."

Turning toward me, she put her hands in her lap. "I really don't know how I'll ever repay your kindness, Nyx."

"You saved my life. We're even."

"No, we're not. If I can ever do anything for you, please ask."

"Actually, I could use some computer expertise with something."

"Anything," she said.

"Can you dig up some information on someone for me?"

"Oh, absolutely. Who?"

"Chief Joseph Magnus."

"Your chief?"

"Yes."

"Sure. What do you want to know?"

"Whatever you can find out about his career before he took the job here. Specifically, if there's anything to do with a man named Elias Nyx."

"Your father?"

I nodded. "The chief told me they met a few times. I want to know if there are any records of their talks."

"Anything else?"

"I'm trying to decide how much I want to trust the chief. Anything interesting on him would be helpful."

She held up both thumbs. "You've got it. Can you give me a few hours?"

"Yeah. I'm going to sleep for a while."

"OK. Hey, if you weren't at work, where have you been all night and all day?"

I looked away.

She gasped. "Oh my god, you've been with your boss."

I tried to stifle a grin and failed.

"You slept with him!"

"Maybe."

With a quiet squeal, she clapped her hands. "I'm so proud of you. How was it?"

"Amazing" slipped out before I could remember I'm not the kind of girl who gushes to friends after sex. Not that there had been any sex to gush about in a really, *really* long time. Or friends to gush to, for that matter.

She laughed and drumrolled her feet under the desk. "I love it. What are you going to do about work?"

That was a damn good question. "I don't know yet. He's thinking of leaving the department, but for now, I guess we'll try to keep it quiet."

"Are you happy?"

I smiled. "I am."

"Of course you are. I barely know both of you and can't believe it's taken so long. Why is that?"

I lifted a shoulder. "Work, mostly. And when we first met, I'd just gotten out of a relationship."

Understatement.

She grimaced. "I have a confession. I googled you before I moved in."

"Ah, so you already know." Strangely, I felt relieved there wouldn't be more questions. And, in a way, that she just knew. It was almost like having a friend.

"Yeah. I'm really sorry about what happened to you."

"Thanks. It was a long time ago," I said, because what else does one say to that?

"He's the guy on the fridge?"

I nodded.

"He was hot."

"Yes, he was. And he was kind." I took a deep breath and smiled.

"Well, get some sleep, and I'll get to work," she said. "And no singing today, I promise."

I laughed. "I'd appreciate that. Are you working tonight?"

"Only on your stuff. I'm off from the Drexler."

"OK." The hallway light flickered. "I'll see you when I wake up."

"I hope your head feels better."

"Thanks," I said and hurried to my room.

"Have fun last night?" Orion had a teasing smile when I opened my eyes in the Boundary.

"I did." I pointed at him. "This had better be good because you're becoming a bit of a cosmic cockblocker."

"I promise I won't ever leave a note on a bathroom mirror if it isn't urgent."

"And no watching me in the shower."

He rolled his eyes. "I wouldn't do that."

"Sure. You have a power that every man on Earth, and probably beyond, dreams of."

"True, but I have two daughters your age."

Thankfully, I was lying down. Orion looked the same age as me.

"Really?"

"Really. So you can stop worrying if I'll respect your privacy. I won't treat any woman any differently than I would treat them . . ." The corner of his mouth tipped up. "Without permission anyway."

I smiled and nodded. "I'm sorry."

"Apology accepted. I can't imagine the shit you must put up with as a cop."

I smiled. "When I do, I don't have to put up with it for long."

We both chuckled.

Using a glove, he picked up my go bag and plunked it down on the bed. "Get dressed." He leaned toward me and grinned. "I'll turn around."

"Smart ass." I dressed quickly with my back to him. "About this shirt." I turned around. "Where's the rest of it?"

Orion glanced back over his shoulder. "It's practical. Imera is always bright and warm."

"But northwest Nevada *isn't*. I'm really tempted to revisit that accusation of you being a typical man."

He shrugged. "Looks like you're headed to the gym."

"It looks like I'm about to raid some tombs."

His eyes narrowed. "I don't know what that means."

Of course he didn't.

"Never mind." I sat down to put on my shoes. "Why'd you come find me?"

"I might have something."

My brow rose.

"I did some nosing around today and found out Kush, formerly your John Doe, has some friends in the illegal horticulture trade."

"That doesn't surprise me. Where?"

He looked at something written on his hand. "South Rock Road, Carson City."

"Have you checked it out yet?"

"I thought I'd see if you wanted to go with me."

"Yeah, of course." I looked around to make sure I had everything. The dagger was still on my calf. The oneiryte vial and light crystal were around my neck. Leaving the flash drive behind, I stuffed the ergane glove into my pocket.

My doorbell rang.

"Who's here?" he asked.

"I don't know."

"You don't know?"

I walked past him toward the door. "I'm sorry. X-ray vision wasn't part of my superpowers package."

He stood beside me to listen. I could hear Bess's footsteps

down the hall. There was more than one person outside. They were arguing.

The door opened. "Hello, can I help you?" Bess asked. "Oh, hi, Ransom."

"My brother," I whispered.

"What's he doing here?"

"If you'd stop asking questions, we might find out."

"Hey, Bess."

"Bess?" a shrill female asked. "I don't know any Bess."

"I told you Nyx has a roommate now. I'm sorry to barge in, Bess. Is my sister here?"

"She is, but she's sleeping. Need me to get her?"

"Yes, dear. You're adorable, but we didn't come to see you," the woman replied, the *click-clack* of her heels indicating that she'd entered the condo.

My heart plummeted to the floor. "Oh god."

"Who is it?" Orion asked.

"My mother."

CHAPTER TWENTY-SEVEN

*L*ike Gran, Mal—whatever the hell her last name was these days—had a slender face, a long nose, and hair so black it refused to turn gray. Unlike Gran, she had a boob job, lip fillers, and a cold, dead heart.

She wore a skin-tight black dress—her mourning attire, I was sure—with silver jewelry and heels that made her as tall as my brother. Her eyelids were painted a shimmering gold, and her bony cheeks had been contorted with the precision of a set square. On her shoulder was her purse, and in her hand a set of car keys and a giant pair of sunglasses.

"Saphera." My name in her hateful mouth made my skin ripple with goose bumps.

"Mal." I closed my bedroom door behind me. "To what do I owe this horror?"

"I'm sorry," my brother mouthed over her shoulder.

Mal was visually inventorying my condo. "Nice place you have here, Saphera. I didn't know you'd moved from your last shithole."

I glared at Ransom. "Thanks for giving me up."

"I tried to call and warn you."

Bess was still lingering awkwardly in the hallway, clearly unsure of whether to stay, go, or maybe call the police or an exorcist.

Mal noticed. "You can go now, *roommate*. This is family business."

Something inside me snapped. "Bess has been here for less than a week, and she's already closer family to me than you are."

Bess smiled. "Would you like me to stay, Nyx?"

I refocused on my mother. "This is your home, so you can do what you want, but my recommendation would be to get as far away from this witch as possible."

I didn't have to tell Bess twice. She turned and made a beeline for her room, slamming and locking the door behind her.

At my request, Orion had left. Mal wasn't exactly discreet, and because she would be able to see him, I wasn't ready to explain to Bess why an invisible man was in our house. He went on to check out whatever growing endeavors Kush might have been involved with, so only the three of us remained. One dysfunctional little family.

"What do you want, Mal?" I asked.

"I had a visit from some of your friends yesterday." She walked over and sat down on my sofa, plunking her heavy designer purse on the cushion beside her.

"I heard you were your usual charming self."

Mal crossed her lean legs, folding her hands over a bony knee. "They told me about your father. I came as soon as I could."

I smirked. "There isn't any insurance money if that's what you're after."

Ransom slapped a hand over his mouth to unsuccessfully stop a fit of laughter.

"You sound just like your grandfather," Mal said.

"At least I got some good sense from somewhere."

"I came to check on my children. Is that so terrible?" She

pushed her silky dark hair back over her shoulder. "You've experienced a devastating loss."

"Bullshit. You came to see which of us inherited Elias's gift." Ransom looked at me. "We had a nice Jerry Springer talk on the drive over here."

"I bet." I jerked my head to the side. "Can I talk to you in private?"

"Privacy isn't necessary. I'm your mother," Mal said.

"Exactly. Ransom?" I lifted my brow.

My brother and I walked down the hall, past the front door.

"Sorry," he said again. "She just showed up at my house."

"What did you tell her?"

"I didn't tell her shit."

But Mal showing up in Reno told me plenty—she didn't know who Ransom's father was either.

"So why did you bring her here?" I asked.

"She wanted to see you. She said the cops questioned her about the plant, but I'm not sure she's ever known much about it. I don't think she even knows that it grows where blood is spilled inside the Boundary."

In my peripheral vision, I saw Mal's eyes widen. She was listening to our conversation.

I turned my back to her and lowered my voice even more. "You didn't tell her about the *other thing*?"

He shook his head.

"Good. Now, how do we get rid of her?"

"You don't!" Mal called from the living room.

"How the hell did she hear that?" Ransom asked, looking over my head.

"I know where the plant is, Saphera."

Definitely not what I was expecting. I spun around. "Excuse me?"

"You heard me. Would you like to know where it is or not?"

"Why didn't you tell the police last night?" I asked as Ransom followed me back to the living room.

"And risk going back to prison? I don't think so." Mal folded her thin arms. "Besides, the information isn't free."

My eyes narrowed. "Of course it isn't. What's your price?"

"I want what's already owed to me." She looked at Ransom.

My brother looked caught.

"Done," I said before he could screw anything up.

Mal turned her evil gaze toward me. "You speak for him now?"

"I know how dangerous that plant is. Whatever you want from Ransom is worth the cost."

Ransom held up a hand. "Hold on now. What exactly do you want, Mal?"

"Oh, please. I'm not telling you anything in front of the police." She cast her eyes toward me. "But that does bring me to my second request."

"More a demand, isn't it?" I asked.

"Call it what you like."

"What is it?"

"Immunity. If I tell you where the plant is, I'm not going back to prison. My name won't be brought into this investigation again, at all."

"Am I supposed to tell them I pulled the plant's location out of my ass?" I asked.

"I don't give a damn what you tell them as long as you leave my name out of it."

"Fine."

"And I want some hypnox."

"What?" My voice jumped up a few decibels. "Haven't you already learned what that shit is capable of?"

She stood and walked the kitchen. "I've learned how to use it responsibly. It would be for personal endeavors, nothing illegal, of course."

"Right," Ransom said.

"I could keep the information to myself and take all the hypnox I want, but as you know, I'm not the only one who knows where that plant is." Mal opened a few cabinets and then the refrigerator.

"What are you looking for?" I asked.

"Something to put my hypnox in. Aha!" She pulled out a brand new jar of pickles, opened it with a *pop*, and dumped the pickles into the trash.

I looked at my brother. His shoulders rose slightly. The important thing was finding the plant. Thousands of people could die if we didn't.

"Where is it?" I asked.

"Do we have a deal?"

I looked at my brother and clenched my jaw. "Deal."

Satisfied, Mal put the jar into her bag and looped its strap over her shoulder. She gestured toward the door. "Shall we then?"

"I need to get my things," I said.

She clicked her tongue. "Not so fast. Give me your phone. I don't need you calling any of your friends at the police station."

I patted my leggings. "My phone is on my nightstand."

"Good. You don't need *things* for this endeavor."

"I need my wallet, my ID, my badge—"

"Fine, but make it fast." Mal followed me to my bedroom.

"There's the phone." I pointed to the nightstand. It was lit up with messages, but I didn't stop to check them.

"Leave it."

I picked up my backpack.

"You don't need all that," she said.

With a groan, I grabbed everything I could from it: my badge wallet, the ergane glove and bag . . .

"Leave your guns here too."

With a sigh, I opened the combination lock and pulled my

gun from its holster. I made sure my mother saw it before I placed it inside the safe. "Satisfied?"

Her eyes drifted over me. I tensed, waiting for her to spot the bulge from the knife beneath my leggings. She missed it. Finally, she jerked her head toward the door. "Let's go."

"I have a bad feeling about this, Nyx," Ransom whispered as he opened the back-seat door to his truck for me.

"So do I." I got in, and he closed it behind me.

Mal got up front with Ransom, and I buckled my seatbelt. Part of me wished I'd asked Orion to stay. It was the same part of me that worried I'd just gotten Ransom and myself in way over our heads.

Ransom stopped at my driveway's exit. "Which way?"

"Turn right," Mal said, staring straight ahead.

Ransom turned onto the highway.

"Where are we going?" I asked.

She didn't look at me. "You'll see when we get there."

I checked the position of the sun in the sky. It was almost sunset. Like a demonic GPS, Mal gave Ransom turn-by-turn directions across town and around the scenic part of the lake.

Ransom's phone rang through the truck. Celise's name came up on his display screen. He touched the answer button. "Hello?"

"Ransom, we need to talk about what happened yesterday," she said through the speakers.

"Can't talk right now. You're on speakerphone in the truck. Nyx and Mal are here."

"Mal is with you?"

I felt Celise's surprise in my bones.

"Hello, dear," Mal said.

"Uh . . . hi, Mal. Where are you all going?"

"I honestly have no idea. Listen, I know we need to talk. I'll come over as soon as I'm free," Ransom said.

"When will that be?"

"No clue. I'll call when I can."

"What are you doing?"

"Being a victim of extortion." He slid a hateful glance toward our mother. "Mal claims to know where the hypnox is."

"It's a family matter, Celise. The last I heard you didn't want to be part of our family anymore." Mal tapped the "end call" button on Ransom's screen.

"What the fuck, Mal?" he asked.

"I'm doing you a favor, son."

"She's already pissed at me enough."

"What did you do?" I asked.

He looked at me in the rearview. "I stopped by there last night to drop off some stuff Milly left in my truck. I guess I was still sore from our conversation, so she opened a bottle of wine and invited me to stay."

I scowled. "Good god, you slept with her."

"Maybe."

"Ransom," I whined.

"I was buzzed. It seemed like a good idea at the time."

I groaned. "You either need to figure out how to make things work or leave her alone."

"Your sister's right," Mal added.

"Relationship advice from the two of you?" Ransom asked. "Really?"

"Speaking of . . . Mal, I hear congratulations are in order," I said.

"For what?" she asked.

"You got married again, didn't you?"

"Oh, yes." She could not have sounded any less enthused if she'd tried.

"To the fine specimen of humanity you brought to Gran's funeral?" Ransom asked.

"You're one to talk, son," she replied with a smirk. "Don't worry. You'll get to know him soon enough."

"Have you told him about me?" he asked.

She ignored him. "Turn right on Sanctuary Drive."

I straightened in my seat. Only one thing was down that road.

Ransom looked at her in horror. "Why?"

"You'll see," she said again.

Sanctuary Drive's literal dead end was at the stone gate of Sapphire Lake Memorial Valley. Since Gran had been buried there, the place had become sacred ground for our family—well, most of our family, anyway.

Nestled beneath the mountains that overlooked the lake, the small valley was a quiet resting place for the departed. Ransom and Paps visited every time they were in town, but I'd only been back once since we'd laid Gran to rest in May.

"You know where your grandmother is buried?" Mal asked Ransom.

"Yeah."

"Go there."

The valley was never a hopping place, but as it was close to sundown, it was especially deserted. We passed an older woman visiting a grave on the lower hill, but we didn't see another car until we reached the upper slope of the valley.

A black SUV was parked on the loop that surround the property.

Essex?

Ransom parked around the curve from it, and the three of us got out. Mal carefully scanned the area, but like me, she didn't see another soul.

Weird.

She eyed the SUV suspiciously as we passed, and I paused to

look in the window. On the passenger's seat was an empty plastic bag marked *Lakeview Comics*.

It *was* Essex.

Mal stepped off the road and started up through a clearing at the base of the mountainside. The three of us walked beneath tall pine trees up the steep incline. Had to give it to Mal, managing the trek in three-inch heels. I'd have been on my ass a few times.

She turned and crossed over a rocky path from a dried up mountain stream. On the other side was a small hill. From its direction, a muffled male voice was carried on the breeze.

She ascended the hill ahead of us and stopped at its crest. Her hand went to her hip. "Who the hell are you?"

Ransom and I picked up the pace to the top, and I saw Essex below. He stood on a wide overlook of the cemetery beside a six-foot black poppy. The growth was as wide as it was tall, covered in four-petal blooms with fresh pods ripening on the long stems. A few of the pods had been scored with a blade. Several others were withered and dead.

"Holy shit," Ransom said, his mouth gaping.

Essex's eyes locked on me. "Nyx?"

Mal turned my way. "You know this person?"

No point in denying it. "Yep." I sidestepped down to the over-grown landing. "What are you doing here?"

"What are *you* doing here?" he asked.

"Being blackmailed. How did you find it?"

"Gramma T was at Sterling Heights with Teek. I asked her about Kush, and she said he'd been spending a lot of time at the cemetery visiting his mother."

I remembered the woman I'd seen in the painting at Borg's house.

"Thought I'd swing by and check it out. I saw this bluff and figured a pothead like Kush might find it a good place to get high. Guess I was right."

On the ground was a broken lighter, an empty package of

rolling papers, and rusty razor blades. All clear signs the drug had a frequent visitor.

I put my hands on my hips. "Stoners always amaze me. Most people wouldn't know a poppy plant if it sprouted from the pages of an actual textbook."

"More shocking still that he didn't die from it up here," Essex said.

"Seriously," I agreed.

He looked back at Mal. "Is that who I think it is?"

"Yes. Have you called this in?"

"Just now. Units are on the way."

"Good. Maybe they can take that witch to jail." I tipped my chin toward Mal.

Ransom, almost in a trance, walked toward the plant.

"Ransom, stay back!" I called, double stepping to catch up with him. "That shit's lethal."

"But have you ever seen opium grow so tall?" He reached for one of the stems, and I smacked his hand away.

"I've never seen opium growing *at all*, and you shouldn't have either." Shaking my head, I walked to the cliff's edge. The sun had set over the lake, painting the sky orange and pink. It would be dark soon. "What was Elias doing here?"

"Watching your grandmother's service." Mal came and stood beside me.

"He was?" I asked, surprised.

"He was right here before the service started."

My eyes drifted toward where we'd all been gathered at Gran's final resting place below. I could almost see us by the casket: Paps clinging to my arm, Ransom holding Milly, Mal walking up as the box was being lowered into the ground.

I faced my mother. "How did you know where Elias was *before* Gran's service started?"

"I saw him, of course."

"But how? You were late."

Mal blinked.

"Where were you before the service?"

"I don't know what you're talking about."

"I saw you coming from this direction. Holy shit." I took a step back. "You killed him."

"What?" Ransom asked.

"Mal killed Elias." Even to my own ears, my voice sounded distant. Foreign, almost like it belonged to someone else.

Mal rolled her eyes. "No, I didn't. Elias died in prison."

I pointed at the plant. "But his blood was spilled here."

I remembered the surprise in Mal's eyes as she stared at Ransom and me talking back at my condo. He'd just said that hypnox grows where the blood of a scion is spilled.

"You didn't know," I said, astonished.

Guilt flooded Mal's face.

"Know what?" Ransom asked.

"She didn't know how to grow hypnox." I folded my arms. "Maybe Elias was smarter than I gave him credit for. He may have allowed you to use the drug, but he didn't trust you enough to tell you how to create it."

Her eyes fell enough to confirm my statement.

"You knew he would come to the funeral. And you killed him so that his power would pass to Ransom."

"The missing dagger," Ransom said. "Did you break into my house?"

"It's really embarrassing that you use your daughter's birth date as a password, Ransom," she said.

"You selfish demon." I walked away, shaking my head. "You killed our father?"

"Oh, please." She gave a disgusted snort. "Don't act like this is some unbearable tragedy. You hated that man."

"That's so far beside the point," I snapped. "Why? Why now?"

She stepped toward me. "Do you have any idea what it's like to be an ex-con? No decent jobs hire felons, and you can't sign a lease or a buy a car without income. I lost *everything*. Would you have me live in squalor?"

"As opposed to murder?" I spread my arms. "Yes! Besides, what about your new husband? Or the nice little nest egg you and Elias socked away?"

"The money's gone!" She pointed at Ransom. "Or would you have wanted me to leave your brother in jail?"

I shook my head. "Don't you dare act like you did that for anyone but yourself."

She didn't rebut.

"And what was your grand plan for Ransom's repayment of the debt?" I asked.

"Only to take back what is rightfully owed to me." She pounded her finger against her breastbone.

"You'd really have him rob Renzo?"

"Your father helped make Lorenzo Bianchi a lot of money. How dare he turn us over to the police after everything—"

"You mean, after you cheated on him and left him for Elias?" I asked.

Her lower jaw shifted to the side, and she crossed her arms with an obstinate huff.

I looked at Essex. "Can we arrest her for murder?"

His jaw went slack. "How would you prove it?"

"You heard her. She confessed!"

"To murdering the spirit of a man who was locked up in prison," he said slowly.

Mal laughed. "Yeah. Good luck proving that one, Saphera. I mean, really, do you even hear yourself?"

I wanted to punch her.

She walked toward the plant, pulling out a glass jar from her purse. "Now, if you don't mind, I'd like to take my hypnox and get the hell out of here." She held the pickle jar toward Ransom.

"You're not going anywhere," I said.

"We had a deal!"

"I guess lying runs in the family."

Her mouth gaped. "You can't back out of this now. Ransom?" She shook the jar at my brother.

"Sorry, Mal. I can't help you."

"But you owe me! You made me a promise."

"And you told me my father was Elias, so . . ." Ransom shrugged.

"What?"

"You heard him." I squared off with her, toe to toe. "Ransom isn't Elias's firstborn." I cut my eyes. "I am."

She stepped back. "That's impossible."

"And yet, here we are." I looked back at Essex. "How about obstruction of justice? She didn't tell Gregg yesterday where the plant was. Surely that's a violation of her probation."

"I didn't know yesterday," she hissed.

"And how will you explain that?" Mockingly, I shook my head. "Really, do you even hear yourself?"

She glared at me.

"If I can't send you back to prison for murder, I will find another way."

She leaned close and lowered her voice. "I hope the night-walkers tear out your heart."

"Well, if I'm anything like you, I don't have one."

Ransom looked up at the sky. "Speaking of nightwalkers, we probably shouldn't be so close to this plant. It's getting dark."

"Because we might have a repeat of what happened at the Drexler?" Essex asked.

"Exactly. Kush is lucky it didn't happen to him sooner." I walked to the plant, and Essex joined me.

He nudged the broken lighter on the ground with his boot. "Looks like he frequented this place."

"Kush?" Ransom asked. "Is that a person?"

"He's the John Doe who died in the fire at your hotel." I

nodded toward the poppy. "He's the one who was bleeding the pods and selling to the Kings."

Sirens wailed in the distance.

"Backup is almost here," Essex said.

"Wanna take bets that it's our guys?" I asked with a smile.

"You think so?"

"I know so." Since they were all on overtime with Charlie shift, they weren't assigned to a zone. They'd all be hanging out together, waiting to respond to whatever came across the radio. Each one would have hit the gas as soon as they heard Essex had called in. "I told you, they'll always get here."

"Saphera, you can't let them take me back to prison!" Mal shouted, hysteria rising in her voice.

"Oh yes I can. And I'm going to enjoy it too," I said.

Mal grabbed my arm. "I can't go back to that hell hole—"

I wrenched my arm free and looked at Essex. "Do you have cuffs we could put her in? Or a muzzle?"

He chuckled. "Maybe in the car."

Mal pulled something from her pocket. The shadow blade she'd stolen from Ransom. She grabbed one of the large round pods.

"Stop!" Essex lunged to grab her wrist.

With one swift move, she drove the blade through the pod like she was going for the heart of an attacking grizzly.

Black sludge bled from the pod, unusual for a regular opium poppy. Even in the US, growing a few plants was still legal because a single one yielded such a negligible amount.

This one bled like Mal had gouged an artery.

Essex released her and jumped back, spreading his arms wide to stop anyone else from advancing. Mal threw the knife down and swept her free hand under the cascade of hypnox.

"Geez, Mal! Have you lost your fucking mind?" I stepped in front of my brother as Essex pulled his gun.

"We had a deal, Saphera," she said again, her words oddly

steady and calm as the powerful narcotic seeped into her skin. She took a few steps toward us.

"You know I can't help you. Don't come any closer," I said, holding my hand toward her.

"Stop screwing around, Mal!" Ransom yelled.

Mal stared at the drug oozing between her fingers. "I'm not going back. I'd rather detach and take all of you with me."

She raised her hand.

Essex aimed. "Don't do it, Mal!"

Her hand sliced sideways through the air as Essex fired. His bullet struck her in the chest. Mal fell back, landing hard on her side, but not before slinging the tar-like substance across all of us.

CHAPTER TWENTY-EIGHT

"Shit, shit, shit!" I threw my jacket on the ground and stripped down to my sports bra, using my shirt to wipe Ransom's face. It was splattered with black specks.

Behind him, a black line of hypnox was slashed across Essex's neck, jugular to jugular. He was panting and staring open-mouthed to where my mother had fallen.

"Tyler, your neck. Get that shit off!" I yelled as I uselessly tried to clean my brother's face. It was like scrubbing sticky molasses. If anything, I was only spreading it to make more contact with Ransom's skin.

"It's on you too," Tyler said.

"I don't think it matters with me, but it can kill you and Ransom. You have to get it off."

"Nyx . . . I . . ." Ransom stumbled forward, and I caught him. His pupils tightened, his jaw slack as he stared through me. "Nyx," he whispered, blinking slowly.

"Ransom, hang on!" I eased him onto the ground.

Still upright, Essex wobbled sideways.

"Tyler, sit down." I was trying, and failing, to stay calm. When he sat, I crawled toward him and grabbed his cell phone. The station was the last dialed number, and dispatch answered on the first ring.

"This is Corporal Saphera Nyx, car number three-oh-three, on scene at Sapphire Lake Memorial Valley on Sanctuary Drive. Shots fired, officer involved. I have a female with a gunshot wound, condition unknown. Myself and two others have made skin contact with hypnox. We have located the hypnox plant. Request additional units, narcotics, a supervisor, and EMS immediately."

I smacked Essex's cheeks. "Stay with me, Tyler!" His head jostled from side to side with each smack, his breaths slowing on every inhale. Terrified tears streamed down my face. "Stay with me!"

"Nyx." Essex blinked a few times. "I can't . . . feel my face."

I cupped his cheeks. "Please, hang on."

Leaning sideways across the bluff, I checked Ransom's pulse. It was there, but it was faint. Too faint.

"Nyx." Essex reached for me.

The instant I touched his hand, he slumped sideways onto the grass. I cradled his head in my arms, jostling him. "Tyler, stay with me. I need you to breathe."

His breath hitched in his throat. His eyes rolled back.

"Tyler!"

His whole body shuddered, and his spine arched unnaturally off the ground as all the air was forced from his lungs. Then he fell flat and silent, staring into nothing. Immediately, his body temperature began to plummet.

I sat back on my heels. "Tyler?" I searched the sky. "Tyler, if you can hear me, touch my hand."

A flash of cold shot through my arm, and I cried out.

I stood at the edge of the cliff, grabbed the crystal around my neck, and screamed, "Orion!" My voice ricocheted around the valley, echoing back with the faint wail of sirens.

A rattling wheeze came from behind the hypnox plant. Mal's leg twitched.

I stormed across the clearing. Blood mist covered my mother's face. The bullet had pierced her left lung, a dramatic injury that was (unfortunately) survivable with modern medicine.

I grabbed a fistful of her hair. "How do I detach?"

She laughed, and blood gurgled behind the sickening sound.

"Mal!"

I dropped to my knees, made a fist, and shoved the point of my middle knuckle into the bloody hole on her chest. She cried and writhed beneath the pressure. "Tell me now!"

"Maybe . . . I would"—she wheezed and blood dribbled down her chin—"if I . . . had a heart." She cackled until a coughing fit choked her.

With an angry and terrified huff, I pushed myself up. Mal caught my arm. "Listen." She closed her eyes.

I heard nothing but sirens too far away. Shoving her hand away, I stood. "Ransom?" I called out.

Nothing.

"Tyler?"

A chill prickled my arm.

I spun all the way around but didn't see anything. "There's some way you can detach me. I need you to try."

A cold hand settled on my shoulder.

"My throat. Go for my throat!" Tears streamed my cheeks.

Cold permeated my neck. Nothing happened.

"It's kind of like a Vulcan nerve pinch!" I jabbed my own fingers into the space above my sternum. "Here! Press here!"

A second later, the cemetery swirled away, and when I opened my eyes, I could see clearly in the dark.

Tyler was wide eyed and staring at me. "Nyx!"

I grabbed him and hugged him. "Oh my god." In all the shit we'd been through together, I'd never seen him rattled. Now, he trembled in my arms.

I looked around for my brother. His spirit wasn't anywhere, though his body lay still on the ground. "He didn't detach," I said, walking toward him.

"Why?" Tyler asked.

"Who knows? Maybe all his past drug use."

Screeches fluttered through the atmosphere. I froze.

"What's that noise?" Tyler asked.

I swallowed. "Don't worry about it."

"Nyx?"

I shook my head.

"They're . . . coming," Mal panted with a bloody smile.

"Shit." He understood. "Nightwalkers?" His voice scratched.

I instantly regretted all I'd told him the night before. Sirens wailed around the corner, and blue lights lit up the valley.

"Look at me, Tyler." He met my eyes. "You have to go back into your body. Remember what happened to Kush."

His eyes searched mine. "I've tried. I don't think I can."

"You have to try harder. Lie down."

When he did, I grabbed his ghostly head and tried forcing it back into his body. I willed and pushed. And focused. And cried.

"It isn't working," he said, more calmly than I felt.

I held both sides of his face and leaned my forehead against his. "I'll figure this out, I promise."

"Don't . . . make promises . . . you won't . . . keep." Mal coughed behind me. "That's what . . . your father . . . used to . . . tell me." She laughed and coughed harder.

I jumped on her again and grabbed her by the throat. "How do I save my brother?"

She twisted beneath me. "You . . . don't."

Shouting echoed through the woods, and Baker crested the hill first with a portable defibrillator in hand. Horror flashed across his face as he grabbed the radio on his shoulder.

"Delta Two, I have multiple casualties at the cemetery. Nyx, Essex, and two unidentified individuals, all unconscious."

As Baker descended the hill, another figure appeared behind him. Jones.

And another. Rivera, who'd even said he *wasn't* working overtime.

They ran to the closest body first, Essex. Jones checked for a pulse. Baker listened for breath sounds. "Rivera, check the others!" Baker yelled.

Rivera went to my body and checked my pulse. "Nyx is unconscious, but she has a heartbeat and steady breath sounds." He went to Ransom next, who was clearly more critical.

"Nyx?" The fear in Tyler's voice zapped all the hope in my heart.

I followed the direction of his worried eyes.

A black spot was growing at the base of the poppy, and hundreds of black tendrils creeped from it, like vines twisting and crawling across the grass.

"What the hell?" I asked, backing up.

Another black spot bubbled up near my body, and another on the hill. The ground rolled as something from beneath pushed to break free.

I rose slowly, pulling the dagger from my calf holster. I sheltered Essex behind me and raised the blade.

"What's happening?" he asked.

My eyes widened as the ground splintered. "The nightwalkers are here."

A head pushed through the first black spot by the plant. The skull, covered in what looked like stringy black putty, had no eyes or nose, but a mouth was fighting to open. Its jaws parted, and the dark flesh stretched until the opening began to shred apart.

The head rolled from side to side, pulling and straining the fibrous tendons holding it up. One shoulder pushed through the surface, but its arms were still trapped. If I was going to make a move, this was it.

Sucking in a quick brave breath, I sprinted forward and dropped to a knee, into a perfect baseball slide, toward the monster. The outstretched dagger sliced its throat, sending a bone-chilling shriek through the atmosphere.

I barely rolled out of the way before a long and slender arm ripped free of the ground, slamming down inches from my face. Like the neck, the arm was more a collection of tendons and veins than bone and skin. Its hand had four fingers—or claws—that were nearly as long as its forearms and needle-sharp at the tips.

It wasn't dead, far from it, but the injury had slowed it down. The reprieve wouldn't last as its friends were coming through the ground right behind it.

A symphony of sirens echoed around the cemetery, and red-and-white lights joined the blue down below. More backup was here. So was EMS.

Plenty of my friends for the monsters to feast on.

The defibrillator hooked up to Tyler's chest beeped, and a robotic voice said, "Evaluating." A second later, "Shock advised. Administering shock. Clear. Three . . . Two . . . One." I heard the pop of electricity travel through Tyler's chest, then, "Begin CPR."

I looked back as Baker started chest compressions again.

Essex's spirit was sitting, staring dumbfounded at his lifeless body.

"Tyler, put your hand on your forehead to go back in!" I shouted.

He obeyed. "I'm trying!"

Even over the hissing and screeching of the nightwalkers, I heard Tyler's ribs cracking and popping under the compressions.

The nightwalker on the hill was free. From what I could make out in the moonlight, it was eight or nine feet tall with a human-ish shape except for extra-long arms and legs and a short torso. It appeared to be inside out, with its bones and tendons covered in something that looked like black crude oil.

Darkness, I realized.

The nightwalker was clothed in darkness.

With its giant claws dragging the ground, it crept slowly toward Mal. As it neared, she began to hyperventilate. "Nyx!" Mal dug her heels into the grass, pushing herself backward. Her left shoe came off, and she slipped on her elbow.

The beast bent over her.

"Don't hurt me! Don't hurt me!"

Its massive mouth opened, and a long snake-like tongue slithered out. At first I thought it might eat her. Instead, it licked the wound in Mal's chest.

What the fuck?

She looked as stunned as I was. "No! Shew! Get them!"

Its sinewy face whipped toward us. The nightwalker crouched, and I readied my dagger as it launched into the air.

Boom!

Something landed so hard in front of me it shook the ground. White light sparkled around the bluff, and the nightwalker burst into flames midair.

Mal shrieked like she'd been set on fire.

A man was on one knee in front of me.

Orion.

His bright blue eyes turned toward me. "I leave you alone for a few minutes . . ."

I exhaled for what felt like an eternity.

"You all have to get back to your bodies," he said.

Shit. I'd been so preoccupied with Essex and Ransom, I hadn't stopped to consider I was a liability too. But between me and my body, the third nightwalker was almost free of the ground.

Orion stood, and a new panic pulsed through me. This magical man had zero qualms about taking human life for the greater good. Tyler's body was now an open gateway Orion would want to shut.

So was mine.

As if reading my mind, he looked past me to Tyler's body on the ground.

I splayed my hands on his chest. "Give him a chance, Orion, please."

Orion looked back at the demons.

Rivera tore open a pack of Narcan with his teeth and shoved its nozzle into Ransom's nose. My brother bolted upright like he'd been shot from a cannon. "What—where—what the fuck happened?" he shouted.

"Calm down, man. You OD'd on hypnox," Rivera said, trying to push Ransom back down.

My brother's frightened eyes landed on my body. "Nyx!"

"We've got her!" Rivera yelled, holding him on the ground.

Orion pushed past me, heading straight for Essex.

"Please!" I screamed, grabbing his arm.

Orion grabbed Tyler's spirit by the throat with his left hand and hooked his right arm under Tyler's thigh. He lifted him into the air and body-slammed his spirit back onto his body.

Nothing happened.

Tyler's spirit sat up.

"No," I whispered.

Orion swore and stood. I threw myself over Essex and his body. "Please don't!"

Orion stepped over us, and I sat up.

The nightwalker closest to my body was free. Snarling and dripping black sludge from its mouth, it stood over my face. Even across the clearing, I could feel its hot rancid breath on me.

I jumped up as Orion ran to my body, but he didn't get there fast enough.

The nightwalker sprang forward. I flipped the dagger around to grab the blade and hurled it across the clearing, burying the blade into the beast's forehead. It stumbled back and fell between two headstones.

Orion looked impressed. "Nice throw."

"I thought you said the dagger would kill them."

"It will."

He grabbed his oneiryte vial, flipped open the top, and poured a line of sand on the ground. Stepping over it, he vanished, and reappeared on the other side of the fallen demon. He grabbed the dagger, and with a powerful jab and rip, cut off its head completely.

The demon stilled, and Mal screamed again.

Baker and Rivera looked over, but of course all they could see was Mal, screaming at seemingly nothing. Essex scooted back away from them.

"You." Orion stalked toward Mal. "I should have known you'd be tangled up in all this somehow."

Mal's eyes doubled with recognition. "How did you . . . ? What . . . are you . . . doing here?" She scrambled away from him like she'd done with the nightwalker.

"You know each other?" I'd known Orion knew *of* my mother, but I wasn't aware they were acquainted.

"Shall I tell her how we met?" Orion asked Mal, standing over her.

"I wanted . . . to help you," she wheezed.

He crouched down. "You wanted an easy payday."

"What are you talking about?" I asked.

Essex stood slowly. "Orion." The way he said his name was full of understanding. "O-rion," he repeated slower. He looked at me. "The officer who died in the fire. Officer Owen Ryan. O. Ryan, like on our name plates."

My uniform's name plate read S. Nyx. I muffled a gasp with my hand.

"It was *Detective* Owen Ryan," Orion said.

"That was you?" I asked.

He gave a slight nod.

"Why didn't you tell me?"

"Would it have made you trust me more?"

Probably not.

He looked at my mother again. "Hello, Malena."

Mal was shaking. Mascara tears streaked her cheeks.

"Damn it, Sarge!" Baker yelled, breathless, behind us. We all turned to see him, still pumping Tyler's chest in the dark.

The defibrillator beeped. "Evaluating."

"It's . . . too late," Mal gurgled.

"She's right." Orion crossed the garden. "He's too far gone."

"That can't be true," I said, putting myself between Orion and Tyler's body.

The machine beeped again. "Shock advised. Administering shock. Clear. Three . . . Two . . . One."

Tyler's body convulsed. Baker pushed the Narcan nozzle into his nose. "Breathe, Sarge."

Tyler's eyes were open, staring into nothing.

Orion shook his head. "There's no bringing him back." He looked at Tyler. "I'm sorry."

"No." I grabbed Tyler's stunned spirit. After a second, his arms closed around me.

"I'm going to die like this?" His voice sounded small. Distant.

I held him tighter.

Something pressed against my thigh between us. I reached down and felt the lump in my pocket. I pulled out the ergane bag I'd stuffed into my pocket. Inside it was a glass vial.

The Water of Lethe.

My wide eyes met Orion's. "You said it would fuse my spirit to my body. That I'd no longer detach."

"Yes." His whole countenance lifted as he understood what I was thinking. "It might work. It's never been tested on a normal human, but he's dead if you do nothing."

I snapped the neck of the bottle.

Orion caught my wrist. "Remember what I told you. There's no going back."

There would be no going back for me or for Tyler. He'd forget, and I'd be doomed to be . . . whatever I was forever.

But there was no choice.

Black saliva drizzled from the closest nightwalker's fangs . . .

I palmed the back of Tyler's neck and kissed him. "I love you."

Then I poured the liquid into his body's gaping mouth.

CHAPTER TWENTY-NINE

The sound of oxygen being pulled into Tyler's lungs was a sweet song in that valley of death. On the pine needles, I slumped forward and held my thighs as I fought to not choke on my tears.

Baker laughed.

Jones fell onto his hip, sighing with relief.

Essex was breathing on his own.

Dani crested the hill with her medical bag. Right behind her was Everly. He lost his footing on the steep terrain and slid down the incline straight for Mal, and the plant, and the nightwalker he couldn't see.

Weaponless now, I pulled on my ergane glove as I dove toward Tyler's body. I reached beneath his shirt, on his right side, and wrenched his gun free of its holster. Seeing the gun, Baker flinched back, unsure of what was happening. I rolled onto my back, curled up in a crunch, and fired.

Pow!

I wasn't fast enough. And I missed. The bullet sliced across Mal's cheek just as she palmed Everly's face with her hypnox-covered hand.

Stunned by the gunfire, everyone packing had pulled their weapons. A cacophony of frantic questions were yelled in every direction.

"Who fired?"

"What was that?"

"Anybody hit?"

"Everly?"

Everly wrestled Mal's arms to the ground. "Ma'am, I'm here to help you!"

After a moment, she stopped fighting him.

Everly sat up, dazed, swaying from side to side. His eyes crossed, and his body face-planted in the grass. At that second, the first nightwalker I'd failed to kill broke free of the hypnox plant.

It spun toward Everly's body as his spirit detached. The demon dove for the body, its flailing claws slicing through Everly's spirit.

The nightwalker vanished.

Orion lifted a hand, and a bolt of white energy ripped through the cloudless sky. When his arm came down, the bolt sizzled across the landing, missing Everly's body by inches.

Everly's spirit crawled sideways across the ground toward the cliff's edge. I ran to him and grabbed him. "I've got you, Brian."

"Nyx?"

"Yeah, I'm here. It's going to be OK."

It really wasn't going to be OK. He had three deep gouges in his torso, open wounds full of black sludge. I dragged his spirit to the edge of the water.

When he saw his body, he panicked. "What's happening?"

Hugging him, I held his head against my chest as I watched in horror as his body arched off the ground. His mouth opened wider and wider until the jaw bones snapped and his face peeled back.

A long clawed hand shot through what remained of his face, and then the head of the demon pushed through his chest.

"What the fuck is that?" Jones screamed, squinting against the darkness.

Orion came closer and reached for the sky again, but another black spot ruptured beneath him, toppling him to the ground.

Through Everly's bloody corpse, the nightwalker stood, leaving a black gaping hole in the center of what remained of the torso. It was a portal, I realized.

A passageway for other monsters to follow.

The rumbling black spots on the ground stilled as the first nightwalker slinked forward. Another followed through the hole. And another.

The demons advanced toward my friends.

"Help me," Ransom said, grabbing the stunned EMT's sleeve. "Help me up."

"Sir, no—" the man tried to argue.

"Help me."

Ransom stood and stumbled forward to face the nightwalkers. My metaphorical heart nearly stopped.

I grabbed Everly's face and turned it toward the moonlit valley. "Stay here. Don't look."

He was crying, but he nodded.

Weaponless, I put myself between Ransom and the seething monsters.

"Nyx, get out of there!" Orion yelled, raising his hand toward the sky again.

"They'll have to kill me to get to him."

"They'll kill you both!"

I didn't care. I advanced, and the nightwalker stopped. It took a step back. A little stunned, I took another step forward. It retreated more.

"Nyx, stop," Orion said, pointing behind me.

I turned just as Ransom stepped through me. My whole

spirit quivered with searing-hot energy that took me to my knees. Ransom's hands were outstretched as he walked forward, and the closer he got to the demons, the farther they moved away.

One by one, the nightwalkers slinked back into the portal, disappearing from Earth's view. Ransom fell to his knees, breathless.

I stared open-mouthed. "Holy shit. Orion, what happened?"

"A scion cannot be heir to more than one bloodline," he said, almost to himself. "Ransom couldn't have been Elias's first-born . . ." Orion looked back at Mal, who seemed as stunned as the rest of us. "Because he was *hers*."

"What?"

"Mal has the spirit of Icelus. She's the God of Nightmares, and Ransom is her heir."

I covered my mouth with my hand. "But Mal's not dead. How's he controlling them?"

"They must recognize and obey the bloodline."

"How do you know?"

"I don't. Not for sure. But it makes sense. The Elders might know."

More spots bubbled on the ground around us.

Orion grabbed my arm and pulled me up. "I'm going to burn this whole place to the ground, and the smoke will be toxic. Get back into your body, and as soon as I set the plant on fire, get everyone down the mountain."

"What about my friend?" I asked, looking back at Everly's spirit, curled in a fetal position on the ground.

"I'll take him to Imera. The Elders can help him, but you must go. Quickly."

I returned to Everly. "Brian?"

He looked up.

"I have to go."

"Don't leave me, Nyx."

"My friend Orion will take care of you. I need to get everyone else out of here."

"Am—am I dead?"

I forced a smile and touched his cheek. "No. You're going to live forever."

Orion touched my shoulder. "He'll be fine. Let him go."

"Will I see him again?"

"Someday." Nightwalker heads sprouted from the black spots around us. "Nyx, you really have to assimilate."

"I'll see you soon," I said to Everly, fighting more tears. I got up and jogged back to my body.

A second later, I opened my eyes.

"Nyx?" Rivera said over me. I held up a hand, and he pulled me up.

Jones had a hand on his bald head. "Boy, did you miss a fucking show."

Ransom reached for me.

I grabbed his hand and pulled him into a desperate hug. "Are you all right?"

"I . . ." he stammered over my shoulder. He pulled back to look at me. "I don't even know. What the hell just happened?"

I shook my head and hugged him. "I'm not sure." But in my mind, Orion's words replayed. If Mal was the God of Nightmares, my brother would someday be too. What the hell would that mean for all of us?

But those worries would have to wait. Mal coughed up more blood as she tried to push herself up.

I lumbered to my feet and snatched my jacket off the ground. "Anybody got tape?"

Dani searched through her medical bag. "Nyx!" She tossed me a roll of white medical tape.

I walked to Mal and knelt beside her.

"What . . . happened?" she wheezed.

Popular question.

Ignoring it, I flipped her onto her stomach, wrenched both arms behind her back, and wrapped the jacket around her hands. I wound the tape tight around, securing her hands and the hypnox behind her. "Rivera, you and Jones take her down. Don't let her get her hands free!"

"Roger that, Nyx," Jones said.

"Saphera!" Mal croaked as my teammates pulled her up.

I didn't respond.

"Sergeant Essex, can you hear me?" Dani asked, adjusting the oxygen mask over his mouth and nose.

I slowly walked over. Baker moved out of my way and put a hand on my shoulder as I sank down next to Essex. I leaned toward his face. "Tyler?"

His eyes slowly fluttered opened and met mine.

"Can you hear me?"

He nodded, barely.

I swallowed. "Do you know who I am?"

He searched my face.

Please, I silently begged, tears burning the corners of my eyes. I wanted to grab his hand, but I couldn't move. I couldn't even breathe.

Please.

Finally, Essex locked his gaze with mine . . .

And shook his head.

The hospital kept all of us the rest of the night. Ransom, because his blood pressure was still low; Essex, because he'd actually been dead; Mal, because she'd needed surgery to repair her lung; and me, because I'd scared the shit out of everyone with an emotional breakdown in the emergency room.

Ransom and I shared a room (Celise's doing), while Essex was taken to the ICU out of an abundance of caution. Paps and Bess both stayed with us, despite my many objections. They were asleep in identical recliners when my spirit woke up.

Orion was seated on the foot of my bed.

The clock above my medical chart said it was four in the morning.

"Hi." My throat was painfully dry, probably from all the crying earlier.

He closed the folder in his hand. "Hi."

"Have you been here long?"

Orion shook his head. "No. I just got back."

"How's Everly?"

"The first few days are always the hardest, of course, but he will be OK."

"Thanks for taking care of him."

Orion bowed his head.

I glanced at the folder on his lap. "What's that?"

"History." He stood and carried the folder to where Bess was sleeping. Carefully, so as not to wake her, he placed the folder on her lap. "Someone's been busy."

"Is it about Chief Magnus?"

"And about me." He returned to my bed and sat on the edge of it, beside my hand. "Joe is a longtime friend of mine."

"The chief?"

He nodded. "We went through the police academy together a million years ago, and though our department didn't have partners, if it had, he'd have been mine."

"Was he there the night my parents—" I stopped myself. "Was he there the night you died?"

"I never died, remember?" He smiled, but there was no joy in it. "He was outside, along with the rest of my brothers who would have died had I not set that fire."

"How did you know to burn it?"

"Elias. He was failing to get my spirit back into my body, and the nightwalker was almost into the Boundary. He told me only fire could kill it. When I heard my guys outside, I begged him to forget about me and kill it. That was when the nightwalker ripped through my body and materialized on Earth.

"Elias panicked and scrambled back, dropping an ergane glove near the fireplace. It sparked, and I threw it at the beast. It blew up, and the rest is history."

I put my hand on his. "I'm sorry."

"And I'm sorry to you for what happened tonight."

"Did you tell Chief Magnus about me?"

"I did."

"How?"

"The same way Elias would talk to you."

I frowned. "Please don't ever do that to me. I hate it."

"It's a useful tool when it's necessary. It's allowed Magnus and me to put away some very dangerous people. He was very excited when he knew he had the chance to work with you."

"I'm not going to take the job." My eyes, and my thoughts, drifted away. "Especially now."

He looked at the floor. "It's probably for the best. You did a brave thing. I honestly didn't think it was possible, but you saved your boss's life. As far as I know, no one has ever done what you pulled off back there with your boss and the Water of Lethe."

Problem was, I didn't feel very heroic. Or successful. Essex was lost to me, maybe forever.

Orion and I were both quiet for a while. Finally, he looked across the room at Ransom. "He changes things."

"What do you mean?"

"I mean, your mother isn't a raging bitch without reason. The power twisted her, sickened her. When Mal dies, it won't be easy for your brother either."

"How did this happen?"

"I think it was your great-grandmother."

"Never knew her."

"I know. Nettie Marcotte was executed before either of us were born."

"The first woman to die in Nevada's gas chamber." I smirked. "Sounds like my family legacy, doesn't it?"

"A little."

I looked at Paps. "But shouldn't her power have passed to him?"

"It should have, unless he drank the Water of Lethe."

I stared at him. "Is that what happened?"

His shoulders rose. "I don't know. Soon, I'll be able to return to the Elders and find out, but all I can do now is guess at the missing puzzle pieces."

"And what's your guess?"

"Mal clearly doesn't know what she is, and your grandfather didn't know to tell her. The only way that's possible would be to not only drink the water of forgetfulness, but to also kill anyone else who knew about it."

My eyes turned toward the ceiling. "Paps's mother murdered her family, so he would grow up without knowing."

"And the gift passed to your mother without anyone being the wiser."

"Mal is the reason the nightwalkers were here."

"And she *and Ransom* will be the reason they stay."

I looked across the room at my big brother, his mouth gaping and his inked forearm draped over his eyes. "Will I lose him too, like Gran and Paps lost Mal?"

"All scions have a choice. I believe it's why the River of Lethe was created to begin with. But when your brother inherits the spirit of Icelus, this life won't be easy for him. You will outshine and outsmart him at every turn. You'll be the star, while he has nothing but a front-row seat to watch all he *should* be able to do. That's a poison that grows from deep within, and for which there is no cure. He will have to continually weed it out. Otherwise, it will overtake him."

"Ransom is a good man," I said with all the confidence I could muster. And he was. But it was no secret that my brother teetered on the very top of a dangerous slope.

Orion nodded but didn't meet my eyes.

He knew it too.

There was also Milly to consider—the next in line after my brother to receive the spirit of a demon. I shuddered. My brain already hurt way too much to think about that tonight.

"What will happen to Mal?" I asked.

"She's out of surgery and recovering. I imagine she'll go back to prison, which is probably the safest thing for all of us until we can come up with a plan." Orion put a hand on my knee. "But don't worry about that tonight. You need to rest."

"I'd like to see my boss while I can. In my body, they won't let me into the ICU because I'm not his—"

Because I wasn't his *anything* anymore.

Orion offered his hand. "Come on. I'll take you."

Unlike most of the patients in the ICU, Essex didn't have tubes and pipes coming out of every orifice in his body. An IV was run through the back of his hand, and heart-monitor pads were stuck to his chest. An oxygen mask had been sloppily discarded onto the pillow next to his head.

He was in a deep sleep, shirtless, with his torso wrapped in stretchy bandages. Pain would be his constant companion for a while. CPR alone was a bitch of a recovery.

Orion nudged me toward the bed. "Talk to him," he said quietly. "I'll be outside."

I inched forward and finally placed my hand on the side of his warm face. He turned toward it and drew in a deep, crackly breath.

"Tyler." With a painful swallow, I sat beside him on the bed.

"I'm so sorry I couldn't save you another way." My face fell. "But hell, maybe this is for the best. I don't see my life getting any less complicated, and the last thing I want is for you to be in more danger because of me."

I put my hand on his. "But the past couple of days, I've been happier than I ever thought I'd be again. Maybe happier than I've ever been. Thank you for believing in me. And for not giving up, even though three years is a long time to wait."

I leaned down and touched my ghostly lips to his. "I do love you," I whispered.

With those words, he wrapped his fingers around mine.

"Don't give up, Nyx." From somewhere far away, I heard his voice. Disjointed.

Detached.

My soul eased.

My heart soared.

His voice continued.

"There's more going on here than what you see. This is only the beginning." His face was serene. Eyes closed. Breaths even and deep. Still unconscious—or maybe *more* conscious than he had ever been—he squeezed my fingers. *"And I love you, too."*

CHAPTER THIRTY

"You can do this, Nyx." Ransom draped his arm across the steering wheel of his truck and stared at me across the cab.

I was sitting on my hands to keep from fidgeting. "What if I imagined everything?"

"You didn't."

"But what do I even say?"

"You don't say anything. You're not here to cross that bridge today."

But Essex *would* be here.

Aside from *whatever* had happened in his ICU bed, we hadn't seen each other since we were on the other side of this same cemetery. And while I'd gotten my hopes up after our beautifully eerie exchange, in this world, Essex still had no idea who I was.

Orion couldn't tell me whether or not Essex's memories would ever surface. According to everything he knew, Essex communicating with me in the Boundary shouldn't have been possible. His memory should now be a clean slate regarding the supernatural, and if he ever remembered, it would be because, like Paps, he created *new* memories with new-to-him information.

But sometimes what we know in our hearts doesn't always line up with what we know in our heads. And maybe the truth in my heart superseded even Orion's experienced perception.

Despite my natural inclination to value facts over feelings, I believed that on some level, maybe even a subconscious one, Essex still loved me. No matter what he remembered when he was awake.

Maybe we are all just spirits masquerading in bodies, unchangeable at our core despite what our brains think they know—or don't know.

Ransom nudged me with his elbow. "Or you can walk in there and say, 'Hi, I'm Nyx, the Goddess of Night. And, surprise! I've seen you naked and I liked it. Nice funeral, isn't it?'"

My laughter surprised me. "Thanks for doing this with me."

Ransom shrugged. "It's nice to finally do something for you for a change." He reached across me and opened my door. "Now go. You'll hate yourself if you don't."

"You'll do what I asked?"

"As soon you get your ass in there. Bess is picking you up?"

I looked at my watch. "She's supposed to already be here."

He grinned. "You really surprised?"

"No."

He pointed outside. "Go."

I took a brave, deep breath and hopped out of the truck. We were far away from the hypnox bluff Orion had scorched into oblivion, but adrenaline seeped into my veins nonetheless when my feet hit the ground. With a hard swallow, I looked across the cemetery. "Wish me luck."

"You don't need luck. You're a fucking goddess."

With a genuine but fleeting smile, I closed the door behind me and straightened my black button-up shirt.

I hadn't attended the service at the church. I was more responsible for Everly's death than anyone, so it seemed wrong to grieve before God and all his witnesses. This would be where I would pay my final respects and hopefully sneak out without too much fanfare.

Our guys were on the second row of white chairs beyond the mahogany casket. I slipped onto the end seat beside Rivera.

I took a quick inventory of who was around.

Essex wasn't anywhere.

I sighed with—relief? Disappointment? Then I waved down the line to the rest of the guys.

Baker reached across Rivera to shake my hand. "Glad you made it," he whispered.

I hadn't seen or talked to anyone much since the battle. Not in person or in the group chat. I never dreamed I'd be so thankful for a doctor's order to rest. There was so much to process. So much more to do.

Mal was back in prison. Attempted murder was clearly a violation of her parole, and with all the new charges, she'd never see the light of day again except through prison bars.

I hoped they'd be strong enough to hold her, now that we knew exactly what she was.

Ransom had many questions, for which I still didn't have answers. After finishing what needed to be done today, seeking out the truth was the next priority on my agenda.

Across the lawn, Ransom's truck rolled toward the crowd of reporters being restrained by the county deputies. He got out and walked around to talk to them. A few moments later, Ransom's truck left the cemetery, and the convoy of news vans followed.

My heart thumped in my chest.

Rivera leaned toward me. "Thanks a lot, Nyx."

I looked at him confused.

He glanced down at my outfit. "I had twenty on you wearing a dress."

"Shut up, Rivera."

He chuckled and settled back in his seat. "Doing okay?"

"Not yet."

He nodded. "I know the feeling."

It was a little hard for me to believe that Rivera had feelings. But if I'd learned anything in the past few years, it was that the armor built around the heart of any law-enforcement officer is there by necessity, not choice. Gods and goddesses aside, we dealt every day with the worst mankind had to offer, all while wearing a brave—or sometimes (in Rivera's case) hateful—face.

"Sarge isn't here," he said, not meeting my eyes.

"Does he . . ." I couldn't even finish the question.

Rivera shook his head. "No. He still doesn't know who you are or what happened."

His words were like a punch to the gut.

"But the doctors say the amnesia will probably fade."

I nodded but couldn't speak.

Thankfully, we weren't a group that asked too many questions—at least not of each other.

In front of us, the casket hovering above a large rectangular hole offered a heavy dose of perspective. It could have easily been Ransom or Essex being laid to rest today. And considering everything, it was probably better that Essex had no memory of the events.

"Plausible deniability is everything," Chief Magnus had once said to me.

Plenty of first responders had seen the nightwalkers on the cliff. The group-chat debate leaned heavily toward the wild-animal theory. It had been dark, and the nightwalkers even darker, so no one was certain what they saw. And if questions lingered, none of our guys would ask.

A black limousine wound slowly through the cemetery. When it stopped, the driver got out to open the back doors. Everly's parents, I assumed, got out first. Chief Magnus and Essex followed.

My heart squeezed.

He walked with a stiff spine, the only way to move and cope with the blinding pain of broken ribs. The shirt beneath his black jacket looked bulky from the bandages certainly binding his rib cage. It had only been six days, but he looked thinner. Paler. Dark circles sagged beneath his tired eyes.

When they were close, his gaze swept down the line of cops until he reached me. Our eyes met, and his perfect lips bent into a polite smile. Beyond that, there was no familiarity. Not one flicker of recognition, let alone anything resembling what we'd so recently had.

I wanted to explode into a million pieces. And yet, I knew the truth: on some level, locked somewhere far away, his soul still loved mine.

"This is only the beginning," he had said.

That truth didn't make this moment any less brutal. He sat at the far end of the aisle in front of me, not meeting my eyes again.

"Nyx?"

I'd been so lost in my own grief that I hadn't noticed Chief Magnus break from the group.

When I'd woken up back in my body at the hospital, Bess had presented me with her full report on Chief Joseph Magnus. As Orion had said, he wasn't a supervillain after all.

In the blaze my father had gone to prison for, Detective Owen Ryan had sacrificed himself to save the other officers. Magnus included.

Magnus had taken the job in Sapphire Lake, in part, to work with me. And, by proxy, to work with his old partner again.

He wasn't going to like how I was about to spin things.

"How are you, Corporal?" Magnus asked.

"I'm alive, so I'm not complaining."

He nodded. "Can we talk after?"

"We'll talk soon."

He squeezed my shoulder and left to sit with the family.

Everly's mother cried through the whole service. I watched her with perplexity and envy. Had it been my body in that box, my mother might have celebrated.

The service ended with a twenty-one-gun salute. I flinched with every bang.

When it was over, I bolted from the group without so much as a goodbye. Bess's green jalopy was parked under a tall sugar pine. She waved from the driver's seat.

"Corporal!" a deep voice called midretreat.

I slowed, but it took a moment to work up the nerve to turn around. When I did, Essex was within arm's reach.

So close.

So far.

"Corporal Nyx," he said so formally I wanted to scream.

I forced a smile. "Sergeant."

"We haven't seen much of you since the . . ." He looked away.

I shifted uneasily. "Uh, yeah. I'm still on leave." I pointed to my head. "Doctor's orders."

"Right. That's a nasty head wound. When do you return to duty?"

That was a complicated question. "I'll have to check my paperwork. How are you feeling?" My eyes dropped to his chest.

"I'm sore." He gingerly placed a hand on his side, under his blazer. "Broken ribs . . ."

"Are the worst," we said in unison.

He chuckled, then winced. "Exactly."

The awkwardness between us returned like a boomerang. We were no longer a couple, if we ever were. We weren't even friends. This whole exchange was Essex in boss mode, trying to address the massive elephant between us without actually admitting he had no idea who I, his subordinate, was. No doubt everyone had told him he *should* remember me.

He just didn't.

"Well, I hope you're back on the shift soon," he said, looking everywhere but my eyes.

"Thanks. Take care of yourself, Ty—" I choked on the name, snapping my lips shut.

His brow pinched, like something locked far away was trying to break through to his memory's surface. "Tyler," he said, surprising us both. "You can call me Tyler."

Hope flickered in my heart before I could tamp it down. My lips curled into a shaky smile. "OK. Take care of yourself, Tyler."

I turned before the moment could shatter. It wasn't until I reached Bess's car that I allowed myself to look back. Essex was in the same spot, staring after me like his brain was trying to untangle itself.

Then our eyes met, and he smiled.

Hope bubbled again.

It was a quiet drive across town. Well, relatively quiet for being in a car with Bess. She hummed "All the Single Ladies" the entire drive. When we pulled into Sterling Frights, Ransom was waiting with an army of news vans.

Word gets around fast in their world.

The reporters started buzzing when one spotted me in the passenger's seat.

Bess pulled into a handicap parking space. "Are you sure you want to do this?"

"Are you sure you want to park here?" I pointed to the wheelchair sign capping the space.

With a groan, she backed out and reparked three spaces over. "If you do this, you won't be able to critique my driving anymore."

"Sure I will."

She put the car in park. "Well . . . good luck."

I smiled. "Thank you. You coming?"

"You kidding? I wouldn't miss this for the world."

Cameras started flashing the moment we stepped out of the car. A microphone was thrust in my face as we walked. Ransom ran over to shield me from the swarm. "Just give her a damn minute!" he bellowed. "Bunch of fucking vultures," he mumbled in my ear.

I walked up onto the steps leading to the hospital and pulled a slip of paper from my pocket. I took off my sunglasses and looked around at all the faces. The microphones crowded in around me.

"Good afternoon. My name is Corporal Saphera Nyx with the Sapphire Lake Police Department. I am not here today representing my department or Chief Joseph Magnus. I'm here as a private citizen with valuable information on the deaths of Ryder Stone, Amber Stevens, and Calvin Fleming."

I gestured toward the hospital behind me. Staff and patients were crowded around the doors and windows, watching the circus happening outside. "For seven days, Corbin Fleming has been held here at Sterling Heights Mental Health Center on medical watch, pending the investigation of what happened at the Drexler. Corbin Fleming is innocent." I held up the flash drive I'd stolen from Birch's office. "And I have proof."

Bess had trimmed and clipped the video surveillance I'd downloaded. Two phone calls and one meeting were particularly damning. She'd even added the bit at the end where the mayor had demanded an arrest before he left for vacation.

"There are a lot of guilty players in all this. Not the least of which are all of you, the media." I glared specifically at Marianne

Clarke from News 4. "Now that you've helped land an innocent man in his own hell, maybe another news network can help set him free." I tossed the flash drive to the tall Hispanic man who'd helped shelter me and Bess at the Drexler.

He smiled.

I took a deep breath and spoke to everyone again. "While I hold the police department specifically blameless in this situation, I'd like to formally announce my resignation from the department, effective immediately."

Murmurs fluttered through the group. From the back row, Bess held up both thumbs.

"Thank you for coming. That is all."

Questions fired from every direction. Ransom shielded me with his arm as he escorted me off the stairs. Overhead, a pounding noise drew my eye. I looked up and saw Teek waving wildly from the window.

I laughed and returned the wave.

"That was exciting!" Bess said when she caught up to us at Ransom's truck.

My heart was still pounding a thousand beats per minute.

Ransom opened the passenger door for me, and I got in. "Proud of you, sis," he said with a smile.

Bess wedged into the doorway beside him. "Me too! But geez, Nyx, what are you going to do now?"

I handed Ransom the second slip of paper from my pocket. It was his business card. I smiled. "I don't know, but Specter sounds like a good idea."

The series continues in Specter.

A FREE Essex story is coming soon for HYDERNATION members. Sign up now at www.eliciahyder.com.

THANK YOU FOR READING!

Please leave a review on your favorite eBook retailer's website!
Reviews help indie authors like me find new readers and get
advertising. If you enjoyed this book, please tell your friends!

★ Want leaked chapters of new books?
★ Want the characters inside scoop?
★ Want to win awesome swag and prizes?

Join HYDERNATION, the official fan club of Elicia Hyder, for
all that and more!

Join on Facebook

Join on EliciaHyder.com

SPECTER

The Saphera Nyx Series - Book 2

★ Want leaked chapters of new books?
★ Want the characters inside scoop?
★ Want to win awesome swag and prizes?

Join HYDERNATION, the official fan club of Elicia Hyder, for all that and more!

Join on Facebook

Join on EliciaHyder.com

Roll into the exciting world of women's flat track roller derby, where the women are the heroes, and the men will make you weak in the kneepads.

A brand new romantic comedy series from Author Elicia Hyder.

THE JOURNEY DURANT SERIES
A Watty Award Winner for Best New Adult Romance

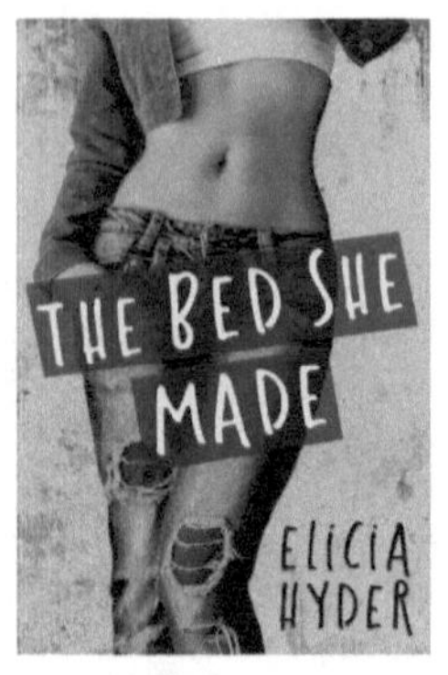

The Bed She Made
Watty Award Winner for Best New Adult Romance
Journey Durant's father warned her that someday she'd have to lie in the bed she made. But she didn't believe him until her ex is released from prison and he threatens to bring her troubled past home with him.

To Be Her First
The Young Adult Prequel to The Bed She Made
At sixteen, Journey Durant hasn't yet experienced her first anything.

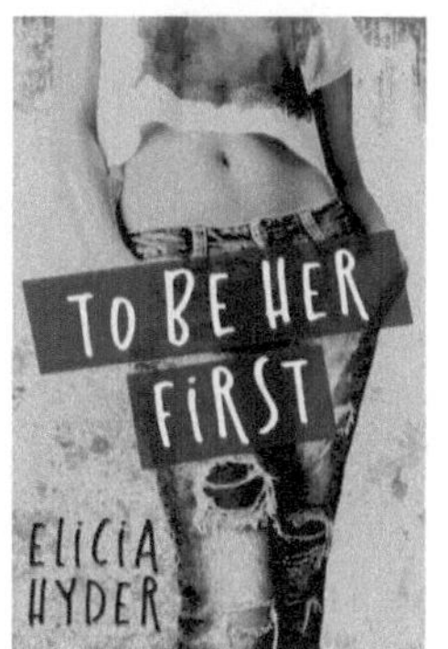

No first boyfriend. No first date. No first kiss. But that's all about to change. Two boys at West Emerson High are vying for her attention: the MVP quarterback and the school's reigning bad boy.

ABOUT THE AUTHOR

In the dawning age of scrunchies and 'Hammer Pants', a small-town musician with big-city talent found out she was expecting her third child a staggering eleven years after her last one. From that moment on, Susie Waldrop referred to her daughter Elicia as a 'blessing' which is loosely translated as an accident, albeit a pleasant one.

In true youngest-sibling fashion, Elicia lived up to the birth order standard by being fun-loving, outgoing, self-centered, and rebellious throughout her formative years. She excelled academically—a feat her sister attributes to her being the only child who was breastfed—but abandoned her studies to live in a tent in the national forest with her dogs: a Rottweiler named Bodhisattva and a Pit Bull named Sativa. The ensuing months were very hazy.

In the late 90's, during a stint in rehab, Elicia was approached by a prophet who said, "Someday you will write a book."

She was right.

Now a firm believer in the prophetic word, Elicia Hyder is a full-time writer and freelance editor living in middle Tennessee with her husband and five children. Eventually she did make it to college, and she studied literature and creative writing at the American Military University.

Her debut novel, **The Bed She Made**, is very loosely based on the stranger-than-fiction events of her life.

www.eliciahyder.com
elicia@eliciahyder.com